CATCHING QAT

Look for the next book in the
Drakkaen Nakkla saga:

Legacies

Catching Qat

Drakkaen Nakkla
Book 1

K.T. Pike

An *Adventures on Oram*
and
Tales of Airdaeya chronicle

Skuulfire
Press

Catching Qat

By K.T. Pike
Copyright ©2025 by K.T. Pike

First Edition

Cover design and artwork by K.T. Pike

ISBN Number(s):
Laminate Hardcover 9781962779005
Jacketed Hardcover 9781962779036
Paperback 9781962779012
eBook 9781962779029

Library of Congress Control Number: 2025914958

Published by:
Skuulfire Press
Sacramento, CA

,

To:
My husband. You are my world.

ALALNGAR
Toithdd Croieanan
Bierenan
Riversmeet
Xophis
Toolium
Cranwood
Craguesport
BABUM
ZEDANA
JUSHUR
Alonard
PUANNUM

Part 1 Riversmeet

Chapter 1 Qat

6TH DAY OF ZAMDI, 14,887
GIFTED ANCHOR, SHIPDURN RIVER, ZEDANA

Why should I bother saving when I live between land and sea and can steal anything I want? Even so, this job will feed me for some time.

If I don't leave a blood trail.

Or get caught.

The *Gifted Anchor* is a large enough ship that I've been able to pose as several different people on board. Tonight, brown contact lenses hide my whiskey-colored eyes. My bronze hair is under a stained kerchief, and my clothes are cabin attendant drab.

If all goes well, this job will be over soon, and I'll have enough coin that I won't need to find another one anytime soon.

I descend the stairs to the passenger staterooms, my sea legs automatically adjusting as the ship lurches slightly. The hall spans the ship's length, with cabins on each side. At the third door on the left, I insert my pick and release the cabin door's lock with an indiscernible click, making much less noise than I would have using my key. Inside, the passenger cabin suite is small compared to a standard hotel room but enormous by ship standards. It's almost twice the size of Captain Rogen's cabin on the *Raven Scream*, where I learned my trade.

Shadows are my friend, but this cabin's lit up like it's the Longest Night celebration. I extinguish the lanterns. In a blink, the room fades into shades of blue and black. Details slowly sharpen as my pupils expand, and I can read the clock on the bedside table within seconds.

I slip my hand drill from my boot and bore several holes in the sides and top of a large trunk. I toss the shavings and a few articles of Truffle's clothing in the bottom to soak up the blood, if there is any.

If there is any.

Ha. There will be blood.

Bernhard Truffle's blood.

I remove all but Truffle's morning suit from the wardrobe and fill several trunks with the stuff. The ship tilts starboard, and in my peripheral vision, I catch something tumbling off the nightstand. I leap forward and grab the back cover of a notebook before it hits the floor, and a sheet of paper slips partway out. The paper is thick and smooth and resists when I flick it open. A distinctive sea serpent crest embossed in gold leaf and a list of items and prices fill the page. The sea serpent crest is familiar. The same one is on Truffle's ring. The ring I need to get paid.

I hear footsteps in the hall and hold my breath, tucking the note into my waistband.

The sole of an open-heeled sandal double-taps and slides on the hallway's wooden floor. Then again and again as the person approaches the room. I exhale a sigh of relief, recognizing the sound. The woman next door seldom flexes her toes enough to lift the shoe's heel off the floor.

I'm annoyed that I didn't hear her coming sooner. It's dangerous to be so engrossed that I don't notice the sound of footsteps. Especially ones so distinct.

Her door opens. She rustles around, and the bed squeaks. Next, a cork pops—probably from the bottle of elixir sitting next to the picture of her late husband.

I smile. One. Two. Three...and she's snoring.

I finish my preparations and settle in to wait. Truffle's usually the last passenger to retire, so I could be here a while.

Next down the hall is the stag party. The university schoolmates are already celebrating their friend's last few nights of freedom, even though the groom is in Riversmeet waiting for them to arrive.

Eventually, the remaining guests straggle to their rooms, mostly in pairs.

Finally, Truffle's unsteady feet and toneless humming stop outside the door. He drops his key. He's sloshed for sure.

I blend into the shadows as he opens the door. A miasma of cheap cigars and expensive wine wafts in ahead of him.

"Thought I left the lights on," he slurs, fumbling for the wall lantern. "Where is it?" He fiddles with the cover.

While he's distracted by the light fixture, I flick the door closed. The noise of the lantern hood opening drowns out the *click* as the door shuts. I creep closer and tap his knees from behind.

"What the—?" His legs collapse, and he falls back against me.

"Ooof!" I can't stop the sound. Bernhard is taller than me by a hand and heavier than I expected.

Before he has time to figure out what's happening, I pull his head back with my right hand, resting most of his weight on my chest while my left arm sweeps over his shoulder, and I slide a *ha-sheesh-shun* blade between his ribs—a little rougher than Captain Rogen taught me. I jerk the handle. The blade is so sharp, I barely feel the tip piercing the heart wall, but I know it does because when he gasps, his full weight falls into me. I stumble before I catch myself and take a step sideways, using my grip around his neck to angle his body toward the trunk nearby. With less finesse than usual, I let him fall headfirst, pulling the blade free.

There is blood. But I'm not finished.

Rogen taught me that bloated stomach gas will bring a dead body to the water's surface in a few days. A few holes in his belly will fix that. When I'm done, I wipe the blade clean and slip it into my sleeve. Next, I fold his legs in, but one doesn't fit. The trunk moves when I push harder. I roll it against the wall and shove hard to bend his leg, using the leverage my new position gives me. The knee finally pops, and I wedge the leg inside.

I should feel something after all that, but I don't. Maybe a bit upset that I misjudged his weight and almost dropped him, but other than that, my pulse is steady, and my breaths are slow and even. Some assassins feel sick or depressed after a job, but not me. I remember when I used to feel a thrill when I executed a perfect hit. Now, I can't remember the last time I felt that good. I can't remember the last time I felt much of anything outside of boredom or irritation.

As soon as I close the trunk, I remember the ring. Annoyed, I reopen the lid.

The band is tight on his swollen finger, but I wrench it free and stare at the gold figure amidst the blue stone. Remembering the note, I remove it and compare the two designs. Yep, the sea monster is the same on both pieces. I congratulate myself on that, at least, and stow them in a pocket. Before closing the lid, I grab the coin purse from his waistcoat, but I don't take anything else. That's another thing the captain taught me. Never steal on a hit job. Nothing will get you caught for murder like hocking a mark's stuff. Coins don't count, though. They can be found anywhere.

The lock clicks, and I do a quick sweep of the room. Servants will empty the room and transport Truffle's baggage in the morning. They've gotten to know Truffle's habits, so the room needs to be perfect. It's not. Something's out of place. I double-check everything again before I realize what it is. The bed. Truffle never makes his bed, and I don't want to tip off the room steward, so I jump on the bed and kick the blankets around, then trample his pillow. That feels better.

Truffle doesn't usually do breakfast, and I overheard him say he doesn't have an appointment in town until tomorrow afternoon. No one will miss him until then.

The room looks packed and ready to be unloaded in the morning. But I still feel I'm forgetting something.

The notepad. I don't remember placing it back on the nightstand, but there it is. I flip through the pages, but it's written in code. That must mean it's important. I tuck it in my waistband and slip back into the hall, hiding my bronze hair beneath a deckhand cap instead of the kerchief—the only difference between them and cabin attendants. I wheel the trunk behind me and time its release into the water to coincide with the disposal of food scraps and galley waste.

I wipe my hands together as if to say, 'Don't pay any attention to me. Just taking out the trash.'

7TH DAY OF ZAMDI, 14,887

RIVERSMEET, ZEDANA

The Bernhard Truffle who debarks the following morning is shorter by a pinch, and the serpent ring on my middle finger is slightly looser than it should be. But no one notices.

I'm that good.

Just in case, I do what I do best. I disappear. I merge with a shadow, steal garments, and alter my appearance often. I change course frequently, using the roof, a busy market, and a cart passing by.

Once I've reached midtown, I climb to the rooftops and head for one of my favorite napping spots. At least, it was when I used to live here. Maybe someone else is using it now? I find the hidden—and empty—nook, lie back, and close my eyes. I've been working double shifts since we boarded, and I'm exhausted. The sun feels so good. I press my arms over my head and stretch my whole body from fingers to toes until my muscles quiver, then melt into the warm shingles.

I wake up a few hours later, refreshed and ready to get paid. Truffle's coin purse is heavy, but I groan when I see what's inside. Not again! Several coins are from a currency I don't recognize, which may mean I won't be able to trade them here in Riversmeet. Thankfully, most are zeds—Zedanian gold coins— plus a few silver shims and copper clinks. There are also a few precious stones.

That'll help, considering that the ship's wages I received still don't compensate me for my work to pull off this job. Not yet, at least.

I sit up and stretch, then drop to street level.

Back to the wharf to check in with the dock rats—children with nowhere to go and nothing to do but watch and listen. That's where all the best news comes from. I listen to the listeners.

Fortunately, there's nothing to hear, so I check for recent marks left by people like me. A few drops of oil, a bent nail, or a charcoal smear on the side of a barrel might not mean anything to the public, but those trained to read the signs—like me—will understand.

There are no signs indicating that a dead body in a trunk was found floating in the river.

Just the way it should be.

The meetup is a few streets over. I enter through the window. It only takes a few minutes to inspect the place. The two rooms are mostly empty, with only a small office and storage area with a few broken and empty crates. I make myself comfortable and wait, keeping an eye on the door.

An hour past our meeting time, I start pacing. Is it strange that I only get impatient on a job while waiting for my pay? I'm annoyed and about to go when I hear someone outside. I melt into the shadows as something bangs into the swollen door. A dwarf stumbles inside when it finally gives.

"When are they gonna fix this fuck'n thing?" he mutters.

The Stripeback dwarf has distinctive white stripes in his black hair. A scar pulls his bottom lip to the left, matching the description of the guy I'm supposed to meet. The holes in his shirt say he needs his commission for this job as much as I need my pay. I wait in the shadows as he lights a lantern and places it on the table.

"You're late," I say.

He jumps back, nearly tripping over his feet. "How'd you get in here?"

Instead of answering, I flip the sea-serpent ring into the air, catching the metal with my nail so it *tings* before it tumbles. That catches his attention.

"Oh," he says, narrowing his eyes. "Are you Qat? Is it his?"

Who else would I be? Without answering, I pocket the ring and head to the door. Why would I be here if it wasn't Truffle's?

"Wait!"

The dwarf's strangled words almost make me smile, but I suppress it, pleased at the desperation I hear in his tone. He wants it more than I want my payment. Or so I want him to think.

I turn and wait.

"What's your problem?" he asks, trying to take back the leverage he gave me.

I raise one brow. He's not getting it back.

"Never mind, let me see it." He holds his hand out.

"You have my gold?" I ask instead, even though the cords keeping his coin purse from falling down his pant leg are hanging over his waistband. From the number of loops tangled together, he has more than one.

"Of course I have it!" The dwarf glares at me as he tugs his shirt to cover the purse strings.

Idiot.

Nearly a minute of forced silence goes by as he peers around the room and over his shoulder. "Don't touch anything," he finally says.

Does he think I haven't already touched everything worth being touched, which is next to nothing? He steps into the storage room and closes the door, leaving only a few inches of space between it and the door jamb.

"Ten, nine, eight." I smile when he swears.

He returns before I reach four. "Keep your boots on." He tosses a small pouch on the table between us.

I don't move toward it. The contents are too sparse. Instead, I narrow my eyes.

"It's your fault," he says, wiping the spit from his damaged lip. "They know he's missing."

He's lying. I narrow my eyes further.

He steps back, and his cheeks darken. With guilt, I'd bet. Who does he think he's dealing with? An amateur? Does he think I've done nothing since the ship docked?

I tamp down my anger. I'm so tired of this shit. If I were with a guild, this wouldn't happen. The guild secures contracts, delegates tasks, and pays timely. But joining a guild means that too many people would know my whereabouts. Freelancing means it's only me and the one who hires me. And possibly the one who took out the contract, although they seldom get involved in the details of who or how.

I move so light from the table lantern shines directly into my translucent blue contact lenses. My pupils adjust to the light, narrowing and elongating as I knew they would. He visibly blanches and shrinks back.

I don't give him time to verify what he saw. I may have gone too far as it is. I've tried to keep my pupils well-hidden since leaving the *Raven Scream*. They're a rare trait except amongst the kadal and a few lesser-known reptilian-like species. I lack scales that would mark me as one of them, among other things, like a tail. Which makes me an oddity. No. Mine are cat-like and could give me away if someone—and by someone, I mean Captain Rogen—has people looking out for them.

"Three," I hiss at him.

He jerks away.

"Two," I say, drawing one of my favorite daggers. The blade is made from several metals combined to create a wavy pattern that twists, turns, and mesmerizes. I point it at his crotch.

"Okay!" He reaches into the front of his baggy pants and pulls out a much larger pouch. "This is the full amount," he says.

It hits the table, and the coins clink inside the bag. Too few coins still.

I raise my brow.

He pockets the smaller bag. "Now, let—"

"I took a closer look at the ring while waiting for you." I watch him closely for his reaction.

Another rule I learned from the captain is to keep people off balance. 'Change the topic lightning fast,' he'd say. 'Interrupt them. Answer their question with a question, but don't wait for an answer. Eventually, you'll wear them down and get an honest answer, even if only from their expression.' I saw him do it so often. I hear his phrases come out of my mouth sometimes, even without thinking about it.

The dwarf doesn't even blink. I doubt he knows the translation for the engraving on the inside of the ring: *Sati lida ane tari takaro.* I don't either, though I wish I did. It might have something to do with why Truffle needed to be assassinated. The same saying circles the sea monster emblem on that piece of paper. The one still tucked away in my waistband.

The phrase and the crest connect the ring and the list. Since I recognized a few items on the list as relics, I'm guessing they're artifacts for sale. Maybe for auction? They're probably mostly fakes. Like the Thunderlight Trident. The real one was used to slay the kraken, Akxoss. That story is one of the oldest myths on Oram. Why would someone like Truffle have access to an artifact like that? He's not *that* wealthy. The auction may not even be legal.

"I know what it is." I'm bluffing, of course, but I say it with confidence.

The ring is special. I feel it. The question is, though, how special? Although Truffle wore several rings, only the serpent one was acceptable for payment.

Maybe I should keep it?

The temptation is brief. I have no interest in hunting down whatever treasure this might bring me. Too much trouble.

Unfortunately, my hook gets no bites. The dwarf looks confused. Maybe he doesn't know about Truffle's dealings, or perhaps he's just a go-between.

Well, it was worth a try.

I fling the ring into the air, and it arcs behind him. I swipe the pouch on the table and the one in his pocket when he reaches for the ring.

I'm gone before he catches it.

Like I said, I can steal anything I want.

Anything, that is, except my life if Captain Rogen ever catches up to me. He's a much better assassin than I've ever been and taught me everything I know. Like how to pick locks, read ship manifests, imitate accents, and drink whiskey straight.

And how to kill from behind with a *ha-sheesh-shun* knife to the heart.

Lucky for me, he's saddled with a ship and crew. He doesn't have the freedom I now enjoy.

I inhale the familiar aroma of moldering rigging combined with fish, sweat, and piss. I've traveled the eastern and central Oram waterways, raiding ships from the frozen lands of Alalngar in the north to Lagash's swamps in the south, and there's nothing like the scent of a busy wharf.

I detour toward the riverbank and along a short dock lined with trees. Tree branches skim the top of the water, giving me a perfect hiding spot to count my loot. The minty, earthy scent of damp leaves is strong, and for some reason, I'm reminded of the first time I met Rogen. I was young when I woke up on Captain Rogen's ship, the *Raven Scream*, with a splitting headache and no memory—not of my name, age, or how I got there—with only a minty smell clinging to my clothes hinting where I'd been.

Where I'd been? Could it have been here in Riversmeet? I shake my head. No. These trees grow all over Zedana. Besides, I don't care.

An ache starts in my chest, and for some reason, I can't catch my breath. I need to get away from here, away from that scent. It's suffocating me.

I jump up and start walking without any thought about my destination.

For twenty years, I've lived blissfully unaware of my beginnings. No ties. No responsibility. No one to worry about, and no one to worry about me.

At least, not since I left Captain Rogen and the crew of the *Raven Scream*.

I like it that way.

The ship's first mate—Goffin the Black—was responsible for my leaving. He took something from me that I can never get back. I keep the memory of what he did tucked away in a chest banded in chains and triple-locked. I open that chest only when I need a reminder to stay on my guard, to keep vigilant, or to stay awake for days at a time when falling asleep could mean the difference between life and death.

If Goffin managed to survive our last encounter, I'll kill him with my bare hands the next time I see him.

Like I might have done last time?

No. This time, there will be no room for doubt.

I'll never forget the rank smell of his fear. His mouth had gaped wide, a half-chewed smill worm seeping black ink and staining his teeth. Those worms are how Goffin got his nickname. The first mate wasn't breathing the last time I saw him, and the whites of his eyes were dotted with crimson when I jumped overboard holding the long end of my favorite scarf still looped around his neck.

I still mourn the loss of that scarf. More than I mourn the loss of my memory.

But Goffin's as mean as they come. I wouldn't be surprised if he were too stubborn to have died. I'd have finished the job if that nosy Uci hadn't flown overhead. His eagle eyes probably saw everything. I was too distracted trying to kill Goffin to notice him until it was too late. It's possible he saw me swimming away.

That's another lesson I learned that day. Keep one eye on the sky.

I've heard rumors that the captain's been looking for me ever since. That's never a good thing, and more evidence that Uci saw me. We were always competing, Uci and I. I spent my time in the eagle's nest on the ship while he flew like an eagle high in the sky. I usually won our competitions. In the time it would take him to fly back to the ship, I'd often already warned the crew of trouble coming or a trophy ship on the horizon.

Uci never liked me or missed an opportunity to malign me. I bet he'd love to be the one who catches me.

Well, you can't catch a cat with a crow, I always say.

So, I keep running.

But before I do, I need to retrieve my things hidden in the *Gifted Anchor's* hold.

Anything to get away from the smell of my stolen past.

Chapter 2 Qrodin

7TH DAY OF ZAMDI, 14,887
RIVERSMEET, ZEDANA

"You don't see me," Qrodin says quietly, hiding the wave of irritation at the intrusion.

"See you, see nothing," comes a whisper from the nearby shadows.

Resigned, Qrodin says, "See it all," completing the secret code he and Talim made up when they roamed the city as orphans. As far as he knows, the Valore—Talim's spies—still use it. "You may as well join me."

Qrodin had sensed Talim's presence some time back but hadn't been ready to see her. Had hoped she'd realize he wanted to be alone and leave. He'd sent her a message that he'd be arriving in Riversmeet soon, but didn't say on which ship. He's surprised she knew where he'd be, but he shouldn't. Like most abandis, her short stature hides a keen brain. And her spies are everywhere. They used to be his spies, too, but he's been away too long to know the members who've joined Talim's network in the last few years.

Talim is Qrodin's oldest friend. They met here in Riversmeet. He couldn't wait to leave this city. She never did. She's been managing the Lightning Strike for him since he acquired the tavern all those years ago.

He's pleased to see her but wishes she hadn't come here. Not to this place.

"I didn't want to bother you." She makes almost no sound as she approaches.

Then you shouldn't have come, he thinks, but doesn't say. "Why did you?"

"I was curious." When Qrodin doesn't respond, she continues, "You used to come here all the time, but I never asked why."

And she's asking now without asking aloud. That's her way.

He can't tell her. The memory is still too painful.

The pier looks much the same as it did twenty years ago. It still smells of spilled ale and mildewed hemp. The only visible changes are the vivid yellow paint on the warehouses and the new light fixtures positioned along the pier. Qrodin, having purchased all the buildings years ago, was responsible for those changes.

Through the tree branches, Qrodin watches a passenger ship sail by with a batch of travelers. Once they're gone, the area is deserted.

The willows are unusually still today, the tips of their branches soaking quietly in the water or lying passively on the ground. There's no breeze to cool the sweat of early autumn from Qrodin's brow. As if the sky is holding its breath, unwilling to disturb his memories of that eventful evening so long ago, the one that changed his life forever. The one that happened right here on this very pier.

20 YEARS AGO
RIVERSMEET, ZEDANA

"Qrow! What are you doing here?"

"What am *I* doing? What are *you* doing here?" Qrodin asks his twin. He'd followed aem when ae'd slipped out of bed, snuck through the window of their traveling home on wheels, and crept into the back of one of the two waiting wagons.

"I want to see a *real* pirate."

Qrodin crawls in under the heavy canvas next to his twin. "What makes you think Ama's meeting a pirate?" Qrow asks, shaking his head at the absurdity, but a little excited that it might be true.

"I heard Quinn say that meeting pirates in the middle of the night was too dangerous, and Ama needed protection. So, I'm going to protect aem."

"Which is it?" Qrodin asks. "Did you want to see a pirate, or are you going to protect Ama?"

"Can't it be both? Why did you follow me?"

"I came to protect *you*, as always," Qrodin answers.

His twin's brow creases. "I don't need your protection."

Qrodin doesn't answer. Rounds of *yes, you do,* followed by *no, I don't,* could go on forever.

The wagon is nearly empty in preparation for the shipment that Ama's picking up. The tarp will cover the items so nothing flies out on the way back to camp. Usually, when ae returns from these nighttime trips, they're full of bales of cotton and wool, food, herbs, and dyes, as well as building materials and tools. Anything that can be used to make clothing, crafts, and musical instruments, fix broken-down wagons, or eat.

"How are you going to protect Ama? You can't even protect yourself," Qrodin says.

"With this!" His twin brandishes a knife.

"Where'd you get that?" The knife looks expensive, and the blade is shiny, even in the near-complete darkness.

"Stole it."

"Of course you did," Qrodin says, scowling. His twin was very skilled in that department, even at barely eleven years old. When ae wasn't running off causing trouble, Qrodin's twin was practicing with blades: throwing, twirling, flipping, and catching them behind aer back. It's a miracle that ae hasn't lost any fingers.

Their family is Karatolii and part of a traveling group that entertains at each city they visit. Qrodin's job is to play music while his twin collects the tips—though with aem, the onlookers don't always know they're tipping. His twin should have given the knife to Ama to be divided among the rest of their team. The Karatolii are like that. Everything belongs to everyone, but stealing isn't acceptable, especially from customers. Ama says it causes animosity and distrust. Townsfolk won't come to watch them if they steal from them when they do. Ama will be upset when ae finds out, but it won't matter. His twin won't change. And his twin steals.

"Hey, do you think Ama will get some fish and chips while we're there?" Qrodin asks. Ama often surprises them with treats.

"I hope so. I want some stingers!" Qrodin's sibling says.

Qrodin grimaces, remembering how the scorpion's pointy tail pierced his tongue once. He couldn't talk for days after.

They are quiet when Quinn climbs into the wagon and grabs the reins. Ama must be driving the other one.

The wagon lurches along the bumpy dirt road, occasionally knocking them into each other. Eventually, they hear waves crashing against rocks. Maybe they *will* get to see a pirate tonight. Qrodin squirms in excitement and discomfort—he probably should have peed before he jumped in the wagon, but he didn't think he had time. He won't be able to hold it until they get back to camp.

Before long, they hear horse hooves on wood, and the wagon bumps steadily instead of dipping erratically. They've reached the docks. No matter how much he strains, he can't hear any of the noises he expects from a busy harbor. He thought there'd be drunken sailors flirting or fighting. Instead, he hears loud clanking, ropes squeaking, and water sloshing. Perhaps it's too late. Even sailors need to sleep.

When the wagon slows, his twin lifts the corner of the canvas. The wagons come to a stop. Qrodin pulls the cloth back down until they hear Quinn jump from the driver's seat and walk to Ama's cart. Qrodin and his twin shimmy to the wagon's edge and slip over the side. They scramble under the cart as silently as possible and watch Quinn and Ama walk to the end of the wooden pier that juts from the riverbank.

The night is so dark.

"Uman's not going to play nice tonight," Qrow's twin says, scowling at the moon. "It's a good thing we're here."

Ama'ani taught us all about the moons and their personalities. Uman is only a sharp red curve tonight, like a hunter's bow pulled taut. Ama'ani says that his mood changes with his shape. The pointier his ends, the more confrontational he becomes. As the God of War, that could mean anything from chasing after a lover to starting a war.

Tonight, Isa is the dominant moon, one night from full and more green than blue. Isa is as mercurial as her color. Green, the color of jealousy, means she'll be looking to get back at someone.

Kuu, the silvery Goddess of Love, isn't in the sky tonight. There's nothing to keep Uman from picking on Isa. And nothing to keep Isa from getting back at him.

Unlike his twin, Qrodin doesn't believe moons can influence events. The stories are just superstitions, but his twin believes them all.

In the low light, Ama's shiny red scarf is nearly as dark as aer jet-black hair, making aem almost invisible as ae gets further away.

His twin rolls out from under the wagon.

"Where are you going?" Qrodin whispers.

Qrodin's twin stops midroll and looks back at Qrodin. "I have to take a piss. I'll be right back." Ae blinks once slowly, then rolls away and is gone.

But Qrodin knows that slow blink. His twin is trying to protect him from something. Ae's probably going to follow Ama.

Qrodin rolls, then crouches low to stay out of Ama's sight as he follows his twin behind one of the warehouses. His sibling is squatting in the bushes. All right, maybe ae wasn't *completely* lying. Speaking of, Qrodin can't hold it any longer. Part of him fears someone will hear them, but he can't wait. He's almost done when he sees a flash of light from the direction of the docks. The area goes dark, then lights again.

When he looks back, his twin is nowhere to be seen. The only thing that remains is the smell of crushed willow leaves.

He fastens his trousers and peeks around the side of the building.

They must have signaled someone. A pinprick of light in the distance. Pause. Two more in quick succession. Quinn opens and closes the hood on the lantern one more time.

Qrodin tries to edge along the side of the pier under the low-hanging willow branches. He flattens himself to the ground to check, but his twin isn't underneath either wagon. Where did ae get to?

While he searches, Quinn jumps into Ama's wagon and maneuvers it down the dock, angling the back end toward the water for easy loading. Once the first wagon is in position, ae jumps down and is nearly to the second wagon when a gasp shatters the silence.

Qrodin recognizes Ama's voice, "Who are—?"

Footsteps pound on wood—at least three sets.

Shouting.

Qrodin's twin is running toward Ama.

"No!" he tries to yell, but a hand muffles his cry. Qrodin is tackled to the ground, and he struggles in vain to free himself.

"Stay down!" Quinn grits out. "It's too late."

Too late for what? "I have to—"

"There's nothing you can do!" Quinn hisses. "Quiet!"

Qrodin looks up to see what's happening on the docks and freezes. Ama is lying on the worn wooden slats. "Ama!" he gasps, not believing his eyes. A sword is sticking up from aer belly. Ama's not moving.

Qrodin struggles to free his mouth from Quinn's grasp. "Get off me!"

But his words are muffled. His arms are pinned to his side. He kicks at Quinn. Where's his twin? Qrodin searches but can't find any trace of aem.

Someone is leaning over Ama. Whoever it is, ae's tall, with huge shoulders and hair so light, it shines Isa green.

Qrodin freezes. Fear spirals through him.

The giant pulls the sword out, examines it, and then grabs Ama's necklace. With one yank, ae pulls it free. Whoever that person is, ae's no friend of Ama's. Aer voice is deep and rough. "Put aem in the boat," ae says to someone holding a struggling child.

No! His twin is tossed into a small boat.

Fear sweat soaks his skin as he fights to loosen Quinn's hold. Finally, one arm wriggles free. He punches at anything he can reach to create an opening to slip out. Once he does, he crabs back as fast as he can, away from Quinn, who's curled up and groaning in pain. Qrodin runs toward the water.

There's no sign of his sibling, but Ama's red scarf is half hanging over the side of the boat. The fabric catches the wind as if waving goodbye while the skiff rows out of sight. He stops at the edge of the dock. He can't swim. Tears blur his vision, and he swipes at them.

He runs back to Ama. Aer eyes are open, but they're empty. Blood soaks aer chest where the ruby necklace had hung for as long as Qrodin can remember.

He drops to his knees, his fear so heavy he can no longer stand. Ama's body is limp and unwieldy, but he inches closer and wedges his knees under aer shoulders as he lifts aer head onto his lap. "Ama," he cries, brushing the hair from aer face and pressing his forehead to aers. "Please don't leave me."

Twenty years still isn't long enough for the memory to have faded. There might never be enough time. How could Qrodin ever forget seeing the person who raised him killed so brutally? Or the sound of aer blood seeping through the gaps in the wooden planks, plopping into the water below? How could he forget the bitter taste of his tears as he held Ama in his arms as aer murderers got away, taking away the only person that mattered more to him than even Ama?

Once Qrodin realized he couldn't save Ama, he ran along the entire wharf after the small boat and scrambled down the rocks beneath the shops along the Hold, losing one shoe along the way. He screamed as the skiff got farther away, disappearing into the wild emptiness of two rivers colliding.

Qrodin and his twin had never been separated before. That night, he felt as if he'd been torn in two. He couldn't feel his twin, who should be terrified or exhilarated. Either way, Qrodin should have been able to feel what ae felt. He always had before.

How long had he stayed there, searching the water, crying, and calling for his twin? Young Qrodin eventually remembered that Ama's body was still lying on the dock. He'd clambered back up the side of the riverbank, his hands slipping and scraping on the sharp rocks, but he'd barely felt it through his anguish. He'd kept the river to his right as he walked, barely acknowledging the late-night stragglers and wandering drunks. He'd thrown up somewhere along the way and dry-heaved a few times before he found the right pier.

Qrodin remembers his shock when he returned to the dock. The only things that remained of Ama were a bloody stain and the black salt the Karatolii sprinkle to release any lingering bad energy. Only later did he realize the significance of the black salt because, at that moment, Qrodin was alone for the first time in his life, and he was terrified.

Qrodin blinks the memory away and clears his throat. "It was a long time ago, Talim. Nothing that can be changed by worrying over it," he says to her, as he always has. As close as they've been, he still can't confide in her. That's one thing that growing up on the streets does. It teaches you to conceal your fears. Your vulnerabilities. Anything that can be used against you later. To keep the real you hidden behind a story you practice so often that it becomes second nature. To survive on the street, you only worry about the things you can control. Otherwise, you die young with a hole burned through your belly.

He wishes he'd known then what he knows now. Qrodin had lain down next to the salt outline and cried himself to sleep, swearing to find whoever killed Ama and make them pay. He'd woken a few hours later as dawn was lighting the sky. He was too distraught and disoriented to find food. Instead, he'd searched between every board, under every willow tree, and behind every barrel. But he could find no clue to explain Ama's murder or lead him to his twin.

He surveys those same warped boards. The willows are larger now, but the long, thin branches still skim the water like fingers desperate to hide what's hidden below the surface. Back then, on that night, they were nearly bare. Most of their leaves had already dropped, transforming the branches into switches whipping in the wind while he searched. They'd lashed him, teasing him for thinking he'd find something.

Qrodin unclenches his hands. It's a wonder he ever returned to this pier, but return, he did. Nearly every night for more than a year, he looked for the men who stole his life and caused him so much pain. He never found them.

He shakes the memories away. The trek through the past has made him hungry, and he can't wait to be back in the sturdy and safe building that once saved him.

The Lightning Strike's customers are tradesmen and locals, so the tavern serves simple fare. It doesn't offer the rare meats, imported fruits, and spices the wealthy insist upon in the north end of town. The ale and whiskey are the less expensive varieties from Qrodin's distilleries.

As such, business is usually steady, with a constant stream of regulars sprinkled with visitors.

Talim has finally taken Qrodin's advice and purchased a pub. The new building is in a better part of town than the Lightning Strike, the tavern she's been managing for Qrodin for the last fifteen years. She's been grooming Xan to take her place. Talim has mentioned him almost daily in her communications with him. It's obvious to Qrodin that she cares for him, and that Xan's more than a little in love with her.

"Tell me about Xan," Qrodin says as they walk to the Lightning Strike. "Has he asked you to marry him yet?"

"Of course he has. You think he can resist this?" Talim asks. She gestures gracefully from her magenta hair and periwinkle eyes to the bottle-green ankles visible above the leather straps on her sandaled feet.

The first time he met her, she was going after the stranger who'd knocked her off a sack of grain. Qrodin got involved when the stranger backhanded her off the pier and into the river. Adult abandis are very short, only ever reaching three feet, but Talim was only ten years old and no larger than a Karatolii toddler. Qrodin had hurried to save her, but she was already climbing out of the water. He eventually talked her out of going after the man, but only after taking a few kicks to his shins and one mighty punch to his groin. He told her that he would help her get back at her assailant in a way that would stick. They did, and she eventually became Qrodin's closest and most trusted ally.

She hadn't needed him back then, but he instinctively felt they would be helpful to each other.

Qrodin stops when he remembers who the stranger was. Is it a coincidence that they were supposed to meet tonight, but the man never showed?

He catches up to Talim, who hadn't slowed. "I couldn't," he teases her.

"Yeah. I was your first love," she says, teasing him back, tilting her head to the side and looking up at him. Then she laughs. The seductive timbre is low and throaty.

Qrodin chuckles at their old joke until he notices where they are. For some reason, he can't keep the memories at bay.

He remembers wandering this street that first day, lost in a fruitless search for his camp, crisscrossing and getting lost in the twisting streets. The search exhausted him, but he'd forced himself to keep moving. It wasn't until late evening that he'd finally found the empty camp where his family's wagons had been.

They hadn't waited for him.

He was shattered. He was thirsty. He was beyond hungry. He cried until no tears remained. Eventually, he found some dirty rags to wrap his shoeless foot, but his heel was already bruised and scraped, leaving him limping.

Ama was murdered, his twin was taken, and his people were gone—he was entirely alone for the first time in his life.

And he was terrified.

Standing here tonight, Qrodin remembers his anguish. Perhaps if he'd done things differently...

Qrodin sighs deeply. He wouldn't change the past, even if he could.

During all those years in Riversmeet, he had waited for another caravan to visit. He had planned on seeking them out to pass on word that he lived and to ask if anyone had seen or heard from his twin. But there had been no visiting caravans, not for a long time. By the time the Karatolii returned to Riversmeet, Qrodin's enterprise had already grown beyond the city's borders. He had taken over failing businesses, created new infrastructure for abandoned children, built his shipping fleet, and started several hotel and retail chains.

Despite his dishonorable beginnings in Riversmeet, Qrodin believes that he's done a lot of good.

Talim shifts her weight, a silent reminder that it is time to get back.

Qrodin still has work to do.

Chapter 3 Qat

The Hold is busy tonight.

Built on a rocky outcrop overhanging the water, the Hold is a string of shops, taverns, and fish houses above the southern shoreline, where the water is too treacherous to navigate—at least, that's what they tell people.

After retrieving my bag from the *Gifted Anchor*, I stashed it in the caves along the shoreline under the Hold. To my relief, the caves were empty and looked as though no one had been down there in years.

Before I go back down there to retrieve my bag, I need to know that I didn't screw up.

Amid the usual noises of ships being offloaded, seagulls grunting and flapping, and vendors hawking their wares, I walk bent over, carrying a pail of fish. I'd painted some fine wrinkles on my face and silver into my hair. My cloak is old and full of holes, and it smells as bad as it looks. The hood will cast enough of a shadow that no one will look twice at an old fisher. There are a hundred of us on any given—

"What's your business here?" The low, clipped inquiry rumbles through me. I recognize the growly undertones of a daga. It's no secret that, in most cities, Daga are recruited by military, police, and investigative departments for their speed and keen sense of smell, especially the more aggressive females. This one's probably an investigator since no one else would care what I'm doing here. What bad luck. "Get your hand out of your pocket and turn around." Yup. Daga. And probably former military, judging by her methods. I've had plenty of opportunities to observe Zedanian soldiers and even posed as one for a job a few years back.

"Don't be triggered, mate. Octopus duty," I say gruffly, not pronouncing the "t" in mate, like the locals. The wording is delicately crafted. An Octopus is a Mimic—an undercover officer who works the docks. Meanwhile, the terms *triggered* and *mate* are military slang. The combination should be enough to put her at ease.

I turn, pulling out a fake ID card I keep on hand for this purpose, and hold it up for her perusal. Her eyes widen slightly, and she dips her head a fraction in respect. Only the best officers are trained to be Mimics, after all. Each variety has unique specialties. I'm most comfortable mimicking an Octopus.

Her furred face relaxes slightly, and she barely glances at my ID again. She doesn't smile. I know her kind. The serious type, always on the alert. Pointed ears on top of their heads twitching toward every sound.

Daga have pronounced noses, sharp teeth, deep chests, and long arms and legs. Their fingers are short, with claws instead of nails. This one's fur is mottled black and brown. She'd blend into shadows perfectly, especially outside of a city. She'd make a great burglar. Or a great Chameleon. Unlike an Octopus, whose job is to be mistaken for a local, Chameleons specialize in not being seen. This one wouldn't be happy with that, though. I can tell she loves the chase. Can practically feel her vibrating with the excitement of this one. Although she's shorter than me, there's no doubt she could outrun me. Even blindfolded, she could locate me from smell alone. Her nose quivers as she sniffs the night. And my cloak.

I'd ditched the skunk dwarf's pouch. I didn't linger long in any one place, either, instead sweeping through the Hold quickly and gathering scents, stopping only long enough to chug a cold ale and grab some deep-fried scorpion to go, exchanging most of the coin. I drenched my meal in hot sauce in case it wasn't as fresh as I remembered. I needn't have bothered. It was practically still wiggling, it was so recently caught. I wrapped the remainder of the coins with my greasy napkin before pocketing them. Then, I'd found the cloak. That was hours ago. There should be no trace of Truffle or the dwarf who paid me. Even for a daga to notice.

I used to think Rogen's extreme measures were a bit overboard. *'You never know what they'll be sniffing for,'* he'd always say. *'You need to look, sound, and smell like a local.'* It's saved me countless times. I'm gambling it'll save me again tonight.

The daga's presence can't be a coincidence, even though Truffle's missed meeting was less than an hour ago. No one should be searching for him for at least a day or two. I wonder what tipped them off.

I breathe slowly and deliberately, keeping my heart rate steady. She'll be able to hear it if it starts racing. Another reason dagas make good investigators.

"So, you know about the missing lawyer," she says, looking at me closely.

Kraken's teeth! As much as I had anticipated the possibility, hearing that someone's looking for him is a surprise.

I press my lips together in annoyance and disappointment and raise one eyebrow. Daga can't see as well as I can in the dark, but they pick up on energy fluctuations. My disappointment is real, but she won't know what caused it. She might not be an interrogator, but investigators are still trained to get information, not give it. She should have known not to say anything about the lawyer.

My perceived age and occupation mean I should outrank her. I'm hoping, like most people, she'll feel compelled to fill the silence.

She doesn't.

I sigh deeply. "Apparently, the Squids haven't reached the docks yet." Squids are runners that pass on information to Mimics.

Her attention switches back to me. She's more relaxed now—too relaxed. I can feel her cataloging my traits in her mind. She sees only what I want her to see, and she'll know I'm in disguise, including my voice, but she'll feel compelled to report the incident.

Her description will describe more people than it will dismiss. Average height, average weight, average coloring. I'm advantageously average-looking tonight, both by nature and design.

She'll list my species as *danaash*. Danaash, similarly to dagas and abandis and many others, are umanids—a group of species intelligent enough to speak Oramische, the international language of Oram. On the other hand, non-umanids—animals—can only be communicated with by some form of magic or telepathy. Some say sign language, too. I wouldn't know. I've never tried.

The daga's description would be partially correct. I've always thought of myself as danaash, but my eyes say I'm something else, too. Hidden beneath my contacts, she won't be able to see them, but I'm not taking another chance like I did with that dwarf. Not until I'm out of Riversmeet.

"What are we looking for?" I ask to distract her and hopefully take her attention away from me, using 'we' so she knows I'm on her team.

She shakes her head. "They've got us searching the ships. Can you believe it?" she asks instead.

Yes, I think, but I shake my head, too. Mirroring your opponent is another Rogen Rule. "They send someone to the Depraved Seductress yet?" I ask with a short laugh. Madame V runs the famous brothel. The establishment is a few blocks landward, about halfway along the western edge of town, where citizens meet sailors. Not too south for the respectable and not too north for the disreputable. More than a few times, I've gone there for information. Madame V protects her 'Tulips' fiercely, and the non-courtesan staff especially enjoy their bouncer duties.

There are plenty of people who have gone missing from that place.

"You know it," the daga practically growls.

Whoa. Heel, doggie.

Her scowl relaxes. A moment later, it deepens again. One ear swivels to her left, and her nose follows the direction of the sound she'd picked up.

That's what I've been waiting for.

"I'll let you know if I hear anything," I say.

"Likewise," she says, but I'd wager she's already forgotten me.

I slip into the shadows as she darts off.

She won't have time to finalize her analysis about me because she'll be distracted by the new scent. One of the dagas' flaws. They remember scents better than descriptions, but scents are more complex to describe to anyone but other dagas.

I will be disremembered.

Which is good because this Truffle disappearance is much bigger than I thought. If they're searching ships, I won't be able to leave by one for days, maybe longer. I should stay away from the docks. I suppose I can sleep in the caves, but I'd rather not, not with the threat of them being searched. This close to the Hold, it's a distinct possibility. I need to find a place to lay low until I get out of town.

I also need to grab my things before there are more people to hide from. They'll eventually get to the caves. And when they do, a daga may find my scent on the bag despite my precautions. I need to camouflage it. The sooner, the better.

On the way, I dump the cloak and steal some gloves, putting them on before stealing enough stuff to litter the caves with distracting odors.

I maneuver the overhanging cliff edge of the Hold and slither down one of many long rock columns, then hop from one column to another to a bank rising out of the water. I call the series of tunnels and caves the *Whaligator* since it's rumored to be the fossilized remains of a giant sea creature. The bank is the tongue and leads to a nearly hidden cave opening that I call the mouth. After making false trails and cleansing all scent from my body with a sea sponge—like Captain Rogen showed me long ago—I head to the cave where I'd stashed my things. The pack is where I left it.

After dressing in dry clothes, I dry off the one piece of armor I own. It was also the first magic item I ever owned. It looks deceptively small, like a child's armor, which is probably why Rogen gave it to me. I doubt the captain knew the armor was magical. It looks like any other piece of armor. It's heavy at first, but as soon as I drop it over my head, it's as light as a cloud. It stretches and forms to my chest and abdomen, or anything underneath. This feature enables me to change shape whenever necessary.

Even without that little trick, I can easily pass as a man or a woman if I choose to. Or neither, as I most often do. No one knows for sure other than me, not even the captain or his crew. I don't care if people are left guessing. I prefer it. Their confusion gives me the upper hand. And I like to have the upper hand.

Right now, I don't feel as though I do.

I need to leave Riversmeet as soon as possible, but it will be difficult with all the ports being watched.

Armored up, I gather my few belongings, but I get an odd sensation before I exit the cave. My danger sense isn't twanging. Had it been, I'd know the severity level and direction of the threat. It starts at the nape of my neck, twitching and tingling. It sometimes feels as though the hair there is attracted to danger, straining toward it with increasing strength as the threat mounts. Despite the lack of sensation, I pause anyway.

Perhaps it's the weather I'm reacting to. Maybe there's a thunderstorm coming? After inventorying my senses, I doubt it. I still feel whatever it is, almost like a hum or an energy vibration pinging in my brain, but not in my body. There's no sound. My arm hair isn't standing on end like in a thunderstorm. I sniff. There's no smell of rain or ozone.

I'm not sure what I'm searching for, so I try to keep an open mind as I move through the corridors. After about a quarter of an hour, the feeling intensifies near a low opening close to the mouth of the tunnel. I've never toured it because it's so tiny. I crouch down and look, but the tunnel's incline prevents seeing anything past a few feet. The feeling is more insistent here.

I lay down and crawl on my belly along the narrow opening. Thankfully, I've never suffered from claustrophobia, but the passage makes me nervous with the incoming tide, and this section is below the salt lines that mark high tide. I need to move fast. About twenty feet in, the path ascends. I continue until I pass more high tide marks and relax a little. At least, if I get stuck, I can wait it out until the tide turns.

A short while later, a slight alcove appears ahead of me. It's so small, a child could barely curl up in it, and an object is crammed tightly into a crevice near the base. I have excellent night vision, but all I can make out is a box shape. Not natural, and my senses are buzzing like I've eaten a handful of sugar cubes.

I peer closer and will my eyes to absorb more light. I scoot closer. The thing is rectangular, but I can't discern its color. I'm only a hand away from it when I finally realize what it is. A small chest, about the size of the one the captain stores his jewels in. My stomach flips as I pull the object out carefully. I can't tell how long it's been here, but it doesn't smell musty or moldy like I expect it would had it been here more than a few days.

I back out of the tunnel, crawling awkwardly and dragging the chest with me. When I get clear, the light is fractionally less dark. There's a two-headed snake with arms and legs set within a pyramid on the lid.

Before I can inspect it further, a tingle prickles the back of my neck. I almost drop the chest, but then I realize the presence I feel is at the mouth of the cave, not in my hands. A presence, but not a dangerous one. At least not yet. Perhaps it's whoever stashed this?

I shove the chest into my bag. There's plenty of time to inspect it later.

I creep forward silently toward the mouth until I see the water around a corner. I hesitate as soft waves splash to shore and retreat, a little rougher than normal. Perhaps a storm is brewing.

There is a loud splash and a thud on the hard surface of the cave's tongue. The resulting silence is filled with flopping and a loud slap. Then, a grunt. Is it a sea lion coming to shore? No, the river here isn't brackish enough for them.

I'm curious, but I don't want to give myself away. Maybe someone is wading in the water or unloading a rowboat. I wait a moment longer, straining for any sound. Thrashing, grunting, scratching against the rock. Then, the unmistakable sound of hooves clopping on rough stone.

Hooves? Like on a horse?

Why would someone bring a horse down here? Reins could get caught on rocks, and a horse could injure themselves on one of the Whaligator's teeth—the long rock columns I used as an entry point.

I listen for a rider, for muttering, or for someone to call out. Instead, I hear a snort. A horse snort.

Around the corner, water droplets appear like mist. Snorting again—a loud one this time, almost like a sneeze.

I crouch and tiptoe forward. If the walls here were rougher, I'd climb them instead. People never look up. It shouldn't matter, though. Who's a horse going to tell?

Resolved, I catch my knife.

That stops me again.

When had I tossed it spinning into the air?

When had I stood up straight?

What is wrong with me? Someone might have noticed. Annoyed with myself, I holster my blade, wishing it were the first time I'd caught myself doing it.

No matter. Holding my breath, I step into the Whaligator's mouth.

Chapter 4 Qrodin

They're almost to the Lightning Strike, but Talim stops walking. "Remember when we met, and you helped me get back at that man who kicked me?"

Qrodin nods. Why is she asking about Truffle?

They'd been children, and Bernhard Truffle had been an adult bully, but Qrodin and Talim got some intel about his gambling debt. The information was shared with Truffle's fiancée's family, who promptly ended the engagement, and there went the inheritance his fiancée would have received as an only child. Talim never mentioned him again, but Qrodin has kept an eye on him ever since. "Vaguely," Qrodin answers now, not sharing that he and Truffle had been scheduled to meet earlier that evening.

"Rumor is that he's gone missing," Talim says, watching Qrodin closely.

Missing? Qrodin tries to mask his dismay. Finding Truffle hadn't taken long, but now he needs to find someone else with a ring. Truffle's absence is a setback to more than just him. Qrodin suspected that Truffle had backed out of their deal when he missed their meeting earlier. Since he wasn't expected at the tavern for several hours, he took a detour to the docks instead. He'd never imagined that it was something more serious.

When it's evident that Talim's waiting for a response, Qrodin says, "And you thought I'd taken him out all these years later?"

"What?" she asks. "Oh, no." She pauses, then continues, "You know that asairtsall down on Lotus?"

"The what?" Qrodin asks, trying to stall while he reassesses his plans.

"They prefer to be called Asairtsall. Stripeback is a derogatory term," Talim says.

He's been telling her that for nearly twenty years, but this is the first time he's heard her use it. In addition to *Stripeback*, she usually calls them *skunks* or *badgers*. Asairtsall are the only dwarf subspecies that can swim and are, therefore, the only ones that regularly work on ships. Most coastal cities have a significant population. They're quite common in Riversmeet and even more abundant in Craguesport. It takes him a moment to place the one on Lotus Street. "Stolgut?"

"Yeah. That's the one."

Unsure how Truffle's disappearance and Stolgut are connected, Qrodin only nods. Talim often communicates in this roundabout manner. She'll get to the point eventually.

"Word is…" Talim pauses again when a group of people approaches, then passes them. "Perhaps we should talk about this back at the tavern? In the office? Where we can have some *privacy*?"

Privacy is Talim's code for activating the spell that makes the office soundproof. Qrodin's head of security puts a switch to trigger the spell under every desk in every office of his.

"Of course," he says graciously, despite not feeling it. They turn and walk in silence. It's still a few blocks away, but Qrodin is used to her one-track mind. Nothing will distract her.

Talim doesn't only manage the Lightning Strike for Qrodin. She's his primary source of information in Riversmeet. *Word is. Rumor is.* Those are how Talim phrases information she's received through the Valore.

Valore, a Karatol word.

When Qrodin met Talim, he vowed to replace his missing Karatolii family with other kids—orphans and children who had been deserted as he had. As they both had. Talim had a way of finding them; some were their age, but others were only a few years old. Some were found a few hours after they were born, tossed in the trash, and meant to die. They banded together, watched out for each other, and taught each other tricks of the street.

It didn't take Qrodin long to realize how they'd get *off* the streets: Secrets. Information was gold, after all. The best part about being an orphan is that—if you're quiet and don't bring attention to yourself—no one notices you. Talim put eyes and ears everywhere, and they all reported back to her. Qrodin stayed in the shadows, perpetuated rumors, disseminated false information, and hid his true self from everyone.

No one on the street used their real name, so neither did Qrodin. He told them to call him 'The Qrow.' It wasn't a lie—his twin used to call him Qrow. That wasn't the only reason he picked it, though. No, he was using someone else's reputation to ensure his success.

The Qrow—the original one—was said to be one of the wealthiest men in Zedana. He'd disappeared a lifetime ago from Craguesport, and his business partners scavenged his fortune. Some rumors claimed that they'd murdered him for his money. Some said he was alive but had turned his back on his riches for love. There were even stories that he'd grown bored and turned pirate instead. When his former business partners started turning up dead, it was widely feared that his fortune was cursed, and anyone who stole from him was bound to die a horrible death.

The day they met, Qrodin and Talim stumbled upon the mystery of Kqrogen's assassination. Solving it not only kept Qrodin sane in the aftermath of Ama's death, but it also jump-started their friendship. Afterward, Qrodin assumed The Qrow's identity.

His plan worked like a charm. The Qrow's curse had become a horror story, even here in Riversmeet. People were too frightened to tell anything but the truth if they thought the curse might beset them.

The stolen reputation came with other perks, too. People came to them. Wives paid for their husbands' late-night whereabouts. Merchants paid for a copy of their competitors' ledgers. If people wanted information, they could find someone who could find someone who could find Talim.

He used the gold to buy the Lightning Strike. It took him years, but he did it.

When Qrodin left, Talim continued running the Valore on her own. She practically ran it back then, anyway. She was the one they reported to. She shared the information with Qrodin, and they decided together how to use it.

He and Talim round a corner, and there it is. The tavern looks different now. Back then, it was a burned-out shell of a building, scorched down to the stone base after an unlucky bolt of lightning. The Valore pitched in. He kept them fed. Talim directed the labor. When the Lightning Strike finally opened, he used the profits to pay them back for all their hard work. Talim still works with most of them. Some prefer to keep working in the shadows—waiting, watching, and listening—as Talim's sergeants. Far more of them took the chance at more honest work. Many are now running their own businesses, while some stayed to manage his.

Still others began learning valuable trades, like the enchanter who designed the special set of ledgers that allows him to monitor his business dealings around the continent. His managers update their business logs, and it's copied into Qrodin's ledger. The information isn't static either; with barely a scribbled command, the numbers rearrange and reorder themselves, tabulating and calculating any metric he wishes.

He carries it with him wherever he goes. The ledger makes traveling more efficient, as he can see immediately which businesses are succeeding and which may need more personal attention. Before that, the managers communicated by burning paper slips while reciting an incantation. The accountant received hundreds of them appearing out of nowhere every night, and their office always looked like a paper storm had just come through. As far as he knows, that's what every other accountant is *still* dealing with since his enchanter has faithfully refused to sell the schematics for his ledgers.

Qrodin and Talim sneak in through the back kitchen entrance.

"Go on up. I'm going to grab a few drinks."

Qrodin nods and turns toward the stairs. When he reaches the office, Qrodin flips the switch for the silence spell and sits, taking a seat across from her chair at the desk. He stretches his long legs before him and gets as comfortable as possible on the hard seat. Talim's taste in decor is hospitable downstairs, but it's bare bones up here in her private space. Not even a throw rug for color. She jokes from time to time that she wants to be the most colorful thing in the room. *'It keeps the attention on me. You know, the boss?'* Not that she needs to remind anyone. No one doubts that she's the boss around here. Even the customers can tell after seeing her walk through the room.

She finally returns. Two plates are balanced on her left forearm, and two glass mugs are in her right hand. Qrodin learned long ago not to offer to help lest he end up with food in his lap. Talim's definition of teamwork is slightly different from his.

She sets the food on the desk and hands him his drink. She doesn't clink her glass with his as is their custom when they haven't seen each other in some time. Instead, she downs the entire pint of ale and sets the glass on her desk. He sets his mug down after a single sip and waits.

She doesn't start talking immediately.

With an ease borne of habit, he settles again into his seat and relaxes the muscles in his face. All outward appearances aside, he's worried. Talim doesn't keep silent like this. Not with him. She delights in telling him all the new juicy news. Office gossip, town gossip—he's known her to talk half the night away.

Qrodin takes a few bites from his plate. Braised lamb chops and baby potatoes smothered in brown gravy melt in his mouth. He almost groans in pleasure.

"Okay," she says, finally. "I'm just going to say it. Word is, Truffle was murdered. His ring ended up back in the city. But he never made it." She pauses again.

Qrodin takes another bite, trying to portray only mild interest in her words. In truth, he's devastated at the news.

"It was a professional job," Talim says. "They haven't found his body yet, but *I* think he's in the water. The last he was seen was getting off the boat this morning." Talim pauses a moment to take a breath. She likes to give information this way: all miscellaneous data points up front before connecting them. "I don't think it was him. One of my crew followed him but lost him in town. Truffle was a clueless bastard. Never knew when we were following him. Whoever it was...they knew how to ditch a tail." She watches Qrodin as she talks.

He takes another bite to hide his expression. She had someone following Truffle? Why? Since when? Has she always done so, or is this a recent thing? Does she know that Qrodin was supposed to meet with Truffle? Qrodin doesn't interrupt with a question. She hasn't sat back in her seat. That's her tell when she's done, as if to say, *'Well, what do you think?'* Trying to conclude anything before she's done is a waste of time. Better to take mental notes and piece it all together when she's finished.

Qrodin nods once to let her know he's following her.

"Okay. So, have you ever heard the saying: *Sati lida ane tari takaro?*" She says it awkwardly.

Even so, Qrodin recognizes it. Stalling for time, Qrodin takes another bite. While he chews, he deliberates. Denying that he knew the phrase would be a lie, and he tries not to outright lie to Talim. There are things he doesn't tell her, but other than the details of his life before he came to Riversmeet, that's for plausible deniability on her part. There are things Qrodin would rather she not be involved in. This is one of those things. Admitting he knew the phrase could put her in danger. And besides, he's not sure he could tell her, even if he wanted to.

A moment later, he realizes that her familiarity with the saying has already placed her in danger.

He nods.

After a slight pause, she says, "Truffle wore a blue and gold and silver ring. Do you know which one I'm talking about?"

Qrodin nods, more than angry that Truffle wore his for everyone to see. They're supposed to be worn only as a key to gain entrance to illegal, underground auctions. It was probably Truffle's carelessness in wearing it that got him killed. He doesn't tell her he has a matching one locked in his vault in Craguesport. Qrodin invested heavily in the acquisition and was meeting with Truffle to learn the date and time of the next auction. Now, he's back to square one.

"Okay. Well. Stolgut got his hands on Truffle's ring." Talim pauses again.

Qrodin nods again and waits for her to continue. Talim's hands are clenched so hard her knuckles are pale. He can't imagine what's made her so anxious.

She's not mentioned Truffle since they enacted their revenge all those years ago, and he doubts the thought of the man's death would upset her.

Not like it upsets him.

"I'm guessing he got it from the person who killed Truffle. Or, more likely, Stolgut hired whoever killed Truffle to do the job and demanded the ring as proof. That's what he does. The thing is, though, Stolgut has no idea what the ring is. The idiot was asking all over town what that saying was. I don't know who hired *him*, but I'll find out." She sits back in her chair. Her thought process is over.

It's now okay for him to speak.

Talim connected the dots for him, and she isn't accusing him of anything, which is good. But he's unsure why she'd gotten so worked up about it. "You always do," he says. And she does, but he hopes she fails this time.

"I know." Talim looks down at her plate. She barely touched it.

He takes another bite. His meal is divine, which means it's Xan's creation; Qrodin's never had anything this good from their previous cooks. He could serve this in his best restaurants.

Finally, Talim nods as though she's made an important decision. She takes a deep breath and leans forward again. "Did you think I never saw your eyes change?" He blinks at the subject change, but she's not done. "That I never noticed that they'd be one color when you woke up, another color a second later? That I could see right through your dark glasses when the light hit just right? Did you think I couldn't see how your pupils changed?" She pauses, then says, "Qrow," in a clipped tone.

His eyes are blue when he wears contact lenses, and when he doesn't: amber with red centers and rimmed in dark brown, with pupils that are slits in the daylight. Back then, to prevent people from noticing his slitted pupils, he'd been careful to wear hooded cloaks or keep them covered with dark-tinted glasses when he could no longer hold the *Deziré* spell to disguise them. Ama had taught him how to use *Deziré*, a spell that alters how light reflects on an object, changing its color, shape, and size. It takes skill to hold the disguise. For that reason, until he discovered contact lenses were being traded in the underground market and acquired his first pair, he mostly slept during the day and did business at night.

But she saw it anyway. And she remembers.

Fear tightens inside him, but he refuses to analyze it and places the blame on her. Why did she never ask him about them back then? Why hadn't she demanded answers from him? He would have told her. Why has she waited until now to be angry about it?

It had become so second nature to hide his eyes that he never considered revealing them to her. But maybe he should have. Regret worms its way in, melting his fear of discovery. Talim already knows him. Has known his secret, and until now, she didn't care that he was disguising himself. Maybe they wouldn't be sitting here talking about it if he had confided in her years ago.

She doesn't continue. Nor has she sat back, indicating that she's done with this new round of questioning. He waits, wondering where she's going with this.

"All those years ago. Did you think I didn't know you were asking about a kid with gold eyes? Eyes like a cat? That you still have people out looking for someone like that?"

Qrodin's heart drops into his belly. This isn't two friends swapping gossip. It isn't a trip down memory lane, either. This is something completely different.

This is about his twin. Out of habit, he stretches his senses, begging the universe to give him a sign that his twin is alive.

Qrodin doesn't get an answer. Nor does he respond to Talim's question. Fear of giving someone the power to destroy him has always held his tongue. And as much as he wants to confide in her, he can't get the words out.

Talim grips the chair arms so hard that her hands and forearms tremble. "Why did you never ask me? If someone or something's in Riversmeet, I can find it."

He's not used to being the target of Talim's intensity. She usually reserves it for opponents, informants, and lazy employees. It's uncomfortable. And terrifying.

He tells himself that his reticence is her fault. Her rules. Rule #5 in her book. He'd met Talim only a few days after he arrived. *'Don't tell anyone anything that they can use against you. 'Cause they will. Remember that.'* He'd taken her at her word.

"It was personal, not business," Qrodin says, as if that should explain why telling her was against those rules. Pointing it out won't help matters.

"So, here's the thing. Qrow." She says his name deliberately. Again. "Stolgut told someone who told someone else that the person he got the ring from carried a knife that swirled like fire. Said they had eyes like a snake. Said they were blue. And gold. And red." She sits forward as she says it, as though she doesn't want to miss his reaction.

Blue, gold, and red eyes. Like a snake.

Like a cat.

Like Qrodin's eyes when he wears semi-opaque blue contacts, which he seldom does because their translucent nature reveals his unusual pupils. But he did when they were growing up.

Qrodin catches his breath at a sudden thought.

Like his twin's eyes?

"What are you telling me, Talim?" It comes out harsher than he intended. He wants it to be light, teasing, just two friends speculating about current events—the way it's always been between them. But this is different. Talim is on the attack.

"What does it sound like I'm telling you? Qrow."

It sounds like she thinks that his twin is here in Riversmeet. He reaches in vain for the twinge of awareness that would tell him she's right. If his twin were here, he should be able to feel it. He's never given up hope of finding aem. There have been times when Qrodin thought he could feel aem, like a tug on a line when a fish nibbles bait. Not enough to hook—just a tremble, just enough to make one think that maybe it was a fish, but perhaps it was only seaweed.

That's what it's been like for twenty years.

He doesn't want to get his hopes up again. Too many times he has heard that his twin might be in one city or another, chased down tips, disguised his travel as business, and covered his tracks by purchasing property or establishing a new source for product. They've never led him anywhere.

But if Talim's correct, and his twin is here, it would be the closest Qrodin's ever been to finding aem. Out of habit, Qrodin redirects the conversation away from himself.

"It sounds like you need a day off," he says, smiling. It's a mistake.

Her eyes narrow to thin strips of cerulean flame, and her breath hisses between clenched teeth. "Why do you even try?" She stares hard at Qrow. "You can't distract me the way you do everyone else. I've heard your verbal acrobatics for too long. I know all your tricks. That you use it *now*? On *me*? Like *I'm* your opponent? That hurts. Qrow." She doesn't look hurt. She looks angry. Furious. "And don't you dare try any of that calming shit with me." Her nostrils flare.

He hadn't been. Had he? Use *Soothe*? Perhaps he would have. Controlling the emotional temperature of a room is as natural to him as breathing. *Soothe* emerges low and soft but with the slightest rumble from deep in his chest. He's been told that the tone massages a person's scalp, sending rivulets of sensation down their spine to their extremities. It's an effective technique when the recipients don't know their emotions are being influenced.

"Talim. I've upset you. I'm sorry for that. We've always been honest with each other. Just tell me—"

"Honest? Qrow? Have *we* been honest with each other?"

Her implication is accurate, but he hadn't *lied*. He'd kept specific details of his life from her. "Talim. If there's something you want to know—"

"What's your real name?" she asks suddenly.

That makes him pause. "Qrow is my real name. As much as Talim is yours." His twin had called him Qrow for as long as he could remember.

"I don't remember what my mama called me. Talim means *alone* in Abandi. Did you know that? Did you know I gave myself that name because people always asked me, 'Are you alone?' before I met you?"

"I did know that."

"Yes. You did. And do you know why? Qrow? Because I told you. And I told you because you were my friend. You know everything about me. Qrow. But I still don't know anything about you. And don't you dare tell me it's because of Rule #1."

Rule #1: Never give your birth name. Not even to your crew.

She slams both fists on the desk. "I don't know if you've noticed"—she sneers, standing on the chair and waving her hands around the room— "but you and I aren't on the streets anymore. We haven't been. For a really. Long. Time. So, now. *Qrow.* I'm asking you. *Again.* What's your *real name*?"

Chapter 5 Qat

I don't know what I expected, but it wasn't the most beautiful creature I've ever seen.

The horse is nearly as tall as I am at its shoulders. Having never ridden one—and I'm pretty sure they're not called shoulders—that seems large.

It's pure silver radiance, as though Kuu—the Moon Goddess of Love—is here in the flesh.

The horse shakes. Water slides over bulging muscles that ripple with every movement. The reflected moonlight turns its sleek coat into liquid silver. Uman and Isa are too small and far away to taint the purity of Kuu's power. I feel her influence over me, even here in the mouth of this cave, shining from this creature.

The horse snorts again, blowing hard out of its nostrils. There is no stringy snot. Of course not. This creature is a goddess. She is tranquility and hope, come to reassure me that I will make it out of this mess alive.

The horse lifts its hooves high as it turns, surveying the cave system. Its tail flicks water and raises to reveal...ah.

Testicles as big as my fist.

Soooo. Not Kuu.

But just as breathtaking. Even in the dim interior, the stallion's coat glistens, his silver mane and tail only a fraction darker than the rest of his body.

Satisfied that we're the only two here, I step out into the mouth of the cave, revealing my presence to this glorious being. Long, elegant ears twitch and send a wave of rippling shivers down its long neck to its back, then beyond to muscular legs until they reach silver-white hooves.

Fascinating.

I could watch him all day.

He turns his head. Cobalt blue eyes send shivers down my spine, and I feel anchored to the stone beneath my feet.

I'm breathless.

We stare at each other.

Mine.

Did I think that? Or him?

I clear my throat, unsure what to do next.

"Hello," I say, stepping closer. "What's your name?"

The horse snorts loudly, stomping its foot. Ah, is he nervous? I take another step closer. The horse doesn't bolt. He tilts his head slightly. Looks me up and down.

That's a good sign, isn't it?

"I bet you'd shine as bright as the stars out there, wouldn't you? I'm going to call you Starshine." I take another step. I'm still about thirty feet away from him. Maybe more. "Is that okay? Do you like the name, Starshine?"

Another quiver runs through him.

I take that as affirmative. I pause, wanting to reassure him. "I won't hurt you." I imagine stroking my hand over his eyes and down his long nose. I want to murmur soothing nonsense and pat him gently along the neck and over his back, chasing the path that shiver had taken through him.

His entire body flinches as if he's been shot.

He gives me one more brief, penetrating look, then races into the water, disappearing under the dark surface.

So much for riding out of Riversmeet.

I wait a moment longer for him to surface for air, but there are so many rock columns between me and the open river that the chances are slim that I'll see him.

Disappointed, I pick up my pack and thread my arms through the straps. With a groan, I grab one low-hanging tooth and start climbing. It's slow going, and I slip more than a few times.

I'm hungry when I reach the Hold, but I can't risk getting seen this close to the docks. I bypass the Marina View Hotel, where I used to stay when I lived here. The view is the only nice thing about it. I effortlessly avoid the streetlamps, steal some dry clothes, and keep to the shadows until I'm well into the city. A few buildings have changed, but the town is much the same as when I lived here while exploring the caves.

Living here was far different than on the *Raven Scream*.

I was tiny as a child. At the time, my size worked in my favor. Rogen taught me to disappear within the folds of skirts, wend my way through a crowd, remove purses, search pockets, and escape without a trace.

I was natural at it.

I would practice on stuffed dummies covered with tiny bells. One tinkling note, and Goffin would cuff me. It only happened a handful of times before I mastered the skill.

There were other lessons. More reasons I was struck. He said I needed to know how to take a hit in case I got caught.

Goffin was mean and harsh, but he took care of me. In his way.

That's what made his betrayal so painful.

And why I hope every day the man is dead.

I'd rather not have to kill him again.

Anyway, I'm thankful for all those lessons, if not for the knocks. Without them, I wouldn't know how to make my way alone.

Deeper into the city, I climb to the roof of a nearby building and move much more quickly. I've spent so much time in Riversmeet over the years that I know the rooftops as well as the street level. And I know the street level by heart, thanks to Goffin's lessons on making mental maps of the cities I visit.

I slide through an empty hotel room window and dump my bag on the bed.

That buzzing feeling is back again, reminding me I haven't looked inside the chest yet. With a strange thrill, I remove it and inspect the latch. Confident that it doesn't contain a trap—my danger sense would warn me if it did—my picks make quick work of the simple lock. My anticipation fades when I lift the lid. A rock sits on a molded bed of velvet. A large, globular green rock about the length of my forearm and a little more than half that in width. The only remarkable thing about it is its pure, lime-green color. I get the impression that if I look hard enough, I might be able to see right through it.

Mine.

Again, the word reverberates in my head.

This time, though, I know the source.

I shake off my strange possessiveness and close the lid. The feeling leaves me. Only then do I realize that the buzzing sensation had stopped when I opened the lid.

Well, whatever it is, I can always sell it. Reluctant to pawn it so soon, I tell myself I won't do so here because I need to keep a low profile. I need to get out of town, and whatever this thing is, I don't want word to get out that it's no longer in the caves. Whoever put it there may still be nearby. Besides, I'll get a much better price in Craguesport.

Comforted by that thought, I slip the box back in my bag.

It's nearly morning, so I should be able to get a few hours of sleep. That's all I'll need. I've survived for days on short, sporadic naps. Several hours will be glorious.

Chapter 6 Qrodin

It was the anguish beneath the anger that got to him. "Qrodin," he finally says. "My name is Qrodin. Qrodin Balaerdo."

Talim's face tightens when she hears his surname, and she blinks quickly. Balaerdo's Fine & Exotic Weapons & Wear was his fourth business. He'd opened it for his twin and filled it with all the things ae adored. Even the sign was designed to attract aer attention. He had hoped that somewhere out there, his twin would discover the shop and know that Qrodin lived.

"And the person you're looking for?" Talim asks, her voice brittle.

Her hardness is a cover for the pain in her eyes. Qrodin hadn't realized how much his reticence would hurt her, but she was right. They weren't on the streets anymore. There had been no reason not to share this with her as she had with him. She deserves more than his name now.

"My sibling." Qrodin closes his eyes for one moment. He reaches into his pocket and withdraws the small vial he uses to store his contact lenses. With a quick pinch, one opaque blue contact lens is removed and dropped into the clear liquid. The second quickly follows. He also drops the disguise, altering his hair and skin. He should have realized that Talim knew about his eye color when they were children. He wonders how many others did.

It's more difficult than he thought it would be to lift his eyes and let his friend see the real him. "My twin," he says.

Their eyes are the same. Gold, like citrine gemstones, with red flecks and a dark halo around the outside. It's not the gold he tries to keep hidden. Danaash have brown eyes that range from gold to near black. But red is only found amongst the Karatolii, in addition to the way his pupils become thin slits in the light. When he was a child, his people called them Nonyx traits since they came from intermixing with Nonyx before the species went extinct. Or so the stories go. There aren't many of those traits left. A tail is the most common, followed by long canines, with whiskers being the rarest.

Talim sits back in her chair. She doesn't say anything. She waits.

What else does she want to hear? It probably doesn't matter. "Our family traveled. My twin and I hid in a wagon when our ama went to the docks." Qrodin's lips press together while he breathes deeply through his nose. He relaxes his shoulders as he exhales. "Ama was murdered in front of us. My twin was taken. Our troupe left. I met you a few days later. Look, I don't know what—"

"That's why you visit that pier?" Talim asks.

Qrodin nods.

"What happened to your twin?"

Qrodin shrugs. "The last I saw, ae was thrown into a small boat and taken down the river. I don't even know if ae's still alive."

"Ae?" Talim asks.

"Our people, the Karatolii, are all female at birth. Some, like me, naturally transform when they hit puberty. We don't refer to each other as male or female. We are all just Karatolii." Even now, Qrodin thinks of the Karatolii in terms of *ae, aer,* and *aem.* Karatol doesn't even have a word for *brother* or *sister, male* or *female.* "My full transformation happened just before the incident. I don't know if my twin..." Qrodin can't finish the sentence.

Qrodin thinks of himself as male, but only after assimilating into Riversmeet's culture and learning the difference.

"It's not the craziest thing I've ever heard? And it explains a lot about you." At Qrodin's raised brow, she says, "Let's just say you were odd and said weird things."

Qrodin's grateful she doesn't press him for more details about his early life. There's plenty of time for that.

They fall silent, and Talim looks at him squarely. "I think your twin killed Truffle. And I think that ae's in big trouble. The city guard is scouring the docks. They're searching every ship."

That's one thing he likes about her; she doesn't mince words. And she doesn't hold grudges. At least, not with him.

"Look," Talim continues. "You're not going to want to hear this, but I don't think you've got much time to find aem."

She's right. He doesn't want to hear that.

Talim leans forward. "There is one thing you can do, though."

Qrodin stiffens at her stern tone, but she doesn't continue. It takes him a moment to realize she's not going to. Maybe she *is* holding a grudge. "Talim. I'm going to need you to help me out here. I have no idea—"

"Finally! Was that so hard?"

Qrodin stops in surprise.

"All you've ever needed to do was ask for my help," Talim says.

Her sincerity cuts him deeply. And she's right. Talim's one of the most competent people he's ever met. He'd never hesitated to ask for her assistance with business transactions. Why had he never felt he could confide in her about his twin? What was it that kept him from reaching out? Habit? Fear? Denial?

Regardless, Qrodin's glad when Talim doesn't wait for him to respond. "Okay. I'm going to send out word right away. If anyone sees...what's your twin's name?"

When he doesn't answer right away, her eyes harden.

"It's not that I don't want to tell you, Talim. My people don't speak the name of the dead. Without knowing if ae lives..." Qrodin closes his eyes, leaving the thought unfinished. He can't say it aloud. He walks to the window and stares out blankly into the night. His twin could be out there.

"Qrow," Talim says.

He doesn't respond. He can't. He's never stopped hoping that he'll find aem. Never stopped hoping that *ae* was looking for Qrodin. That's why he named the store Balaerdo's. His twin would have recognized the name. Would have known how to contact him.

"Qrodin."

Startled to hear his full name on someone else's lips, he turns. He's been Qrow for so long, it often seems there is no Qrodin. He raises his brows at Talim in inquiry.

"Did your twin call you Qrow?"

He nods.

"Did you have a nickname for aem?"

He frowns.

"Look. I think your twin is still alive. But I don't want to go against your customs or anything. I was wondering if using a nickname would count."

He nods, then shakes his head, starting to follow her reasoning. Do nicknames count? Probably not. Their custom is to change the name slightly when naming a child after a loved one.

"Well. What did you call your twin?" Talim asks.

Chapter 7 Qat

8TH DAY OF ZAMDI, 14,887
RIVERSMEET, ZEDANA

Avoiding the sightlines from taller buildings, I traverse the rooftops, more cautious during the day. Sundown won't be for another half hour or so, and I don't have the cover of night to disguise my movements if someone happens to be enjoying the view from their fourth-floor balcony. Thankfully, most tall buildings are further north than I plan on being today.

"Hold up!" Abaft of me, perhaps one building over, is the unmistakable sound of a female hablis. Her voice is high and robust despite her tiny stature. Hablis are about half my height, usually no taller than my waist, and nearly as round as they are tall. Maybe that's why they wear such tall hats—to make them look taller. Their small eyes and pointy noses remind me of the rats in the *Raven Scream*'s bilge that threatened to eat all our grain stores.

The hablis turns a corner and bobbles straight down the middle of the alley, determination stamped on her face, bent nearly double from the giant pack on her back but doing her best to stay upright. Unfortunately, her head-forward posture only reinforces the rat resemblance.

As I watch, she stops walking, plants her fists on her knees, and tries to catch her breath, glaring ahead of her most adorably. With her nose scrunched up and twitching slightly, she looks less like a rat, and more like—I tilt my head to study her face—more like a chipmunk with puffy, round cheeks and soft brown eyes. And an adorable little nose.

No long and ornately styled and pinned updo for this hablis. The short, blond locks are sticking out in all directions and look like they've been hacked off by a dull knife.

Hablis, by nature, are chubby little creatures, but this is the thinnest one I've ever seen. The most bedraggled, too. The sad, green tunic is enormous on her, like a child wearing her mother's clothing. The garment is missing all the puffy stuff it must've started with. The hablises I've met wouldn't be seen in public without at least three ruffles and lace at both neck and wrists, nor one of their famously tall hats.

Maybe she's homeless. It looks like she's carrying everything she owns in that pack. The bag is big enough to topple her any second.

I can't help but smile. Hablis are as cute and harmless as sea lion pups.

"Llani! Slow down; I'm going as fast as I can!" The high-pitched tone sounds authoritative yet polite at the same time.

Who is she yelling at? I change my position on the roof to view the street directly below me. An elf. One with long black hair that falls past her waist. What isn't braided is curled so tight, I bet it would touch the ground if pulled straight. The elf turns and waits for the hablis, and I stifle a gasp. She's purple, the color of a sea urchin delicacy sold and eaten in only the most exclusive restaurants. I've never seen a purple elf before. Never even *heard* of a purple elf.

"We are behind schedule, Bell. Kasaandra is going to blame me."

Her words are spoken precisely with short pauses between them, like someone speaking a new language and hasn't learned to smash all the words together. Although she's dressed simply in black leggings, tall boots, and a fringed vest, her skin color and long, pointy ears are so unusual that I can't look away. Especially when she tosses one long, raven-black ringlet over her shoulder, revealing a necklace with a stone the same color as her aquamarine eyes, and twice the size.

Mine.

No doubt about the source of that claim. I want that necklace.

"I'll tell her it's my fault," the hablis—Bell—says, still not moving forward.

Before I can get a better look at the necklace, my danger sense kicks in, unexpectedly directing downward. It takes a moment to realize the danger is coming from below. A hand emerges from the eaves beneath me, poised in a very familiar way.

A thief.

But the danger isn't to me. It's to the necklace I'd claimed. *Mine*, I think again as the hand grabs it.

A bright flash. Without thinking, I leap away from the blast, expecting the roof to cave in.

There's a crack and thump below me, but no *bang* of an explosion. No hole in the roof either, so I scramble back to the edge and look down. A person on the ground way off to my right. Ae'd been thrown far. The feet aren't moving. Is ae dead?

A moan answers my question.

Where's the necklace? I search the ground around those feet, then back to where the elf had been.

I don't find it. Or her.

A purple hand appears on my left. Then another. The elf flips onto the roof without taking her eyes off the street. "Bell! Run!"

I go completely still, not making a sound, but her ears twitch in my direction anyway. She tenses and turns her head.

She stares at me.

I stare at her throat. Luck is on my side. The necklace is still there. I step closer, eyeing the gem from a few paces away. It's large and oval and, now that I'm closer, several shades darker than the elf's eyes. The color reminds me of the sea before dusk when the sun's reflection glints off the water. Spectacular. I've never seen anything quite like it.

I blink away the glittering thoughts, coming back to my current surroundings. I'm on the roof. *She's* on the roof.

How did she get up here so fast?

And what was that blast? Where did it come from? Why hadn't it made any sound? I don't smell blasting powder, so it hadn't been dynamite. And I can hear fine. No ringing. There was just light and...

The elf's hands are shaking; she must be terrified.

I put my hands up so she can see I'm not a threat.

There's a scuffle below me, the whizzing of something being thrown, and a sharp *thwack!* I glance down and see the hablis across the street, glaring at the downed attacker and picking up another rock for ammo.

"Llani!" the hablis calls out. "Where are you? Are you okay?"

"Yes," she responds, still in that clipped manner. "I'm up here. Be careful. He has a knife."

He does? Another glance at the body below me. The feet haven't moved. I look back at the elf—at 'Llani.'

Something small and sharp hits me square in my temple.

I pivot in place, trying to draw my dagger but realizing I've already drawn it. Only my lightning-fast reflexes keep it from clattering to the road below.

What the fuck is happening?

The elf is staring at the knife in my hand.

"Hey!"

I glance down.

The hablis's face is red, and her eyes scrunch to mere slits when she looks at the knife. Brave girl. And a good shot. How can she be so accurate with that pack on her back? How did she even pick up the rock?

Bollocks, my head hurts! I rub it where the rock hit me. I'm going to have a bruise there later.

I flip my dagger and make my voice as low and menacing as possible. "Did you hit me with a rock? I've killed people for less, you know."

If she were my size, I might say her eyes narrowed dangerously. But, well, she's not my size.

Suddenly amused by the whole thing, I bite my lip to keep from smiling. I take a step back and sheath my blade. There's no threat here.

When the elf peers back into the street, I slide out of sight behind the chimney. But I don't leave. Instead, I follow them.

I want that necklace.

It's the only thing of value I can see on her. The elf looks put together, but her knapsack sags down her back in an empty way, starkly contrasting with the hablis's bursting-at-the-seams bag.

It doesn't take Llani long to notice that I'm no longer on the roof, and she tells Bell to meet her around the other side of the building. When the little hablis complies, I drop to the street and rifle through the would-be thief's pockets before trailing them. There's not much. Hardly worth the wait and risk of losing my prey.

I almost miss them as they round two corners in quick succession. If it weren't for Bell's *'That was soooo cooool!'* and Llani shushing her, I might have kept going down the wrong alley. Llani doesn't walk ahead of Bell this time. They whisper between them, but I'm too far behind to hear anything else they say.

They turn down a street. I move closer, wending my way through the crowd. A few blocks later, they slip into the Lightning Strike tavern.

I debate the benefits of following them inside before reconciling it to fate. I reach into my pocket for my dice bag. Gambling is an easy way to earn a few bucks—especially when the dice are loaded—but I also keep a few true ones on hand for this kind of thing. The inside of the bag glitters in an array of colors. I grab a random die, an amber, twelve-sided one.

Odds for *Follow*, evens for *Leave*.

A nearby crate makes a decent enough surface to roll on.

I roll odd.

The Lightning Strike tavern is a two-story building, but only the first floor is for customers. The walls are a rough mix of old charred stone and newer wood. A short, cobblestone walkway surrounds the building, leading to a solid oak front door. There aren't any windows. I'm familiar enough with the tavern to know that the inside is still dim despite the many wall sconces and oversized chandelier.

I remove the faded brown scarf I'd been using to cover my hair, letting the tresses fall past my shoulders. I tie the scarf around my neck instead, then roll the long sleeves of my shirt to my elbows. Minor changes are often all that's required to avoid detection.

I wait until someone exits and glance inside, but the door shuts before I can scan more than a few tables near the entrance. When I enter, I circle to the left, keeping to the dark spots between the lights. Had the tavern been located further north, there would have been candles on each table, and about a dozen more chandeliers. But the food wouldn't be as good. Besides, the half-lit atmosphere is why I like it here.

The tavern is busy, as are most establishments around here, good catch or not. Every seat is taken, and there's standing room only near the bar. In addition to Oramische, there is a smattering of other languages. I've got an excellent ear for accents and can imitate any I've heard, but I seldom know what they're saying.

When impersonating someone, I often need to study other languages, but I don't bother trying to remember them when the job is done. I can keep accents forever, but simple phrases and greetings for only a few days. I'm sure that says something about my personality, but I don't care what. Other than Oramische, I understand only three languages. One is Grimmsche (the bankers' language, although why or how I learned that one is a mystery). The second is a language used solely by pirates and thieves.

And the third one? I've only ever heard it used by the captain and an old woman he used to visit in Craguesport. Rogen never spoke it around me, and I only heard them because I followed him one day while we were in port.

"You're late," I hear a dwarf say. The place is full of dwarfs—black and white stripes everywhere—but the accent is slightly different. The tone is forceful, but not loud, and the last word sounded more like 'la'e.' Curious, I scan the interior for the speaker.

It's so crowded that I hear Bell's unmistakable "We almost got robbed!" before I see her, followed by Llani's attempts to shush her.

The hablis is sitting at a table near the bar with Llani and two others.

"Are you all right?" The dwarf's voice isn't nearly as deep as the breadth of aer chest suggests it would be, but the accent is the same as the one I'd heard.

Ae has flaming orange hair—almost red in the dim light—and is facing away from the door directly across from Llani. Orange hair, not a Stripeback, then. And the size of those arms is impressive. All adult dwarfs can grow lush beards. This one's beard is full but shorter than I'd expect. I can't see features like wide hips or a round ass to determine if ae's male or female. Not that it matters, but I think this one is female. If so, she must be Kasaandra, who Llani said would blame her for their tardiness.

The last person at the table is an ukulu with curved lower tusks the length of my middle finger and thick but sharp upper canines. Even sitting down, I can tell he's on the small side. Most ukulus are at least six feet, with a humpback and bulging muscles. And bald. But this one has hair. His alert gaze flicks my way. I let my eyes roam past their table as I change direction away from them. From my periphery, I can see the ukulu's shoulders ease slightly. Usually, that would indicate someone is relaxing, but I sense it's the opposite with him. He's storing his energy like the sea retreating before a tidal wave strikes.

I wonder if that makes me the tidal wave and hold back my smile at the thought. But then my pleasure recedes. I wouldn't be the tidal wave. I'd be the beach.

"Okay!" Bell says in response to something I didn't hear. "Let's just say that you'd have loved it! All these lights shot out. Pew! Pew! Pew!" Bell punches her arms out with every sound effect as if words aren't enough. "Then they *exploded*! Like BANG, BANG!" Her hands transform into little explosions. "It was just like a bunch of shooting stars...or *fireworks*! But they didn't make *any* noise."

Llani's ears fly back and then creep up slowly. So expressive. I'd love to learn how to read them.

But that would mean sticking around.

A shame. As soon as I have that necklace, I'm out of Riversmeet. Well, as soon as I can figure out how to avoid the patrols scouring the docks and searching the ships.

A vision of that horse in the cave flashes briefly. If only...

I slink around the perimeter, keeping to the walls until I'm behind the ukulu, who's too observant for my liking. I notice his hair is only growing on the top of his head. The sides and back are either shaved closely or lack hair completely. This one has got to be half danaash. Ukulus are usually bald and only have hair along their spine, something I got used to seeing on shirtless ukulus onboard the *Raven Scream*.

A tiny abandi server takes their order, her shockingly pink hair piled high over her green forehead. "Well, if you're looking for fireworks," she says, grinning, "our crab cakes are the bomb."

"The bomb?" Llani asks, sounding skeptical.

"Yeah, they're killer," the server says.

"We will avoid the crab cakes, then. Thank you for the warning. Do you serve innocuous crab?" she asks.

"Innocu-what?" the orange-haired dwarf asks.

"Innocuous," Llani explains as if she's talking to a child. "It means something safe."

Why didn't she just say 'safe'?

"Why didn't you just say 'safe'?" the dwarf asks, as if ae had read my mind.

Bell is laughing out loud. "I'm a killer crab! I'm going to pinch you in the belly after you eat me!" She's making pincer fingers at Llani.

This is going to take a while. I glare at a couple until they abandon their seats, then sit down, far back enough that I'm hoping they don't notice me. Unfortunately, it also means I can only hear them when they speak loudly. From my vantage point, all but the ukulu's face is visible.

The verbal sparring continues throughout the meal, mainly between Bell and Llani, with a few comments from the dwarf. The dwarf acts fond of Bell but barely tolerates Llani for some reason. The ukulu doesn't speak.

Once the food comes, Bell takes a sample of everyone's meal, wraps it in a napkin, and hands it to Llani to put in her bag. If they weren't so small, I'd think she's taking leftovers, but each piece is barely bite-sized.

After the meal, Bell screeches when the abandi returns to the table, "You were right. The crab cakes *are* the *bomb*! They're just *exploding* with flavor!" She laughs at her joke, and I can't help but inwardly chuckle along with her.

The dwarf gives her a look. "They gonna *blast* out yur ass, you keep ea'in' 'em."

I recognize that accent now. The dropped t's. The k's that sound like she's clearing her throat with her mouth open. It's northern. Probably from Alalngar, or what most people call Dwarf Mountain. How original.

"Blast! Ha-ha!" Bell laughs, skueeeee-ing with each inhale until she finally settles. "That's a good one."

"Well, I, for one, can't eat another bite. I feel ready to burst," Llani says, rubbing her flat belly.

Bell starts hiccupping through her laughter until tears run down her cheeks.

"What?" Llani says. "That lacked hilarity."

The ukulu's hands move fast, flicking through various gestures. Bell starts shaking and nearly falls off her chair.

Is she having a seizure?

"Akin! Stop! You're killing me!" Bell states breathlessly.

Is he casting a spell on her?

Tempted to come to the hablis's defense, I wait and watch, but no one else at the table is interfering.

Chapter 8 Qrodin

After nearly an hour of watching Xan, Qrodin's ready to leave. Xan is more than capable of managing the tavern, helping where needed, but not to the point that he loses sight of the rest of the establishment. He stays mobile between the kitchen, the bar, and the dining area and assists shorter customers with the modified furniture he designed. The double-hinged boosters swing out from under the chairs, and the pullout panels allow diminutive patrons to step up to their seats. Xan also has a good rapport with the employees and customers without being overly friendly or giving away free food and drink.

Qrodin will visit Xan tomorrow to make it official, but for now, he may as well return to his room at the Viridian. The conversation with Talim took a toll on him, and he wants to sleep it off. Besides, holding his disguise in place requires more concentration than it should, a sign that he should have left long before now, and he should have reinserted his contacts, but he hadn't thought he'd need them for the short time he'd planned on being here.

A movement in the mirror grabs his attention. Behind him, someone is flipping a dagger in one hand, catching it, and flipping it again.

His twin used to do the same thing.

But this isn't an eleven-year-old child. This is an adult with sun-darkened features and blazing amber eyes rimmed in black. When ae twirls the knife and starts to stand up, Qrodin's stomach cramps, and he feels light-headed.

The knife twirler catches the blade, and aer eyes snap to him in the mirror. Qrodin clenches his hands to avoid visibly reacting. Glass shatters, and a shard cuts deeply into his palm. He feels his disguise slip. His mirrored reflection mutates, and two of him are side-by-side in the glass. Dozens of them are twirling and intertwining in a kaleidoscope as dizziness overtakes him.

Qrodin takes a deep breath and refocuses his disguise, feeling the illusion wash over him.

"Qrow, what is it?" Talim asks, standing on the raised platform she'd installed behind the bar and scanning the room behind him.

Qrodin's hands are still shaking, and Xan silently hands him a clean cloth for his bleeding hand.

Qrodin wraps it while he searches the room in the mirror.

Chapter 9 Qat

I catch the knife's handle out of reflex, and a shiver runs down my spine

Someone's watching me through the mirror behind the bar.

With pale blue eyes.

Rogen? Here?

Fuck!

But no—dark hair and a startled expression.

My heartbeat slows back to normal. Not Rogen. Nothing startles that man. Though considering how much taller this man is than those around him—even sitting—he rivals the captain in height.

The stranger has heavy brows that slash sharply outward and end in a high, hooked arch. Like mine. We have the same mouth with a wide, full upper lip, thicker than the lower. Unlike mine, his nose is broad and narrows to a point at the tip, like an arrow aiming for his mouth.

The man looks familiar, but I've never met him before. I'd have remembered seeing someone who looked even a little like me. So why do I feel as though I have?

"Are you coming or going?" A patron near me asks, breaking my hold on the mirror.

When did I stand up?

"Going. Help yourself," I say, releasing the tension in my stomach.

I hate the feeling that I should recognize the man.

I re-sheath my dagger and smile, disguising my uneasiness through years of deception. I melt into the shadows and glance back at the mirror. The person sitting there doesn't look anything like me. I dismiss the whole incident as a figment of my imagination brought on by exhaustion. Apparently, my nap was shorter than I needed.

The brief adrenaline rush drained the last of my energy reserves, and I rub the spot on my temple where the hablis had struck me with a rock. I've made enough of a fool of myself for one evening, and I still need to find a place to stay tonight. I'm not too worried about losing track of that motley crew. By morning, word of a purple elf with an intriguing necklace will be all over town.

The door bangs open, and two daga younglings push in.

"We're under attack!" they say in unison.

"Dragon!" says one.

"Manticore!" says the other, slamming the door as they leave us all in shocked silence.

I push toward the door, dodging the crowd as diners hop out of their seats. Dragons are extinct, but manticores aren't, and they often come out of the hills from across the river. I know from experience that manticores can't be reasoned with; they're ruled by instinct and hunger and will keep killing. The invasion must be dealt with, and while the townsfolk are dealing with it, I can get away. No sense in getting wrapped up in that mess.

I jump over someone crawling to get under their table and finally reach the door. Two men are holding it closed, so I push them away and yank it open. About half of the street lanterns have already been lit. The three crescent moons aren't bright tonight. I should have left sooner and avoided all of this.

The townsfolk are panicking. A few of them have torches, trying to keep a giant creature with rust-brown wings from going deeper into the city.

A horse and cart overturning catches its attention, and the beast turns toward me.

As I thought. A manticore. Brown wings are raised high behind it, one bent at an odd angle, and its tail is flailing violently, hurling tail spikes like darts.

My danger sense warns me too late to avoid one of them. Pain shoots up my leg, and I grit my teeth. *Bollocks!* I hadn't even seen it coming.

I duck to my left. Another one thunks into the wall behind me.

Not wanting to risk it, I slip around the corner of the tavern. I yank the first spike out and toss it as a third whizzes by.

The wound in my thigh pulses as I peel my breeches to the side to get a better look at the damage. That thing had dug deep, but at least the blood is seeping rather than spurting. As fast as my heart is beating, I'd be dead in no time if it were.

Hurried footsteps pound on the wooden porch of the Lightning Strike, then on the stone slabs of the street. I peek around the corner. The townsfolk are shouting at the snarling manticore. It turns in wide circles, tail thrashing, keeping onlookers at bay. Sharp teeth in an enormous maw pervert the strangely danaash-like face. The beast scrambles awkwardly, trying and failing to take flight with one wing listing to the side. The beast turns toward my hiding spot.

I scramble back to get out of sight.

Lancing pain in my thigh causes me to stumble and drop one of my daggers. Damn, I forgot I was hurt.

A flash of light pulls me back. In the center of the beast's chest is a hole the size of my fist. The creature rears back in pain.

An ukulu smashes feet-first into the manticore's belly, and a moment later, an arrow lodges in the creature's neck. The manticore's shriek of pain drowns out everything else. Its dagger-sharp teeth snap shut only a breath from the ukulu's shoulder as he rolls out of the way. His black eyes meet mine as he emerges from the roll on his feet.

It's the same ukulu who had been sitting with Llani.

The creature screams again, and I hear the dwarf from the tavern taunting, "—get for going after my friend!" I don't know whether to be impressed or afraid of the *whoop* that follows. Either way, I'm grateful for the reprieve.

The manticore turns toward the dwarf, its side bleeding profusely from a giant gash courtesy of the dwarf's battleaxe. Where had she stashed that during their meal? The injured wing is now dragging on the ground.

I move closer. This isn't my first time being outsized in a fight. On the *Raven Scream*, I was small but quick with my fingers. I discovered sensitive areas like the nose, groin, and throat, and learned how easy it is to get in close, take my shot, and get away fast.

I doubt I could get close enough to hit one of those spots. He's too fast. Not that I have any plans to fight this thing. That's someone else's problem. I need my knife. And I don't want to leave my bag lying around. That green rock is too valuable.

After watching and assessing, I dive for the blade and barely miss the swinging tail. My thigh gives an agonizing jolt as I roll awkwardly, grab the knife, and land in a crouch, ending up closer to the melee than I'd intended.

Time to leave.

The spiked tail comes back, quick and low. There's no time to duck away—I leap at it as it swings my way, ignoring my thigh's protests as I straddle it, my hands grabbing above the base of the spikes. I hang on tight, hoping my weight will slow it down, but it's like riding a sail's crossbeams in a thunderstorm!

The tail spikes curve close as it whips me around, and I lean back as far as my arms can reach so I don't get skewered in the face. As the fight continues, I do my best to bend the tip of the tail away from me, but I may as well be wrestling a sea serpent.

I grip tighter with my legs as the tail swings again.

A flash of orange hair catches my eye on one of the swings, and I look back to see the dwarf block both claws with the flat side of the axe's blade. *Kraken's teeth*, even Rogen would be impressed by that!

The tail changes direction. At the last second, it whips back.

I can't hold on.

The world flies by in a blur.

So does the ukulu as he rolls underneath me.

Following his lead, I roll into my landing and use the momentum to stand up awkwardly, nearly falling when I put weight on my injured leg. I shove my hair from my face and cough up dust from my lungs. My thigh is on fire, my ribs hurt, and the roaring in my ears has nothing to do with the creature.

I feel alive as I haven't since leaving the *Raven Scream*.

Chapter 10 Qrodin

Qrodin is out of his seat before he realizes it.

A hablis girl nearly falls as she jumps from her tall seat to the floor ahead of Qrodin. "Llani! Get my bow!" she yells, dragging her companion out from under the table and toward the door, slowing Qrodin down. "Hurry!"

The diners and drinkers are panicked. People jostle back and forth; someone topples a candle that—thankfully—extinguishes underfoot, and bowls and platters tumble as customers scatter.

As the elf weaves through the chaos, she draws a longbow from a backpack. The bag must be enchanted, as the bow is many times the length of the pack. At another time, he would have asked her to show it to him. Now, he wants her to get out of his way.

"Here!" the elf says as the hablis stops inside the doorway. The elf halts behind her and peeks over the hablis's shoulder, blocking the exit.

Qrodin's manners prevent him from pushing her aside. Outside, a flash of light briefly illuminates the ukulu flying feet-first into the underside of a golden creature with a feline body, spiked tail, and broken wings. The beast roars in pain.

"Oh!" the elf says, still blocking Qrodin's path. "A manticore! How fascinating!"

"Llani! My arrows! I don't want to miss this!" With speed he doesn't expect, the hablis bends the bow, attaches the string, snatches an arrow out of the offered quiver, aims, and fires. All in the blink of an eye. "Got it! Don't just stand there, Llani. Help them!"

Qrodin searches for his twin in the fading light and feels his stomach drop. The creature is so close, but his twin is nowhere to be seen. Qrodin doubts ae would have run. Sparring was in aer blood. And fighting monsters was something ae used to dream about.

"Stand aside," he says as he brushes past the elf. Usually, he would leave the fighting to those trained for it, but he isn't prepared to face losing his twin just as he's possibly found aem.

Coax is a deep hum—so low it can't be heard by most danaash—layered beneath Qrodin's command. The ability, like *Soothe,* can lull most people into doing as he wishes. For it to work, he needs to project the words deep into a person's subconscious.

In his mind, the space between him and the manticore shrinks until he imagines he's looking out of the beast's eyes. He *Coaxes* the creature silently, intoning: *Your bite is harmless; your claws are mist. Your tail missiles are certain to miss.* The rhyme isn't necessary, but he's learned that it penetrates a person's subconsciousness more effectively, like an old and familiar song. They do as he *Coaxes* without realizing it's not their thought.

His commands aren't so concrete; he's trying to destabilize the beast. To make it falter enough to give the fighters an opening. He hopes it's enough.

His sight returns as the dwarf slices into the manticore's back. The creature tries to retaliate with teeth and claws as it turns, but thankfully, the dwarf evades them all.

Perhaps the *Coax* worked.

"Llani!"

At the hablis's cry, Qrodin turns to the doorway.

The elf's gaze is steady, and her lips are moving. He realizes she's casting a spell and moves out of the way as her long, erect ears wilt.

She frowns. "I tried Bell. It was unsuccessful." The elf seems far less moved by the danger of the situation than the hablis next to her. She looks more academically interested in the proceedings than worried about the fighters on the field.

"Try again!" The hablis says, then gasps.

Qrodin turns and finally sees his twin. Any joy is overridden by the realization that ae's riding the injured manticore's tail. Spikes are hurled erratically now. The creature is clawing mindlessly, in survival mode now. *Coax* won't be enough to stop this thing. *Coaxing* requires the target to have some executive function. Qrodin needs something more potent. Something that can get straight through to its core.

Something primal.

Like *Terror.*

Qrodin hesitates. Spells that cause pain and fear take much more energy than gentle persuasion or misdirection. The Karatolii call it *deformaenti* magic. The first time he'd used that spell was also the last. At the time, he'd thought it was the answer to their problem, but it ended up causing him and Talim more trouble than it was worth. He'd vowed to find a better way to handle difficult situations.

But his twin needs him.

Once again, he plants himself securely in the mind of the creature. This time, rather than taking the subtle approach, Qrodin imagines a hand thrusting into his chest and yanking out his heart. *Terror's* hum vibrates his vocal cords, allowing Qrodin to transfer and manipulate energy. Some call it magic; others call it divine intervention. The Karatolii call it Itan. No matter what it's called, it's accessed in unique and personal ways. What works for one person may not work for another. No matter how Itan is called upon, faith is the essential ingredient.

Qrodin focuses his concentration like he never has before. This *will* work. It must. He envisions himself—and, by extension, the creature—screaming in pain and fear as he squeezes his fist. The heart bursts, splattering blood like raindrops.

The manticore screeches, and Qrodin releases control of his spell. He retreats around the side of the tavern, his hands shaking and his belly churning like he's eaten rotten fish guts. Barely able to stand, he heaves up the contents of his stomach. Shaking violently, he slides down the wall until he's sitting on the wooden deck.

What was he thinking?

He's a businessperson, not a warrior. The dangerous scrapes he used to get into with Talim and the Valore are nearly two decades behind him. He's out of practice—not that he had the stomach for fighting anyway. Even the duels he and his twin reenacted for crowds were for entertainment purposes, at least on his part. Qrodin prefers carrying instruments over weapons. His magic comes from his voice and music, not any skill with a sword or staff. He inherited the ability from Ama, just as his sibling inherited Ama's love of horses and fashion. He has no idea where aer love of weapons and fighting came from.

Qrodin talked his way out of things; his twin was the fighter.

Speaking of which, he glances around the side of the building. His twin is alive.

He sighs heavily. This time, it was worth it.

Unapologetically, his priorities change when his sibling's life is on the line. Again.

Chapter 11 Qat

The stench of burnt flesh reminds me I haven't eaten since this morning. No wonder I feel so weak.

The manticore flees toward a crowd of onlookers who scatter and race for cover. A few brave folk wave torches to keep it from retreating far. The beast turns our way again, but has gained enough room to avoid the dwarf's giant axe. It lobs several tail spikes, but they fly over her head as she evades them while running.

The ukulu catches one of the spikes and throws it back at the monster.

I've never seen anything like it.

He'd been knocked aside when I had, and I'm still trying to catch my breath while he's back in the fray. I limp forward, but I can barely feel anything below the injury.

Every breath is torture. I must have broken at least one rib. I wrap an arm around my ribcage and try to slow my breathing.

Thankfully, the creature is in worse shape than I am. A gash in its back has painted its gold fur and the street a dark red. No wonder the beast had screamed; that battleaxe did some hefty damage.

And I haven't even bloodied one of my blades!

Speaking of which, I've dropped my blade. Again.

It sparkles with reflected lamplight on the other side of the street. Fuuuck! I can't make it that far.

Can someone retrieve my dagger for me?

In time, I wipe the sweat from my eyes to see the ukulu hit the beast with a charging, five-fingered death punch to its temple. The manticore's head whips around so far that it's facing backward. The beast stumbles forward.

A collective gasp rolls through the crowd as they take a few steps back.

The street trembles beneath my feet when the manticore drops to the ground. Its wings fly forward, almost crashing into the ukulu before he jumps free.

I count silently to three. It still hasn't moved.

The dwarf approaches slowly. She—I can tell that now—hefts her battleaxe high and brings it down on the manticore's neck, cleaving through muscle and bone. The clang of steel against stone breaks the silence, and I wince at the damage that'll have done to the edge.

The townsfolk cheer. Like cockroaches when the lights go out, they emerge from their hiding places and scurry forward. One grabs the head and holds it high. Another kicks at a wing. I almost laugh when he rubs his foot in pain, but my ribs hurt too much.

"Everybody, stand back now!" A daga pushes through the crowd and takes the manticore's head away from the reveler. "You know the rules! The champions get dibs on the prize!"

The dwarf wipes blood from her face. Her emerald-green eyes hold mine for a second before she examines her blade.

Now that the fight is done, I take the scarf from around my neck and tie it above the wound, tightening it until the bleeding slows. The tourniquet is the best I can do for now. I'm tempted to sink to the ground, but my pride has been beaten enough tonight. There's no way I will show more weakness in front of these townsfolk. Or in front of the ukulu and the dwarf.

You'd think that a town of sailors would be skilled at fighting. But no. They've learned to hoist sails and empty a full hold, but nothing about combat. That's why we pirates are so successful.

The town guards push their way through the crowd. Too late, as usual.

Pain sears my leg as I take a step. I need to get inside before the guard sees me. I search nearby, but my knife is gone. Something twinges inside me as I realize I may never see it again. The blade was one of a matching set. One is good, but the two are better together.

Blood squishes along my thigh beneath my breeches. Damn it! These were expensive leathers. Other than my breastplate and fake IDs, they're the only clothing I keep.

A fortnight ago, I doubt I would have cared. But today, for some reason, the damage bothers me. Had I become bored lately? Aside from this battle, I don't remember the last time my heart raced.

So why do I feel caught in the ropes of a net I'll never escape?

Llani is rushing toward me, looking anxious. She isn't looking at my face, though. Instead, she's examining my leg, her slanted aquamarine eyes somber, and her long, pointy ears twitching nervously.

Beautiful, you can touch me anywhere you want, I think, instinctively trying to manipulate her, even if only in my head. She reaches toward me but pulls her hand away before making contact.

I step forward. As I do, the pain from my wound flares. It's been so long since I've been injured, I forgot how much it hurts to be stabbed. I frown at my carelessness. I'm not used to fighting alongside people anymore. That must be why I was hit.

Oh, who am I kidding? I'm exhausted. That's why I got hurt.

I convince myself it wasn't the events that occurred before the fight. It wasn't the man in the mirror or the wonder on his stunned face as he looked back through the tarnished glass. Or seeing my face on another person.

Wait. My face?

My eyebrows, for sure, and my mouth. But I don't remember thinking it was *my* face.

"You need to sit down. The bleeding is quite severe," Llani says, putting her arm around me.

I wince in response to the pressure on my ribs as we approach the Lightning Strike. I look around for the man I'd seen earlier, whose presence caused this mess.

"Glad to see you made it out of the doorway, Princess," the dwarf says to Llani from my other side.

"I have stated repeatedly, Kasaandra, that I am not a princess." Llani looks behind us but continues addressing Kasaandra in her odd, overly enunciating way. "The Tumi do not have royalty. The Xandri were the last elven species to have a royal line, and it died out over two thousand years ago."

Maybe it's blood loss, but the dwarf looks elated despite the scolding, practically thrumming with excess energy and bouncing up and down on her tiptoes.

"Stop teasing Llani," Bell says. "One of these days, she will have to heal you. You wouldn't want her to do the wrong kind again *accidentally*. Would you?"

Llani is ignoring them, stealing glances behind us. I doubt she even realizes that she's supporting me.

Kasaandra holds the door of the Lightning Strike open for us. The tavern's not as crowded as before, and the group sitting around the nearest table gets up quickly and offers it to us.

"Oh, Akin! You're hurt, too!" Llani drops me abruptly and rushes to the ukulu. "Kasaandra, locate a compress to stem the blood flow."

I stumble over my feet before I reach a chair. I stare at the closest one, trying to stay upright while the floor tilts and rolls, and I fall, more than sit, into it. The room starts spinning. I try to focus on the elf to keep me steady.

The ukulu—Akin—points at me.

What does Llani see in him, anyway?

He's a good-looking guy, I guess, but intimidating. Aside from the tusks, his hair and skin are the color of a whiskey barrel bleached from the sun, somewhere between grey and brown, and his eyes are entirely black. No whites at all. They're so penetrating, I almost don't notice the scars on his forehead. The small dots above each brow were done intentionally. I wonder if they're cultural marks. The scar on his neck, however, is not decorative and instead looks as though someone tried to rip out his throat.

Or maybe that's just how I feel.

"Of course," Llani says, still obviously more concerned about him than me. She glares at the dwarf. "Kasaandra! Why haven't you put pressure on that leg? Hello?" she says, turning back to me. "Stay awake."

Llani tightens the kerchief above my wound, grabs a cloth from somewhere, and holds it against my torn skin. I barely feel it. Maybe it's already healing.

The dwarf is pacing back and forth, making me dizzy. My head hits the back of the chair, and I close my eyes, suddenly tired.

"Kasaandra, perhaps you can put your battle euphoria to good use by carrying the injured party upstairs? Otherwise, I may be tempted to do as Bell suggested. I could use the excess energy."

"Over my dead body," the dwarf says.

"If you were dead, I would be incapable of seizing it."

The dwarf huffs and lifts me over her shoulder like a sack of grain, and I'd bet my lost blade another three ribs break. The pain barely registers.

Then it does. It hurts so much I can't breathe.

I come to lying on a short couch in the upstairs office with Llani bent over me. I reach for my daggers out of habit, surprised they're both there. While I was unconscious, someone must have returned the blade I lost when the manticore tossed me. I'll have to remember to thank them later. Right now, speech is too much to manage. Breathing is more than I can manage.

"Are you in pain?" Llani's voice quivers slightly as she looks down at my leg. She looks frightened, which is silly. I've been in worse shape. I'll be fine as soon as I can take a breath without passing out.

Again.

A groan. Was it me?

My leather breeches are split open at the thigh, exposing my torn flesh. The compressions and tourniquet slowed the bleeding, but now Llani pokes and prods at the wound.

"If you would like, I can try to heal it," she offers hesitantly.

"Where is ae?" The man from the mirror barges in, sees me, and then leans against the doorjamb. Three lined grooves between his brows are scrunched tight in a scowl. I've seen that same scowl in the mirror. My mirror. I feel my frown deepen and try to relax, afraid someone might see a resemblance. The effort makes me frown more.

The man addresses Llani. "Did you say you can heal?" He nods at me.

I try to relax, but my teeth are clenched hard enough to crack a molar, and I'm near panting now. The air hisses out between my teeth, and I can feel my lips stretched wide like a sailor trying to stuff their intestines back into their abdomen after a bloody battle.

"Oh!" Llani says. "Certainly. My apologies." She kneels in front of me and takes a deep breath. A slick of moisture forms on her upper lip. She's nervous again.

I focus hard on the necklace twinkling at me like moonlight on the ocean when the wind teases it.

"Relax, sweetheart," I say to Llani when I finally get a breath. "I'm good, but I'd be great if you just—Oh, ballast!" I gasp when Llani places a hand lightly on the wound.

She closes her eyes. Her fingers move quickly, and she mumbles something I don't understand. A dark purple, nearly black cloud extends from my leg, separating and swirling in ever darker, whirly tendrils.

My energy fades, and my vision turns black around the edges. Worry and pain recede.

"Llani, stop! You're going to kill aem!" Bell cries.

"Oh!"

I don't feel any more pain. I don't feel much of anything at all. Is this the magic they spoke of earlier? Why would Kasaandra not want this? I focus on turquoise eyes. They slant up to her temples. The irises are so tiny that she looks perpetually surprised.

"What happened?" the man asks.

His face is suddenly above me, so close. His eyes are blue, almost white. His irises are so large that the white is but a small triangle in the corners.

The opposite of the elf.

And just like mine.

Look at me. I urge him.

He does.

The light hits his face from the side, highlighting the edge of his contact lenses.

He's not who he wants us to believe.

"Llani. You have to try it again. This time, make it green!" Bell pleads.

"Yes. Green. It was supposed to be green," Llani says.

"What's happening?" Qrow asks again. His mouth tightens. He looks and sounds like he's in a long, dark tunnel.

Why does he care?

What color are his natural eyes?

I feel fine. Better than ever.

My vision narrows further. Ripples inward.

I can no longer see the room, just him.

I don't care.

I'm underwater.

I love the water.

No details through the ripples now. Colors intermingle in and out of the light.

Drowning feels like this. Peaceful. Or so I've heard.

Chapter 12 Qrodin

Qrodin hasn't been this frantic in years, if ever. If this is his twin—and Qrodin is almost convinced ae is—he can't lose aem. Ae's passed out again. The bleeding has resumed.

That means ae's still alive, right? Corpses don't bleed.

Qrow checks for a pulse and releases his held breath when he finds one, thin and unsteady. "I thought you said you could heal." Qrodin's voice is deep. And loud. And angry. He doesn't usually lose control like this.

"My education has been more...theoretical...than practical until recently," Llani says shakily. "I'll try it again."

"Green," the hablis urges.

Green tendrils seek out the wound. Torn pieces of skin knit together, leaving several raised, dark red scars that fade nearly as fast as they were formed. Qrodin is so focused on the leg that he doesn't realize, at first, that aer breathing has gotten stronger.

"Oh, good. It worked," Llani sighs, her body slumping heavily before she reaches over and unties the kerchief tourniquet.

She looks exhausted.

Qrodin barely acknowledges the murmurs of the other three inhabitants of the room. It takes him a few moments to reassure himself that his twin will live. When he does, he finally releases a breath he didn't realize he was holding.

Manners dictate that he should thank them for their assistance. They did, after all, defeat the manticore before it could do any more damage to the town and people. Finally, he pulls his attention from his twin.

When he looks up, they're all staring at him. He takes a moment to recall what they were discussing before the manticore attack. They had been sitting behind him, he remembers.

There had been some talk about being robbed. An explosion. They're staying at the Broken Bed & Barrel. They've been here a fortnight. They're leaving for Craguesport soon.

"I thank you for your bravery this evening," he says unsteadily. Clearing his throat, he continues. "If there's anything that I can do for you during your stay, please let me know. You will, of course, be compensated for your assistance. The carcass has already been retrieved, but there's still time for you to claim some of the spoils. I informed the butcher that I would send word if you do." Why is he rambling on? The details aren't important right now, but he's afraid he will collapse if he stops.

Immediately after the battle, the excess of emotion had been more than he could mask, so after arranging for his probable twin to be taken to the office, he'd advanced on the manticore corpse outside. A tanner who had a shop nearby was on his way to skin the beast, and a butcher was standing by, urging him to hurry so the meat didn't spoil in the evening heat. Per the laws of Riversmeet, first dibs on the carcass go to the combatants who defeat it. If they aren't interested or don't claim the spoils, it goes to the landowner, if one exists. After, it's a mad dash for anyone else, and—like seagulls on fish guts—they swarm the remains.

Since Qrodin owns many buildings nearby and was one of the combatants— though no one would likely have realized it since he didn't use a weapon—he announced his claim on the carcass, to a general groan of displeasure.

He wasn't interested in the head, like a hunter would be. It looked too danaash for his tastes. Instead, it was the tip of the tail with the spikes he was after.

"Can I get the heart?" the hablis asks. "I want to make a stew with it." When the dwarf clears her throat, she adds, "And the liver?"

"Certainly. I'll ask Talim to allow you the use of the kitchen downstairs if you'd like."

"Yes, please," she says.

"How long will you be in Riversmeet?" Qrodin asks, not wanting them to discover he had eavesdropped on their earlier conversation.

"We intend to depart tomorrow next," Llani replies.

The day after tomorrow. "There may be just enough time to tan the hide, in that case."

Qrodin looks over at the person lying on the couch. Ae's still asleep. Qrodin's quite confident that ae is his twin. Until tonight, he had avoided even thinking aer full name. Thinking it would be the next step to voicing it. He almost had, downstairs.

"Can I get the tail spikes?" the dwarf asks, bringing Qrodin back to the present.

The hablis squeals. "Oh! You could carve them!"

"I was hoping to keep those, but—"

"The hide, then?" Kasaandra says quickly, almost uncertainly, in direct contradiction to her actions during the fight, where every action was deliberate.

"I will make the arrangements," Qrodin says. "Anything else?"

Chapter 13 Qat

I don't open my eyes right away. I flex my leg experimentally. No pain. My breathing is no longer labored, either. A wave of relief washes through me.

I flinch when a hand touches my face.

Llani is leaning over me, examining my temple where the hablis's rock had hit. She pulls back as soon as I open my eyes. "How are you feeling?"

I don't want her to realize I'm the person she'd run into on the rooftops earlier. I try to sit up, fully expecting to be greeted by pain, but I'm not. I swivel until my feet hit the floor and take a deep breath. The pain in my ribs is gone. "Better than a few minutes ago," I say. *Was* it just a few minutes ago? I scan the room, refusing to pause at the person who'd leaned over me, whose eyes are still on me. Everyone is still in the same spots as before. I wasn't out long.

I smile as though I normally wake up in a crowd of people, but inside, I'm anxious that I was unconscious around all these strangers. At least on the ship, I had my hiding places to escape the crew.

"Maybe we should introduce ourselves properly now," the elf says. "I am Llani of the Tumi, and these are my acquaintances: Kasaandra of Toithdd Croieanan, Akin of the Owanulafa band from Iletitun." Kasaandra is sitting in Talim's desk chair, and Akin is leaning against a wall. "And, of course, Bell of clan Tubaks of Bierenan."

Sitting on a trunk against the wall, Bell waves with the drumstick she's eating.

Llani's eyes flicker my way. "And you are?"

"At your service." I wink.

"Well, that is most unhelpful. And incorrect, as it was I who serviced you." Ouch.

Llani looks around, straightens her shoulders, and lifts her chin slightly. Her gaze pierces the man I'd seen in the mirror. The one who had been leaning over me earlier. "I heard the bartender call you Qrow," she says.

"Yes." He watches me closely from the door as he continues, "Most people here know me as Quentin Browning, but my closest friends call me Qrow."

Hmm. I wonder which, if either, is his real name. Qrow. I close my eyes. He's not *The* Qrow. The man is a legend, as he has been for longer than this man has probably been alive. The Qrow must be at least twice my age, or maybe even three times, and this man can't be more than a few years older than me. If that.

"*Sueh ba' mira*," Qrow says, holding his arms crossed in front of him, wrists out and stacked one on top of the other, facing Llani.

Llani's cheeks darken to deep amethyst, and she returns the greeting and the gesture.

Showoff. If this *is* The Qrow, he's using a disguise to make himself appear younger. I can't believe he's Quentin Browning, the big-time merchant in Riversmeet who owns most of the ships I've stolen from when visiting.

"What are you doing *here*?" I ask Qrow.

"This is my tavern"—he gestures to the office—"and I arranged for you to be treated up here." He glances briefly at me, his eyes searching, but for what, I have no idea.

I have nothing to discuss with The Qrow. Or Quentin Browning. Especially all the goods I've stolen from his ships and warehouses over the years. But he wouldn't know about those.

I search for something to change the subject.

Llani beats me to it, speaking to me this time. "My apologies for my error before healing you properly."

What error? I search my memory, but the last thing I remember is realizing that Qrow was wearing contact lenses, then falling into blissful sleep.

I must look as confused as I feel because Llani explains how she had drained my energy before healing me. I shrug it off, but inside, I'm both impressed and a little afraid of her skill. "Don't worry about it," I say, trying to make light of it and ease the guilt I can see on her face. "You would've been handy to have around on the ship. Especially if you can do that first part intentionally." I wink to show I'm joking. I'm not, though. Taking people's energy is a skill I'd love to have. I didn't even know someone could do that.

"What were you doing on a ship?" Qrow's deep voice is cautious. Why is that? He's far more concerned about me than he should be. I don't like anyone knowing my business; saying even this much is unlike me.

"You want my life story?" I ask, expecting him to back down.

"Do you *know* your life story?" Qrow asks in return.

He says it softly, but it flays me open. The fact that I don't remember my earliest years is something that I've never revealed to anyone other than Captain Rogen. I don't even know how old I am.

"Do you not know who I am?" Qrow asks when it's clear I'm not going to answer him.

"I know *exactly* who you are," I say to hide my annoyance. Who around here doesn't know The Qrow?

"I mean, who I am to *you*?" Qrow says softly.

My heart stops beating. I remind myself to breathe. I'm no one to him. He can't know anything about me, but his expression says otherwise. His eerily familiar expression.

Fuck this! I'm out. Whoever this guy is, and whatever he thinks he knows, he can keep it to himself. My pack is on the floor near me. I grab it and lift Llani's hand to my mouth to kiss it softly. "Thank you, my sweet. Until I see you again." I nod at each of the others and approach the door.

Qrow refuses to move out of the doorway. He's tall enough that his head almost brushes the top of the frame, and his shoulders span the entire opening.

This isn't the first time I've dealt with his kind, and it won't be the last. I unsheathe one of my daggers and flip it once before catching it. "We can do this one of two ways. The easy way." I flip the knife. "Or the fun way." Flip. "I know which way I'd like it to go." I spin the dagger and give him my fighting grin.

"You don't remember me?" Qrow asks.

"Should I?" The hair on the back of my neck is at full sail.

"*Yu nu pot prita o Qat tu o Qrow,*" Qrow says so softly that I doubt the others heard him.

Blood drains from my face even before he finishes speaking, leaving only a cold numbness in my cheeks. *You can't catch a cat with a crow.* It's the same language Captain Rogen spoke with that old woman. Hearing them speak had given me a sense of comfort I could never explain.

There's no comfort hearing it come out of Qrow's mouth.

Only dread and an eerie sense of foreboding.

Whispers across the room draw my attention.

"—know you heard him. What did he say?" Bell asks.

"I am unfamiliar with the language."

How had Llani even heard him from there?

"What? I thought you knew every language!"

"Well. I doubt anyone understands *every* language," Llani says, clearly perturbed.

Distracted though I am by their conversation, the current situation has me more on edge than I'd like to admit. I flip my dagger again and raise my left brow, hoping I look unconcerned at Qrow's scrutiny.

He scowls. "You understood me, though, didn't you?" he asks softly.

He's searching for signs that I recognize him, but other than knowing his name and reputation, I haven't a clue how we could be connected.

"Sorry, bud. I got nothin.' Now, if you don't mind, I've a lady I'd like t'go see," I say in my best sailor-about-town accent. I take a step forward.

"You're my sibling," Qrow says. "My twin." His voice deepens slightly on the last word.

I stop. Who does he think he's kidding? Why would a wealthy man like Quentin Browning want to lay claim to someone like me? "That's bollocks." I move away from the door—away from him. The desk is nearly empty, but I pick up and set down each item to keep my hands busy and my expression hidden from Qrow.

The whispers from across the room kick back up in force.

"You don't remember being taken?" Qrow asks.

"Taken?" When I woke, the captain said I'd fallen and hit my head. Said I had a concussion. But he never said how I fell. "That's a fanciful tale, but it's not mine."

"Fanciful? Do you think Ama being murdered in front of us is *fanciful*?" Qrow stalks forward, his brows nearly meeting and his nostrils flaring sharply. "You think seeing you dragged away and not being able to stop it is *fanciful*?"

Before my eyes, his face alters slightly. His upper lip fills out. A chin dimple appears. I'd missed that detail before. He's been using magic to change his appearance, the way I use makeup to alter mine. I wasn't imagining it back in the tavern.

"Sorry, *Qrow*. You've got the wrong person," I say, but Qrow looks too familiar for him to be making it up. Hadn't I been thinking that earlier?

"How could you have forgotten?!" Anger and something else I can't place are stamped deeply on his features before he turns away.

I glance at the others to see how they're taking this. Bell and Kasaandra look startled, but Llani and Akin don't seem phased. Had they seen his altered appearance before?

"Your mom was killed in front of you?" Bell asks. Tears are welling in her eyes. "I'm so, so sorry." She jumps off the trunk and runs toward me. She crashes into me, wrapping her arms as far around my legs as she can, and presses her ear to my abdomen.

Unprepared for the assault, I nearly stumble but right myself against the desk. What is she doing?

Her arms squeeze tighter before she releases me. She sniffles and wipes tears from her eyes.

I hand her a kerchief from my pocket, stunned to realize she had been hugging me. Me. A pirate and assassin. She blows her nose and offers me the kerchief.

"You keep it. I have another."

Llani touches Bell's shoulder. "We should leave these two alone." When nobody moves, Llani's voice hardens slightly. "We should *all* leave them to their discussion." She drags Bell behind her and stops in front of Qrow, "I apologize for our intrusion into your reunion, for it is apparent we are unnecessary witnesses to a most awkward situation for you both. Please excuse us while you deliberate on your circumstances. If you have further need of our presence, our accommodations are the Broken Bed & Barrel."

"*Tama musari vasidara*," says Qrow.

"*Siroha suskirta*," Llani replies automatically. Then, without looking at me again, she leaves, pulling Bell behind her.

Bell stops at the door and stares at me. "But I don't even know your name!"

I should lie. "You can call me Qat," I say, surprising myself.

Her answering smile melts away the annoyance I feel at telling the truth.

Chapter 14 Qrodin

This *is* his twin. The fact hits him like a fist in the gut. The feeling is quickly replaced by anger. How dare Qat act like ae doesn't remember anything.

Qat doesn't move away as Qrodin approaches the desk and pushes the switch to activate the *Silence* spell. *"What do you remember?"* Qrodin asks in Karatol.

Qat doesn't respond, but Qrodin can tell ae understands the question, and that's all he needs to know. Karatol is a language that has long been kept secret by its people.

The Karatolii are danaash, and after their country dried up and could no longer sustain them, they left and began earning their livelihood traveling in caravans. They trusted only those who could speak their language. Children were taught Oramische—and spoke it as fluently as Karatol—to communicate with outsiders, even practicing different accents before visiting a city so they didn't sound like foreigners. The practice made it easier to gain the trust of the townsfolk.

It's why he had spoken it in a whisper earlier. The elf shouldn't have been able to hear him. He still shouldn't have spoken it with others in the room, but Qrodin had to know if Qat understood him.

"I ask," he says, "because you're using the same name. The one I called you because I couldn't pronounce your full name."

"And what name is that?" Qat finally asks.

"Qatzsi. Qatzsi Balaerdo," Qrodin says, pronouncing the familiar *Cat-zee* for the first time in decades. *Qat,* a shortened version of his ama'ani's name, and *Zsi* from Zsiara, Ama's best friend.

Qat's eyes widen slightly.

Qrodin nods. "Yes. That Balaerdo's."

"And you say I'm your twin?"

Some of the tension leaves Qrodin's shoulders. He nods, grateful Qat stayed. Ae could have left when the others did. Qrodin's even more grateful ae's asking questions.

"How old are we?"

"Thirty-one," Qrodin says. "We were born the thirteenth day of Kazamee, eight fifty-six."

"Who's older?"

Surprised by the question, Qrodin tells aem the truth, "You are." He then tacks on, "By three minutes."

Qat doesn't say anything else for so long that Qrodin gets nervous. He doesn't want to frighten aem off. "I see you still like scarves." He nods to the one in Qat's hand. "Is red still your favorite color?" Why did he ask that? Indeed, there were more important things to talk about. He'd imagined their reunion hundreds—possibly thousands—of times. There was nothing, however, that could prepare him for the possibility that Qat didn't remember him.

He pictures Ama's red scarf, waving as Qat clutches it. His last memory of aem. Maybe that's why he asked it.

Not wanting to bring up that particular memory, Qrodin continues. "You took a couple of Ama's satin ones once. Tied them on your feet and skated in a hotel lobby where we performed. Completely ruined them. Ama was so angry, ae started to yell at you in Karatol before ae remembered where we were."

"Performing?" Qat asks. Aer brow knits familiarly.

Qrodin breathes a little easier. Every question equals a few more minutes of aer time.

"Ama played the violin. Ae specialized in playing string, but ae made the best flutes. Ae was teaching me before ae..." Qrodin swallows hard and clears his throat, surprised at the emotions he can't suppress. "I played the lute, sometimes a flute. I enjoyed singing best, but it depended on the audience."

"And me? What did I play?"

Qrodin almost laughs at the memory of Qat being forced to sing. "You didn't. Couldn't sing a note. No, you mostly performed stunts. Acrobatics. Knife throwing." Qrodin glances at the knives tucked into aer waist. "You always loved knives."

Qat's lips press together. Ae's annoyed.

Time to change the subject. "I understand this might be hard to believe. I can't imagine what you're going through right now. Maybe this will help convince you." In a repeat of last night, he pinches one of the contacts, removing it easily. Then the other. He drops them into their case and meets aer eyes.

For a long moment, Qat stares. Qrodin tries to read the myriad emotions flickering across aer face, but they're changing too fast for him to keep up. Aer fingers twitch, and Qrodin can feel aem tensing.

Afraid ae'll leave, Qrodin finally speaks. "I travel extensively, but my home is in Craguesport." He suddenly realizes that with Bernhard Truffle gone, he no longer has a reason to stay in Riversmeet. If Qat is the one who dispatched Bernhard Truffle, ae might need to escape the city. He ignores his lack of concern that Qat may have committed murder. "I'll be leaving for there soon. You're welcome to join me."

At Qat's panicked look, Qrodin recalls the other four strangers, Llani, Bell, Kasaandra, and Akin, saying they were going there by land, leaving in two days. Accompanying them could provide both cover for Qat and protection for them, considering the dangers of overland travel. "I thought I'd go by horseback this time. It's been a while since I've had some time off."

After a moment, Qat replies, "I don't ride."

Qrodin looks at aem in surprise. "Of course you do. You've been riding since before you could walk."

Qat looks stricken.

"I'm sorry," Qrodin says quickly. "Have you not been on a horse since…?" Qrodin doesn't know how to say it.

"Since I was taken?" Qat asks quietly.

Chapter 15 Qat

Taken.

I was eleven years old when I was taken.

Taken. Taken. Taken.

The word keeps echoing in my head.

I'm the one who takes. Not the one that's taken.

I still can't believe it. But everything he said fits. The red scarf I pulled out of my pocket that first morning. That language. His eyes.

My eyes. My eyes in his face.

I think that's what clinched it for me. The same whiskey-colored eyes with red-brown bands framing pupils that narrow to thin strips in the sunlight. That's one rumor about The Qrow I've never heard. I would have gone in search of him if I had.

"Yes," Qrow says. "You used to do most of your stunts from the back of your horse."

I had a horse? Unbidden, the silver horse from the caves comes to mind. Could I have ridden him out of the caves?

"What kind of stunts?" I ask to keep from regretting circumstances I had no control over.

"You'd ride backward, standing up, or standing up backward. You'd flip off its back. Sometimes, you'd jump onto a galloping horse from the top of a moving carriage."

I'd do that? Jump onto a running horse?

"Is that all?" I was only eleven, so maybe it is.

"No. You also trained the horse to do tricks. There was nothing you couldn't get a horse to do." He looks at me for a moment. "You had a few other skills as well."

I feel him studying me closely.

"What kind of skills?"

He pauses a moment. I can see him debating with himself over something.

My curiosity piques, and I realize I'm holding my breath for his answer. I deliberately release it, refusing to give him power over me. "If you weren't going to tell me, you shouldn't have brought it up."

His face softens, and he nearly smiles. "Let's just say that if you wanted something, you'd take it."

He means stealing. I raise one brow. "Was I good at it?"

"One of the best."

I guess that's why I learned so quickly not to set off many bells when Goffin was training me. I wonder what else I was already good at. "What about knives? You said I always liked knives."

"You'd practice tossing them, flipping them, throwing them. After Ama gave you one for our birthday, you were seldom without one. You'd started throwing them at targets while you were riding, too. You hadn't done a show with it yet, but you were working on it."

Still thinking about things I'd picked up quickly, I ask, "Did we ever fight?"

"We argued all the time."

"No. I mean, fight. Spar. With fists or weapons?"

"Sure. Not so much with fists, unless you were angry at me. But for the show, we used weapons. I used a staff most of the time. Long weapons were the only way to keep you at a distance. Otherwise, I'd end up nearly naked." He laughs. "You'd use—"

"A knife," we finish together.

"Yep. You'd remove buttons, cut ties, slice my shirt from neck to hem. All without touching the skin."

Like I did on the *Raven Scream*. The crew sparred to stave off boredom at sea. Even as small as I was, I joined in. I started developing trademark moves the day I sliced through my opponent's drawstrings, and his pants dropped around his ankles. Before long, I learned how to do it in the most creative ways.

Or rather, my body remembered how.

I'm suddenly uncomfortable with the conversation.

Not remembering my origins meant I could be anyone I wanted to be. *I* made myself, not my mysterious past. Now, I'm finding out I may not have. At least, not in the way I remember. Will discovering more about my past be a blessing or a curse? Will learning more make me question who I am going forward?

Possibly. But maybe it could help me right now. Maybe my body will remember riding? For some reason, I've never been comfortable around horses. Even when I saw that horse in the caves, I was nervous about approaching it.

Was I afraid of finding out there was something else I was naturally good at? The crew already gave me a hard time about my knife skills. Said I was cheating. Using magic. Magic frightens most sailors—they think using magic at sea is bad luck.

But I've never had magic. Most people don't. "You're leaving in two days?"

Qrow appears to take the change in topic in stride. "Yes. I was going to ask the group that just left if they wanted some company on their journey. I don't believe they've been there before, and there is safety in numbers. I'm meeting with them tomorrow to distribute the items and reward them for killing the manticore. When I see them, I'll ask if they wouldn't mind some company. They agreed to meet me at Balaerdo's tomorrow morning so they can purchase what they need for the journey. Part of the reward is yours, by the way. You're welcome to accompany me—or us—if they agree."

I don't say anything. Out of habit, I don't share my plans with anyone. "Thank you for the offer," I say instead.

9TH DAY OF ZAMDI, 14,887
RIVERSMEET, ZEDANA

In an instant, I can be male or female or both or neither, walk with a limp, or glide effortlessly across a dance floor. If I study someone long enough, I can pick up their mannerisms, speech patterns, postures, and expressions. The subterfuge is how I blend into a crowd. How I hide in plain sight.

But Qrow had recognized me.

And he hadn't seen me in twenty years.

That makes me nervous that Rogen will be able to do the same. After all, he taught me everything I know—that is, everything I remember learning.

It's all very frustrating.

I didn't sleep much last night. After I left Qrow, I checked for hidden messages and eavesdropped on gossip.

When I stayed here all those years ago, I discovered the street kids have a code:

"You don't see me."

"See you, see nothing."

"See it all."

I learned to stay out of sight and listen when I heard that exchange.

I heard it again last night. Every outgoing ship is being searched before it leaves, even if it's already been searched.

Who knew Truffle's disappearance would prompt this level of investigation? Had I known, I would have asked for triple the rate.

I've debated back and forth the wisdom of going with Qrow and the others. On the *pro* side, they already know my relationship with him. I wouldn't have to hide my face. I'd be off the water and, therefore, more challenging for the authorities—and Rogen—to find. I'd also be able to relearn how to ride a horse.

I always loved to sail fast on the *Raven Scream* as it chased after a ship. I'd never tell Uci, but I always envied his ability to fly. He was free to go *where* he wanted, *when* he wanted. If I could fly like him, would I have tied myself to the captain for so long?

Probably not.

I miss that feeling of speed. Would it be the same on the back of a horse?

I imagine that silver beauty from the cave. His mane and tail flying behind as he races along the shore. He'd be fast.

Does he belong to someone? The thought makes me strangely jealous.

Mine. I remember thinking when I saw him. But then, I remember thinking the same thing about Llani's necklace.

I add it to the list of pros for going with them. I'll be able to keep an eye on the necklace.

As for *cons*, well...

I've never been one to worry about the consequences of doing something. I prefer to think of the consequences of *not* doing something. Like, *not* going to Craguesport on horseback *might* get me caught here.

And that's plenty good enough for me.

"Is Qat going to be here?"

Bell's hopeful question is unwelcome. But it's my fault—I shouldn't have *told* her my name if I didn't want anyone to *hear* it.

The answer to her question is *yes,* though.

I'm still wearing what I wore last night. I'd been too distracted by my thoughts to grab some different clothes. Besides, I need to replace my leather pants. And Balaerdo's carries the best kind.

I'm outside the building next to the store, which gives me a good view down the street. Bell's leading the way toward me, and the group is getting more than its fair share of curiosity.

Riversmeet is a mix of most species. Despite that, Llani's ears and coloring are drawing attention. Or it could be the long raven-black curls nearly touching her knees this morning. Or the intricate braids woven throughout. You don't usually see something so exquisite here.

Kasaandra is talking to Akin, and he responds with his hands. I watch for a while longer. Yes. With his hands. No wonder I never heard him speak. And no wonder I heard odd starts and stops to some of the whispered conversations while I was half out of it last night. I thought I was hallucinating. Or maybe I'm hallucinating this morning.

Bell looks awful. Her dress looks like it snagged on every thorn and bush as she rolled down a hill. Usually, hablis are meticulous in their dress. Both men and women sport ruffles and frills, buttons and belts, tall hats, and shiny shoes. Bell's hair looks like it underwent the same treatment as her dress, and her shoes look like mud-encrusted clogs.

Perhaps that's why Qrow suggested they come here this morning. Balaerdo's Fine & Exotic Weapons & Wear has something for everyone and is one of my favorite shops in Riversmeet. And in Craguesport. And in nearly every other port town I've been to. Balaerdo's is everywhere. A shop full of all the things I like best.

Strange to know that my surname is Balaerdo.

"You look very pretty today, Bell," I say, stepping into their path.

"Ae is mocking you," Llani says.

"I don't care," Bell replies, sticking her tongue out at Llani. "Oh, look! A cat! Just like you," she says, pointing to the Balaerdo's sign.

They disappear inside.

I don't follow them right away. Instead, I stare at the sign: a carved and painted cat, long and slim, with a light body, dark ear, and dark extremities. The feline is sitting, licking the back of one paw with its claws extended sharply forward. Around the cat's middle are a leather belt and a dagger. Around its neck and cloaking one ear is a blood-red scarf.

The scarf first caught my attention when I saw the sign more than a decade ago. It wasn't this sign on this shopfront here in Riversmeet. It was the one in Alonard. The scarf was the same color as the scarf I had found when I first awoke onboard Captain Rogen's pirate ship. Pulling it from my pocket is one of my earliest memories.

Qrow stops next to me.

Without glancing his way, I ask, "Why did you think I was your long-lost twin? What did you see last night? It wasn't my eyes." When he doesn't answer immediately, I say, "According to you, it's been twenty years since you've seen me."

"It was the knife," he replies. "You were flipping it and catching it by the blade. A habit when you were nervous, or debating a course of action."

His speech sounds so formal this morning.

"A lot of people flip their knives."

"With your left hand."

"A lot of people are left-handed." Captain Rogen was left-handed. He'd said the best assassins were. The commonality was why he taught me how to use a *ha-sheesh-shun* knife. *'Due to the shape of the handle,'* he used to say, *'and the blade's curve, only left-handers can use it correctly, reaching around from behind to drive the tip just left of the breastbone, through the ribs to the beating heart behind.'* I find myself repeating the mantra while performing the act. Like I did with Bernhard Truffle.

"They don't twirl them once they've come to a conclusion." Qrow's comment brings me back to the present.

Do I do that? Twirl my knife? I remember it twirling last night at the tavern. Was I deciding on a course of action? If so, I don't remember what it was. Had I been conscious of it, I'd have probably used dice. I'll need to watch that in the future. If Qrow noticed it, Rogen would, too.

The shop has a single front door with display windows on each side showcasing new arrivals on stands or tables. I slip inside while Qrow's attention is on the display, but he follows me almost immediately.

The shop isn't tiny, but it's not massive either, and it's lit from above by opaque portholes in the overhead rather than by hundreds of candles. They reflect off a polished, white wood deck. Dark-paneled bulkheads are draped with fine silks; clothing is portside, and weapons are starboard. Tables and racks are scattered seemingly randomly around the boutique, but I know every area of the room can be viewed from the counter using strategically placed mirrors. Whoever designed it had an intimate knowledge of a thief's tricks.

Even so, I pocket a purple and gold flask out of habit. Hocking it will feed me for a few days, at least.

"You don't need to do that. Not now. Not anymore."

I startle at Qrow's voice whispered over my shoulder. How had he gotten so close? Few people have been able to sneak up on me since Goffin the Black. This situation must have rattled me.

"You don't know what I need," I say, working my way to the weapons. They are of exceptional quality. Blades made in the depths of Dwarf Mountain, elvish braces, monk's throwing stars, darts, and so many more handy items. I acquired my favorite whip from Balaerdo's. They have jewelry, perfume, shoes, and...scarves.

So many scarves.

Llani and Bell are examining some. Bell is oohing and aahing over the many shades, but Llani doesn't look impressed. "They serve no purpose whatsoever other than vanity, which isn't useful. Or to draw attention to oneself." Llani folds a metallic blue, satin headscarf at the original creases and sets it on a stack of others like it, lining up the corners precisely with the one below.

Bell hands her a sunny yellow one.

"Not that one either." Llani starts folding.

Bell giggles. Llani ignores her.

Intrigued, I approach them. "There are several uses for these beauties. Scarves are the most versatile item I own." I take the scarf from her and drape it over her black curls. Her ears, higher than the top of her head, make two points in the satin. "You could use it to tie your hair back or cover your head from the sun and shield your eyes." I had observed her shielding hers with one hand as she approached the shop.

"Oh. That is *quite* brilliant." Sarcasm? Probably. The example was an obvious use for a scarf. She doesn't, however, remove the item. Instead, she tosses one end over her shoulder. Perhaps it wasn't sarcasm. Bell hands her a green scarf. Llani ignores it, setting it down.

The little hablis's face falls. She wants the scarf.

I pick it up and unfold it, holding it out to Bell. "This is probably large enough to make a new dress for you," I say. "I know someone who can do it, and they owe me a favor." I motion her to a mirror and drape the cotton before her, leaning down to match my height to hers, one of the many tricks I've learned to manipulate people's emotions. In this case, to make her feel less nervous and more of an equal. "I think emerald is your color. What do you think?"

Her brown eyes sparkle as she views herself. "I love it!" She throws her arms around my neck, and I freeze. Pirates don't hug. And this makes two in as many days.

Llani narrows her eyes and taps her lips with one finger as though the decision to purchase the green fabric is up to her. Bell waits anxiously for her response. "The emerald would be better suited to Kasaandra, with her coloring. You would look better in jade or sage green."

"No! I like it!" Bell says, pulling the fabric away before Llani can take it. "I—Oh." She stops suddenly. Her eyes widen, then her lip trembles. She swipes a hand across her face and sniffs loudly. She shakes her head and stuffs the scarf between two piles on the table. "I don't have any way to buy it." She bows her head. "I left home without any coin."

"Oh. That's unfortunate," Llani says. "You should have said something earlier." She pulls the cloth out and shakes it before folding it. "Now the cloth is wrinkled. How did you expect to replace your gown if you lacked the means?"

"Don't worry," I say to Bell. "Qrow's buying." Whether he'd planned on paying or not, he said he would give them reward money. He may as well start paying up now.

I turn around to look for him and instead see something that pitches me sideways like I'm walking on deck in a storm. I grab a nearby table to steady myself.

Behind Qrow, a wooden ball tops a stand of pegs crammed with metal bangles. Tied around the ball is red-on-red satin, the rough design woven to contrast with the smooth and shiny background in a design I recognize all too well—stars of various sizes alternating with the moons in all their different phases.

I approach it slowly and rub two pieces of the fabric together, back and forth between my thumb and first two fingers. The alternating friction and slip, friction and slip, releases tension between my shoulder blades. I used to do the same thing when huddled in my favorite hiding spot on the *Raven Scream*. Something about the rhythm, or maybe the vibration on my fingertips, is hypnotic.

Qrow's sudden stillness snaps me out of my reverie. He's like a shark that's caught the scent of blood in the water.

"It was hers, wasn't it?" I ask, without realizing I'd spoken aloud until he answers.

"Whose?" His face is unnaturally blank, but I can feel his tension like static electricity before a storm.

"Mm...ah...our mother? She had one like this, didn't she?" I ask.

He nods. "Ama had one."

Ama. Did I call her Ama, too? I test it out a few times in my head. Ama. Ama. *Ama, can I go...?*

Can I go...what? Go play? Did I ever play as a kid?

Suddenly, I'm pissed that I don't remember. Then, I'm angry about being pissed. *I don't want to know!* I've never wanted to—

"Do you remember it?" Qrow asks softly.

I do, but not for the reason he must think. I had lost that scarf, *Ama's scarf*—my gut tightens at the thought—twelve years ago on the last day onboard Rogen's ship.

I had hung over the side of the ship, released one end of the scarf while holding onto the other, bouncing, hoping it would unwrap from Goffin's neck folds—or he'd tumble overboard. I finally gave up and dropped into the water when I heard someone walking along the pier. I probably would have gone back to finish the job had I not seen Uci flying overhead.

And I've been ducking Captain Rogen ever since. He wouldn't care why I felt it necessary to off his first mate. He'd've probably even taken Goffin's side. I couldn't take the chance. I ran and never looked back.

I shake my head to clear it. I should thank Goffin, truly. He taught me never to let my guard down.

"Qatzsi." Qrow's impatience probably would have made me smile if I weren't amid a cyclone of memories. But the name doesn't amuse me.

It takes a moment to remember what he was asking about. Oh. Yeah. *Do I remember Ama had that scarf?* "No. I told you. I don't remember anything. Stop asking. You think it will all come back to me now that I've met you? And my name is Qat! Not Qatzsi!"

"You didn't *just* meet me!" Qrow's comment attracts the attention of the others in the shop. He compresses his lips, then continues more quietly. "You've known me your whole life." He practically hisses it, and his blue eyes smolder.

"No! *You've* known *me* your whole life. *I've* known *you* two days!"

His jaw muscles clench tight, and a vein pulses above his right eye near his hairline.

Not my problem. "You want to have this conversation here?" I ask.

Qrow closes his eyes, takes a deep breath, and shakes his head. "No."

"Neither do I."

The Qrow stalks behind the counter and flips aside a brown curtain. He looks over his shoulder at me before proceeding. I wait a few beats before slipping through the doorway myself, timing it to avoid any contact with the fabric as it slowly settles back into place.

We've entered a storeroom. Near the back door are neatly stacked unopened crates, most likely a recent delivery. Beyond the pile of boxes stand a couple of wheeled racks stuffed full of hanging robes, cloaks, and overcoats. Along the walls are bookcases full of more of what is already stocked out front.

Beyond those racks is another door. The office? The safe?

Qrow is watching me, studying my every expression. "What?" I ask. Qrow doesn't answer. Not at first, but I can feel his frustration mounting. "Ask me already," I say, but I don't care what he wants.

I strain to hear him when he finally speaks. "Not even in your dreams?" He takes a breath and holds it as though trying to listen to my thoughts.

My dreams?

I shake my head. No. Not even in my dreams. I usually dream about letting go of that red scarf and falling, watching as the ends flap in the wind, waving goodbye. I always wake before the water closes entirely over my head.

"What happened to her? To Ama?" Now, why did I ask that? "Wait! No!" I close my eyes and cover my ears when Qrow opens his mouth to answer. "Not yet! Not yet! Not yet!" I repeat out loud quickly in case he answers. "Give me a bit."

I walk away from him. I open my eyes but see only the red scarf waving in the distance, getting smaller and smaller as I slowly disappear below the waves.

That's how I feel now. As if I'm underwater. If I take a deep breath, I'll drown.

I hear my pulse pounding, loud and fast in my ears. My hand automatically seeks out my dagger's hilt as if my current troubles could be stabbed to death.

If I go there, there's no going back.

Flip. Catch.

That's how I am. It's all or nothing with me.

Flip. Catch.

I'll be all in. No more running away.

Flip. Catch.

I inhale through my nose slowly. I don't drown. Instead, I hear my pulse slow. I exhale through my mouth. Again. In. Out.

I've felt my heart race more in the last two days than in the previous decade.

Flip. Catch.

Maybe it's time I do something about it.

Spin. Catch.

With my dagger sheathed, I slip past the curtain to the table and remove the red satin from the stand. I tie it around my head like I do when I'm high up in the crow's nest watching for enemy raiders—cocked to cover one ear and wrapped around my neck to keep it secure. I can almost feel the wind on my face. Hear men screaming as we overtake them and board their enemy vessel. I swing down from above like a shadow, slicing in time to my heartbeat, alive as I've never felt since.

I want to feel that way again.

Maybe it's time to run toward something rather than away from someone.

All I have to do is ask.

I'm not a coward!

Just ask.

I turn around. "Okay. Tell me." I take a deep breath. "What happened to Ama?"

Chapter 16 Qrodin

Years ago, Qrodin invested in a lightweight set of clothing made of something the dwarfs called *sia'damhalla*. The fabric looks and feels like silk but is more durable than leather armor. The clothing was enchanted so he could alter its appearance at will, transforming each article with a touch.

This morning, he had changed them into a plain cotton top and trousers. Before Qat approached, he'd been looking for a few extra changes of clothes to bring on the trip. He hadn't been prepared to talk about Ama.

Qrodin stops in front of the naked display ball on the table. He selects a random scarf to replace the one Qatzsi...Qat...is now wearing. He realizes he's stalling, but old habits die hard. Even those twenty years out of use. Not even twelve hours into their reunion, he's cleaning up after his twin. He nods to the back room. This time, Qat precedes him.

"Ama was murdered," Qrodin says, "but I already told you that."

"By whom?"

"I never discovered his name; it was too dark to see his face, but I remember his hair looked green." At Qat's confused look—few species have green hair—he clarifies, "My best guess? He must be blonde or all grey because it was Newkuu. Isa was nearly full and green, and Uman was a thin crescent."

"That's never good," Qat says.

Aer voice is distant. Is ae seeing that night? Does ae remember any of it?

"I'm confident I'd recognize his voice," Qrodin says. He can still recall the smell of rotted fish from where he'd pulled himself up from the dock while a man crouched down over Ama's crumpled form at the end of the pier. The deep baritone saying, *'Put aem in the boat,'* has never left him. The voice has revisited him in his dreams, so he never forgets.

"But you saw him?" Qat grabs his arm and then releases him. "You saw it happen?"

Qrodin closes his eyes. "I saw him standing over Ama as he removed aer necklace." And the sword, although he doesn't say it.

"What necklace?" Qat asks loudly.

"A large ruby," he finally answers. The ruby was suspended from the chain by wire wrapped loosely around it, like a cardinal in a birdcage. "In a gold cage."

"What did the ruby look like?"

"It was about the size of an egg. Uncut." Ama liked them better that way. Said they had more power when they were raw and unpolished. Qrodin's belief that rocks have energy or influence of any kind died that night. If they had power, wouldn't the ruby have saved aer?

Qat's eyes narrow ever so slightly. "When did it happen?"

Qrodin hesitates a moment. "The night you were taken."

He turns and watches Qat closely for any reaction. There is nothing. Not a ripple or flicker of recognition in those eyes. That hurts.

How can there be no memory of a night that has been burned into my brain for two decades? he asks himself.

After a few moments of silence, Qat asks, "And you saw it? You saw him kill her? How? How did he do it?"

"A sword through aer belly."

"How?"

"What do you mean, how? Ama's stomach was slit open!" Qrodin clenches his hands, trying to forget.

"I mean, left side, right side? Did he do it from behind? How was the blade held?" Qat pulls a blade to demonstrate and continues as if it were a stranger, not their ama, slaughtered in front of them. "Like this? Or this? Was it a stab? Like this? Or a slash?"

"Enough!" Qrodin says with more force than volume, conscious that only a thin length of fabric separates them from eavesdroppers, and unsettled that he can't control the conversation.

Qat's eyes flash gold.

Hoping to calm the situation before it gets further out of control, Qrodin takes a deep breath and counts to three before asking softly, "What does it matter how it was done?"

"It matters!" Qat hisses, pacing three steps away and back, expertly spinning the knife in aer palm.

Qrodin doubts ae even knows ae's doing it. "Why?"

Qat holsters the knife and turns away. "It just does."

Qrodin has learned a lot about getting people to talk, such as the power of silence. He uses it now to encourage Qat to continue, but the technique doesn't work.

Qrodin remains as silent as his twin, unwilling to reveal that he hadn't seen the actual strike that had killed Ama; he had been trying to get away from Quinn.

"If you want me to keep asking questions, you're going to have to learn to answer mine," Qat finally says, then slips into the main room to join their companions.

Qrodin slams his hand on a nearby crate, then reprimands himself. He takes great pride in his composure, always staying calm in the face of adversity, able to charm the cantankerous and stubborn. Why he can't do the same with Qat is beyond him. Maybe it's because he never could, even as a child, get Qat to do anything ae didn't want to. Qrodin is as impressed as he is frustrated by Qat's stubbornness. And aer recklessness.

Most of his earliest memories are their adventures and the trouble they got into, all because Qatzsi was bored. When ae was taken, Qrodin was lost. His whole life—all eleven years of it until then—had been about chasing after Qatzsi and keeping aem safe—and having the best time doing it.

Without Qat, Qrodin's purpose had become finding his twin, no matter how long it took. It was his motivation to make enough money to get out of Riversmeet. It drove him to travel to every major port on the east coast.

Year after year, his hope slowly became a growing resignation that Qatzsi had not survived aer captivity. Now, he wonders what's worse. Qat not surviving? Or the reality of aer not remembering him?

If yesterday's events tell him anything, it's that Qat is as unpredictable and impulsive as ever. There's nothing to stop aem from leaving, and if that happens, Qrodin may never see aem again.

He was surprised and relieved to see Qat at Balaerdo's this morning. He's afraid Qat won't stick around or come with him back to Craguesport just because he asks. If it's going to happen, it must be Qat's idea. He must also be far more prepared for trouble if he can convince Qat to travel with them.

Qrodin reenters the main room as the others are ready to pay for their purchases. He selects a few items for himself and then settles the bill.

Qat has offered to take Llani and Bell to a tailor, and they're splitting into two groups when they leave here. Kasaandra will be going with Akin to the Tiolapin Monastery. Despite Qrodin's desire to keep an eye on his twin, space may be what Qat needs now.

And a visit to the monastery is long overdue. Like the Varsome orphanages, the monastery provides a home and training for wayward children. Participants strive for inner peace through meditation combined with *Idajmbe*, a form of martial arts practiced by the Owanulafa (danaash from Uruk, a country in western Kish). *Idajmbe* is an integral part of the Tiolapin religion. The monasteries are entirely self-sufficient. They only receive income from surplus food and goods sold at the market, so they live a spartan existence. Unless one counts their magnificent robes.

"The monastery?" Qrodin asks Akin once their plans are settled, belatedly recognizing Akin's robe as Tiolapin. "If you don't mind my accompanying you," Qrodin says, "I would like to see Anada again." Anada is the high priest in charge of the monastery and an old friend. "I haven't been there in years and would like to see how much of the compound walls have been completed," Qrodin explains, leaving out that he had donated live bamboo plants for the wall and the land itself.

Akin nods in agreement.

"Wonderful!" Qrodin bows his head to the group. "Now, allow me to repay your bravery last night with a meal at the Blushing Swan after we finish our errands. The manticore could have done quite a bit of damage to the neighborhood, but you prevented it. What do you say?"

"Yes!" Bell says eagerly. "I didn't know the hotel was real! Did you know the Blushing Swan was in *Rapturous Heart*? I've read that book at least five times. Even though he is engaged, the owner falls in love with his baker's daughter, but he doesn't know she loves him back. But it all works out in the end. They get married," Bell sighs dreamily. "I do hope that happened in real life, too!"

Qrodin owns the Blushing Swan, and since the only person he fell for rejected him many years ago, it hasn't happened. But he needs Bell to convince Qat to stay with them, so he doesn't ruin her hopes.

"Hey! Does it actually have a statue of a swan in the lobby that blushes if you talk to it?" Bell asks.

Qrodin laughs. "Yes, it does."

"We're going for sure! Right, guys?"

"Sure. Why not?" Kasaandra replies.

"Yes!" Bell jumps up and down, clapping her hands. "Qat, you're coming too, right? Please!" She grabs Qat's hand and bats her eyes.

"Who knows what will happen by tonight?" Qat says. "I, for one, like to keep my options open." Then, at Bell's frown, tacks on quickly, "But I'm not saying 'no.' And if you're going there tonight, we'd better get going so you have something nice to wear. You'll want to look your best for the Blushing Swan."

They reach the monastery shortly after the sun reaches its apex. The area is sandwiched between the Karleris River and vast stretches of farmland. A cut bamboo wall taller than Qrodin curves gently back and forth, spanning most of the southern border of the compound, more for privacy than protection. As they near it, Qrodin is astonished by how tall the bamboo along the riverbank is, almost two times the height of the wall.

The entry gate is open, and they enter a courtyard lush with potted and planted greenery bordering the interior of the twisting wall. Qrodin suspects every plant has a nutritional, medicinal, magical, or mechanical purpose. The monks are very practical, after all.

The courtyard's centerpiece is a giant sundial surrounded by pavers carved with symbols, statues, and rocks, all arranged to communicate the time of day and year, the seasonal solstices, and the waning and waxing of all three moons. Perhaps even more.

Several buildings weren't here when Qrodin visited a few years ago, all made from bamboo.

Members are working, planting, watering, and training. There are many people here, both children and adults, and that weird phase in between. Some workers are shaved entirely bald, and some are shaved like Akin, with hair only on the top of their head and pulled back into a braid or ponytail. Several have their hair very short, with designs shaved into the stubble. Many adults also have facial modifications, such as scarring and tattoos.

Imolena was the first Tiolapin practitioner he met, a priestess having difficulty gaining recruits. They met in Craguesport.

Eventually, they struck up a partnership: a Tiolapin monk or two would be housed at Varsome, and in exchange, they would work with the children, especially the unruly ones who challenged Qrodin's staff.

The monks didn't judge or try to change them. Instead, they listened to them and taught them meditation and *Idajmbe*. Any child who chose to would move to the monastery. The arrangement was so successful that by the second year, Qrodin had priests and monks in Varsome establishments all over Zedana. When the need arises, as it often does in large cities, Qrodin donates land and supplies for their expansion, as he did here and in Craguesport.

A flutter of burnt sienna robes from around a corner brings him from his thoughts. Anada is a tall, very dark-skinned danaash with perpetually smiling, sapphire blue eyes and a belly that's thickened nominally since the last time Qrodin was here. His robes are embellished, like Akin's, but with colored cords that outline the bright sash. His bald head shines as though he recently polished it.

Akin drops to his knees and bends at the waist, touching his forehead to the ground in front of Anada.

"*Iniki, keka*," Anada greets Akin in Owanulafa, the language of the Tiolapin monks.

Qrodin remembers that *keka* means *student*.

"*Edi*," Anada says, motioning for Akin to stand.

The ukulu does so, and Anada embraces him in a warm hug. "You look well, Akin. How was your trip home?"

Akin frowns and signs in response.

"Forgive me. Of course, it's no longer your home. You were still small when you and your aunt came east. I have been anxiously awaiting your arrival since I heard you were coming. But that can wait. I'm being rude to your guests." He faces Kasaandra first. "I am Anada, the *gia faa* of this temple."

"*Gia faa* is a high priest," Qrodin explains to Kasaandra. She ignores him and stares instead at Anada, who has kindly moved slightly to shade her eyes from the sun.

Kasaandra stands taller. "Kasaandra, daughter of Casinn Casmorlaid and Curis Lamlaiir of Toithdd Croieanan."

Anada's face crinkles in a smile, and his eyes twinkle mischievously. "Welcome, Kasaandra. It takes a strong arm to wield a mighty hammer," he says.

Kasaandra responds with apparent approval. "Indeed, it does!" she says with more respect than she's shown anyone other than Akin.

Finally, Anada addresses Qrodin, "*Iniki, ero ami*, Quentin." *Hello, my friend.*

"*Iniki, gia faa*," Qrodin says.

"It has been far too long, my friend. I hadn't heard you were in town. What brings you here today?"

"When I heard my companions were coming, I asked to tag along. I had to see the wall. It looks even better than your descriptions." Qrodin hasn't seen bamboo on this scale before, he's quite impressed with how fast it's grown. "I hope we have time to walk through the groves. I've heard it's like being in a different world."

"It is. It is. But first, you must eat. I imagine you left before your noon meal and are probably famished?"

Kasaandra nods.

"Then we will eat first. After, you will have a tour," Anada says, turning and leading the way.

After a meal of savory vegetables and fragrant bread, Anada asks one of the helpers to show Qrodin and Kasaandra around, explaining that he has some business with Akin. Kasaandra narrows her eyes at Qrodin, then follows their guide outside.

Qrodin initially trails behind the two, but curiosity gets the better of him, and he sidles up beside the dwarf. "Kasaandra. What did Anada mean about a strong arm and mighty hammer?"

"Casmorlaid is 'Mighty Hammer.' Lamlaiir is 'Strong Arm.'"

"Do I understand correctly that he made a saying from your parents' surnames?" When Kasaandra nods, he asks, "Is that a common way to greet one another?" At Kasaandra's affirmation, he wonders how he never knew of the custom. He makes it his business to discover as many as possible, considering the diversity of his staff and clients. He will need to learn the language or study the most common surnames. "I would like to learn this custom." Kasaandra's look says he won't learn it from her. He makes a mental note to remind himself to find a mentor.

"How long have you known Akin?" he asks, mostly to change the subject.

Kasaandra shrugs before replying, "Summer."

The autumnal equinox—also the first day of autumn—was eight days ago, which means they met between nine days and three trit'quarters ago. A span of one hundred and seven days isn't very specific. "How did you meet?"

"Fighting demon dogs."

"Demon dogs? That's intriguing." Demon dogs—or dire wolves—often travel in packs. They aren't demons, just giant wolves, but their eyes glow red at night when the moons' light reflects from within their depths. "Where was that, if it's not too forward of me to ask?"

Kasaandra's shrug is more pronounced this time. "Middlequet," she finally says.

"Middlequet, you say?" Kasaandra must have traveled south from Toithdd Croieanan—or *Dwarf Mountain,* as most people call it—to the valley where the Biennora and Abfil ranges overlap. Together, the two mountains bisect the entire continent of Kish from north to south. Most refer to them as the *Biennora-Abfil*—or *Bien'fil* for short.

"I visited your city when I was a child—Qat and I both did—for the harvest festival during Proximan," Qrodin tells Kasaandra.

Without slowing, Kasaandra nods several times. "Thought so."

"Really? How...?" Qrodin stares at Kasaandra. Her nose and cheeks are flushed from the walk. Suddenly, he remembers a young dwarf with skin so burnt from the sun that it's darker than aer red-orange hair and emerald eyes that pierce stronger than a dagger. Ae was throwing the carcass of a giant spider into one of the wagons of their caravan. The memory so surprises him that he stops and then rushes to catch up. "That was *you*? With the spider?" Qrodin asks.

"Yup."

The revelation that he and Kasaandra met nearly twenty years ago keeps him silent throughout the tour. Why didn't she say something earlier? Is it because she isn't comfortable talking? Or maybe she's very private. Or perhaps it's because he's a stranger. Then again, he and Qat had continued wearing contacts around the group, so maybe she hadn't recognized them.

When they arrive at the bamboo groves, he realizes that he was so preoccupied with the coincidence that he was blind to the many buildings they were shown, doesn't remember any of the names of the garden attendants they were introduced to, and hadn't registered the statues and fountains they passed. He lets the others get ahead of him when they reach a point on the path where bamboo trees surround him with long, grass-like leaves as high as he is tall. The trees are dense, leaving only a thin strip of sky above the path and a mottling of sunlight within the groves.

It's like a fantasy world. He wouldn't be surprised if a faerie flew between the trees and landed on a fence post. He could sit here for days, fortnights, years. Maybe he'd finally have the peace to compose his music, as he seldom has the time or environment for such a luxury.

Qrodin uses a post for balance and closes his eyes, letting the serenity of this place cleanse his mind and body of stress and worry. Thoughts of Qat, Truffle, and the upcoming journey dissipate with the scent of bamboo, moist soil, and herbs. A tune starts to compose itself from birdsong, buzzing insects, and cool breezes. This isn't a place for words. Those will come later.

"I thought I'd find you here," Anada says, his voice barely louder than a whisper.

Sorry that his solitude is over, Qrodin is still pleased to see his friend. "Anada, this is breathtaking. More beautiful than I could have imagined."

"Yes, it is. I often come here when I miss my home." Anada takes a moment to survey their surroundings before continuing, "I have something for you." He reaches into his robe and pulls out a slim flute with a body of blonde wood and a reddish-brown mouthpiece, both shimmering with a satin finish. "It is made from white and red mahogany and is more than just a flute. Let me show you. You hold it by the mouthpiece like so," he says, holding it at arm's length before he hands the flute to Qrodin. "Then, say '*Aagut.*'"

Qrodin adjusts his grip on the fine instrument and repeats the phrase. Instantly, the flute expands into a staff. Unprepared, he almost drops it.

Anada chuckles. "I guess I should have warned you."

"But then, you wouldn't have witnessed me almost drop it. Admit it. That was more fun." And a lesson that he should be prepared for anything. Anada is always teaching.

"Guilty."

Qrodin tests the weapon's weight by twirling it, holding the red mahogany at the center, and making the white mahogany ends look like they're two staves instead of one. "This is very nice, Anada. *Aagut!*" Qrodin waits, but nothing happens. "How do I turn it back to a flute?"

"The same word backward."

"*Tugaa*," Qrodin says, watching it shrink into its flute form. "That's spectacular, thank you. You didn't need to do this. It is very kind of you to remember I play."

"I also saw your skill with a staff the last time you were here."

Qrodin had been testing a newly made staff for balance. Many years had passed since he had practiced with one, and he had been pleased he hadn't lost his skill.

"Will you play something?"

Qrodin brings the flute to his lips and tries a few notes. The volume is louder and more penetrating than others he's played. He's impressed with the balanced sound despite the volume. He plays the song he started composing.

"That is very peaceful," Anada says in response to the short piece. "Play it again?"

Eventually, Qrodin and Anada leave the groves. "You know that Akin is Imolena's nephew, no?" Anada asks as they walk.

"I knew she had a nephew but never learned his name." Imolena confided she had never married, and her nephew was her only family.

"Yes. Yes. Akin's the reason she came east of the Bien'fil all those years ago. Said he needed to experience the world, and what better way to do so than assisting her? Oh, he's been all over. Just came back from visiting the West for the first time since he was a child." Anada sighs deeply. "Ah. There they are, as I expected."

Akin and Kasaandra emerge from a path to Qrodin's left as he and Anada near the sundial.

"I think it would be good for you two to spend time together. You could learn a lot from each other. And that dwarf," Anada adds.

"I was thinking I could accompany them to Craguesport." If Qat doesn't disappear before then.

"Try to convince yourself," Anada says quickly and quietly, then louder, "Akin. It was good seeing you, as always."

Chapter 17 Qat

Captain Rogen was an honest man. For a pirate, at least. He treated me well. There's always a possibility it wasn't him. I'd be surprised if it was.

The thing is, though, Rogan kept jewelry as trophies. He wore chains from his enemies around his neck and sewed pendants onto his jacket like scale mail. More than once, a saint pendant or holy talisman saved his life by stopping an arrow or blade. He said it was the only time he believed in religion.

And he kept a rough-cut ruby encased in a wire pendant—just like Qrow described—in an interior pocket of his jacket.

Doubt crushes my faith in Rogen's character.

If Qrow's memory is correct, Rogen may have killed Ama. The thought makes me sick to my stomach. Is it because—deep down and hidden somewhere I pretend doesn't exist—I carry a long-lost hope that my mother still lives? Maybe it's because I can't imagine the captain hurting a defenseless woman. He loved women. He couldn't get enough of them. And he was a charmer, but he didn't force anything. Refusals didn't bother him. If a woman said 'no,' there was always another woman willing enough.

He was attractive enough that he didn't hear 'no' often. Tall and broad-shouldered with platinum-blonde hair and a golden tan, he attracted attention wherever he went. His ice-blue eyes were flecked with yellow. I overheard one woman tell him that they reminded her of the sunrise. *'Perhaps you'll let me compare the two in person?'* she hinted.

The more I think about it, the more conflicted I become. I was hoping that accompanying Llani and Bell to the tailor would get my mind off the conundrum, but my brain circles back time and again, even as Bell gets measured for two outfits and a cloak.

I wrench my thoughts away from Rogen and try to be present for Bell. Llani means well, but she can be overly critical. I've designated myself the peacekeeper. Ironic, I know, but the task comes naturally.

The green silk scarf will be used to make a dress from scratch. It will be ready tomorrow. An outfit Bell purchased from Balaerdo's will be altered to fit and picked up later today.

Afterward, we shop for utensils, extra plates and bowls, and a few pieces of cookware that Bell insists she needs if she's going to cook for us properly. And the food! So. Much. Food. Flour and sugar and herbs and spices and dried fruits and salted meats and nuts and seeds.

"Why do we need coffee beans?" Llani inquires when Bell asks a shopkeeper where to find them. "None of us drinks coffee."

"Because Qrow drinks it every morning for breakfast," Bell says.

I groan. Does everyone cater to him like this?

I've never cared much for coffee. No captain would waste precious coin on coffee for his crew. Not even Rogen.

When Llani and Bell disagree about which coffee shop we should visit for the beans, I grab my dice bag, randomly selecting one. "How about we roll the dice," I say, noticing the blue one I picked out is loaded for sevens. "Odds, we go to Rabble Roausters; evens, the Coffee Cabinet."

I roll before they have time to decline.

Llani glares at me when it comes to a stop on the shopkeeper's counter. She'd been arguing for the Cabinet.

Ah, another fan. My job here is done. I look deeply into her eyes. "Mmm. Don't be upset, beautiful. Your forehead scrunches there when you are." She pulls away before I touch the frown.

"I will thank you for keeping your hands to yourself. Is everyone in Riversmeet as forward as you? Let us go now, Bell. We still have more to do." She tosses her hair over one shoulder as she turns, motioning for Bell to follow her.

"Forgive me if I was rude," I say when we get outside. No need to alienate her if I'm going to be traveling with them. "I'm not used to meeting someone as lovely as you, and I've quite forgotten my manners," I say.

She turns, her eyes narrowed to slits. "Are you saying your insolence is my fault? That if you found me undesirable, you would be courteous? That logic is flawed. And you are insulting and obnoxious." Her overlarge ears rotate slightly. During her speech, they pulled forward.

Whoa! Now, that's a tell if I've ever seen one. I could fleece her in a card game with ears that are that expressive. I wonder what they do when she's lying. Despite that, I'm rather impressed. Few people have the cannonballs to call me on my bullshit, and none of them with such a vocabulary.

At my stunned silence, Llani again attempts to leave, but Bell tugs at the bottom of her vest. "Llani!" she says urgently, stamping her foot when Llani doesn't stop.

Bell motions Llani closer and down to her level. When she complies, Bell whispers in her ear while sneaking peeks in my direction.

Llani's ears tilt down, which must mean something, but I can't see her face to determine what it is.

"You're right, Bell. I shouldn't be so harsh. Ae probably has no idea ae's being insulting." Llani rises to her full height and looks up at me imperiously. "You are forgiven."

There's a curious rigidity to her. Ah, she hates being wrong, doesn't she? Which, in this case, she isn't. I *knew* I was insulting her. I guess I wasn't as unobtrusive as I thought. Of course, I'm not around many people as observant as she is. I'll need to remember that.

"I accept your apology," I say, bowing slightly to hide my smile. I steal another glance at her necklace.

"Apology!" She turns to leave. "I retract my forgive—"

"You are absolutely right," I say, cutting her off. "Let me make it up to you."

She turns back around to face me. "How do you propose to do that?"

Her bag is loosely draped over one arm as though it weighs nothing. "Let me carry your pack," I offer.

"I think not," she says, threading both arms through the straps. "You must take me for a fool."

"It must be heavier than a horse with all that you've placed into it," I say, eyeing the small bag. It still looks empty.

"I am quite strong," she says, but her eyes shift away from mine.

Does she think I haven't noticed all the crap we purchased today fit into that bag? I've never seen anything like it. What I wouldn't kill to get my hands on it. Well, *apparently,* anything except a know-it-all, bossy slip of an elf. Inexplicably, the thought of anything or anyone hurting her makes my fists clench and my jaw tighten.

"You can carry mine!" Bell pipes up.

Well, I asked for that, I think as I heft her giant pack. It weighs a ton.

As I lift it, a familiar feeling along my spine makes me look around. Three elves are watching us from across the street. Young and beautiful. And green. They quickly look away and keep walking. Elves are still rare enough in town that it's unusual to see them. I wonder why we caught their attention. Llani, maybe? Perhaps they've never seen a purple elf before, either.

I'm just glad to have escaped the all-seeing eyes of *that man*. I refuse to think of him as my brother. There's something about his stare. When he looks at me, does he see what I've hidden deep down in that locked chest buried below the changing currents and sea monsters in my head?

You can't catch a cat with a crow.

The Qrow knew the phrase. And he spoke in the same mysterious language.

Could that mean Captain Rogen and Ama might have known each other? I mean, I've been all over eastern Kish. If I've never heard the language spoken by anyone else, it's got to be rare. Even Llani said she didn't recognize it, and from what Bell noted earlier, she recognizes most languages.

Wouldn't that make it less likely Rogen killed Ama? Could he have killed a woman he knew? Would he have continued to meet with others who spoke the same language if he had? What is his connection to them?

What is his connection to Qrow?

And me?

Had Rogen known me back then?

After all, he was the one who named me Qat. He said it was because of the crew's comments about my cat-like eyes, but was there another reason? Had he already known my name?

Part of me wants to find him and confront him. But to do so, I'd have to ditch Qrow. There's no way he would let the captain live if he knew Rogen might be the one who killed Ama. I can tell by the tension he radiates when he speaks of Ama's death. All it'd take is the captain opening his mouth. I'd never get any answers that way. And I must get answers. Besides, the captain would wipe the floor with Qrow.

And what if Rogen *was* the one who killed Ama? It's not like before, when I'd do anything he asked without question. Can I dispatch him as indifferently as I have other marks? Could I slide a *ha-sheesh-shun* knife between *his* ribs? Could I even sneak up on the bastard? Maybe. He's twelve years older than he was last time I saw him. Perhaps he's gone deaf from his blasted cannons.

Right, and maybe I've gone daft to think so.

I've never been able to surprise him. And it wasn't his hearing that told him I was there. It was that sense you get when you're about to get pounced on. Like those fish that act like they don't know there's a shark abaft of them. But the second the shark opens its mouth, the whole school changes direction, leaving the shark with nothing to swallow but water and disappointment.

Well, except that it's hard to see him as a little fish. Captain Rogen is the *shark*.

A shark with a wide-ranging diet.

A diet that doesn't include killing women. At least, not one that isn't already trying to kill him.

I'd bet my blades on it.

After an hour in Tangali's Tinderbox & Tentage supply store, where we'd ended up after going across town to get coffee, I feel another warning. We're being watched. I move through the racks, following my danger sense to the watchers. I find them almost immediately. The three elves I'd seen earlier stare at us through the shop window. Or rather, they're staring at Llani. I don't like their expressions. I maneuver my way to the windows, keeping out of their sight until the last minute, and then I step into their path. They startle. The one in the middle says something to the others. They both look at me intently, and a warning tingle flares hotly. Before I can reach for my daggers, they move on.

"Qat!" Bell calls out to me. "What's your favorite color?"

"Purple," I respond before remembering I don't have a favorite color. Qrow said it used to be red. But after? It never occurred to me to pick one. And why does she want to know? They're picking through sleeping bags. The last thing I need is a purple sleeping bag. Nervous that the elves will come back, I change the topic. "Shouldn't you be getting ready for dinner?"

"Is it that late already? Llani! Hurry! We can't make Qrow wait! And you're going to dinner, too, Qat!" Bell impales me with her tone. "Don't think you're getting out of it!"

I can't even tell where she is. Her voice is coming from all directions; it's so loud. How does such a little thing make so much noise?

"You better hurry. It's raining," I call back instead.

The packages are stowed safely in Llani's bag before I can get a look at what they bought. Not that it matters. I still don't know if I'll be joining them. Maybe I can wait out the inspections at the docks.

A moment later, we scurry outside and keep to the sides of the buildings as much as possible to avoid the drizzle.

I let them get ahead of me. I scan the area for the elves, but they're nowhere in sight, and I don't feel any danger. I follow Bell and Llani until they enter the front door of the BB&B and then make my way to the Hold.

My favorite street vendor, Alf, is still alive somehow. He's an old dwarf, shorter than Bell, with a sun-weathered face, a full head of coal-black hair, and a beard so long he tucks it into his belt to keep it out of the fire. He's one of the few vendors that will cook anything you bring him (as long as it's seafood), so he's the local fishers' favorite. He takes fish for trade, too, and since most of it is fresh off the boat, it's the best stuff around. He's been here for as long as I can remember and tells stories of meeting Linn "Golden Teeth" and "Handsome"

Newboy, two local pirates who died before Captain Rogen was born. I wonder what stories he'll tell of the captain long after we're gone.

I order deep-fried crawfish on a bed of roasted garlic, chives, and red peppers, drizzled with a spicy red sauce. The delicacy is layered on a medium-soft flatbread that I usually fold around the meal and eat on the go.

Tonight, though, I hang around while I eat. Eventually, Alf gets around to talking about the holdup at the docks. "Did you hear all travel south will be halted for several days? Seen it before, and I'll see it again. Least the fishin'll get through. Did I tell you about that time—"

Bollocks! I thought they were inspecting the ships leaving port. Now, they're holding them?

When Alf finishes his story, I purchase some crab cakes to go. Before wrapping them in a cloth, I dig out a chunk in the middle and fill them with the spicy red sauce. "Later, Alf," I call out as I leave.

I slip in and out of a clothing store. Around back, I change into my newly acquired blouse—this time something that doesn't scream dock rat—and throw on a long cloak.

Bell will be mad that I didn't make it to dinner in time, but maybe she'll forgive me when I give her the crab cakes. If I can catch them before they finish their meal, that is. If not, I'll see them when they return to the BB&B. Staying so far from the others doesn't make sense, so I stop off and get a room at the BB&B, stashing my things there so I don't have to carry them. I brush my hair and leave it loose, then fish out my brown contact lenses. A bit of makeup and some fake breasts later, my mother wouldn't recognize me.

That thought stops me cold. Goffin used to say that phrase all the time. Back then, it hadn't meant anything. I hadn't known my mother. Now, though, the phrase stings. I look at myself in the mirror. Is this what she looked like? Qrow said I look like her. Did she wear her hair down? Did she wear makeup? I wear it to disguise myself. To change into whomsoever I want at will. Did she wear it when she went out the night she was killed?

I shake away the thought and leave through the window.

I've been to the Blushing Swan once before, but that was for business. This, on the other hand, is personal. I'm not looking forward to spending time with Qrow, but I think a few days to pump him for information is just what I need. Then, I'll join another caravan and be on my way to find the captain and get some answers.

The hotel's entrance is a deep archway that opens onto a huge courtyard. Three horseshoe-shaped floors and balconies overlook the central courtyard and the iconic swan surrounded by potted trees and plants. The last time I was here, the swan wasn't, so Bell's description is my only preparation. The figure is as fabulous as she said it would be. Behind it is a fountain that cascades into a pool surrounding the statue's base. Wings arch over the water on each side and form the backrest for two benches. It looks so alive, I touch a wing as I pass. Expecting it to be cold, I'm surprised it isn't. I trail my hand in the water. It, too, is the perfect temperature, whether you want to cool off on a warm day or warm chilled hands during the winter.

I act as if I belong here, and no one questions me as I veer to the right of the swan and back to the dining area near the rear of the hotel. That's one room I'm familiar with. That, and the kitchens. The job wasn't my best—I almost got caught. Of course, it wasn't my fault, but it caused quite a stir. I'm not worried about being recognized, though. I wore a disguise, as usual, and it was long ago.

The dining room is about half full. I don't have Bell's laughter to zero in on tonight, and it worries me until I see Kasaandra's hair flowing out this side of a booth. At least I didn't miss them. Qrow is at the head of a table with a wraparound bench, with Llani and Bell on each side of him. Akin sits by Llani, with Kasaandra across from him.

The table across from them is unoccupied, so I pull a chair across the aisle and sit down, straddling the chair back. No need for them to shift themselves and their food, even though it looks like they're about finished.

Oil from the crab cakes has stained the cloth wrapping, but I set it on the table before me.

All conversation ceases, and Kasaandra and Bell look at me in confusion.

"Hey, guys!" I say.

"Qat," Qrow says.

"Wow! I didn't even recognize you!" Bell says. "I *told* you Qat would be here," Bell says to Qrow before looking back at me. "They said you wouldn't make it, but I *knew* you wouldn't let me down."

I stand up, intending to flip the chair around to be more comfortable.

"You're late," The Qrow says with a frown.

I plop back down and pick up Kasaandra's extra fork to pick at my teeth. The three lines between his brows become deep grooves. Score one for me.

"Bell. I brought you something." I toss the crab cakes, which land on the table between her and Qrow, exactly where I aimed.

"What are they?" She sniffs the package, then squeals, "Crab cakes!" She struggles with the knot, and Qrow helps her untie it. She carefully lifts one of the cakes to her nose, sniffing at the red sauce. "Roasted tomatoes, garlic, vinegar, horseradish, paprika, black pepper. Oh, this is going to be good!"

Before taking a bite, she pulls off a bit, ties it up in a fresh cloth napkin, and hands it to Llani. "I'll take this one, too!"

Qrow raises an eyebrow. "You already have one from each of our meals. What are you going to do with them all? Have a late-night snack?"

"No, silly! When I return to our room, I'll write down all the recipes for later." She smiles sweetly. "*Then* I'm going to eat them."

That surprises me. "How will you know what they're made from?" I ask her. I didn't get the information from Alf.

"By smell! Isn't that how you do it?"

"Uh. No. I don't cook."

"Well, then. It's a good thing I'll be able to cook for you!"

I don't respond because she takes her first bite, and the look on her face makes the trek to the wharf worth it. Besides, what can I say?

"Mmm! These are soooo gooood! Where did you get them? I didn't see them on the menu. And I looked! How does a luxurious place like this not serve crab cakes? Hey! How did you know I wanted some? I didn't think you were listening to anything we were saying today."

"I heard everything you said." And I had. It's what I do. I listen, and I watch.

Kasaandra clears her throat loudly.

"They have garlic," Bell says as if that's all the explanation needed for not sharing any with the dwarf. "Would anyone else like one? They're delicious."

Llani and Qrow take one, but Akin declines. His expression hasn't changed from a grimace since I sat down. I'd take it personally, but I think he had it before he saw me. His only communication has been declining the cake, which was the slightest shake of his head. From the looks of his plate, he didn't eat much of his meal, either. To test the water, I snag a green bean from his plate.

I feel the slightest twinge in my neck, but it's gone so fast that I wonder if I imagined it. Regardless, I won't be doing that again.

I turn to Kasaandra to hide my reaction while the others enjoy the crab cakes. "You don't like garlic?"

"I do," she says.

"You do?" Bell sputters, her mouth still full. "Why do you always ask to hold the garlic when we go out? And you never let me put it in any of your food. Not the whole way here!" Bell looks quite put out.

"I just do. That's all."

Kasaandra is saved from any more questions when a very young server comes to clear their plates. "Would you like coffee and dessert?"

"Yes!" Bell and Kasaandra say together.

"Coffee for me, thank you," Qrow says.

Coffee for breakfast *and* dessert? Well, isn't he fancy? Bell might need to buy more coffee.

"I doubt I can eat another bite," Llani says.

Dessert sounds good. I wonder what they've got.

"What are the desserts, again?" Kasaandra asks the server.

"You don't remember?" Bell asks. She lists them by memory before looking at the server. "I want the deep-fried coconut dumplings drizzled in dark chocolate sauce, please!"

Wow. This girl is serious about her food.

I got the impression today that she should be wearing glasses. She would squint at whatever she held, except when she caught me looking. Like a blind person, she touched everything in detail, running her hands along seams and zippers, pot handles and fork tines. How was she able to read the menu? Maybe she could smell it from the kitchen?

Kasaandra is almost shy when she asks for two oatmeal cookies. Her discomfort is evident. I almost can't believe this is the same person who slayed the manticore with such ferocity.

Qrow generously urges her to take another. "Get as many as you'd like," he says.

Her wide-spaced, green eyes tilt downward, accommodating her wide, bulbous nose, while her beard covers most of her cheeks. A faint blush obliterates her freckles. She clears her throat. "Could you make that three?"

"Absolutely," the server says before turning to Akin. "And how about you?"

Akin is motionless, not even a headshake this time. He doesn't look at her. What's up with him? If his eyes were closed, he'd look like a statue.

"Uh. No. He's good," Kasaandra answers for him.

"Wonderful, then. And just the one coffee?" the server asks, her voice rising high at the end of the question.

"I'll have coffee," I say, just to see Qrow's expression. He nods as if to say he knew we were alike.

"Would you like cream or sugar with that?"

She got me there. I have no idea.

"Molasses with cream," Bell answers for me. "Trust me," she says at my raised eyebrow.

The server finishes our order and walks away, heels clicking on the marble floor and high ponytail swishing with each step she takes to the kitchen.

"Thank you, Bell. I like your new dress," I say to fill the silence. She's wearing the one she'd had altered today. The dressmaker was surprised when she told him she didn't want any frills. A middle-aged hablis himself, he did his best to convince her to keep at least one ruffle on the neckline. *For modesty, Miss Bell, you being a maiden and all.* She wouldn't have it. Nor would she purchase a hat. *It gets in the way when I shoot my bow,* she said. He was so scandalized that I feared he'd refuse to alter the gown.

"So! What did I miss?" I ask, cutting off Qrow as he's about to speak.

Llani dabs her lips with a napkin. "We are leaving tomorrow for Craguesport."

Qrow opens his mouth. I cut him off again. "The river's closed for at least a few days."

Bell snorts. "Kasaandra doesn't like boats."

"Qrow has generously offered to provide us with horses," Llani says.

I want to puke. "I can't ride." With a pang, I recall my encounter with the silver stallion. I'd try if I could ride him.

Silence.

Llani breaks it. "I have never ridden, but it cannot be difficult. Kasaandra can do it."

Kasaandra harumphs at the back-handed compliment.

"Me either, but I can't wait. I love horsies!"

I smile at Bell while Qrow eyes me. "You'll pick it up again." He looks around at the others. "You should have seen aem. Qat'd ride around town standing on the back of a horse and snapping aer whip to get people's attention, then yell at everyone to come see the show."

I feel the blood drain from my face. Anger, pleasure, and confusion compete for supremacy inside my head. Anger at Qrow for revealing things about me to strangers, especially information I don't know about myself. Pleasure at the thought of riding that silver stallion. And confusion because I travel on foot or by water. Only. The same as the captain. We never needed a wagon because our goods were removed from the ship only after they'd been sold. Delivery ended at the docks. Before meeting Qrow, I'd never considered learning to ride. I've never wanted to go somewhere I couldn't sail to.

And I thought I was naturally good with a whip when I started using one on the *Raven Scream*. Besides, I never seek a crowd's attention. Just the opposite.

"What kind of show?" Bell asks.

Qrow was prevented from answering by our server's arrival. "Here's your coffee, Mr. Browning. I asked Cook to brew it with a bit of cinnamon, like yesterday."

"Thank you, Twyla. That's very kind of you."

"Very kind," I say, mirroring Qrow's flirtatious smile, just to see her reaction.

She stumbles at my tone, blushing. She places the cup and saucer down so quickly that a few drops spill over the side and pool in the saucer. "And your cream. And your molasses. And a little coffee spoon, too. I'll be back with your desserts!" This time, her ponytail swings faster as she walks away.

Qrow is frowning at me. Oh, well. He'd better get over it. Or maybe not. They're leaving tomorrow. Now that I know they're riding, I might have to change my mind about joining them. If only I could find that stallion again.

I frown down at all the little pouring containers in front of me.

"Put your molasses in first and stir it in," Bell says. "That way, it melts. Then, you can add your cream. Otherwise, you'll have a mouth full of molasses on your last sip." She scrunches her nose in distaste.

"I've never sweetened my coffee," Qrow says. "Why do you think Qat will prefer it sweet?"

"Maybe because you don't?" I say under my breath. Akin makes a sound as if he's choking, but his eyes are laughing when I glance his way. Only his eyes, though. The rest of him is still rigid.

"Oh. I *know*," Bell says. "I can always tell what someone's going to like. It's like I can read their food aura."

"Their food aura?" Qrow asks.

"Yeah. It's like a feeling or something. I can hear what their body wants."

"And what does my body want?" I ask.

"Duh! Molasses!" Bell says, then bops up and down in her booster seat. "Dessert's here!"

Twyla doesn't even look at me this time as she places the desserts in front of Kasaandra and Bell. Before she leaves, she touches Kasaandra's arm. "I warmed them up for you a bit. I hope you like it." And she's off! Like one of those horses that Qrow wants me to ride.

Bell sniffs in Kasaandra's direction. "Don't be impressed. Those are a day old. She only warmed them up so they wouldn't taste stale."

Kasaandra tastes one, then wraps the other two in a napkin and tucks them into her belt.

"If they are not satisfactory, I'll have her bring fresh ones," Qrow says immediately.

Seriously? Day-old cookies? I'd have given my right arm for trit'quarter-old cookies while we were out to sea. They would have been better than hardtack soaked in fish broth, which was all we got sometimes.

Kasaandra shakes her head. "Just saving them for later."

Bell is leagues more impressed with her dessert. "Oh, I just love chocolate!" She flops into the cushioned back of her seat and spreads her arms dramatically.

Instantly, she pops back up and picks off a piece of her dumpling. "Llani. I need another napkin!"

"Here." I hand her one from under my saucer. "What did you do, ask for a stack?"

"Of course! I told her I was a *really* messy eater."

Considering the chocolate already staining her dress, she wasn't lying.

I smile. "Isn't that steal—"

"Shh! You can never have too many napkins. You'll see once we're back on the road."

The reminder kicks me, and I no longer feel like teasing her. They'll be gone tomorrow. I should probably go with them. It's too dangerous to stay here. But a horse? Can I do it?

I still haven't decided. Why can't I ever make up my mind? I'm confident one second, then do the opposite the next.

"What's wrong?" Bell asks. "You don't like your coffee?"

I forgot I had it. I flip the lids on the containers, then start pouring in the molasses.

"That's enough!" Bell says. "Now stir it."

And here I thought Llani was the bossy one. I sneak a peek at her. She's also been reticent tonight. All day today, the two of them were non-stop. Tonight, she's almost as quiet as Akin.

I add cream and lift the cup. A drop from the bottom of the cup lands on my leather breeches. I almost don't bother wiping it off. Almost. But they're new leathers.

"Well?" she asks.

I finally take a sip. "This is good," I admit.

"See? I knew it! You needed molasses."

"Oh, yeah? What's molasses good for, then, that I need it so bad?" I don't care about the answer. I'm just trying to avoid more talk of them leaving.

All but Qrow and I stare at Llani expectantly. So, we do, too. She finally notices. "I apologize. What were we discussing?"

"Qat," Bell says, speaking each word slowly as she continues. "Asked what molasses was good for."

"Molasses? Oh. It's good for your bones." She looks back down at her hands.

At her concise answer, Bell narrows her eyes. Something's up there. Too bad I'll probably never find out what. I like to keep moving. Stay in one place too long, and someone you don't want to see'll find you.

"Will you be accompanying us?" Qrow finally asks me.

That is the question, isn't it? He's been waiting all night to put me on the spot. I shrug. "I'll have to rearrange my schedule if I do."

Another cover-up-cough from Akin. He must be feeling better. I bet I'd get to like this guy if I stuck around.

"Oh, Qat! You *have* to come with us! Please!"

I wonder if Bell's begging works on everyone.

I want to say yes.

I do.

But I do *not* want to ride a horse. I'm not scared of them. I just don't like to do something I'm not good at in front of others.

What if I fall?

Then again, what if? I mean. I jump from the rigging all the time—and at three times the height of a horse.

But I'd be traveling with Qrow.

I *had* decided I needed a few days to pump him for information. What better place to ask him than a deserted road?

Better than on a ship where *anyone* may be listening.

That could get back to the captain.

And *that* would be bad.

And what better place than a long ride between towns?

Like Llani a few moments ago, I suddenly realize everyone is staring at me. And my left hand is in the air, flipping my dagger. They must think I'm crazy. I would if I were them.

"Well? Can you come with us?"

I stare into Bell's tear-bright, chocolatey-brown eyes. "Sure. Why not?"

Chapter 18 Qrodin

A knock at the door disturbs Qrodin's thoughts. He bids the visitor enter, and Xan hands him several packages wrapped in leather and tied with twine, along with a bottle of Qrodin's favorite wine.

"Thank you, Xan. I've been expecting these."

"Of course, Mr. Browning."

"One other thing, since you're here. I fully support Talim's choice of you as her replacement here. I can see that the staff respects you, and your handling of the other night's excitement was impressive. I look forward to collaborating more closely with you as you fully transition to the role."

Xan stands a little taller. "It will be my pleasure." Xan closes the door on his way out.

A man of few words. Maybe opposites do attract, considering how Talim is.

Qrodin moves a quill and ink jar to make room for the packages. He removes the twine on one and peels back the leather, revealing six long manticore tail spikes, each the length of his hand from fingertips to wrist. Two nights ago, he had been a roiling mix of emotions. Shock, doubt, and joy that he had finally found his twin, fear and helplessness when he witnessed Qat wounded in the battle, and relief when ae had survived it.

He still doesn't understand his motivation for taking the trophies. It was the act of a hunter or warrior, not a businessperson. He passes the objects from one hand to the other and back again, listening to the distinct, almost hollow-sounding tone as they tumble about, protesting in death what had happened in life. Despite their deceptive sound, they're heavier than he thought.

Qrodin spreads the long spikes on the desk. Perhaps they could be carved or attached to short handles or made into throwing darts. Maybe all of those combined. Qat would probably like that. Qrodin smiles as he carefully wraps them back up and ties the package closed. He'll store them until he finds an artisan in Craguesport capable of the task.

Qrodin is still hopeful that Qat will accompany them. If ae doesn't, he'll spend the rest of his life looking for another sighting of his elusive twin. If Qat told Bell the truth and shows up this morning as planned, they'll probably argue the entire trip. Every time Qat opens aer mouth, ae says something to make Qrodin angry, just like when they were children. It's hard to believe that Qat doesn't remember anything, but the flashes of doubt on aer face when they've talked seem genuine. Qrodin must accept that his past is no longer their shared past.

If he thought Qat didn't want to know about aer life before the incident, it'd be easier to let aem go, but he's seen the curiosity behind those eyes. Eyes that had morphed from pain to peaceful acceptance right here in this room after the manticore attack. Before Llani had finally healed Qat.

He looks down at the spikes and remembers what it felt like when he realized that Qat might die from aer injury. Fear, anger, and hatred fill him again at the thought. The feelings aren't foreign to him. He used to be afraid all the time. He used to get angry at the injustice of being left behind. And he used to hate the strangers who abused the children they found alone on the streets.

Maybe that's what drove him to request the trophies in the first place, even before he knew the extent of Qat's injury. He wanted to get back at the manticore.

"Because they hurt you," he says to his absent twin. *And that is unacceptable.*

Qrodin takes a few minutes to return the room as he found it. With a final glance, he closes the office door.

Downstairs, Talim is cleaning tables but comes over to say goodbye— without saying goodbye. The knack is something you learn on the streets.

"Next time you're here, I'll be in my new place," she says. "You sure you don't want to stick around and help to rebuild it? It'll be like old times."

"You mean, where you boss everyone around, and I hide from you?" Qrodin prods, hoping they're back to normal.

"Ha! You're right. This *is* like old times. You were never around to tell those lazy rascals to get back to work. I had to do *everything* around here."

"That's why I made you the boss. To take care of things when I'm gone." Qrodin is thankful that Talim's not holding the other night against him.

"Which you always are, nowadays. Things sure have changed since you left. Did you see the new clock tower? Looks sharp!"

"I did." Qrodin donated some funds but didn't return for the unveiling last year. He and Talim exchange a glance, remembering how the previous clock was destroyed many years ago. Depending on who's inquiring, they may or may not have had something to do with that unfortunate event.

"How's it going with Qat?"

Qrodin had stayed after Qat left the other night and told Talim what had happened. His way of showing Talim that he was taking what she said seriously. He was confiding in her. A pang of guilt stabs at him that he can't tell her about his arrangement with Truffle. "Ae's coming with me when we leave. If ae shows up." He's giving it a fifty-fifty chance.

"Ha. One of those, huh? Well, I'm glad you found each other," she says with a slight tightening of her tone. "Even if you'll probably screw it all up."

She's probably right about that. "I'm going to miss your messages on the reports. Some days, it's the only thing that makes me smile."

"I'm not leaving yet. And who says I can't send you messages after I'm gone? You might end up with a dictionary full of all my new cuss words after I start remodeling."

"I look forward to it." He removes two notebooks from his inside coat pocket. "That's why I had these two made up for you."

Talim eyes them momentarily, then takes them hesitantly, as if they are poisonous snakes he's handing her. "Why two?"

"Turn them over," he says.

She does. The top one is twice the thickness of the other and has her name embossed on the leather cover. The second one says, "Xander."

"I get the bigger one because I've got more to say?" she asks, only half joking.

"Open it," he replies instead.

When she does, there are two tabbed separators. One is labeled "Xander." The other "Qrow."

They're similar enough to the notebooks the managers all possess. What she writes in the Xander pages will appear in his book and vice versa.

"Why is your name on top?"

Qrodin hefts a small bag over his shoulder and strides toward the door. "Well, I was your first love."

"As long as you're not my last," she calls back after him.

Qrodin smiles at her quip as the door closes. If she's back to insulting him, she's forgiven him.

He goes straight to the stables. He wants to ensure everything is ready when the group arrives. They had decided against a wagon, so Qrodin had arranged for four horses, two ponies, and a mule for extra baggage.

He selected the stable on the Shipdurn side, north of the city. The horses there seldom have names, as they're bought and sold for short legs of overland travel rather than used as permanent mounts. They're usually older horses that have spent a lifetime carrying people from one town to another. They should be docile enough for Llani and Bell.

Qrodin arrives an hour early to select the best horse for each rider. He chooses mounts that won't spook easily for Bell, Llani, and Akin. Last night, Kasaandra said she's been riding ponies since she could walk, and Qrodin's confident that when Qat places aer feet in the stirrups, muscle memory will take over, and ae'll have no problem controlling aer mount.

The one he wants for himself is the tallest and most spirited horse available. The stallion is in a small paddock fenced away from the rest of the horses. The speckled grey coat is so pale it's almost white, and his mane and tail are a few shades darker. But every time Qrodin approaches him in the yard, the horse pulls away, raises his head, and kicks out before running to the opposite end of the enclosure.

"He's a persnickety one," Harlan, the stable owner, says, laughing at Qrodin's attempts to catch up with him. "Won't take a rider. The darn thing is an eating and pooping waste of my time. I'd pay you to take him if he'd let you, but he's kicked out at every damn thing that's got near him. No one's been able to mount him."

"Where'd you get him?" Qrodin asks, intrigued that such a beautiful beast hasn't already been claimed.

"Pulled him out'a the river a while ago. I roped him easy enough when he came to shore, but he fought me every skootch of the way 'til I got him into the yard. He knows who's boss now."

Considering Harlan's short, wiry frame, Qrodin's surprised he hadn't been dragged off.

"He won't take to bit or saddle. Or anything. I'd let him go if it weren't so fun to watch y'all try 'n ride him. What do you say?"

"I wish I could, but I'll be traveling with a group, half of which have never ridden. I wouldn't want him to—"

"Oh! Aren't you a striking one!" Llani says as she joins them. "Hello, sweet thing. You want to go to Craguesport with us?" she says to the grey.

"That one's not for us," Qrodin says. "He's not sweet, and you should stay back from the fence. He's already tried kicking me this morning."

"Smart horse," Qat says from the rear of the small group, walking up from the stable. "So, this is where you got up to," ae murmurs, staring at the horse. "I've been looking for you for days."

Qrodin is pleased that Qat showed up, even if aer comment is strange. "Good morning to you, too, Qat."

"It is now. In addition to Bell's breakfast, that is. I can't believe they let her in the kitchen this morning."

Qrodin had asked Talim to make a special request to the hotel. He's glad to hear that the BB&B accommodated her.

"Here, Qrow. I brought you a raspberry and cheese pastry." Bell hands him a small package and then pulls him down to whisper in his ear. "Two. But don't tell anyone. They only got one." She winks and releases him.

"Thank you, Bell. That was very kind of you." He takes a bite and groans in pleasure. Divine.

"You're welcome!" she says as she pokes her head through the fence. A small earthenware jar swings forward from a leather cord looped around her neck. "Here, horsey, horsey!"

Qrodin addresses her when the grey approaches again. Afraid she'll be hurt by the spirited animal as it prances toward the group, Qrow attempts to distract her. "Bell, would you like to meet your pony? It's the golden one with the blonde mane and tail." Qrodin points him out in another pasture and watches her skip to the ponies.

"Mine?" Kasaandra asks.

"The chestnut."

The dwarf nods once and follows Bell to the pony paddock.

"What is your name?" Llani asks the grey. "Starbright?" The horse shakes its head while a fly buzzes around its eyes. "Starlight?" The fly lands on the horse's ear. Another head shake. "It has Star in it, though, correct? Hmm, Starshine?" This time, the horse bounces up and stomps down on both forelegs. "Starshine! That is a lovely name. I would wager you do shine in starlight. Will you let me pet you?" The horse drops his head, blowing forcefully out his nostrils. "No? I will be gentle."

The horse sneaks frequent glances at Qat but mostly stares into Llani's eyes as if communicating directly to her. And maybe it is. Horse lips twitch on one side, then lift and wiggle as if trying to pronounce a tricky word. Qrodin smiles, but Llani's ears suddenly drop. "You are in pain? Would you like me to heal it for you?" The horse raises its head and looks sideways at her through one eye. "I can," she assures him. "Now, show me where it hurts."

Starshine's lips quiver and twitch and pull back from his teeth in an odd grimace. Then he sneezes and snaps at a fly.

Llani gasps, then gently lifts his lip, exposing a pus-filled pocket bulging from the gum.

"Whoa! I didn't know that was there," Harlan says quickly. "E's too young to have bad teeth, and he eats all the time. Never had no sign his mouth was buggin' him."

Llani glares at Harlan, obviously blaming him for the stallion's condition.

"Not making excuses. I should'a checked." Harlan bristles. "I guess that's why he's so cranky."

Llani erases her frown before turning back to Starshine. "Oh, you poor thing. Now, hold still. I am going to heal you." Like Qat's wound two nights ago, the abscess shrinks until it disappears, and Starshine's gums form back over the exposed root. "There. Does that feel better?" Starshine nudges Llani's shoulder with his nose, and she scratches him behind the ears.

"Did she just…?" Harlan stutters to a stop.

"How long did you say you've had this one?" Qrodin asks.

"Oh. Uh." Harlan scratches his head, but is looking Qrodin up and down. "A year, maybe?"

Starshine, if that is his name, raises his head and snorts.

"More like two days," Qat says.

Starshine nods vigorously. Then nudges Qat's hand. Ae scratches between the stallion's eyes and rubs aer hand down his nose. "Didn't you hear me say I've been looking for him for two days?"

Qrodin's pleased to see that Qat hasn't lost aer touch with horses. Just like when they were children.

"No. You can't take that one. He's never been saddled. You can tell that by the hair on his back. There ain't no rubbed spots or nothing. Now that sore's gone, I'll have to work with him to get him broke. That'll take me a full season, at least." Harlan rubs his hands together. "Maybe two!"

Qrodin's guessing Harlan's already calculating how much he can sell him for.

Starshine breaks from Qat's attentions. He bounces away, then stomps back with his hind legs in front of Harlan.

"Qat rides bareback," Qrodin says.

And it's true. Qat always did prefer to ride without a saddle. *'It takes too long to put it on, and it makes too much noise,'* ae used to say.

"You said earlier that you'd pay anyone to take him if they could ride him," Qrodin reminds him.

"Well. Sure. But that was before. He's fine now."

"It looks to me like Starshine already has an owner," Qrodin says.

"There ain't no proof," Harlan says, clearly not wanting to lose the opportunity to break in a wild horse. Qrodin's seen the type.

"Do you have any idea how much healing like that costs? I'll make you a deal. If he lets Qat ride him, we'll take him off your hands. Otherwise, you can pay us for healing him minus the cost of the rest of the horses."

"No deal! I could'a pulled that tooth for free. Now, let's get you saddled up so you can get on your way."

As soon as he says it, Starshine spins and kicks his rear legs back, smashing into the paddock's top rail. It explodes outward in a flurry of wood chips and splinters. Everyone jumps back.

Harlan yelps and grabs his arm. "What'd you do that for? Now I'm gonna have to fix it! I swear you cost me more than you're worth!"

"As I said, we'll take him off your hands," Qrodin offers.

"What? No. I'll just put him in with the others. Come here, you shit!" Harlan grabs a coil of rope and climbs over the busted fence. Starshine bounces away, kicking back in Harlan's direction, then races to the end of the enclosure. Harlan runs after him, but as he corners the horse, Starshine kicks again, bringing down the rail between his paddock and the larger one. He leaps the fallen remains of the fence and squeals, racing toward a group of about two dozen horses. They scatter immediately, and Harlan curses when two of them gallop toward the break in the enclosure. He waves his hands at them to get back and tries to tie the broken beam with the rope.

Qat whoops and cheers Starshine while Llani encourages the horse to 'be good.' Bell and Kasaandra have left the ponies and are watching the action on the fence rails. Even Akin, who'd stayed near the stables, watches the debacle.

"Changed your mind yet?" Qrodin calls out.

The stallion halts his antics and stares at Harlan, his head and tail high as if to say he's ready to cause more mischief. When Harlan hesitates, Starshine tenses, lowers his head, and paws the ground.

"Fine! Take the damn horse!"

Starshine does his double-hoofed stomp, tossing his mane forward and back, then races toward them.

Qrodin leans close to Llani. "I've not ridden bareback since childhood, but I did well enough. Qat was better, but I don't think ae's up to it yet."

"I could try. He seems to like me."

"It takes extraordinary balance and strength. If he spooks, you'll be thrown. It could be dangerous."

"Well. I *have* extraordinary balance and strength," the elf says.

Starshine prances up to the fence, obviously pleased with himself. He nudges Qat's shoulder.

Llani strokes Starshine's nose and looks him in the eye. "Will you let Qrow ride you, my Starshine?"

The horse blows out sharply. So does Qat.

"Do you want me to ride you?" she asks next.

He nudges Qat's shoulder.

"Qat?" Llani asks, surprised.

Starshine stares at Qrodin's twin.

"I'll ride you," Qat says.

The thought of Qat being thrown isn't a pleasant one, but Qrodin isn't going to dissuade Qat now. Qrodin and Llani step back to give them some space.

"How are you communicating with him?" Qrodin asks Llani when they're alone.

"Oh. Well. I am merely reading his body language. Growing up, I spent more time with animals than people. I had a fox that was very expressive. And Starshine is quite clear. I expect you knew what he was communicating as well as I."

Not really. It seemed to Qrodin that Starshine's actions were pure coincidence. "But what about his name? You knew it had a star in it."

She shrugs. "The name just popped into my head."

Qrodin is still skeptical. He's heard of people who can talk to animals. Perhaps she's reticent to acknowledge the rare ability. Qrodin glances at Qat. "Lead him into the corral over there, and we'll see how he does."

Once there, the stallion stands still while Qat hops onto a mounting block, grabs his mane, and vaults onto his back. Qrodin asks them to circle the corral a few times, and Starshine is as docile as can be. Satisfied the horse will behave, Qrodin takes Llani and Akin into the stable and shows them how to rub down their mounts, hoping they'll all get better acquainted. They're more nervous than the horses.

He leaves them alone to check on the ponies. Kasaandra has them both saddled and ready, and Bell is feeding them carrots. Where she got them, he can only guess. Qat and Starshine are still riding in circles. To give them more time, he saddles his mount—a beautiful bay gelding he'd initially selected for Qat—before returning to help Llani and Akin saddle the two mares. Once mounted, he adjusts their stirrups and leads them out of the stable. He shows them how to sit correctly. "Keep your toes up and hold the reins loosely enough you don't strain their mouth."

Kasaandra and Bell join them before he realizes that he has completely forgotten to select a pack mule. "Where are the rest of your supplies?"

"Everything is in our packs and the saddlebags," Llani says, nervously gripping the reins of her horse.

"Everything? I thought you said you purchased—"

"It's all in Llani's bag," Qat explains.

Oh, that's right. Llani had pulled Bell's longbow out of the bag the night they met. The accessory must hold more than he had thought. "Then I think we ought to be on our way. We're making a much later start than I expected. Qat, can you lead them to the bridge while I settle with Harlan? I'll catch up with you in a moment."

"Sure thing." Qat and Starshine move as one toward the exit.

"Which way?" Kasaandra asks at the road.

Qat points to the left. The other horses, obviously anxious to be elsewhere, rush to follow Kasaandra. Starshine pushes his way in front of them all, and Qat takes the change in speed in stride, sitting up straight, legs falling relaxed to the horse's sides. The others follow behind without any further commands from their riders. Bell is latched on tightly to her pony's mane, and her eyes are wide—from excitement or fear, Qrodin can't tell. The small pot around her neck bounces with every step.

Rather than worry about everyone, Qrodin searches for Harlan, who is still swearing at the broken fence and trying to keep the horses from leaving. Qrodin tosses a bag of coins. The pouch falls to the ground after bouncing off Harlan's hand, and several coins scatter in the dust. "That should cover the horses, gear, and fence. I'll send help and supplies on our way out of town."

Thankfully, he has plenty of resources in Riversmeet. So, after writing a note to Talim to send a crew to take care of the damage to the corral, Qrodin nudges his horse into a trot. He catches up with them quickly.

At the bridge, two mounted guards and two dagas block the entrance.

Qrodin moves to the front, surprised to see them. They've never obstructed the bridge before. "Hello," he says. "Is there some danger we should be worried about?" The guards likely want to avoid panic. The question should put them on the defensive.

"Not at all, sir. We're investigating a missing person is all. We're searching all carts and wagons leaving the city," says one mounted guard. The two dagas are sniffing the group.

"Well, as you can see, we don't have a cart or a wagon," Qrodin says with a smile.

"When did you come to town?" a male daga asks.

"My companions and I arrived twelve days ago," Llani says.

"All of you?" a female daga asks as she reaches Bell's pony. She sniffs at Bell's dangling pot rudely.

"That's my Pure Gold," Bell says to her.

"Well, no. Pardon me," Llani says to the daga, still sniffing at Bell's pot, "but that is quite unnecessary."

"Oh. It's okay," Bell replies, her wobbly smile revealing her discomfort.

Qrodin is worried. They're probably looking for Qat. That they have dagas at the bridge means they probably have a scent they're following.

"What about you?" says the male daga. "When did you arrive?" Unlike the female, he doesn't appear to be concerned about them.

Qrodin inflects his voice with *Soothe*, just in case. "A few days ago, on board the *Banshee*."

The guard retrieves a notebook and flips through the pages. "What's your name?"

"Browning. Quentin Browning," Qrodin says.

That gets all their attention. Quentin Browning is the alias he used to purchase the Lightning Strike and a few other businesses in town. He mainly uses it to make donations, so although the name is known, his face usually isn't. He has different aliases for different cities, but he is careful not to let too many people put a face to the names.

"Oh! Mr. Browning," says one of the mounted guards. "I'm so sorry to inconvenience you. We're just doing our job. You understand."

"Of course," he says. The female daga has finally moved on to Qat and Starshine. "That is my sibling," Qrodin says, hoping they assume Qat was with him on the *Banshee*.

"Is this your horse?" the female asks.

Qat nods. "Got away from me a few days ago. Down by the Hold?" Qat says easily. "Got spooked and jumped right into the river. Gone before I could get to the water." Qat points back toward Harlan's stables. "Found him at the stables a few minutes ago. Boy, was I glad to see you." The last is said to Starshine as Qat strokes his neck.

"We never did get our fish and chips," Qrodin says to corroborate Qat's story. He's not worried that the daga will pick up on his falsehood. It isn't one, not really. Ama never did bring back fish and chips. "You didn't happen to get any stingers while there, did you?" Blackened scorpion on a stick was one of Qat's favorites.

"How'd you know?" Qat says, looking up in surprise.

"You never could pass them up," he answers.

Qat laughs out loud. "You caught me."

The female daga, finally satisfied they're not the ones she's looking for, shakes her head at the two mounted guards.

"You have a fine day, Mr. Browning," the closer of the two says as they move aside.

Part 2 Cranwood

Chapter 19 Qat

10TH DAY OF ZAMDI, 14,887
ROAD TO CRANWOOD, ZEDANA

I can ride a horse.

And riding Starshine is now my favorite thing to do.

I followed Qrow this morning when he left the Lightning Strike. I couldn't believe my luck when I saw Starshine in that corral. I'd stayed out of sight until the others got there and watched him. When Starshine snubbed Qrow, I nearly laughed out loud. There was no way I was going to leave him behind with Harlan.

Mine.

I hear it again every time someone asks if he's mine. The intensity of the feeling I get is unnerving, but present all the same. I'd also felt Starshine's muscles relax when the daga asked if he was my horse, almost like he wanted to tell me he was. That it was okay for me to say yes.

I admit I'd been nervous about riding him, but from the moment I climbed on Starshine's back, it was as if we were one being. I may not speak to him like Llani, but we understand each other perfectly. As soon as I think about trotting ahead, we're on our way, and he turns instinctively, without me needing to tug on his mane.

It's even better than flying high in the crow's nest.

We follow a broad, winding road for most of the morning, bordered by gently sloping hills starting to turn green after the recent rain. Speaking of, we're only a few hours into the trek when a touch of rain falls.

When the sun is high, Qrow suggests we move off the road and dismount near a copse of trees. Even with a light sprinkling of rain and a steady breeze, it's a hot day, and I'm glad to stop.

When we do, I dismount without thinking about it, as though my body already knows what it's doing. When my feet hit the ground, my legs buckle. Only my lightning-fast reflexes and a grab for Starshine's mane save me from landing on my ass. "Sorry, buddy," I tell him when he chuffs. I relax my grip and pat his back. Embarrassed, I hope no one noticed.

My leg muscles feel like water, and I struggle to stay standing.

I can barely walk. Who knew sitting on a horse for hours would tire your muscles? How is it even possible? We didn't do any hard riding. I could have *walked* faster.

Starshine isn't challenging to manage, either. Just the opposite. Much easier than Llani's mount. Her mare doesn't move unless another horse is in front of them. Llani clicked and clucked and wiggled and jiggled and nudged her mare with her heels, but the horse wouldn't budge. I'm surprised she didn't talk to her like she did Starshine, or maybe she had, but the horse didn't care.

I volunteer to help Kasaandra with the horses. I have no idea why, except that I am equally clueless about setting up camp. That, and I'm hoping to keep some distance between Qrow and me.

She recommends we not remove the saddles until we stop for the night, but she says we should clean the dirt from the horses' legs and haunches before letting them loose to graze nearby.

Kasaandra's sweating profusely. Her face is tanned, but her furry knees—visible between her short skirt and tall, laced boots—are burnt pink. Riding must have exposed them to the sun, whereas walking usually wouldn't. They'll be painful this evening, but at least it's the only patch. Her sleeveless blouse shows off tanned and muscular shoulders, and she's wearing wide metal armbands above bulging biceps. The designs circling the center stone remind me of those on her double-bladed battleaxe.

And that reminds me. "You're skilled with that battleaxe of yours," I say to the dwarf. "You did some hefty damage to that manticore."

Kasaandra grunts in response.

"It's a beautiful piece," I say, nodding to her battleaxe. I remember that Llani said Kasaandra was from Toithdd Croieanan—Dwarf Mountain. It's the best place to get the finest-bladed weapons, made with steel that holds a sharp edge longer than any other. My twin blades are from there. Working on a hunch—and the burn scar I spy on her forearm—I continue. "The artistry is superb. I'd love to meet the person who made it."

"You have," Kasaandra says.

"You?" My hunch was correct. "I'm glad they're finally allowing women to become blacksmiths."

"They're not." Her brow wrinkles in a dark scowl, but her hands stay gentle as she finishes with her pony.

"Ah. That why you left?"

The dwarf nods once, and the topic is closed.

I give it a few moments for the heat to leave her face—it'd gone as red as her knees—and for Bell's pony to stop swishing her tail at Kasaandra. I've heard that horses can read a person's energy. It's a wonder Starshine let me close to him in the beginning. "So, what's up with you and Llani?" I ask the dwarf quietly when I hear Qrow and Bell start a conversation away from us and the horses.

Kasaandra's orange curls are dark and damp and obscure her face as she leans down to brush the pony's legs. After a few swipes, she shoves her hair out of her face and glances my way. "What do ya mean?"

"Why do you call her 'Princess'?" I switch to Qrow's horse and copy the dwarf's actions. Starshine and Kasaandra's pony shake themselves and wander a short distance away to graze.

"Oh, that." The scowl is back in her voice. "She's lazy."

I search the temporary camp. Qrow is helping Bell get a meal together. Akin is walking back with an armful of wood. Llani is nowhere in sight. "Oh, yeah?" I ask, hoping Kasaandra will expand on her comment.

"What is she doing right now?" she asks instead.

"Gathering wood?" I suppose she could be helping Akin with that task, but we already have enough wood.

"In the tree. Reading."

Surprised, I follow the direction Kasaandra indicates with her chin. I'd made the same mistake most people do by assuming she'd be on the ground. I search the oak tree up, up, and nearly to the top before seeing her. I thought her coloring would have made it easier to find her, but nestled as she is with her back against the trunk and long, thin legs stretched along the branch she's sitting on, she blends in with the shadows of the leaves and branches. "Does she always do that? Climb trees?"

"Yup."

No wonder she was able to climb to the roof so quickly. I'm not used to being around someone else who can climb as well as me. I'm impressed, but I don't want Kasaandra to realize it. "What does she read?"

The dwarf shrugs, moving on to Akin's horse. No favoritism there. I'll be taking care of Llani's horse in the future. At least for a few days.

I haven't decided how long I'll stay with them. I noticed that most people travel in groups. Although the road isn't crowded, several had passed us on their way to Riversmeet. We had also recently passed a clearing used as a rest stop. There were three different traveling groups there. If they have one so close to Riversmeet, there'll likely be more along the way. I'll have plenty of opportunities to join a different group.

I decide to change the subject and keep Kasaandra talking. "Have you always known how to sign?" I demonstrate with my hands when Kasaandra steps around the horse to look at me questioningly.

She shakes her head. "Some. Not the same. Akin is teaching me."

"He seems like a good guy."

"He is."

"Are you a couple?" I didn't think so, but I *had* discovered that Akin and Kasaandra shared a room at the BB&B while Llani and Bell shared another. I hadn't told them I was also staying there in case I left in the middle of the night. Instead, I'd spied on them from across the street until the lights in their rooms went off.

There hadn't been anything to indicate that the dwarf and ukulu slept together, but I wanted to lighten the mood.

Kasaandra snorts her answer, then pulls some jerky out of her pony's saddlebag and takes a bite.

As we remount, Qrow says, "The road will run parallel to the Shipdurn River for the next few days before it veers east and away from our current heading. If the weather holds, we should reach Cranwood in about six days."

I groan. Six days before we reach another town? At least I have Starshine to entertain me. For the rest of the day, he makes trouble wherever we go, nipping at the other horses, trotting ahead, wandering off the road. He nudges Llani's legs, swishes his tail at Qrow, and more than a few times tries to knock Kasaandra off her pony with his nose. My balance gets less steady, and my reflexes get slower as my muscles try to keep up. Even so, my confidence in riding him only gets stronger with each of his pranks.

Llani's mare pays as much attention to Starshine as Llani pays to me, which is hardly any at all. Her mare ignores Starshine's antics and keeps trudging along at her steady pace. At least she's sure-footed. No matter how often Starshine bites, bumps, or flicks at her with his tail, she ignores him. The elf, on the other hand, has found it more difficult to ignore. After a day of trying to get Starshine to behave, Llani's voice is hoarse from correcting him, and she is visibly exasperated.

We finally find a place to spend the night. After dismounting, I crab over and follow Kasaandra's instructions to unload, unsaddle, and brush the mounts. They don't care what we do; their entire world is centered on satisfying their hunger.

Except for Starshine.

Llani is still annoyed with him, and he picks up on it, lowering his head when she comes near and keeping it there as she walks away.

"I know how that feels." I reach my hand out to him. He raises his head and snuffs slightly but doesn't move away.

I *do* know how that feels. I've been wanting to get a closer look at that necklace. I'd gladly sacrifice any knowledge I could gain from Qrow if I could figure out how to get it off her neck without her blasting me like she did that thief. I'd be out of here a second later. Starshine is the fastest horse in the group. They wouldn't catch up with us. But even as I think it, something tells me I'm lying to myself.

With the other horses groomed and grazing, Kasaandra joins the rest of the party. I stay with Starshine and watch my companions as they organize their sleeping areas. A fire is going, and in one swift move, Bell skins and guts the first of the rabbits she shot with her bow earlier today. The second and third follow just as quickly.

Impressive.

It's...much different from the last time I traveled with a crew.

During my inattention, Starshine must have nudged my hand because I find myself petting the bridge of his nose, rubbing my hand in circles over his eyelids, and straightening his mane over his forehead. Then, without conscious thought, I start talking.

"Don't get me wrong," I tell him. "Sailing on the *Raven Scream* wasn't all bad. I was lucky the captain liked me from the beginning. As a kid, he gave me easier duties, like cleaning his cabin. I think he did it to keep me away from everyone. I was pretty good at finding hiding places, though. And when Rogen found out I could see in the dark, he stationed me up in the crow's nest to keep watch at night. Sometimes, I'd stare at the sky and create stories about the constellations. My constellations, at least; I never cared about learning the real ones until Rogen taught me how to navigate by them."

Starshine nickers softly. The sound makes me smile. I gently work at detangling his mane, pulling stubborn strands apart, alternating between using the brush and my fingers to tease out the tangles. I don't discuss my recent suspicions or plan to locate the captain. Saying it aloud would make it more real. And for now, I need it to be...not real.

It's fully dark by the time I finish his mane. The moons' combined red and blue crescents give him a dark pearlescence. Kuu—the silver moon—won't appear tonight, as it's Newkuu, and Isa and Uman are waning. Isa is blue tonight, so she'll be in a generous mood and spend the night playing tricks on Uman. They will be so embroiled in each other's escapades that they won't have time to bother us.

That makes it the perfect night for an assassin, even though Assassin's Night is two nights from now, when Isa and Uman are so thin they resemble an assassin's blades. It never made sense to me that Assassin's Night doesn't consider the size or color of Kuu. Two nights from now, Kuu will be nearly a third of the way whole and too bright in the sky for an assassin to go sneaking around town. Real assassins pay more attention to Kuu's phases than anything else when we need to do shadow work. Luckily, Kuu has a new moon every fourteen days, once a fortnight.

Of course, when you're one with the shadows, as I am, it doesn't matter what stage the moons are in.

I tell all of this to Starshine as I regard him. In this light, he's nearly the same color as Llani is during the day. How could I not admire him?

The sensation along my spine alerts me to Akin's approach before I see him. His soundless steps are even and controlled, smooth, and light. Even so, he clears his throat to announce his presence. He hands me a carrot, demonstrating that it's for Starshine. I break off pieces and feed them to the stallion. Akin indicates that our meal is also ready, so I give Starshine a final rub on his nose and join the others.

I was expecting dried-out rabbit on a stick. I didn't imagine herb-roasted veggies and rabbit pie with a crust so flaky it dissolves in my mouth. How does Bell make something like this over a campfire? "If every meal is like this, Bell, you may never be rid of me." I lick my fingers clean, then spit out the silvery strands of horse hair.

"Oh, they are," Llani says. "When we met Bell in Bierenan, Kasaandra initially rejected her request to join us. Bell's tracking skills are impeccable, however. She snuck into our camp late that night but was first up in the morning with breakfast." Llani sniffs primly. "Kasaandra faked being hurt the following day so that Bell could keep up."

"I wasn't faking. And it was hot," Kasaandra says, eyeing Akin's leftover pie.

Huh. I'm surprised to learn that Llani had joined Akin and Kasaandra before they met Bell. I had thought Kasaandra only tolerated Llani because of Bell. Curiouser and curiouser.

"At least we're not walking to Craguesport," Bell says beside me. "I don't know if I'll ever gain back the weight I lost on the way to Riversmeet. I'll never find a husband if I'm so scrawny."

"Ha!" I can't help but laugh. "I don't think that's going to be a problem. Not with your skills." I lick my fingers again.

"Aww. Thanks, Qat."

After the meal is cleaned up, Akin signs something. Kasaandra shrugs.

"Oh! Yes. We should determine the watch order." Llani includes Qrow and me in her look. "On our previous journey, Bell always took the last watch to start the morning meal. As I need only a few hours of rest, I took the one before her, and assisted her with her morning duties. Akin and Kasaandra alternated the remaining shifts. If you agree, the two of you can be added to the rotation."

"It's going to be a long journey," I say. "Do we all need to be on watch each night? Perhaps we can rotate giving one person the night off so they can get a full night's rest."

Akin nods in agreement.

"Who gets tonight off?" Qrow asks.

"I volunteer," Kasaandra says.

"Me too," Bell yawns her answer.

"I have an idea," I say. I dig out my dice—the true ones, even. "We roll. High score wins."

After the watch order is established, with Qrow getting tonight off, we agree to travel at dawn.

I drew first watch, and surprisingly, Llani stays up with me. "I only need a few hours of rest," she reminds me when I question her. She removes a book from her bag and settles close to the fire. The stone at her neck catches the light.

I'm reminded of the way she had flung the thief back. *What in a tidal wave was that, anyway?* But thinking back, was it she who had done it? She'd seemed as surprised as I was, and I hadn't seen her move her fingers or lips like she does when she heals. Reacting to a hunch and hoping that surprise will loosen her tongue, I say, "I saw what your necklace did to that person in the alley. I've never seen jewelry that could do that."

"Oh! I expect it is a protection spell of some sort." Llani bites her lip.

It *was* the necklace! Hmm. I doubt it was a protection spell. More like an anti-theft spell. Which is another surprise. Why would a twig necklace need that?

Maybe because I want to steal it?

True, but just the gem. What's so special about that stone, anyway? What else could it do that would be so valuable that it warranted an anti-theft spell?

And why did Llani say she *expects* it's a protection spell? Shouldn't she *know*?

And why didn't the blast push her away? In my experience, anything that gives off that kind of power should have flung her back with the same force. And those spindly-looking strands holding it should have been blown to pieces. There's more to that odd piece of jewelry than I initially thought.

"What else does it do?" I try to make the question casual, just mere curiosity.

"Well...I..." Llani looks down and away from me.

Hmmm. She doesn't know the answer. Interesting. And she's not used to lying.

"If you would be so kind as to defer questions until another time,"—she sweeps her hand toward our sleeping companions—"I prefer to read before I retire."

"Certainly."

When I'm not watching her, I use the time to check on the horses, inspect our surroundings, and find a good place for my hammock.

Before my watch is half over, Llani packs her book away. She says goodnight and climbs the tree she'd been in earlier. She's even better at it than I am, scaling the trunk as easily and swiftly as a lizard. Unlike me, she doesn't need to use the branches as her primary hand and foot holds. I'd heard tales that some elves live in trees and can somehow carve into them and live inside their trunks without killing the tree. What's more likely is that they live up in the branches. Llani settles herself on the same branch she had perched on earlier.

I'm still watching her when, a moment later, she lowers herself into an upside-down, hanging position. Her hair is knotted to keep it from hanging low. After several minutes, I realize she plans on sleeping that way.

Later, I'm both surprised and thankful when Akin wakes up for his watch. I'm used to shaking sailors awake and arguing with them to take their turn.

I fall asleep in my hammock before he finishes his first round.

11TH DAY OF ZAMDI, 14,887

The smell of coffee pulls me from sleep, which was better than expected, even though I woke at each watch change and when Bell started cooking.

It doesn't take me long to roll up my hammock and pack it away. The equipment is light and compact but robust and dwarven-made. I catch Kasaandra's expression when she looks at it. There's almost a satisfied smirk there—maybe even a hint of pride?—but I must be imagining it. She hadn't looked the same way when she saw my blades, which are from her city.

Remembering Kasaandra's complaints about Llani, I wonder how I can help. I'm many disreputable things, but *lazy* is not one of them. At least, not when there are chores to do. I've never cooked, so breakfast is out. And there's no deck to swab or rigging to mend. On a ship, there are countless chores. Here, there's not much that needs to be done that isn't already being done.

I gravitate to the horses and help Kasaandra until Bell hollers that breakfast is ready. She hands me a cup of coffee and a plate of food. The meal looks fantastic.

Traveling with them has its advantages after all.

After a few hours on horseback, I change my mind. Bell snaps at Llani when she pulls over yet again for some rare herb or mushroom or whatever it is that catches her eye. Llani snaps back. Kasaandra defends Bell, then spends the rest of the day complaining about the heat, then the rain, then her sunburn. Akin spends most of the time clutching his stomach and growling at anyone who speaks to him. The space between the horses gets further and further apart. Eventually, I decide to take advantage of the situation, and Starshine and I scout ahead.

All the squabbles today remind me of sailing with Rogen. There were always arguments and heated outbursts. Most of the time, I'd retreat to the crow's nest and observe everyone from above. They always forgot I was there, and I'd learn the most intriguing things.

I escape with the chest and stone when we finally stop to make camp. I hear it thrumming and want to see if opening it stops it again. I traverse a safe distance and climb up into a tree. It's the closest thing to a crow's nest I can find.

I get comfortable on one of the branches. As soon as I open the box, the buzzing stops, and I hear Akin groan. His hands are clenched to his side.

"Oh!" Bell cries, rubbing her bottom.

"Are you okay?" Kasaandra asks.

I close the box quickly. Akin relaxes instantly.

Interesting.

"Yes, but I think I got bit." Bell scratches. "I hate spiders."

"I was asking Akin," Kasaandra snarls. "No one cares about bug bites."

Bell sticks her tongue out at Kasaandra.

"What happened?" Qrow asks.

Akin shakes his head and signs too fast for me to follow.

They fall silent, and after a few minutes, everyone returns to what they were doing. Qrow pulls out his notebook. Llani reads. Akin meditates. Kasaandra whittles. And Bell sniffs the pot she wears around her neck when we ride. I've caught her putting sticks and berries in it. The oddity is nothing compared to the rituals of superstitious pirates.

I open the box again slowly, but this time, I watch them all for a reaction.

Llani's ears twitch in my direction.

Qrow stops writing and looks at her with a frown.

Bell scratches.

Akin doesn't move.

Maybe I was wrong.

I watch him as I close the lid. Nothing. I open it and close it again. He opens his eyes and stares in my direction. The look in them sends a shiver down my spine, and my danger sense twinges, then fades. In another blink, he looks normal.

Had I imagined it?

Had he seen me?

I glance at Llani as I open the chest again. Another quick twitch of her ears—kraken, they're sensitive—but she doesn't look over.

What kind of rock is this that people unconsciously react to it?

Hours later, when Kasaandra wakes me for my watch, I quiz her about gemstone properties. I figure she may be the most knowledgeable. After all, she has several gemstones hidden in her beard alone. Maybe she's heard of it or seen one.

I tell her I had a dream about a strange gemstone. I describe it to her. "Do you know what it is?"

"Hmm. Maybe prehnite."

"I've never heard of it."

She shrugs.

"Someone told me once that they could hear gemstones. You ever heard of something like that?" I ask her.

"Some people are sensitive to them. My father can feel when they're charged. I know someone who got migraines. Another got arm cramps." She shrugs as if it's of no concern. She obviously isn't affected by them, considering the enormous indigo-colored stone embedded in the armband on her left arm.

And the fact that she didn't seem affected earlier.

Chapter 20 Qrodin

14TH DAY OF ZAMDI, 14,887
ROAD TO CRANWOOD, ZEDANA

The last few days have been a challenge for Qrodin. He's had to use *Soothe* more often than he can count.

Llani and Bell are barely speaking. Bell has also refused to join Akin for morning and evening stretches, something Llani said they used to do on the way to Riversmeet. Qat and Kasaandra still look out for the horses but seldom share more than a word or two.

Llani spends even more time reading up in a tree or off by herself. Bell practices with her bow. Akin meditates. Kasaandra sharpens her giant battleaxe. And Qat? Qat does what ae always did best when they were kids. Disappears.

Qrodin spends most of his non-travel time catching up on business.

Sometimes, he observes the others, but most of the time, like now, he reviews each page of the journal, sends inquiries to business heads, and responds to complaints about product shortages and other inquiries.

After Qrodin had given his blessings on Xan's promotion, Talim said she'd spend only one day in five at the Lightning Strike to focus on constructing her new restaurant. He turns to the page that pulls from Talim's new journal. Then almost laughs out loud.

Under his How's it going? she had scribbled, What the fuck was I thinking doing this again at my age? This is your fault!!!

Abandi can live two and a half centuries. She's barely considered an adult at her age, something that she's very good at hiding from the Valore. He responds, *I'm glad to see that things are back to normal,* then closes the journal and looks up.

Qat's napping—or pretending to.

Eventually, Qrodin hopes Qat will be comfortable enough with him to initiate a conversation. But waiting isn't easy. They always shared everything.

They were like two halves of a whole. He's heard people say that about their spouse, but he can't imagine ever feeling that way about anyone other than Qat. Not even Doscia, the woman he once thought he'd marry.

It was like he and Qat had a bond, like a rope, that connected them. When Qat was in trouble, Qrodin would always feel the rope wiggle. When Qat was taken, that rope was severed. Or nearly completely severed—except for one tiny thread. A thread so small that he often thought it wasn't there at all. Occasionally over the last twenty years, he'd feel something—an infinitesimal pull—that'd kept his hope alive.

After twenty years, he's an entirely different person, but around Qat, he's still a twin following around and looking after his other half. Unfortunately, without that rope, he doesn't know where to be.

So, he waits.

It starts raining heavily in mid-afternoon, and it doesn't look likely to let up anytime soon. With no dry wood to be found, they can't make a fire. After a hasty meal of local greens and raw, citrus-marinated fish that Qat catches in a nearby stream, they all crowd into one giant, makeshift tent fashioned from many tents Llani pulls from her bag. Qrodin wonders why they haven't been using them up to this point. He has to admit, though, that it was quite lovely to sleep under the stars. Not that he can see them tonight.

The heavy cloud cover obliterates the stars and moons. Qrodin's night vision reveals that everyone's expressions are as closed off as the lantern they'd only lit for Bell's sake.

She's watching Akin closely.

Akin is staring into the night. He has first watch, but it doesn't start for another few hours.

Their stillness makes Qrodin slightly uneasy. He puts it down to the bad weather.

A few moments later, Kasaandra yawns loudly. Then Bell and Akin follow suit. Finally, Llani stretches and wraps another blanket around herself.

Qat finally breaks aer silence, slowly sitting up. "I know it's my night off for watch, but if you all want to get to bed early, I'll stay up until it's time for Akin's watch. We may as well get some extra sleep tonight, what with the rain and all."

"You don't have to tell me twice." Kasaandra curls up in her sleeping fur. Before long, her snores rumble through the tent, competing with the thunder outside. Not long after, Bell's soft snoring joins Kasaandra's.

Qrodin tosses and turns on the hard ground. At least when they slept apart outside the last few nights, the snoring wasn't so loud.

When Akin wakes him hours later for his watch, Qrodin is surprised at how deeply he slept.

The heavy rains had also succumbed to sleep, for when he steps outside to check on the horses, the night is quiet and clear enough to see Isa's teal crescent moon and Uman's red sickle. Right now, Kuu is still hidden behind something—a hill or a heavy cloud—for Qrodin cannot find any of her silvery light.

He finds the horses by Starshine's iridescence, huddled together for warmth under a nearby oak tree. They nicker lightly at his approach but don't move. Qrodin takes a quick lap around the tent and campsite to wake himself up.

He catches something out of his peripheral vision and wonders if he's wake-dreaming. A light is coming from the west side of camp. Straight for him.

He reacts too late. It strikes his left side. Every muscle in his body convulses and contracts. His jaw clenches. It feels like every molar cracks. He doubles over in pain, clamping his arm to his side.

He can't breathe. What's happening?

He gasps for breath.

A crackling boom bursts something in his left ear.

He clutches at it. His legs give out. He falls to his knees, barely catching himself before his face hits the ground.

Everything disappears in a black haze.

His sight returns suddenly. A putrid-smelling substance fills the air near him. Noxious fog is roiling through the air, a fetid mist that drifts ever closer to Qat.

Wait, Qat?

Qrodin crawls toward his twin.

Qat's lying prone on the ground with a dagger through aer heart.

"No!" Qrodin reaches for his twin. His arms pass through aem, striking the ground. The vision shimmers and then fades.

He's dreaming. He must be.

But something tells him he's not. He was attacked. He rolls away out of instinct and slumps against a nearby oak, shielded from whatever—or whoever—targeted him. He looks for his twin.

Qat isn't there. The vision was a hallucination, not a dream.

His ears ring like an alarm inside his head.

He peeks around the tree trunk, afraid of what he'll see. The ground around the lightning's origin bursts into shimmering green fire. Two figures approach the camp slowly. Fiery green specters with long hair and even longer robes, one taller than the other.

What can he do? He has no weapons, not even the staff Anada gifted him. He's not a warrior, but he's supposed to be on watch to look out for danger. Why hadn't he prepared himself? He'd never have walked into a board meeting unprepared.

He shakes his head to clear it. Okay, if this were a hostile takeover attempt from another company, what would he do? Divide and conquer. Sow dissent.

He needs to separate them.

Qrodin hears Bell *oof*. Llani shushes her. They're by the horses.

Kasaandra laughs. Amid the green fire, her battleaxe slices through the night.

How did she get to them so quickly?

The shadow of a third assailant walks nimbly to the left of the others, beyond the verdant fire that's blanketing everything nearby. Two fiery green creatures, bent with age, are fighting with Kasaandra. They're all small—about Kasaandra's height—with pointed ears.

Qrodin focuses on the shadowy dark one. His vocal cords tremble with a low hum while he composes a *Coax* command. As with the manticore, he sends the command telepathically.

Of the three, you must flee.

The figure runs away. She falls. Skeleton hands are emerging from the ground near her. They catch and hold her while she struggles and fights. There are a hundred or more between her and the neon green figures.

The shorter of the two goes for Kasaandra, her clawed hands grasping as she lunges forward. Akin tries to trip her, but it barely slows her as she leaps. Kasaandra swipes at the tall one, but she's quick. The axe swing should have removed a limb, but it barely skims her.

In the distance, the dark, shadowy one escapes the hands holding her. She steps agilely around more of them.

Qrodin crouches low and circles the melee to the left, moving closer to her. In his mind, he rushes to her and stares deeply into her eyes. There's no time for a rhyme. *Stop fighting and stay away from your companions,* he commands.

When she complies, Qrodin moves closer to Kasaandra and Akin in case they need his help.

Strangely, the taller of the two fiery creatures is waving her hands around her head and screaming, like she's batting away vicious insects or bats, but there's nothing there. Qat's blades are nearly invisible as ae attacks the shorter one from behind. The taller, crazed one shrieks and flails her arms, flinging blood and spittle everywhere. Everyone moves back to avoid the mess. As they do, several arrows pierce her chest. A dozen more arrows come down like rain, catching nearly everyone in their path.

Closer now, the fiery ones' appearances don't match their flaming green outlines. The apparitions look as if two beings are overlapping each other—young and nubile elves in flesh, hunched and crippled ones in flame. They are disguising themselves, and Qrodin suspects the fire is revealing their true nature.

He can't understand what they're saying, but Kasaandra laughs and taunts them, and it sounds like the same language.

Her axe swings, and the taller one's head falls. As if in slow motion, the face morphs as it arcs to the ground, going from young and beautiful to wrinkled and twisted. An elf. An old elf. The emerald fire is still engulfing her head as it stares blankly into the night. But the flames don't burn her, and her sightless eyes seem to see through to his soul.

He gets no satisfaction that he was right about them disguising themselves. That they could do so during battle tells him that they are far more powerful than he is.

Qrodin stumbles. His strength is nearly depleted. His scorched side feels stripped to the bone. He can't tell if he's bleeding. He only hopes the strike cauterized the wound.

The short one spits a string of vicious sounds at Kasaandra, but the dwarf doesn't back away.

Out of habit and unable to stop himself, Qrodin murmurs: *Intercept and perceive, from their lips I now receive.*

"Where is it?" the elf screeches, the language sitting archaically in her mouth. "Give it to us, or I will take my vengeance. I will turn your blood to fire. I will slice the heart from your chest!"

Kasaandra points at the lifeless and headless body on the ground, responding in the same tongue. *"You, if you don't stop. I will dance on your body."*

The vengeful creature turns her back on them. She screams. Remembering the dark one, Qrodin searches the night and finds her standing in the distance.

"Traitor! Coward!" the vengeful one screams at her. He can sense the Itan in her words.

"No!" Qrodin yells. "Stop her!" Can she end Qrodin's *Coax*? If she does, there will be two of them to contend with again.

A sizzling fireball comes from behind Qrodin, small but accurate, igniting the vengeful one's robes. She turns and claws at Akin, scoring his face and neck deeply, then twists violently to avoid his parry. *"You haunted my sister,"* she screams in that other language, staring at Kasaandra. *"She will haunt you until you die.*" Her hair is on fire, orange flames competing with the green. Smoke is swirling about her, almost obscuring Qat as ae creeps up behind her and strikes. The elf gasps loudly, the wound making a sucking sound as she struggles to breathe around the dagger in her ribs.

Arrows whiz overhead again. Everyone scatters. The vengeful one clutches at her chest when an arrow pierces it fletching-deep.

She falls to her knees.

"Yybyiehk will return! You cannot escape his wrath!" she curses.

Kasaandra takes a step to the side and swings.

Another flaming green head arcs and transforms.

The dark one is running fast toward Qat. "I smell him on you," she growls. "You will regret it. He will turn your blood to acid. You will rot from the inside out, and maggots will eat your heart."

The vengeful one's words are ringing in Qrodin's ears. *Blood to fire, slice, dance.* He copies her cadence and twists it into a horrifying tune, then hurls it into the dark one's mind. A brief glimmer of a green gemstone flashes in her mind. Instinctively assuming it's important to her, he pictures himself shattering it between his hands. She halts in her tracks and clutches her head. She pulls at her hair, screeching loudly.

Another ball of fire lands behind her, but this time, it bounces before striking her from behind. Her hair and clothes ignite. As they do, she stands tall and points at Qat. Her words fly so fast that Qrodin can barely keep up.

"You think you have won, but he will destroy you! Your skin will melt off your bones. Your—"

A white beam hits her, bursting into tiny stars that wink out. Qrodin is blinded again, but only for a few seconds.

Another arrow sings through the cacophony of her words, cutting off her maniacal ravings.

Kasaandra's final axe swing is deafening in the sudden silence. Her sightless head hits the ground, the third one tonight, before rolling to a stop.

Had this been a dream, Qrodin would wake up and forget it before he got out of bed. Instead, their words burn into Qrodin's brain like flaming script on black parchment. Hate in the hue of each word. Discord in the line of each letter. Scratched by an ember so deep, the parchment is rent through and slowly burning.

He'll never be able to forget them.

Chapter 21 Qat

Kasaandra is moving at twice her usual speed, but the rest of us are exhausted and listless around camp.

"Wanna join me?" I ask Akin and point beyond the clearing. "I'm going to search for any more threats."

I wait until we are beyond even Llani's hearing. "Have you ever seen anything like that?" I ask.

After a moment, Akin shakes his head. His face and neck have several long, deep scratches that are still bleeding. Where the skin is torn, a grey, mucus-looking ooze mixes with the blood.

"Whoa! Kasaandra said you like scars, but you should have Llani look at that. It already looks infected." I hand him a kerchief from my pocket. "Here. Hold this against your jaw."

Akin presses it to his face.

That'll hurt tomorrow. I've been lucky over the years, but I've seen my share of battle injuries. He'll live.

I'd only gotten a few splinters. At least I redeemed myself after how badly I'd performed when we fought the manticore.

Akin and I go slowly, even though we can see well in the dark. "Could you understand what they were saying?"

He presses his lips together.

I take that as a no. "Kasaandra could."

Akin bends and picks up one of Bell's arrows without answering.

A shiver ran down my spine when I saw Kasaandra laugh and respond to the elves. I may not have understood the words, but I could tell they understood each other. The same structure to the words. Was Llani close enough to hear them?

We search from the river to the hills but find nothing else. I smell cooked pork before we return, and my mouth waters in anticipation. When did they have time to hunt a pig?

When we round the tent, I almost gag. It's not a pig. Three elves are piled on a burning pyre. I hold back the reflex to vomit. My mouth was watering for cooked elf? That's just wrong.

I move closer. They're old, but they looked young when we were fighting them. I'd bet my blades that these are the same elves that followed us in Riversmeet. Things had happened so fast, but when that last one approached me, she looked familiar.

"Llani said we needed to bury the ashes." Bell scrunches her nose. "It's kind of gross, but we don't want to take any chances either."

"Why do you think I took off their heads?" Kasaandra says as she tosses broken arrow shafts into the fire.

"Where did you get the wood?" I ask. We couldn't find dry wood earlier. How did she find some tonight?

"Llani asked the trees to donate it." Bell's eyes open wide. "And they did!"

"She didn't help lug it over to the fire, though," Kasaandra grumbles. "Or put the bodies on top."

Llani is sitting on the other side of the camp, but since her ears twitch in our direction, I figure Kasaandra was loud enough for her to hear. I'd kill to have hearing that good.

Akin signs something to Kasaandra. I only recognize the sign for Qrow.

"He went to bed soon as the fire was lit," Kasaandra says with the same disgust she'd used when complaining about Llani.

Akin looks nearly as disgusted as Kasaandra, and I feel an odd twinge of annoyance. Qrow's not like us. He hasn't been trained for battles like this.

"Llani?" I call out. "One of them got Akin. It's deep."

I ignore his growl.

"And it needs to be cleaned," I say. "It stinks like rot." I back away from the group while Kasaandra's attention switches to Akin's wound.

Why do I feel defensive on Qrow's behalf? He's more than capable of standing up for himself.

I decide not to dwell on it and move to the far side of the clearing, taking a lap around it again to keep moving. I decide to check on the horses. My spine tingles before I get there. Someone's watching me. The sensation is gentler than my danger sense. I turn in a slow circle.

Bell is sitting huddled on the ground.

"Hey, Bell." I walk over and crouch down next to her. "Are you doing okay?"

I see immediately how stupid that question is. She's shaking. Her brown eyes find mine in the dark. She tries to smile. She's not okay.

"You don't have to pretend you are," I tell her. "I can see that you're not."

She nods her head. Her eyes are haunted. Tonight's battle was probably the worst thing she's ever witnessed. I've been in hundreds of battles, and even I'm shaken at the weirdness of it. At one point, it looked like that last elf had been talking to me, specifically. "Come on," I say, wanting to distract us both. "Let's see to the horses and make sure they haven't run away."

She nods again and slowly gets to her feet.

I'm worried about her continued silence. "Do we have any more of those apples?"

Without answering, Bell disappears inside the large, makeshift tent.

Llani and Akin follow her inside, then Kasaandra.

"Is Akin okay?" Bell asks as she comes back out a moment later.

"He'll be fine." And I don't want to be there when Llani's done with him if he holds a grudge. "It's just a scratch."

"That's good." She hands me a couple of carrots. "We're out of apples."

The horses nicker at our approach. Starshine bumps his nose on my chest.

"Hello, there." I place my forehead against his and scratch behind his ears. For the first time since the attack, I feel the tension in my shoulders relax.

Bell silently feeds her pony. One by one, the others surround her, nudging her for their share. I can barely see her beneath the horses' heads. I run my hands along Starshine as I circle him, looking for any sign of injury. When I get back to his head, his lips fluffle.

"What are you laughing at?" I say, switching my attention back to the hablis.

Akin's horse sniffs Bell's hair from above, then snuffles her ear. I hear her giggle. "Don't worry, Cinnamon." She pats the nose that's resting on her shoulder. "You'll get one." Her pony prods her. "Ginger! You already had yours. You, too, Nutmeg." She pulls a carrot away from Kasaandra's mount and waves it back and forth. "This one is Clove's."

"You named them all spices?" I ask her.

"No," she says, peeking beneath Cinnamon's head to look at me. Her smile is infectious. "Llani's is Hot Chocolate."

I laugh out loud. Llani will hate that.

By the time we return to the tent, Bell looks much better. Color has returned to her cheeks, and her head is higher.

All but Llani have retired. She's tending the fire.

"You go on in, Bell. I'll stay out here with Llani for a bit."

"Night, Qat."

"Night, Bell."

"Hey, Qat?"

"Yeah?"

"I'm sorry for shooting you."

"Don't worry, Bell. Your arrow barely grazed me." I turn my forearm to hide the wound. "I think Kasaandra got it the worst."

Bell touches my arm, just below the hole in my sleeve. Her bottom lip trembles slightly, but then she removes her hand. "Thank you." She says it so sincerely that I feel myself blushing. Gratitude is something I seldom get. How am I supposed to respond? I'm spared when she smiles and ducks through the tent flap.

"I can't believe those are still burning," I tell Llani when I join her by the fire. The largest bones are still in the coals, including the skulls. They stare up at me.

"The fire needs to be at least..." She pauses as though she's trying to calculate the exact temperature. Finally, she sighs and continues, "extremely hot to disintegrate the bones to ashes. It's taking more wood than I anticipated."

She sighs again, and her shoulders slump. It's not like her to look so unsure. She turns slightly away from me. Now *that* is like her.

I leave her be.

I think it's supposed to be Qrow's watch, but since I can't sleep, and he's passed out, I may as well finish it. I spend most of it walking the perimeter, thankful that at least my danger sense had warned me of the attack earlier tonight. I'd gotten the others up and slipped under the tent. But even with my senses clanging like alarm bells, I couldn't see the threat until the green flames illuminated the elves. I hope there aren't more of them out there.

Llani stands up and approaches some trees. I follow her, hoping to see if the trees drop their branches for her, as Bell described earlier. Llani looks tired but embraces one of the trees. She stays there for several minutes, her forehead to the trunk. Nothing happens. I'm about to turn away when several large limbs sway gently and tumble to the ground.

Llani finally steps back and raises her face toward the sky. Tears fall in glistening streaks.

I'm surprised. The only emotion I usually see in her is irritation.

I don't hear what she says to the tree, but when she's done, she grabs the smallest of the fallen limbs and drags it toward the fire. She should have had no problem carrying it, but she stops halfway to rest.

At this rate, she'll never get to the remainder.

I grab two limbs and haul them to the fire.

15TH DAY OF ZAMDI, 14,887

Storm clouds blot out the sun, and the rain pelts down so thickly I can barely see well enough to relieve my bladder. Llani and I have spent the last two hours trying to keep the wood dry as sprinkles turned into light rain. The fire is so hot, droplets hiss and sizzle when they fall on it, but it still burns. I helped her cover the wood pile, but it wasn't enough. When I return, Llani is pulling the water out of the wood before placing it into the fire. Every time she does it, the magic seems to age her.

"You need to rest now," I tell her. "I'll stay up until Bell's watch."

She only nods in answer. She pokes at the ashes to verify there are no more bone pieces, but is too weak or too tired to stand up.

"Do you need help?"

She doesn't respond. Her eyes gloss over, and she sways slightly.

I approach her slowly, afraid I'll startle her out of whatever daze she's in. Is it exhaustion, or is she suffering a form of delayed shock? I've seen it happen before. Usually to young sailors after their first fight. Sometimes to veterans. When the adrenaline is pumping, you have no idea what you're putting your body through. When it wears off, you pay the price. At those times, Rogen directed those of us still standing to help the others. We'd triage the injuries. We'd make necessary repairs. We'd get the ship moving. We'd work in shifts. Eventually, everyone would be back on their feet and back to full speed.

Llani has no more wind in her sails.

"Do I need to carry you?" I ask. "Or do you just need help?" I'm betting that Llani's pride won't let me carry her. I'm right.

There are a dozen leaks, and half of the bedrolls look soaked when we get inside the tent. At least Llani's is dry.

I dry off as much as possible, settle down by the tent flap, and watch the rain. I can't tell what time it is without the sun or stars, so I let Bell sleep in. We're not going anywhere today.

"Is the fire still going?" Bell asks about an hour later from within her bedroll.

"For a little while longer, I think."

She crawls out from a mound of pillows and blankets and peeks outside. "Oh. Maybe I'll just make coffee. We have enough for another cold breakfast."

Kasaandra and Akin finally wake up and slip outside the tent to take care of business. Neither stays outside long, even though it had stopped raining. They do their best to drape Akin's wet bedroll over his bag. He finds a comfortable spot and sits down to meditate. Kasaandra paces. Sleep did nothing to alleviate her adrenaline from last night. I wonder how she was able to sleep. I didn't bother waking her for her shift, either. Eventually, Kasaandra gathers a few items from her bag, then shakes out her giant bear fur before draping it around her shoulders. "I'll be outside. Call me when breakfast is ready?"

"Sure." Not that I'll need to. Kasaandra has a sixth sense when it comes to mealtime.

"Where's Qrow?" Bell is carrying his coffee in from outside. A drop escapes over the side.

"Still sleeping," I tell her.

"Did he take an extra watch?" Bell frowns.

I shrug.

"You tell us." Kasaandra scowls at Bell as she says it, pausing at the tent entrance.

"Only Qat was up when I woke up," Bell says. They both look at me.

"I couldn't sleep, so I stayed up the rest of the night," I say.

"He's been asleep this whole time?" Kasaandra's question is filled with even more disgust than she usually shows for Llani.

"You were," I remind her, annoyed at her intolerance when she was no better.

"Maybe he got up already." Bell lifts his blanket. "Oh, there you are."

Bell pulls back a corner of the bedroll, and a tangled mass of sweat-soaked hair falls over Qrow's face. She shakes his shoulder. "Qrow?"

At Akin's whistle, Bell glances at him. "I don't know." She looks at Kasaandra and me. "Was he hurt?"

Kasaandra shrugs, still waiting near the tent flap.

He'd avoided the fight, so I assumed he'd been spared. I shake my head. "Not that I know of." To be honest, I'd barely been aware of him.

Bell crouches down next to him. "Qrow?" She pats his shoulder again. "I have your coffee." When he doesn't wake, she touches his forehead. "Oh no! He's burning up!" She rushes toward Llani, spilling coffee on her hand in the process.

I take the cup from her.

"Llani! Wake up! Something's wrong with Qrow." When Llani only groans, Bell shakes her again, then touches her forehead. She looks back at us. "She's not getting up, but I don't think she has what Qrow has."

Akin turns Qrow on his back.

I get a terrible feeling when I see how pale he is. Akin struggles with the blanket. It's almost as if Qrow had rolled himself in it before slipping into the bedroll. I see the blood before he gets it completely off him.

"Oh, Qrow!" Bell cries.

Kasaandra leans in to look. "That's not good. I'll get your pack," she says to Akin, dropping the fur on her way.

"Bell," I say, wanting to distract her. "Can you get us some clean water? And do you have any clean rags or something?"

"I think so." She jumps up and hurries to her pack, then digs through it. "Yes!" She yanks several items out of the bag. "I told you, you can't have too many napkins!"

"You sure did." I set the coffee down and help Akin remove Qrow's arm from his jacket. At the sweet, metallic smell coming from him, I steel myself. I use one of my daggers to cut his shirt from the hem up to reveal a wad of cloth soaked in blood at his side. When I try to remove it, it sticks in places. Beneath it, skin and muscles are damaged clear to his ribcage.

My stomach tightens. I've seen injuries like this onboard the *Raven Scream*. They get infected often, and the healing process is quite painful. I glance back at Llani. We're going to have to deal with this ourselves. Whatever Llani had to do to keep the fire going last night took a toll on her.

When Bell returns, I soak the section of cloth enough to remove it and clean the wound. I'm thankful Qrow doesn't wake up. Akin coats it with a salve while I search Qrow for other injuries.

"What do you think caused it?" Bell picks up Qrow's coffee cup and starts drinking from it. I doubt she even realizes it. The hot drink is likely more for comfort than thirst.

"He was probably the first one hit." Kasaandra takes the cloth Akin hands her.

I try to remember the order of events from last night. "Kasaandra's right. I remember a bright light whizzing past. Whatever it was, it only happened one time." I hadn't seen where it went. The tent had blocked the light's trajectory. Shortly after, the two elves closest to me were lit up with green flames, and I forgot all about it.

Akin signs, and Bell nods. She returns with a cup of water.

She dribbles a few drops into Qrow's mouth. When his lips close and he swallows, Bell crouches almost nose to nose with him. "Qrow? Wake up."

I hold my breath, but he doesn't move again.

"Wasn't it her night off watch?" Kasaandra gestures to Llani, who's curled up in her blankets. Kasaandra picks up her fur, and with a flick of her wrist, it falls around her in heavy folds.

I nod. "She stayed up all night to keep the bonfire going."

"I' shoul'n've 'aken all nigh'," Kasaandra says, her accent stronger than usual. She gathers the items she'd discarded earlier.

How would she know? Does she burn bodies as a habit?

"It does if you aren't using *fiery ho' magma*." Bell imitates Kasaandra's accent.

"Then she didn't' build it right. It would've gotten hot enough if she did," Kasaandra says, disgust in her voice.

Akin frowns at Kasaandra and signs something.

I need to learn sign language.

I dismiss the thought as quickly as it comes. I probably won't be with them long enough for it to matter.

The dwarf takes a moment before responding. "Even if I had helped her, it's not a big deal to throw a log on the fire. She's just being lazy, as usual."

"She kept running out of wood and had to keep collecting it," I say. We had made three more trips to the trees after that first time. "And it was raining."

"So, the princess had to get her hands dirty. Big deal."

"Kasaandra," Bell says, exasperation clear in her tone as she points outside. "The wood was *wet*. And she had to collect it from the *trees*. You *know* that!" She flings a hand toward the tent opening with each point.

"So!"

"*So*? It took *magic*! Trees are *sacred* to her. She didn't just go chop a tree down like you would have." Bell's eyes fill with tears, but her frown is as fierce as Akin's.

I don't know enough about magic to entirely understand what's going on, but Llani had been exhausted.

"It's not like she helped in the fighting. She had plenty of magic." Kasaandra crosses her arms.

"She did so!" Bell yells. "She saved *your* life, and *your* life, and *your* life," she says, pointing at the three of us. Before Kasaandra can respond, Bell continues. "*She* was the one that lit up everything green. *She* was the one who threw fire at them. And even though one of them was an *oopsie*, it *still* slowed one of them down enough that *you* could actually *hit* her." She takes a deep breath. Kasaandra opens her mouth, but Bell beats her to it again. "*And* she did those hand things that kept the other one from joining in, even though *that* was an *oopsie* too."

Kasaandra looks over at Llani. She hadn't moved—even with the yelling. I'd been watching her ears. Not one twitch.

"Why are you always so mean to her? She just wants to be your friend." Bell's lips tremble, and her tears finally fall.

"She did all that during the fight?" Kasaandra stares at Llani, who's sunk into a slumber so deep, she looks dead.

The hablis nods. Her short, choppy hair flops forward over her eyes. She brushes it off her face.

"And kept the fire going?" Kasaandra asks with a frown.

"Until about an hour ago," I say.

"No help from *you*." Bell blows her nose into one of the extra napkins. "If you knew she was doing it wrong, you should have shown her how to make the fire right. Instead, you just went to bed."

Kasaandra walks to Llani's side. "Why didn't she ask me for help?"

I wait for someone else to state the obvious. "If you were her, would you have asked someone like *you*?" I finally ask.

Kasaandra scowls, then turns and walks away again. She turns back. Her lips press tight as she stares at the unmoving lump inside Llani's bedroll. She dumps her stuff again, throws off her fur, and stomps to Llani. "You idiot. How many times do I have to tell you we're all on the same team?" She yanks Llani's blanket down and turns her onto her back. "Llani, you lazy elf, you get that scrawny ass out of bed."

Bell gasps, but the dwarf doesn't pay her any attention. Akin pulls Bell back when she steps forward, a steely glint in her eyes.

Kasaandra shakes Llani roughly. "I need you to heal me, and I need you to do it *right* now."

"Heal *you*?" Bell pulls her arm back to throw Qrow's half-empty cup, then changes her mind and swallows the last of it.

Llani's eyes flutter open. "Kasaandra?"

Bell stops struggling in Akin's arms.

"I need you to heal me, Princess," Kasaandra says, putting her face close to Llani's. "I need that purple healing. You hear me?"

Bell gasps and leans her weight back into Akin's arms.

I remember what it felt like when the 'purple healing' drained me. What is Kasaandra thinking?

"Green. Like your eyes," Llani says weakly.

"No, I need that purple stuff. Like you did before. Remember? When that boar gored me? Like you did with Qat?" Kasaandra lifts Llani's hand to her face.

"Purple?" Llani asks, obviously confused.

"Yeah. Purple. Like this." Kasaandra shakes Llani's hand.

Llani tries to sit up, but Kasaandra holds her down. "Hurry up, Princess. We don't have all day," the dwarf goads her.

Llani's eyes narrow, then close. Her lips move, but I don't hear any words come out. Even so, purple swirls around the hand on Kasaandra's face.

"More," Kasaandra says when it stops. "Or are you too lazy to do it right?"

"You—"

"I've got all that *battle oof* stuff," Kasaandra says, interrupting her. "You know what that does to me. I need you to take it away."

"Battle euphoria? You need to be more precise, Kasaandra," Llani says with more strength. "Hold still." She searches Kasaandra's face for a moment, then closes her eyes again. This time, without touching the dwarf, she runs her hands down over the length of Kasaandra's body, sitting up mid-way as purple tendrils escape Kasaandra and converge on Llani like eels attacking their prey.

Bell's mouth opens in a silent O.

I can hardly believe my eyes.

"One more time, Princess," Kasaandra says with much less acerbity when Llani pulls away.

"I have removed the euphoria, Kasaandra. You should be much more amenable now. Thank you for coming to me. Please accept my apologies for neglecting you last night."

"Yeah, yeah, yeah," Kasaandra says ungratefully. "I still need you to take more. This time, don't stop until I tell you." She sounds almost drunk. Her words slur, and she sways before catching herself.

"This is unprecede—"

"I need you to shut up and trust me, Princess," Kasaandra says roughly, placing Llani's hand back on her face.

Llani's mouth tightens. She starts the process again. This time, she keeps her eyes open. Purple tendrils extend from Kasaandra to Llani for a third time.

Kasaandra's legs start shaking. She collapses from her kneeling position and lands awkwardly. "Remember, don't stop until I tell you."

A moment later, she slumps sideways, barely catching herself before hitting her head. She rolls onto her back and closes her eyes.

I'm about to interrupt and tell Llani to stop when Kasaandra finally opens her eyes. "You can stop now, Princess."

Llani does. "Oh! I took too much."

Kasaandra shakes her head and turns toward Qrow's still body. "Help Qrow."

Llani whips around. Her irises are tiny dots in her wide eyes.

Bell points to Qrow, then bursts into tears. "He's hurt real bad."

Llani crawls swiftly to Qrow's side. "Where is he? Oh." She prods lightly at his wound. "What happened?"

"We don't know," I say. I glance briefly at the wound. Llani places her hands over Qrow's injury.

"Llani," I say softly. "No *oopsies*. He's barely hanging on. We didn't know about this until a few minutes ago." I may not want him around me, but I don't want him dead, either.

"I understand." She looks worried, though. She stares at her hand as though afraid she might do it wrong.

I sit down next to her. Her hands are shaking. "Llani." I hold her gaze momentarily when she finally looks up at me. "Remember. Green. Like Kasaandra's eyes."

I see doubts in her aquamarine ones. She takes a deep breath. I gently place a hand on her arm. "I believe in you." I step back to give her room.

"Don't have...all day, Princess." Kasaandra says weakly.

Llani's lips press tight. Leave it to Kasaandra to get Llani riled up enough to perform. Again.

She closes her eyes.

Green. I try to embed the thought into her mind.

"Green," she says.

And it was.

The wound doesn't fully heal. There's a depression where the muscle has disintegrated, but the skin scabs over, and his ribs no longer show. His breathing becomes stronger, and his fever leaves him. Llani sits back when she's done, exhausted again.

Bell washes Qrow's face and chest with a wet cloth to remove the fever sweat and remaining blood. When he's as clean as she can make him, Akin helps me put a fresh shirt on him, then we cover him and let him sleep while Bell brushes his hair. When she's done, she twists the damp locks around her fingers, then slips them out, leaving perfect, individual curls.

I watched a candy maker at the fair one year making taffy, and it looked like caramel and melted chocolate twisted together. Qrow's curls look like that shiny, saltwater taffy.

Behind me, Kasaandra groans. I help her with her sleeping fur and pull one end to cover her. I wait until she looks comfortable. "Thank you, Kasaandra. What you did was brave."

"I know," she replies and closes her eyes. She turns on her side and sighs. The heavy sound is followed by a light snore. It's as if she doesn't have enough energy to snore in her usual loud way.

I rejoin Akin, Llani, and Bell and catch the end of Llani's instructions. "We still need to pulverize any remaining bone before we bury the witch ash."

"I'll do it," Bell says with a determined look. "Just like I crush nuts." She grinds one hand into the other.

In the following pause, I bring up the topic that has been worrying me since I saw Qrow's wound. "I think we need to have sparring sessions. We used to do them out at sea." I glance over to Qrow. "He needs to be able to defend himself if something like this happens again." Who knew traveling by land would be so exciting?

Akin's hands fly fast, and Llani interprets for me. "He says Qrow defended us. He sent one away several times. And he stopped her from attacking you. That must have been very difficult with his injury. We don't know what else they did to him before we got out there."

"Oh! Qrow did that? I was wondering why she ran away." Bell pats Qrow's face gently.

I hadn't seen any of them run away. Akin nods.

"What are you talking about? Those freaky hand things you did kept her from us." They almost caught me when I was trying to sneak around to flank the elves.

"He sent her there. My hands held her there."

"How did he do that, exactly?" I ask. I don't doubt them, but all I saw was Qrow standing there, away from everything.

Akin signs haltingly and ends by touching his fingertips to his forehead, then thrusting his hand away like he's flinging water from his fingers.

Llani pauses a moment before speaking. "He believes Qrow uses a specialized form of magic. He speaks telepathically to his opponents using either words, images, or both. Is that correct?" she asks Akin.

He nods.

"Whoa! That's cool!" Bell says.

"Why do you say that?" I'm still confused. "He just stood there."

Akin signs again. Llani says, "Did you not wonder why the last one stopped before you and screamed in pain?"

Well. Sure, I did. "Of course. I figured..." I have no idea what I thought at the time. I remember wondering what tactic would work best to evade her headlong run. When she stopped, I reacted.

"I heard him," Llani says. "He stopped her. I suspect he did something similar against the manticore."

"I was there. He didn't say anything," Bell says.

"He doesn't use words, exactly."

"Then what did you hear?" Bell whispers as though it's a secret.

Llani frowns. "He hums. Though not with his lips, it's in his throat. Perhaps it is more like a purr."

My lips twitch. "He purrs at the enemy?"

Llani nods. "I believe that is how he accesses his ability."

His ability. His magic. A word creeps into my consciousness. *Itan*. That's what the Karatolii call it. I'm almost certain. Qrow purrs to access his Itan. There have been times during our journey, particularly when we've been short with each other, that I've caught his throat working oddly, as though he's holding himself back from lashing out. But then things settle down, and he relaxes.

Has he been using Itan on us? On me? Did he use it on me to convince me to come with them? The thought rankles.

Llani's brow knits in thought. "But perhaps, as Akin suggests, he manifests his intent using images or words either imagined or"—she frowns—"commanded."

Commanded? I almost laugh at that and dismiss the idea that Qrow can command me. I defy him every chance I get. The conviction clears up any doubts I had about him manipulating me in Riversmeet.

Bell gasps. "Oh! That reminds me," she whispers. "Was Kasaandra talking to the witches? 'Cause it seemed like it to me."

Bell looks between me and Akin, who glances away quickly, but I defer to Llani for the answer. After all, they were elves. Maybe they were all speaking Elvish.

Llani looks uncomfortable. "I do believe that it was Ancient Elvish. I recognized several words. I am not fluent, though, as the elders discouraged me from my studies." At our puzzled looks, she explains. "They locked the texts away. They said it was a complex language that should be learned only by adults."

"Was that normal?" I ask.

Llani shakes her head. "It goes against everything I've learned about language. Attempting to learn a language as an adult is more difficult than as a child. I am puzzled by their decision. The ancient texts of our history are written in the ancient language, after all." Her fingers twist together. "And I heard several classmates bragging that they were learning from the texts."

"Were you doing *oopsies* back then?" Bell asks.

Really, Bell?

"What?" she asks, seeing my look. "She's said before the elders were always mean to her because of her *oopsies*. It only makes sense that they would hide stuff from her, too, especially if it has anything to do with magic. They wouldn't want their old books to go *poof*." She punctuates the last word with her hands.

Llani nods once. "Thank you, Bell. That is very insightful on your part. I do believe you are correct."

So, how does Kasaandra speak Ancient Elvish? I can't be the only one thinking it. How could a dwarf with no magical ability, who grew up inside a mountain that doesn't let any other species penetrate the inner caverns, learn to speak a language so ancient that only elven elders—and a select number of acolytes—have learned it?

Chapter 22 Qrodin

16TH DAY OF ZAMDI, 14,887
ROAD TO CRANWOOD, ZEDANA

When Qrodin wakes up, he can't tell what time of day or night it is. The pain is gone, but there's a stiffness in his side he's never felt before.

He's still in the tent, but most of the gear is rolled up, packed away, or removed from the structure.

Bell drops a handful of berries into her small earthenware pot and swirls it gently. Since leaving Riversmeet, she only ever takes it off when they're in camp.

Qrodin yawns. "Good day, Bell. Would you mind telling me what time it is?"

"Qrow! You're awake!" She rushes over and throws her arms around his neck. "I was so worried about you." She finally releases him. "We just finished breakfast. It wasn't much. Qat couldn't catch any fish. Llani found some wild berries, though. I saved you some 'cause she said we had to let you and Kasaandra sleep."

She sounds tired, not at all her usual exuberant self, despite the effort she's making. He touches his side. The cloth he'd put there to stop the bleeding is gone.

"Llani healed you. Well, Akin did first, and Qat helped, but Llani did after Kasaandra yelled at her and made her do that purple thing until Kasaandra passed out. Then she did you. But don't worry, she did it green for you."

Is his confusion due to her explanation or his lack of sleep?

"I washed you, but only your face and chest, so it was okay," she says, blushing furiously. "It was all very proper, and they were here." She motions outside.

"Thank you, Bell," Qrodin says. "I'm certain you did so with the utmost decorum."

"I did. And you're welcome. How do you feel?"

"I have a bit of a headache, and I need to step outside for a moment," he says.

"Oh! I'm sorry about your head. Do you want some coffee?"

"That would be wonderful," he says. "I'll be but a moment."

Outside, the rain is gone. Everything was flattened by the storm. Several trees that were there yesterday are missing entire limbs. Even the remnants of Llani's bonfire have been washed away. All that remains are a few rocks.

He hopes the storm is over for now. The horizon looks clear, so that's promising.

Qat and Kasaandra are tending to the horses. Llani and Akin are nowhere to be seen. After relieving himself, Qrodin decides to wash and change his clothes. He can smell himself, and it's not pleasant.

He returns inside, and Bell greets him with coffee and fresh fruit.

"You must be starving!" she says.

He was. Surprisingly so. The coffee is nearly cold, but he gulps it down. "Thank you, Bell. I apologize for my lack of manners by sleeping in this morning."

"That's okay. After what happened to you, it's understandable." She washes his empty cup and puts it away, along with the last of her things.

"That's very gracious of you. I should also apologize for not noticing that we were being ambushed. You weren't hurt, were you?"

"Oh, no. I'm good." She doesn't look it. "You got it the worst." She looks around furtively. "I ended up shooting Kasaandra, Qat, and Akin with the arrows Llani made for me. I don't want her to know it. It was my fault. I didn't know they were going to spread out like that." She looks around again, but they're still alone.

"They were very effective," he assures her. "I think we can work out a way for you to warn us next time, so we're prepared to get out of the way."

"Yeah. That's a good idea." She thinks for a moment. "Maybe I can just yell, *'Don't look now!'* Then you all can scatter."

"That sounds good. I'm surprised everyone is up so early after last night's skirmish," he says, wondering at the relaxed feeling of camp. It's as if nothing unusual had happened.

Bell's eyes widen. "Oh. That wasn't last night," she says. "You slept all day yesterday. It rained, and no one wanted to leave."

"That explains a lot," he says to her, rubbing his forehead. He always feels muddle-headed when he sleeps too long, and he can't believe he slept the clock round. He scratches at the stubble on his cheeks. He hasn't shaved since leaving Riversmeet, and it's starting to itch.

Despite Bell's curiosity, Qrodin feels like something's bothering the little hablis. There are purple smudges under her eyes and dark shadows within them.

"Are you certain you're okay, Bell?" he asks.

Instead of answering, she looks away and squints into the rising sun, peeking through the tent flaps.

"Yeah. Me too," he says. When she doesn't react, he touches her lightly on the shoulder. He injects *Soothe* into his voice when he speaks. "Would you excuse me? I'd like to clean up and change my clothes so we can be on our way. I should be back in time to help take the tents down."

She looks up at him then and nods.

Qrodin retrieves his pack. Usually, he piles things onto his left arm and shoulder to leave his main hand free. Today, he's so weak on that side, he can't lift or swing the bag with his left hand alone.

This is going to take some adjusting to.

Wanting to avoid the others until he can inspect the damage to his side, he chooses to go to the stream. Once there, he strips to his waist. The wound looks like it's been healed for a year or more. The scar is shiny and discolored, and the skin is stretched oddly, distorting and elongating his birthmark on that side. Both he and Qat have two birthmarks, each located high on the sides of their ribcages. The left and right marks are different but similar to each other, resembling little cat faces. His and Qat's marks are identical. As if Ama had branded them both at birth with the same irons.

He tries to flex the muscles there, then makes a mental note to ask Akin for exercises that might help him strengthen what's left.

Yesterday's rain swelled the stream, but it's still too shallow to sit in and bathe. He strips down and does what he can, lathering with a pinch of mountain lilac Llani gathers whenever she finds it. He rinses his long hair, then combs it back and secures it in a low ponytail.

After getting dressed, he inspects the burn in the traveling jacket he'd purchased, glad that it wasn't the dwarven-made jacket he'd been wearing in Riversmeet. Then again, it *is* armor. He may not have been injured so severely had he been wearing it. Perhaps one of the others can mend this one.

He eats the berries Bell had given him as he returns to camp. They're sweet and juicy with a white, powdery coat that smears when he rubs them.

Once back at camp, he shakes out and rolls his bedroll, wincing at his lack of strength. It unsettles him, and for the first time, he wonders if it's permanent.

He's dismantling the tents when Llani and Akin join him. Akin looks fresh from yesterday's rest, but Llani is noticeably exhausted. Her cheeks are sunken in, and there are bags under her eyes. Instead of the many elaborate braids she usually weaves, her hair is pulled back into one thick braid wound several times around her neck as if to keep it warm.

"I understand I have you two to thank for healing my injury. You have my eternal gratitude," Qrodin says.

"I imagine you would have done the same for us, had you the skill," Llani says.

Qrodin doubts that it's a compliment but decides to take it as one.

Before he can respond, she continues, "We were fortunate you isolated one of the witches. Well done of you."

"Witches?" he asks.

"I believe so. Elves that mostly keep to themselves, away from society in something they call covens; a consortium of three to eleven individuals."

Qrodin finds it interesting that she says so, as elven societies are themselves secreted away from other communities. "Really? Only elves?"

"We possess innate magic with a connection to nature that enhances over time. We were fortunate that there were only three of them and that you were skilled enough to temporarily dispatch one. Pexri elves are virtually impervious to suggestive manipulation."

Now, that sounded like a compliment.

"I'm surprised you were successful," she says.

Qrodin decides to ignore the insult. He may not be a proficient fighter, but he is a skilled negotiator. He's spent years perfecting his talents. Very few people perceive his ability to access Itan.

Llani's brow wrinkles slightly. "Their unprovoked attack puzzles me. I am positive I saw them in Riversmeet while Bell and I were purchasing supplies. They were wearing their youthful illusions at the time. I assumed they were on their *sodafari*."

Qrodin has heard of elven sodafaris. Most elves embark on their sodafari upon reaching adulthood. The elders encourage young adults to travel the world. Many return home, but sometimes, they choose to make their home elsewhere.

"I had wanted to speak to them, but Bell was worried we might be late meeting you."

Bell shifts and looks away. Sometimes, it's hard to tell if Llani's stating facts or placing blame.

Qrodin's not so certain about the lack of provocation. He recalls what the witch said last night—or two nights ago. '*Where is it? Give it to me,*' she'd said. And they spoke of someone returning. "They were looking for something," Qrodin tells them. "Or someone. Maybe that's why they were in town."

Bell gasps. "Do you think they were following us?"

"What makes you say that?" Llani asks Qrow, dismissing Bell's question entirely.

"I heard her ask Kasaandra where 'it' is, and to give it to her."

"You understood them?" Llani says, blushing hotly. Her ears tilt to face the ground and dip low. A moment later, they shoot straight up. "Do you read minds? Could you read their thoughts?" Her expression changes from excited about the possibility to worried.

"Fear not, Llani. Your secrets are safe," he assures her as the others join them. "I have an ability that allows me to temporarily understand and speak any language spoken. I find it quite helpful in my line of work." He doesn't tell her he started using it when he was young. Ama had taught him. The skill was quite useful growing up in Riversmeet. No one ever suspected a homeless boy could understand them.

Llani looks intrigued, but her expression changes to confusion when she glances at the dwarf. It doesn't take a mind reader to understand why she's disturbed. Kasaandra said she doesn't have magic, so she hadn't used a spell to understand them as Qrodin had. She even spoke back to them.

"Wow! You can understand every language? Can you do it any time you want?" Bell asks. She had been disconnecting the green tent from the others but had stopped to look up at him.

"That depends on several factors, but usually, yes, I can access it anytime."

Akin takes the rolled, purple tent and tosses it to Qat, then looks at Kasaandra and points to a rock. Kasaandra's eyes close, and her lips disappear into her beard and mustache. She shakes her head.

The last time Qrodin had seen Kasaandra, she was practically vibrating. This morning, however, she's pale and shaky. Qrodin tries to recall Bell's disjointed rambling this morning. Llani had told them to let him and Kasaandra sleep.

He goes to her. "Kasaandra, are you still injured?" Qrodin asks softly when he reaches her. "Bell said she shot you with one of her arrows. Are you not healed? We can wait another day if you need it."

"I'm good. We'll be riding. I can rest on the way."

"Please let me know if there is anything I can do for you. I understand I owe you for my current state of health."

Kasaandra blushes and looks away, obviously uncomfortable with the comment.

They finish sorting and stowing the tents in their saddlebags and finally mount their horses. It takes Qrodin three tries to pull himself up because of the weakness in his side. Everything's going to take some getting used to.

As has become aer habit, Qat takes the lead. Akin and Kasaandra take their positions at the rear, leaving Qrodin, Bell, and Llani in the middle. Depending on the width of the road, they often ride three abreast with Bell in the middle. Today, she speeds up and joins Qat.

"I apologize that my injury delayed us a full day of travel," Qrodin says to Llani.

"It rained all morning yesterday," she says. "It took the remainder of the day to dry everything out and pulverize and bury the ashes. How is your injury? I apologize for being unable to heal you completely. Even with Kasaandra's battle euphoria, I was incapable."

"Battle euphoria?" Qrodin asks.

"Yes. Her vitality increases during battle."

"That's fortunate for her. What causes it?"

"It is a rare psychological condition sometimes found in warriors, particularly close-quarter combatants. My grandmother has the same condition. She claims the resulting exhilaration is uncomfortable, but my observations of Kasaandra indicate the degree of discomfort varies. We discovered I can siphon off the excess."

Despite her reluctance to admit that last part, he's curious. "How did that happen?"

"I attempted and failed to heal an injury she had sustained during a clash with an enraged boar." She looks away. "She has declined assistance ever since."

And that bothers her. "This is the same thing you did to Qat?"

She nods.

"How did you use it to heal me?" Qrodin asks, intrigued with the concept.

"I siphoned the excess vitality from her and infused you with it."

"I'm fortunate you thought of doing so," Qrodin says, feeling humbled they'd gone to that extent for him.

Llani shrinks in on herself again. "It was Kasaandra who thought of it. I was unaware of your injury until after she insisted I draw more than necessary to drain the euphoria."

So that's why Kasaandra's as tired as he and Llani are. Qrodin stretches his arm out to his side to stretch his injury. He curses his wince when she apologizes.

"I regret it was insufficient. I will have adequate strength by this evening to finish the job."

"Can you regrow missing muscles?" he asks, knowing she cannot.

Llani frowns. "I can repair muscles, but I cannot replace them."

He realizes too late that his question may have made her feel inadequate and berates himself. He should have known better. They are quiet for some time. Qrodin tries to appreciate the beauty of their surroundings, but he's too distracted by thoughts of the last few days. They had been completely vulnerable. He tries to remember the battle, but most of it is hazy. He had imagined Qat dead. "Llani, you said the witches are nearly impervious to psychic manipulation. Can they use it? Could they make a person see something that isn't there?"

"Did you have a hallucination?" she asks instead.

"I believe so, yes."

"A description of the vision would be helpful," she says.

Hesitantly, Qrow describes it.

"Interesting. Mayhap they tapped into your fear of losing your sibling."

"I fear you may be right," he says. "Do you have any siblings?" he asks her.

"I do. After my birth, Mata." She hesitates and looks at Qrodin. "Forgive me. My mother formed a union with an old schoolmate named Chladd. They have one son and one daughter together. Ki-Ssani still lives at home."

He recalls that Elven custom is to form contractual unions instead of marrying. "And your father?" Qrodin asks.

When she doesn't answer, he glances in her direction. Her ears have dipped low, and she's staring ahead unblinkingly.

"I'm sorry, Llani. Has he passed?"

She visibly starts. "We have yet to meet. Mata met him on her sodafari."

"I see. Are you on yours?" he asks to steer them away from another painful subject.

"I am."

"How long have you been gone?" He's heard they last upwards of ten years.

"I left shortly before meeting Akin and Kasaandra."

Her home must be in the forests of Babum, where Kasaandra had earlier told him they met. The three had later stopped in Bierenan, Bell's home. Since elves are private about the locations of their homes, he changes the subject again. "And your destination is Craguesport?"

"It is, for now. I would like to visit the library there."

"There are several libraries in Craguesport. At least one in each district."

"There is a library in the Jalu district. Do you know of it?"

Qrodin is transfixed by her transformation. Her eyes are bright, and she's smiling. Tiny points catch his attention. She has fangs. "Ah, yes," he finally says. "It's not far from my home."

"You live in the business district? That is logical, considering your occupation."

He hums in agreement. "Do you know the history of Craguesport?" he asks.

"Only what I have read in our history lessons." She sighs heavily. "I have tried discussing it with Bell, but she gets distracted easily. She's only interested in the food and the races."

Qrodin's impressed. "Well, she's in luck. We should get there before the Longest Night celebrations. The races run all night long."

"I've heard the entire city is lit with candles during Longest Night."

"It is."

"Ki-Ssani would love to visit the crafting district. She is very much an artist like Mata."

"Ki-Ssani is your sister?"

She nods. "Yes. My brother Ssaro is not interested in large cities like Craguesport. He recently left on his sodafari with his pata. They are going to visit Chladd's ancestral home in the desert."

That would mean that Llani delayed her sodafari. Most leave shortly after their one-hundredth birthday, or *nascency* day, as they refer to it. Some elves are so impatient that they leave the same night. If her younger half-brother is already on his, then Llani must've waited more than a decade to start hers, as most elves often require ten to twenty years between births.

He wonders what was so vital that she delayed hers for so long.

"Will you be visiting an ancestral home, yourself?" Qrow asks after a slight pause. He is very curious about her. She seldom talks about herself. This is the most she's spoken to him.

Her pause is long, and he almost decides she isn't going to answer when she finally does. "I intend to do so."

Something in her voice tells him their conversation is over for now. "Let me know if I can be of any assistance. I have many contacts from all over the world. I would be happy to help."

"My thanks to you," she responds.

They fall silent after that.

17TH DAY OF ZAMDI, 14,887

"Look! It's Sorbslles Marvelous Menagerie!" Bell is practically hopping in the saddle. "I've always wanted to see them." She looks back at Qrodin. "Do you think they're open?"

A blur of emotions assails Qrodin at her words. *These are our people*, Qrodin thinks silently at Qat. A part of him wants to give the Karatolii troupe a wide berth. What if Qat wants to stay with them? He watches Qat's face for a reaction. Other than a look of curiosity, there is none. Does ae not recognize anything?

Even now? When Qrodin saw them from a distance, he was confident Qat would finally remember.

He crushes his disappointment behind a smile before glancing at Bell. "I'd say they're always open. Sorbslles is the largest Karatolii troupe, nearly ten times the size of Balaerdos." There are several hundred or so people. Qrodin counts more than fifty carriages and wagons, and twice the number of horses needed to pull them. There are also camels and elephants. Even a bear. The vehicles are in a large circle, and the road goes right through the middle of the camp. Unless they make an awkward detour around it, they'll be passing right through the party. That's done intentionally, they want to attract as many people as possible. The camp opens like a flower when visitors come through.

Bell looks excited. "Your Balaerdos? These are your people?"

He nods.

"Is there a customary greeting that we should be following?" Llani asks.

"Yeah. Say, 'hello'," Kasaandra says as she rides past. She and Akin lead the way toward the menagerie.

Qrodin decides to elaborate on Kasaandra's answer. He's nervous about how Qat will react to suddenly being surrounded by aer people after learning of aer heritage. It's possible that ae's visited one of the troupes in the meantime, but ae wouldn't have realized they were family. "They will shake your hand if you offer it. Hand touching is quite common. Don't be surprised if they attempt to kiss your hands or stroke your wrist." He doesn't tell them how the Karatolii interprets changes in pulse or body temperature when they do. "They may also stand very close and make prolonged eye contact. Like I said, they are very friendly."

"Just like Qat!"

Qat frowns at Bell's observation.

Qrodin pulls alongside Qat. "When you were mad at Ama, you'd say you were going to run away to join them."

"Why would I want to join Sorbslles?" Qat asks.

"The horse shows." They had only ever seen them twice as children; both times during *Bucuatoari*, the annual Karatolii gathering in Jushur. Balaerdos didn't go every year, and neither did Sorbslles. "They're why you started doing horse acrobatics."

Qat doesn't respond.

"I'm sorry. It's a lot to dump on you all at once. Had I known we would run into them, I would have prepared you better." Qrodin sighs deeply, then winces when he feels scar tissue pulling on his side.

He hopes things don't get worse before they get better.

Chapter 23 Qat

17TH DAY OF ZAMDI, 14,887
SORBSLLES CAMP, ZEDANA

Qrow's right about this being a lot to dump on me. I've heard of Sorbslles Marvelous Menagerie. Everyone has. I've even seen them a few times from afar. We were never in town long enough to attend any shows, but I'd seen them from the ship as we sailed by their camp. People riding horses, camels, and elephants. For some reason, Captain Rogen didn't like them.

"You all go ahead. I need to talk to Qrow a moment." This is the first time I've initiated a conversation with him.

The others ride ahead. They're immediately greeted by children who run out to meet them, talking over each other in their excitement.

"Welcome to Sorbslles Marvelous Menagerie!"

"Hello!"

"Welcome!"

"If you'd like, we can take care of your mounts while you browse?"

Bell breaks into a large grin and scrambles down from her pony. Almost immediately, she's surrounded. One of them takes her pony's reins and touches the braids Bell wove in its mane. "Please tell me you have food. I'm starving!"

I turn Starshine around, placing our backs on the retreating group.

Qrow and I wait until they're out of earshot.

"Sorbslles is Karatolii," I say.

"They are. Nearly all traveling troupes are. Balaerdo's had horses, but not the other animals you see here. If they accept you as *valore*, they will share anything they have. After all, everything belongs to everyone."

Valore. Extended family. My belly cramps. "And how will they know that?"

"Your eyes will give it away. But they won't accept you as such until you introduce yourself properly. In Karatol."

I close my eyes and picture Captain Rogen and the old woman. I remember them touching their foreheads when they meet. I wonder if that's what he means by a proper greeting. I thought it was strange at the time. At first, I thought they were going to kiss. He never greeted anyone else that way.

I take a deep breath to slow my pounding heart. "I'll follow your lead." I motion for Qrow to go ahead of me. At least that's something I'm familiar with. I used to follow Rogen's lead whenever we came to a new location. I'd mimic his body language, his tone, even his words, if necessary. Once I was on my own, I'd emulate my marks, townsfolk, and anyone I needed to blend in.

I will do the same here.

"Can you handle this?" Qrow asks.

Qrow says we belong. That we're one of them.

Perhaps he is.

I'm not. I don't belong anywhere.

At the same time, I belong everywhere.

The Karatol words roll off my tongue as though I've always spoken them. *"Of course I can. I can do anything I want."* A wave of emotion hits me all over. It's the first time I've spoken the strange language out loud. If I were standing, my legs would have given way. I squeeze my legs around Starshine's ribcage to keep from falling. My fingers tighten in his mane to control my trembling hands.

I need to calm down.

Starshine relaxes beneath me. Tension recedes from his head to his tail. I feel it in every fiber of my body. The release finds my fingers, and they untangle themselves from Starshine's mane. My legs unclench. I run my hand along his satin-smooth coat and finger-comb the mess I'd made of his mane. *Thank you, big guy*, I tell him silently.

Time to see what trouble I can get myself into.

Wagons, tents, carriages that resemble domed houses, and giant wheeled cages face inward in a large circle, creating an arena-sized area in the middle. The road cuts the ring in half. Everything is banana yellow, from the tents and carriages to the clothing.

Beyond the circle on each side are huge boulders.

Everyone scatters around the place, lifting and securing the carriages' side panels. One person hangs clothes from an awning, making a curtain that blocks the sun. In another carriage, someone tugs and pulls out a drawer that is the length of the vehicle. Additional drawers are stair-stepped above it.

In the time it takes to ride in, the inhabitants transform the camp into a small town, complete with a blacksmith, food stalls, and plenty of shops.

Once we turn our horses toward camp, more children—or maybe the same ones—run out to meet us. I feel like I've been kicked in the gut.

Several of them could have been me at their age. There are slight variations in our looks, of course. They have rich, golden-brown skin just a shade darker than mine. Their hair is straight rather than wavy and lacks highlights, but they wear it long and tied back with ribbon or string like I do sometimes.

Qrow and I share a glance. He nods. Does he know what I was thinking?

We halt the horses as they draw near. They smile and wave but don't greet us. I wonder why. They'd been overflowing with welcome to the others.

"*Oiy.*" Qrow dismounts. He holds the reins lightly and pats his horse as the children gather around us, preventing us from moving forward.

"*Oiy,*" the tallest one says to Qrow.

One of the smaller children smiles. "*I told you!*" ae says in Karatol.

"*Oiy. I like your horse.*" I look down toward the voice, to the child who had boasted earlier. Ae is no taller than Bell.

"*Thank you,*" I answer back in Karatol. It feels surreal to be speaking it aloud. I slide one leg around and sit with both legs dangling from Starshine's back. I look down at them from above, nervous to be around so many children. I have to admit, they weren't part of my training. I was the only child aboard the *Raven Scream*. How do you talk to them?

"*Are you going to do a flip?*" The child shields aer eyes as ae peers up at me. I move to the right to block the sun and am rewarded with another smile.

"*Do you want me to?*" I gauge the distance to the ground. I'd need to stand on Starshine's back to do a proper flip, but I've never stood on his back before. How will he react?

"Bragdin always does."

I can land on my feet if I fall backward and bring my legs over. I might also land on my ass. Or my head. "And who's Bragdin?" I ask, trying to give myself more time to decide how important it is to impress this kid with a flip.

The child points at a person walking toward us. Ae's about my height and probably a few years older than me with a hard, athletic body and slightly bowed legs. Ae's wearing a white top that wraps over both shoulders and crosses at the waist where a wide, yellow band keeps it snug to aer body. Tight black pants have padding along the inside of aer thighs.

I have no idea if ae's a man or a woman. I'm not used to that level of uncertainty with danaash. It's disconcerting until I realize it doesn't matter.

I guess now I understand how others feel when they look at me.

"I be Bragdin." Ae eyes me and Qrow unblinkingly.

"Oiy, Bragdin. I'm Qrow, and this is my sibling, Qatzsi. We are Balaerdo and entrepreneurs," he says.

I understand what he's saying but can't connect the words to myself. *"Call me Qat,"* I say quickly.

"Oiy varsome shae valore, Qrow," Bragdin says slowly and sincerely, finally blinking. It is pronounced oi varso shay valoo, and something stirs inside me. I shake it off, uncomfortable with the feeling.

Bragdin and Qrow clasp each other's forearms, and their foreheads meet briefly before separating.

So. The forehead thing is a thing. At least they don't hug. I'm not a hugger.

"Oiy valore," Qrow replies. He motions for me to come down, eyeing me closely.

I jump down. Or rather, I slide down Starshine's side until my feet hit the ground.

Bragdin looks me up and down slowly. *"Oiy varsome shae valore, Qat."*

Even with that brief sensation when ae greeted Qrow, I couldn't have anticipated the impact of those words directed at me. A warm feeling starts in my chest and spreads throughout my body, to my fingers and toes. There is no Oramische equivalent, but I feel their meaning just the same. A proffered shared bond as an extended family member. But it's more than that. It's a feeling of welcome and belonging such as I'd never felt before.

I step forward and grab aer forearms as ae grabs mine. Our foreheads meet, and the greeting flows between us through the touch. Bragdin stares into my eyes, so I stare into aers, allowing each of mine to focus separately instead of going cross-eyed. I smell mint on aer breath and horse on aer clothes. Aer eyes are a dark sienna, almost as red as they are brown. A smile forms in them. Ae slowly blinks and softly strokes aer thumb along the sensitive skin inside my elbow. My pulse lurches, and desire races through me.

Ae pulls away slowly, sliding aer hands down to my fingers before letting go. The smile on aer lips matches the one in aer eyes.

Starshine blows out sharply, and he stomps his front hoof.

I laugh. *"Oiy valore."* My voice is hoarse. I turn to scratch the horse behind his ears, belatedly trying to hide my response from this stranger. I clear the roughness from my throat and, trying to change the subject, say softly, "Be careful not to stomp on someone's toes, Starshine. There are little people around."

Starshine steps between me and Bragdin, skillfully avoiding children as he does so.

"Ae's a protective one," Bragdin says. "And as exquisite as aer rider."

My cheeks warm. Ae's flirting with me. It's strange to be on the receiving end of a flirtation. I remember how my pulse had jumped when Bragdin brushed my arm. I've done the same thing—stroked a finger along a pulse point. I love to feel the pulse jump when I do.

Starshine turns his head and side-eyes me. He steps out slightly with his rear hoof, nudging our host further from me.

I smile when Bragdin sighs.

"*You didn't do a flip*," says a little voice behind me.

I turn around. "*Neither did ae*," I say, motioning to Qrow.

"Yeah. But that horse isn't a good one for flipping," the child replies.

"*And* Starshine *is?*"

The child nods.

"How do you know that?"

Ae shrugs. "*I just do.*"

The child's breeches have pads on the inside of the thighs, just like Bragdin. The strange attire must be a horse-riding thing.

"I hope you will extend your welcome to our traveling companions," Qrow says.

"Of course!" Bragdin replies in Oramische. "They are welcome inside our circle. We have food and clothing, and crafts for sale."

The switch in languages is a deliberate signal that I catch but don't understand the meaning of.

"We have a tent where you can leave your fine protector," Bragdin says to me over Starshine's back. I already miss the musical quality of Karatol. "He will be fed and cared for while I show you around." Ae takes a few steps backward, watching to see if I follow.

I do.

I spend the next several hours with Bragdin. Ae introduces me to every member of the camp we come across. When my traveling companions aren't near, the introductions are in Karatol. With each meeting, I feel more comfortable with the greeting.

I'm mildly jealous of the fluffy tails a few of them have, although I don't understand my emotions. I've never wanted a tail before.

At the same time, strange things keep happening. I know things without remembering how I know them. I recognize foods I've never eaten. I know how they will taste before I've taken a bite. I know I love *bramzi*—a pepper stuffed with meat and thick, creamy cheese—and to stay away from the black, pickled eggs. I know the wine-colored jelly they serve me on stiff crackers is sour, not sweet, and is usually only presented on special occasions.

I know the mushroom-shaped carriages are homes called *cobilas*, and the rectangular ones are mobile shops named *magilas*. I know that the large tents are for livestock, not people. I know the yellow clothing everyone is wearing is called Sorbslles yellow, and that the color is derived from a seed. That Balaerdo's color is blue and is made from green leaves ground into a fine powder. That lying in the back of a wagon looking up at the stars would remind me of being in the crow's nest.

I know that I used to live in a community like this one, even though I can't remember doing so.

I know that the old one approaching me should be called *Ama-nu*.

I don't know why ae's crying.

Chapter 24 Qrodin

The expression on Qat's face worries Qrodin. He's seen it countless times on the faces of orphans who have stepped inside a Varsome orphanage and realized that food, a bed, and companionship are theirs for the asking. Around him, Qat has mostly been reserved, often riding ahead and spending time alone with only Starshine for company. Qat clings to the horse the way Qrodin has seen orphans cling to one of the many stray cats allowed to wander inside all Varsome buildings. Frequently, children open up to a cat long before they feel comfortable talking to another child or staff member.

Now, Qat follows Bragdin around like a puppy while Starshine trudges behind them.

Akin whistles two notes softly to get Qrodin's attention, then signs, *Kasaandra is hungry.* The gesture has been repeated often enough in the last few days that he has no difficulty understanding, even with Qrodin's limited new sign vocabulary. He nods, and the two walk toward the smell of grilled meat.

Qrodin continues watching Qat. One part of him is happy ae is so comfortable here, but a more significant part worries that Qat won't want to leave. This would be the perfect place for Qat to avoid any trouble that might follow from Riversmeet. Unless Sorbslles is heading there next.

He hasn't talked to Qat about it, but Qrodin's suspicions have only gotten stronger that Qat was responsible for Truffle's death. He's worried that word of Truffle's assassination will beat them to Craguesport, and a handful of guards will be awaiting their arrival at the gate.

He wouldn't blame Qat for staying. After all, it was aer dream growing up to ride with Sorbslles. But Qrodin's not ready to lose his twin again so soon. Today's the first day that Qat hasn't gone out of aer way to avoid him—had actually approached him.

Qrodin feels a touch on his arm. Two wrinkled hands offer him a plate of food. Cabbage rolls and thick slices of warm, fried bread topped with freshly chopped tomatoes, onions, and peppers. His stomach growls. He can smell the spicy meat hidden in the rolls.

He looks into warm brown eyes surrounded by hundreds of wrinkles. "*Oiy. Thank you, Ama-nu,*" Qrodin says, using the term of respect for a Karatolii elder. He catches himself short. He'd automatically answered in Karatol. He glances around quickly and sighs in relief when he realizes Llani and Bell have moved on without him.

"*Oiy varsome shae valore.*" The elder takes Qrodin's forearm with one hand and hands him the plate with the other.

Qrodin reciprocates, touching aer forehead with his own. "*Oiy valore.*" *Valore.* Extended family. The knowledge that someone will always be there. There were members in Ama's group that Qrodin had known his whole life— people they could count on to help if a wagon wheel broke, or if they ran out of water, or if they needed someone to drive the wagon so they could work while there was still light to work by.

It's one of the reasons he named his Riversmeet street gang *Valore* (although he used the Oramische pronunciation for it). The sentiment is one he wanted for his new family: trust, companionship, loyalty, and friendship.

Varsome is the bond that holds the *valore* together. Bonds reinforced through companionship, compassion, inspiration, support, and balance. Something every parentless child craves. And it's why he named his orphanages after it.

At the time, he knew it was a risk to use Karatol words openly, but he did it anyway. His troupe betrayed him when they left. Had they embodied varsome, he would be with them still. Even so, he couldn't bring himself to go entirely against custom. The Karatolii deliberately inserted silent letters in their written script so strangers couldn't learn the language from books. By naming the orphanages Varsome—and pronouncing it as written—Qrodin could send a message to any Karatolii child that gets left behind in the future that they have a home and will be welcomed—all while keeping the proper pronunciation from everyone else.

"*Eat. Before it cools.*" The elder barely comes up to his armpit. Aer shoulders are hunched as if ae's persistently cold. A shawl is wrapped around aer shoulders, adding to the impression. A bronze beaded necklace reflects the sun as it peeks through the folds of the shawl.

Qrodin doesn't bother looking for a place to sit. The meal is easy enough to eat standing up. He takes a bite of a crispy, deep-fried roll, and he's immediately transported in time. Thin pastry, spicy meat and vegetables, savory juice that drips down his chin and along his fingers. He devours the meal, starved for traditional cooking. He could eat another two servings, at least.

The elder takes the plate when he finishes. "I am glad you are found. And your sibling, too. I heard about what happened to your ama. I am sorry for your loss."

He'd been stunned the first time someone had expressed a similar sentiment at an annual Bucuatoari. The twins were somewhat well-known when they were young. Twins are common enough, but Nonyx eyes on twins? He remembers how often he and Qat used to be the center of attention when attending Bucuatoari. He hadn't thought anything of it at the time. He was used to attracting townspeople's attention, so why would it be any different amongst his people? Realizing that some still remembered him was a kick in the gut.

How could no one have ever found him? Found Qat? Hadn't they looked?

Throughout the three days he'd attended his first Bucuatoari as an adult, it seemed like half the attendees approached him. They expressed their condolences for his ama and delight that he was found.

Found. As if he'd been lost. He hadn't been lost. He'd been abandoned. They never found him. *He* had found *them*.

The next time he went, he thought wearing Karatolii clothing and pulling his hair into a ponytail would allow him to escape notice. He hadn't realized his height was an even bigger giveaway. By then, word had gotten around to even more troupes. Not only was he found. He was very tall. That wasn't a Nonyx trait. Or a Karatolii one.

Perhaps that's why he had been abandoned. He had been tall for his age. Despite his eyes, had there been speculation amongst their troupe? He wonders if Ama had suffered any condemnation. Do they condemn him still?

As if reading his mind, the elder touches his bearded face. The Karatolii don't have facial hair. He should have shaved like he had in the past. Qrodin hadn't thought of it, nor the possibility they might reject him. Or Qat. At least aer height is closer to theirs, if also on the tall side. And Qat wasn't cursed with facial hair.

"I hadn't heard you found each other. I am happy for you, motas."

Kitten. Qrodin dismisses his doubts at the endearment. Ae wouldn't call him *that* if ae were rejecting Qrodin's right to be here. Had ae called him *pisitas*, on the other hand, he would have continued to worry. Another Karatol word for kitten, *pisitas* is used for babies and toddlers, while *motas* is for youngsters who haven't yet reached their teenage years. "Thank you, Ama-nu. It was quite recent. You are probably the first to know."

Aer eyes twinkle at the words, and ae pats Qrodin's face. "*Then it will be our secret.*"

Qrodin laughs and winks at aem, hoping it stays that way for a bit longer. But Qrodin suspects that by the time he and his companions leave, everyone in camp will have heard that the missing Balaerdo twins are reunited. The news will likely only mean something to the elders, but it will be fodder for the next Bucuatoari.

He may skip the annual event for a few years.

Qrodin stretches and winces at the pull in his side.

The elder notices. "Are you in pain?"

"It's nearly healed." Qrodin smiles, not wanting to explain that the injury was barely three days old. "I remember when sleeping on the ground didn't bother me so much."

"You do not have a *cobila*?"

"Unfortunately, we do not. We are using tents. Sometimes, we connect them to make a large one."

"And you carry a heavy pack?"

"I do, although my horse usually carries it for me."

"Come with me."

Qrodin follows aem across the clearing and the road. The elder climbs the steps of a *magila*, one of the shop carriages. Ae waves Qrodin to follow aem inside. Dozens of floating balls dimly light the interior. With a flick of aer hand, the balls get brighter.

Drawers of all sizes line the back of the shop, while shelves with ornate rails line the sides. Each shelf is stuffed to its fullest with jars, boxes, bowls, and vials. Storage trunks line the edge of the floor. Smaller ones occupy the top shelves, stacked to the ceiling and kept from falling by a coarse net with sizeable mesh.

The elder roots through a trunk near the back and pulls out a wooden container. Ae removes the fitted lid and tilts it in Qrodin's direction. "Pick one." Inside are different colored pouches. He pulls out a blue one.

The wooden container is stowed away. "This is a *reasacobila*. You shouldn't be sleeping in the rain." The elder nods to the pouch. "Open it."

Qrodin drops the item into his palm. A blue stone about the size of a chicken egg with a flat bottom.

"Only the person who erects it and those you invite can enter it. When you are ready, trace the symbol here"—she points to her temple—"onto the ground and place it inside the symbol."

"What is it?" Qrodin asks, referring to the item rather than the symbol. Runic magic—something he's already familiar with—must first be seen in your mind and is as different and personal as the people envisioning it.

"A pocket home. It will blend into the surrounding area. No one will guess you are inside."

"The giant boulders, I presume?" He'd been wondering why they'd been in such a convenient circle around the outside of the clearing.

The elder shrugs. "You are perceptive."

"I can't wait to see it. Is this a one-time use, or can it be dismantled and reused?"

"You redraw the symbol anywhere on the structure, inside or out. It will transform back into this shape at the place you redraw the symbol."

"That is unbelievable. I've never seen these before." Not even at the last Bucuatoari.

"They are quite new. I have only shared them with Sorbslles, your sibling, and now you."

"You make these?"

Ae nods. "Two more things. If you want to share the space, your companions need to stand near you when you draw the symbol. It is best if you are all touching."

"Will this be large enough for six?"

"I have already gifted your twin with one, but it will be a tight fit if you decorate them as we do."

"In that case, I would like to purchase four more for my companions." At aer hesitation, Qrodin decides to confide in aem. "The weakness you noticed earlier is from an injury I received three nights ago. We were attacked, and I nearly died." Qrodin lifts his shirt to show her the damage to his side before lowering it. "They saved me, at great risk to themselves, even though we've known each other only a short time. The healing took a great deal of magic; more than one person could handle. It left three of us quite vulnerable to attack. I want to show my gratitude and prevent a recurrence."

The elder pats Qrodin's arm. "You are a good person."

"I owe them my life."

She names a price, and Qrodin counts out the gold zeds—far fewer than the reasacobilas are worth, he's certain.

Four pouches are pressed into Qrodin's hands. "Place your rocks simultaneously in a circle about ten feet from each other, and the space will be shared."

"That's extraordinary." Qrodin tucks the five pouches away before he remembers what ae'd said earlier. "What's the second thing?"

"I recommend you be outside when you take it down. Everything you leave inside will remain inside here." Ae points to the blue rock.

"Everything?"

Aer eyes twinkle. "Including your clothes. Living things will not, of course. You can decorate the pocket home inside like you would your home. They are very comfortable."

"How can I thank you, Ama-nu, for your generosity?"

"*Totine apa tomea*," the elder says. *Everything belongs to everyone.* "Now. I have taken up too much of your time. Find your friends and give them their pocket homes. You will stay with us tonight and as long as you wish. After all, you will need time to furnish them. *Manot su manot, Motas.*" *Tomorrow or tomorrow.*

Qrodin once asked Ama what that meant. She said the saying embodies the Karatolii belief that optimism is the key to success and stability. You must believe that everything can be accomplished by staying strong and true to your vision. He had tried to remember that every time he was ready to give up the hope of finding Qat.

The elder reaches up and gently clasps the back of Qrodin's neck.

Qrodin leans down and presses his forehead to aers. "*Manot su manot, Ama-nu.*"

Qrodin climbs out of the magila and searches for the others. Before he finds them, two more elders approach him. They must realize he was offered the reasacobila, for they gift him a metal wash basin and matching pitcher—items that don't fit inside saddlebags. They invite him to their shop, pointing it out to him. He thanks them and excuses himself.

He finds Llani and Bell, and they eye the gifts with curiosity. "Can you help me find the others and meet me over by that rock formation? I have a surprise for everyone."

"I know where Qat is." Bell rushes off.

Llani goes in search of Akin and Kasaandra. It takes a few minutes for everyone to rejoin him.

Qrodin presents the reasacobilas but refers to them as 'pocket homes' rather than their Karatol name. Bell chooses the green pouch and hands Kasaandra the orange. Akin takes the red, which leaves the yellow for Llani.

Qrodin explains the process and ensures they are all within ten feet of each other. Kasaandra succeeds first and slips inside it while the others struggle, testing and failing until all six domes are formed and deconstructed. Finally, together, they draw their sigils on the ground and place their colored stone eggs in the middle of their respective runes. The air shimmers around them and settles like a giant soap bubble. The grass beneath their feet and inside the bubble is flattened.

Qrodin's unsure what he expected, but it wasn't this. The structure is nearly transparent from the inside. Qrodin can barely discern its outline.

Kasaandra dumps her bag on the ground. "Not very private, if you ask me."

"You should see Bragdin's. It's amazing. Ae's had it for years." Qat looks around.

"I was told that setting it up as we did would allow us to share the space. Of course, we don't have to if you'd rather not." Qrodin shares the elder's instructions.

He turns away to open his pack and hide his frown. Why does talk of Bragdin upset him? He should be happy that Qat's made a connection to another Karatolii. Every connection adds protection. Karatolii take care of their own, after all.

Which is why he's still wondering why he was left behind when Ama was killed. Quinn had known Qrodin was still alive and should have waited. The Balaerdo troupe should have stayed and looked for Qrodin, not left Riversmeet immediately. He hasn't run into Quinn in all the years since and wonders what excuse Quinn would give him for leaving.

Bell throws her arms out to her sides and dances in circles. "I love it!"

It only takes a few minutes for everyone to unroll their bedrolls. Qrodin sets out the wash bin and pitcher. The area is much too large for the few items they currently have. He imagines items he can purchase that will make the space more usable. Like a table for Bell and some chairs or stools. Perhaps a few trunks for clothes and supplies. The latter he can get from the elder. She had them available in every shape and size imaginable.

Qrodin returns to the conversation when Bell tells Qat she saw aem doing some trick riding on one of Bragdin's horses.

He wishes he'd been able to see it. Qat had been remarkable back in the day. Fearless. There was no such thing as too fast or too reckless. Qat would stop a horse in full gallop, then vault from its back before it skidded to a stop, flipping on the way down.

Qrodin has always been more cautious. He rides at a safe speed. He never jumps from anything higher than the side of a wagon. Truth be told, he's afraid of heights. Too risky, and he's not a gambler. He doesn't put so much as a copper down on anything he doesn't believe is a sure bet. Qat was forever betting dice or cards with anyone who would play.

"Bragdin says if I stay, ae'll teach me more."

The group goes very quiet.

Qrodin waits for someone else to say something, but they don't. "Where are they going next? They don't usually winter further than a day's ride from a town."

"I'll ask Bragdin. Anything else we need to do here?"

"Unless you want to stay and continue unpacking." Qat's gone before Qrodin finishes the sentence.

"Oh! I *totally* saw this place where we can get some furniture. It had these super big pillows, and they said they have beds and everything!"

"Do they have an oven?"

"Really, Kasaandra?" Bell says. "Is food the only thing you ever think about?"

"You have to ask?" says Llani.

Kasaandra and Akin leave shortly after.

"Beds?" Qrodin would pay just about anything to sleep in a bed tonight. He still hasn't recovered from his injury. At least they'd had one night of sleep, and the arguing that had been frequent before the battle hadn't resumed, though no one seemed ready to talk. "Lead the way, Bell."

"Sure! What are they called again?"

"Pocket homes," Llani says as she approaches them. "Really, Bell, you need to pay closer attention."

"Right." Bell taps her chin while inspecting the combined structure—a dome larger than most others in the area. "Maybe when they're small, but it doesn't feel right when it's big." Doubt floods her face when Llani frowns and walks away toward the Sorbslles camp.

Bell glances up at Qrodin. "You think I'm silly, don't you?"

"Not at all," he assures her. "Words have power. What would you call it?"

"Home Dome. When we're done decorating, I think it will feel like a home."

"Then Home Dome it is. We should start looking for things to fill our Home Dome with." Qrodin looks down at Bell's choppy hair and dirty green dress as they walk across the clearing toward the shops. "What else would you like for yours? We can get anything they have. They also have beautiful clothes. I need to replace a few of my things, and you are welcome to do the same."

"Oh. Yeah. I don't know."

"It's on me, Bell. You all saved my life the other day. And besides..." He turns to face her. He doesn't continue until she stops and looks up at him.

Bell narrows her eyes. "Besides, what?"

"I'm rich," he says with an encouraging smile.

Bell frowns. "But I didn't do anything. Llani did it all. And Kasaandra."

Qrodin drops to his knees so he's at her level. "Bell. You helped kill the witches."

Dark shadows form in her eyes. "I've been calling them the Twisted Sisters."

"That's a good name for them. They were twisted."

"And Kasaandra said they called themselves sisters." She wrings her hands.

"They did." Their words had run through his head since they returned to the road yesterday. Only Sorbslles Marvelous Menagerie has distracted him from those thoughts starting back up again.

"I never had a sister." Bell stares at the ground.

"They aren't all like that."

"I never killed anyone before, either." Her voice is so soft that he strains to hear it over the noise of the camp.

"It was my first time, too." He tries to inject *Soothe*, but it's difficult when he's hurting, too.

She looks down at her feet. The toe of one shoe is rolling a rock back and forth. "The others don't seem bothered by it. Does that mean I'm weak?"

"Bell." Qrodin waits until she looks up at him, then shakes his head. "I think you're strong for talking about it. Everyone deals with this kind of thing differently."

Bell places both hands on each side of his face. "Do you think we were all fated to meet?"

He doesn't believe in fate but doesn't laugh at her question. "Something brought us all together. Don't you think?"

She studies his face closely and then nods slowly. "I don't want Qat to stay here."

"I don't either. But Qat must decide what's best for aem."

"Yeah." Bell sighs. She puts her hands on her hips and stares at their Home Dome. Her face creases into a cheeky smile. "But that doesn't mean we have to make it easy."

"No. It doesn't."

Chapter 25 Qat

"Stay with us, Qat." Bragdin slides a lock of my hair away from my eyes.

I feel pulled in two directions. Would I like to get to know Bragdin and Sorbslles better? Of course. The thought creates equal parts curiosity and excitement inside me. But there's something else, too. Something I can't identify. I glance around, not knowing what I'm searching for until I spy crazy red curls and a crumpled green dress, and something inside me relaxes.

Bragdin introduces me to most of the vendors as we walk around. There are jewelers, wood carvers, potters, and basket weavers. I recognize large tubs for dying cloth. There is even a clockmaker. One of my favorite vendors is a blacksmith with a mouthwatering display of knives.

And that's when I realize something. They don't need an assassin or thief, and that's the only thing I know.

Bragdin notices my sudden stillness. "Why do you hesitate?"

"What would I do?" That's the question, isn't it? Everyone here has a job or purpose, even the children have chores.

"Whatever you want. I've been looking for a partner. We'd be great together."

I suppose I could be a performer. I've spent my whole life trying to hide my true self from people, either behind a disguise or by my absence. Isn't performing another way of putting on a disguise and hiding, but doing so in plain sight? Would I want to do it forever?

The crying elder who approached me earlier said ae remembered me and Qrow. That ae and my *ama'ani*—if I understand the word correctly, an *ama'ani* might be like a grandparent—had been good friends before my ama'ani died. Strange to meet another person who knew me before I lost my memory.

According to my ama'ani, the Balaerdos had been told Ama, Qrow, and I had all been murdered. The person who brought back Ama's body said Qrow's and mine had been tossed into the river and couldn't be found. That person was found dead the following day in camp, stabbed to death like Ama. They packed up quickly after, worried someone was targeting them. The elder said ae always suspected that Qrow and I lived.

At first, the story made me anxious to leave. To ride away and not come back. Then, I thought of Bragdin and wanted to stay.

Why am I feeling so torn? Why am I tempted to stay? Why now? And why Bragdin?

I've never felt like this before. Not the way I feel about aem. After all, we only just met. When I look at aem, there's something there—a warmth in my chest. My heart races, and I feel short of breath. But it's more than that. It's all of it. The feeling of familiarity when I'm walking around the camp. The taste of the food. The ability to hide in a crowd without putting on a disguise first because everyone looks like me. I don't feel like I need to be in control of every conversation. I didn't feel like this onboard the *Raven Scream*. Only Rogen treated me like everyone here treats me, as though I belonged. Qrow doesn't treat me this way. He's always watching me. He doesn't trust me.

Maybe I don't exactly blame him for that.

Bragdin shifts aer weight from one foot to the other, and I realize ae's waiting for me to respond.

Bell's laughter rings out behind me, and I feel myself smiling. "I don't like to stay in one place for long," I say.

"Sorbslles is always on the move. A different place every season."

A part of me wants to say I'll stay, but I don't always leave a place because of the location. I go because of the people. Years ago, I could have stayed in Riversmeet for several years before Rogen sailed there again, but I didn't want to be a known entity.

I don't want anyone to ever discover so much about me that there are no secrets between us. I'm most comfortable when no one knows who I am. And right now, no one does.

Qrow doesn't know *me*, only the *before* me. And the other four we're with? Well. They don't either. We're all practically strangers. I was surprised that Kasaandra did what she did for Qrow the other day. Of course, Qrow is one of the wealthiest men in Zedana. It probably doesn't hurt to have him owe her. I don't think Llani understands the significance of that, though. She's so stuck in her books and studying that she has no concept of the real world. Bell is infatuated with him. And Akin doesn't have anything to say one way or the other.

Normally, I'd laugh at that last pun, but I can't summon the mirth. This decision has me rattled.

It's not like I plan on staying with Qrow and crew for long. I'm just using them for cover right now. Once we get to Craguesport, I'll be on my own again. Before that, if I get the chance.

Isn't that what Bragdin is offering?

Well, sure. But it's too soon.

"We'll be attending the Bucuatoari this summer."

I file that information away for later.

They're heading west, Bragdin said. West is towards Riversmeet, and I can't go back there for at least three to five years. Not until after the mess with Truffle has settled down. I suppose Sorbslles might continue west instead of making the short detour north, but Riversmeet is the closest town.

I won't ask. I don't want the answer to sway my decision.

Which doesn't make any sense.

"You don't have to decide tonight," Bragdin says. "And speaking of tonight, you should join me."

Ae'd asked me to earlier. I hadn't answered. "When Kuu reaches her Zenith," I say, surprising myself. Why did I agree?

"What time is that?"

Instead of answering, I smile and excuse myself, then find a tree in which to hide.

Staying with people is too much of a burden. I wouldn't have any choice about our next destination if I remained with Sorbslles. I have some say, currently. I'm one in six, after all. If I stay with Sorbslles, I'd be one in...well... it may as well be one in a million. I'm the newest member.

I settle back against a branch and notice Qrow and the others walking toward our new combined rock home. I'm glad I brought my things with me. I don't trust any of them near my stone. The box makes a palpable bulge in my bag. I'm tempted to open it to ensure it's still inside.

As the procession nears the structure, they space out in the clearing around it. One after another, they draw their sigils on the side, and each structure disappears like bubbles being popped. Everyone catches their shrunken dome except Bell. She drops hers, then accidentally kicks it toward Akin, who doesn't see it coming in time to catch it. The pocket home falls behind him and rolls into a shrub, where Bell stoops to fish it out.

Only mine remains standing. It had morphed into a solitary rock.

What's going on? Are they leaving?

My limbs jerk in response, and I almost jump down and run to them. I stop myself only when I realize I'm too far up to land safely.

I take a deep breath. Besides, Qrow wouldn't leave me without saying goodbye. That much is obvious.

I stand on the tree limb and brace myself for a better look. I move a branch out of the way, as I'd hidden myself deep in the foliage. At least I'm high enough to see most of the wagons on the far side of the camp.

Bell is skipping, and Llani and Qrow follow as they return to the Karatolii camp. Kasaandra and Akin follow along more slowly. Several people come out to greet them when they get to the ring of vendors. Pocket structures appear. Most of them are longer than our combined one.

More than a few minutes after entering one, Kasaandra and Akin come out carrying furniture. Those aren't homes, they're *warehouses*. How ingenious.

Before I realize it, I'm on the ground.

I've got to see this. And maybe get a few items for myself. After all, if I leave Sorbslles, I won't mind being a bit more comfortable on the road. And if I stay with them, I'll have a place of my own.

I put my bag inside my pocket home. I'll be the only one able to enter it when I set it up again, so the rock will be safe. Once outside again, I trace my sigil on the outside of the dome. It shrinks down like the others had, but when it does, the witches' green stone falls to the ground next to it. Thankfully, there's plenty of flattened grass to cushion its fall.

I look around quickly. Across the way, Bell steps out of her pocket home and scratches her bottom, and the others are either in their own homes or inside shopping. No one else is paying attention to me. I don't think anyone saw it. I pick up the green stone. When I sketch the symbol on the ground and place the pocket home stone, it pops up quickly, and I step inside.

I study the green gemstone more closely. I shake it and hold it to my ear. I don't hear anything. Holding it up to the sun doesn't reveal anything new. Thankfully, it's not broken or cracked from the fall.

I quickly stow it back inside the box inside my bag, annoyed that my new hiding place for the green gem won't work unless I keep the pocket home intact.

I throw the bag over my shoulder, step back out, and shrink the pocket home again. When I try to catch it, it drops to the ground and rolls.

Fucking fantabulous.

Chapter 26 Qrodin

The inside of the warehouse domes—what the vendors call *reasamagilas*, or pocket warehouses—is a surprise. There isn't much that Sorbslles doesn't have. Ama would have loved having the extra space to store aer instruments, and privacy would have been welcome while Ama was teaching him the complexities of voice magic. He remembers them constantly needing to look for spots away from the troupe to practice. No one wanted to be Qrodin's target while he was learning how to manipulate people.

Ama'ani would have used them to store the large vats for dying cloth. Qat used to help aem pick out colors, especially when Ama'ani painted designs onto the fabric with dyes or wax resists rather than dyeing them solid. Qat particularly enjoyed dotting and splashing hot wax onto the fabric. Having a protected area large enough to spread out lengths of cloth would have been ideal.

"What about flooring?" Bell asks.

"I have the most beautiful rugs you've ever seen, made special for pocket homes." One of the shopkeepers waves her to follow aem over to a selection of area rugs.

"The way you drop stuff? I don't think so."

Bell sticks her tongue out at Kasaandra.

"I have some fine wood flooring," another says. "I can have it installed before dark."

Bell looks at Qrodin, a question in her eyes.

"Anything you'd like, Bell." Qrodin and Bell follow the vendor. Bell selects tulip poplar for its beautiful, variegated pattern. Qrodin chooses walnut. When he notices Qat approaching, he steps outside. "Qat. Are you joining us, or do you have plans elsewhere?"

"I go where the action is, and this looks interesting."

"We are furnishing our pocket homes. Please feel free to select anything you desire. I have already made payment arrangements." He'd like to get most of the selections made tonight, but he's prepared to finish tomorrow if necessary. As comfortable and welcoming as Sorbslles has made it for them, Qrodin can't shake the worry that the longer they stay, the more likely Qat will remain. Qat has always been unpredictable, and Qrodin's opinion seldom affects aer decisions. As children, Qat was more likely to roll the dice than listen to any advice Qrodin had.

Two Karatolii merchants follow Qat inside.

"Will you require wall covering? I have tapestries next door," the taller of the two says.

The smaller of them steps forward. "I can texture your walls. I have samples here."

The taller salesperson elbows the shorter one out of the way. "Tapestries can be changed out. Get tired of one? Select another. I see you have combined yours. They work well for privacy screens, too."

Kasaandra approaches Qrodin, looking confused. "I thought this was a circus."

He smiles. "The animals attract attention and bring in visitors. But they make their money by selling their craft."

One of the vendors nods.

An hour or so later, the hardwood installer finds Qrodin. He and Qat are inspecting some of the tapestry samples. "If you have a moment, come take a look. I had help, so your flooring is ready. I think you will be thrilled! The walnut is glorious!"

"Wood flooring?" Qat asks.

"Oh, yes. Best there is! We harvest the wood ourselves from forests all over the world. What color would you like?"

"You have pink?" Qat winks at Bell, who had followed the installer in.

"Four kinds! Would you like a deep or pale pink?"

"Neither," Qat says. "I don't care for pink. Do you have any teak?"

"Do you like teak?"

"That depends," Qat says, following the installer out.

Qrodin shakes his head. "It looks like we have been abandoned. Would you like to join me? We can inspect the progress of your flooring."

"Sure!" Bell takes his hand. "This is going to be so much better than those flimsy tents."

Kasaandra's space is completed first. She had declined the wall texture but purchased the supplies to do it herself. Out of everyone, Kasaandra refused to allow him to purchase her furnishings.

"I could have done yours, too," Kasaandra tells Bell.

Bell shakes her head. She had requested a simple plaster design. "You're not tall enough to go all the way to the ceiling."

"I'd use a ladder."

"Would you do it tonight?"

Kasaandra doesn't answer.

"Exactly! There's no way I'm going to move everything back out again. I want it all done now so I don't have to worry about it later."

Kasaandra shrugs.

"That is a wise choice, Bell." Llani frowns. "You lack the housekeeping skills to—"

"Where are you going to sleep?" Qrodin asks Kasaandra, using *Soothe* before an argument can ensue.

"In my fur, like always." Kasaandra unrolls it with one swift motion, places it in the middle of the room, and then folds it in half. Qrodin had never really looked at her sleeping fur closely. The fur is white as snow and thick. The head of the animal had been skinned and sewn into a hood, but the ears are still intact, and someone had sewn fake eyes in place.

"Is that a bear?" Qat asks before Qrodin can get the words out.

Kasaandra nods.

"It was a baby." Bell looks ready to cry as she says it. "Kasaandra said the mommy bear died, and the baby bear starved 'cause it wouldn't leave its mommy."

"What killed the mama bear?" Qat asks.

"Bell, weren't we going to see the completed flooring?" Qrodin asks, increasing the *Soothe*.

In addition to a hablis-sized bed that doubles as a couch (and triples as wardrobe storage), Bell chooses a cabinet to hold cookware and dishes, and a low table with stools that tuck underneath and out of the way.

As soon as they move the furniture into their reasacobilas, Bell removes the small pot around her neck, opens it, and sniffs. She smiles and sets it carefully on a small cabinet shelf. She turns it slightly, then pats it.

After days of travel, his curiosity finally gets the best of him. "I've noticed the care you take with that pot. Do you mind me asking what it contains?"

She smiles. "Pure Gold."

"You feed berries to gold?" he asks, recalling the small handful she'd dropped in the container yesterday.

"Only when it's hungry."

Chapter 27 Qat

I sneak out while my flooring is being installed, and everyone is busy with their pocket homes. After seeing everyone else's, I didn't know how to furnish mine.

Kasaandra had a forge, Bell a kitchen, Llani a library, Qrow an office, and Akin a meditation space. What do I need? I have no trade outside of killing and stealing. No craft. My hobbies are gambling and spying.

Ultimately, I'd opted for a table spacious enough for the six of us, two matching table benches that double as storage trunks, and a cushioned settee that can be laid flat into a large bed. At least we can eat our meals in relative comfort. The table was Bell's idea, and I couldn't say no to her.

But what will I need with a large table when I leave them?

I wish I'd thought of that before selecting it. I guess I can always sell it. It's not like it cost me anything. I had chosen teak flooring, the kind used on ships. I'm happy to keep that.

And the bed. Though not as elegant as Bragdin's, it's a nice one.

I can't stop thinking about aem. I need to be in control, and when I agreed to meet aem tonight, I felt like I was being swept along in a rowboat with no oars.

I'm not in love. I don't believe in love at first sight. But I am interested. And I don't believe in denying myself.

So, why am I?

If tonight is the only night I get with aem, why am I delaying it?

And if it isn't the only night?

Who cares?

I catch my twirling blade and sheathe it.

I change direction. The horse tent is an excellent place to start looking for Bragdin.

It's a clear and cool evening. Every other tent flap is rolled up to let in fresh air. At the far end, horse trailers for the show horses—those not used for pulling wagons between shows—are backed next to each other. About half of them are occupied. Temporary corrals and stalls have been resurrected around the perimeter, leaving the center ring available for practice riding.

The place looks empty for now, so I stroll over and greet Starshine, who had eventually stopped insisting on following me and Bragdin, but only because we put him in with three other mares in addition to Qat's companions' mounts.

"What do you think of your new friends?"

Starshine snorts and swishes his tail.

"That much, huh?"

Starshine's ears flick back and to his left.

"What do you hear, big guy?" Listening with him for a moment, I hear something in one of the trailers. I wink at him. "Is someone playing in the hay?"

His head swings toward the sound, then back to me. His body is stiff with discomfort.

"What's up?" I walk around the corral toward the noise. The hay trailer is rocking. I hear a low moan and stop. Someone *is* playing in the hay. I walk back to Starshine. I don't want to ruin someone else's good time.

"I don't blame them. I'm going to go find Bragdin and see if I can get some of that myself."

Starshine doesn't react.

"Nothing to say? Does that mean you've decided to like aem?"

His ears flicker again.

I glance toward the trailer. It's not rocking anymore, so I slip into the corral to hide behind Starshine and run my fingers through his mane to keep him from moving.

I bend just enough to peer beneath his chin as someone strides out of the trailer.

Wow. Ae's gorgeous. Aer hair is long and thick, and as glossy as Starshine's the day he came out of the water. Ae smiles and turns back to aer companion.

Bragdin walks out of the trailer.

I feel like I've been gut-punched.

The two of them share an embrace. Their kiss is hot, wet, and deep.

My hands fist in Starshine's mane. A hot knot of anger starts in my belly and spreads up and out.

Why ask me to stay the night and then come here to be with someone else? Ae couldn't have waited one night? Not even that long. I overheard Qrow telling Kasaandra and Akin that we are leaving tomorrow afternoon.

It's not like there was a chance I was going to stay.

Okay. Maybe a tiny chance. Wasn't there? I'd thought so, but while we were picking out furniture for the pocket homes, Bell kept talking about different foods she'd make in her new kitchen. And she kept asking me about Craguesport and saying how much she was looking forward to me showing it to her. Every question pierced my temptation to stay. My gut twists into knots at the thought of not being there with her.

I wish we could leave now. It's what I'd do if I were alone. It's what I do best.

I successfully talk myself out of sneaking behind them and knocking their heads together. How do people do relationships? I can't handle even one day of a *maybe*.

I fix the mess I'd made of Starshine's mane.

Slipping through the horse tent and into the clearing beyond, the two finally leave. I give Starshine one final pat and slip out behind them. Not expecting either of them to have lingered, I nearly walk into Bragdin's lover outside the tent. I'm close enough to smell the spicy scent of aer lotion—or maybe aer hair oil.

Ae waits until Bragdin gets halfway across the clearing before straightening aer clothes and walking toward the camp. The sun set hours ago, and the smell of woodsmoke fills the air. Bragdin's companion joins a group of people sitting around a campfire. Ae picks up a child and hugs aem.

I return to the corral, grab a brush on the way, and spend a few minutes with the horses. I brush first one, then another, and a third before the repetition of the task calms my racing pulse.

I leave when I no longer want to slip a knife into Bragdin.

The clearing is bright. Kuu is brilliant this far from town. Turning away from the bright, full moon, I glance back at Bragdin's pocket home and nod goodbye.

Mine is where I left it, of course. When I reach it, I trace the symbol on the outside of the rough surface. The purple stone brushes my fingertips as it falls and hides in the tall grass.

I sigh.

Just like the rest of my night has gone.

At least Qrow and the crew returned to the same location as before. As I approach, I wonder if my pocket home will combine with theirs.

Nope. It pops up around me, and I breathe a sigh of relief. I elected not to cover the sky, and Kuu's glow illuminates all my new furniture.

I set my bag down and take out the knobby green stone. Moonlight glints on the weird protuberances.

I hold the rock up to Kuu. Like before, there are some spots darker than others, but nothing stands out.

So why did it fall out of the pocket home?

"What are you?" I ask it.

Mine, is the answer that comes to me.

Chapter 28 Qrodin

18TH DAY OF ZAMDI, 14,887
SORBSLLES CAMP, ZEDANA

Combining the five domes gives Qrodin the impression of an odd little home. Instead of five individual pockets, the outer walls shift to form a smooth transition between adjacent spaces.

When inside Bell's kitchen, the plastered wall ends where it meets Llani's home on the left, and Kasaandra's home on the right. However, from Qrodin's space, the plastered surface delineates Bell's kitchen from the rest of the space. Despite this, whether by nature of the material or—more likely—the reasacobila's magic, the plaster can be passed as though it's not there. Unfortunately, that's not the case with the furniture, as Qrodin discovers the hard way. They must take care when entering Bell's space until they learn to orient their furniture when erecting the combined structure.

When Kasaandra finishes plastering her space, it will likely look the same.

Qrodin had decided to replicate the business hotel rooms he usually stays in while traveling. The effect required a few changes due to space, but the Karatolii make their furniture compact and efficient to fit the cobilas—and now the reasacobilas. Like Akin, Qrodin's bed collapses, but he chose one that folds up and out of the way. He also selected a tall, narrow wardrobe with space to hang his clothes above, with drawers below. To finish the setup, he selected a matching desk and chair. Privacy screens tuck behind the bed when not in use.

All they're missing is a table. Qat's table. Last night, they had left a space for Qat's reasacobila. Although Qat came back and set it up in its space, they can't access it, as they didn't set it up simultaneously.

Bell was up hours before, if the mess in her kitchen is anything to go by. He tries not to touch any of it as he leans against her new hutch and watches her.

"What are you making?"

"Bread! You're going to love it!"

"You've been making bread this whole time." Almost daily, Bell placed flattened dough into hot oil and fried it golden brown. Sometimes, they ate it with meat, vegetables, and cheese piled on top. Other times, she added herbs and mushrooms to the pan, then placed the dough on top, infusing the bread with savory goodness. Qrodin's favorite is topped with fresh fruit and honey. She says once they get to Craguesport, she'll make it with chocolate.

"No, not like this. I've been making flatbread. Not Pure Gold bread." She raises the cover on a bowl and pokes a finger into the lumpy dough, leaving a finger dimple. "Hmmm. I'm going to check the oven. Don't touch anything."

"I wouldn't even think about it."

"Qat's back," Bell says from the stove.

"Yes, I noticed. Where is everyone else?"

"Kasaandra said she wanted to look for more metal or something. Llani had to pee."

Qrodin doubts Llani mentioned such a thing. She'd think it was inappropriate.

They all return a few minutes later. Only Kasaandra doesn't bump into furniture on the way inside.

Qat walks out of aer reasacobila and knocks on the wall of Akin's space.

"Oh! We're going to need to reset everything." Bell sticks her head outside. "Qat. We're going to reset the Home Dome."

Once they have them all reassembled, Bell returns to the bread in the bowl. "Something's wrong."

Kasaandra joins her and nods. "Did you use your kneading board?"

"Of course I did. I've been making this since I was a little girl."

Llani approaches. "What is the problem?"

"My bread isn't rising."

"Did you starve your starter?" Kasaandra asks.

"No, I fed it yesterday. And while we were in Riversmeet. And a couple times in between." Bell opens the small jar she'd nurtured since leaving that town. "I don't understand. Yesterday, it was fine. There were bubbles and everything. Now, it's just..."

"Dead." Kasaandra shrugs. "I told you. You starved it."

"Have not! I know how to keep it alive."

"Smell it. No bug farts. Sometimes, it just happens."

"What are you talking about?" Qrodin has never baked. He has no idea about the process or how to troubleshoot bread-making problems. He's out of his depth.

"Pure Gold," says Bell.

"Bug farts," says Kasaandra.

"Yeast," Llani corrects. "I've explained to you that leavened dough is formed by gas—"

"As I said. Bug farts."

"Pure Gold is magic, not bugs." She glares at Kasaandra. "And not farts!"

"Bugs?" Qat curls aer nose. "You put bugs in your bread? Are they alive or dead?"

"Initially, they are alive," Llani states as Kasaandra opens her mouth. "The heat from the oven kills the organisms." She walks away from the group and returns with a book. There are more books than he would have thought possible for one person to bring on a *sodafari,* even one with a magic bag. "They are not bugs. They are single-celled microorganisms."

Bell rolls her eyes. "Smaller words, Llani."

When Llani only raises her chin in defiance, Qrow offers, "*Micro* refers to organisms so small you are unable to see them with your naked eyes."

"Then how do you see them? With your—"

"By enlarging them with magic." Llani interrupts Qat before ae can say something obscene.

Qrodin is intrigued. And confused. As far as he knew, the only way to study them was with expensive contraptions made of mirrors and lenses. "I have been told that such magic is impossible. How can something that small be made large enough to be studied?"

"You were told incorrectly, though it takes a consortium to accomplish such a task."

"What is that?" Bell asks.

"Three to eleven elves capable of advanced sciencecraft."

Akin whistles and signs.

Llani frowns. "A consortium is not a coven."

"Do they secret themselves away from society?" Qrodin asks, remembering what she'd said about witches.

"Well. Yes. Privacy and confidentiality require seclusion."

"Do they know Ancient Elvish?" Qat sneaks a glance at Kasaandra.

"Of course." Llani presses her lips tightly, clearly not happy with the turn of the conversation.

Bell scrunches her eyes. "But they're not witches?"

"Of course not. They are scientists." Llani returns to her space and places the book carefully in the gap left by its absence.

"Sounds like witches to me." Kasaandra looks at Llani. "We're taught that the bread breathes life from the volcano in which we live."

"None of this explains what happened to my Pure Gold." Bell lifts the cover off the bowl. The bread is still lumped at the bottom.

Qrodin recalls something the elder had said about the reasacobilas. "Llani. You're saying that tiny organisms…ah…"

"Fart."

Llani glares at Kasaandra. "They expel gases that allow the bread to increase in size."

Qrodin nods his head. "Then they are probably no longer in the dough."

"Why not?" Bell says.

"We moved the Home Dome a few times yesterday while trying to find the best configuration. I recall seeing your jar on the table. Nothing alive can stay inside when they are shrunk," Qrodin says, feeling confident in his theory. "Whatever was in the bread dough would have stayed outside, like us. I'm sorry. Did I forget to tell you that part?"

"Uh. Yeah. I'd say you did," Bell pouts.

Qrodin frowns. "That's why I told you we needed to dismantle the pocket homes from the outside. So your clothes don't remain inside. I suppose I hadn't given much thought to other types of organisms."

Bell picks up the earthenware pot and holds it to her chest. "I'm so sorry, Pure Gold. I didn't mean to kill you." Tears roll down her cheeks.

"If what Qrow says is true," Qat says, "then you didn't kill the yeast. They escaped into the air."

Bell looks heartbroken, as though she's lost a loved one. Qrodin's thoughts are confirmed when she finally responds to Qat. "Pure Gold is more than just yeast. It's a lifetime of care and nurturing and love."

"Don't you have one of the samples you saved? You can restart it with that," Kasaandra says.

Bell shakes her head. "They would have died, too. They don't work after being kept in Llani's bag, remember? I tried to start a test one before. Now we know why it didn't work. Her bag probably does the same thing."

"You can start over." Kasaandra opens the ceramic pot and snorts, then wrinkles her nose. "Mamair and Mili started over several times."

"It won't be the same." Bell sniffs loudly.

Llani throws a braid over her shoulder. "It would be different regardless. Yeast strains are specific to their environments, and the yeast adhered to the berries and bark you have been adding will have already changed the flavor."

Bell glares at her. "I know what I'm doing. I know what they need. I told you, I can sense food auras." She looks through her meager supply of cookware. "I'm going to need more pots. I can't start with just one. I need to test different ingredients."

"I know where I can get you some." Qat is gone before anyone else responds.

Chapter 29 Qat

The rock is *alive*. That's the only explanation.

The thought is equally exciting and frightening.

It doesn't *look* like an organism. It looks like a rock. Like a gemstone.

But it won't stay inside the Home Dome. That means it's alive.

Maybe it's like an insect encased in amber. Captain Rogen has a set of four of those he uses to hold down map corners. But those insects aren't alive. And even if they were, wouldn't they miraculously end up outside the amber? Qrow did say we'd be standing there naked if we drew the symbol while standing inside.

There were darker spots inside when I held it up to the light, but no different from most rocks, even semi-transparent ones.

But it's alive.

Could the rock be an egg?

I guess that would depend. Is an eggshell like clothes or like skin?

A shadow materializes between two carriages as I enter the space between them, and all thoughts of shells dissipate.

"You didn't come by last night. I waited up for you."

Bragdin. Beautiful, heart-racingly gorgeous Bragdin.

I search aer face for tell-tale signs of a sleepless night. No bags under reddish-brown eyes. No extra crease or tension through the forehead. No paleness or squinting or pinched lips.

The discovery makes me feel better about my decision not to spend the night. Yesterday, Bragdin had an advantage over me. I was vulnerable. Yesterday was the first time I'd spoken my native language. The first time I'd met people who had known of me from my time before Rogen. I was assaulted by smells, sights, and knowledge of things I have no memory of.

But today is a different story.

I've had one whole night to sleep on it. I should have been up tossing and turning, running through the pros and cons of each decision. But I wasn't. I slept better than I have in as long as I can remember. This morning, I didn't even need to roll the dice.

I'm still attracted to Bragdin. I am. Bragdin is a beautiful being. But I no longer feel overwhelmed by aem like I did yesterday. Aer sad eyes don't make me feel guilty for having passed on our meeting.

"Oh, don't be sad." I stroke aer face lightly. "Your forehead scrunches here when you do."

Bragdin's eyes crease in a slight smile. I can't tell if ae's puzzled or amused.

And I don't care. I'm just relieved I no longer feel the need to please aem or be pleased by aem.

This morning, I'm free to make my own decisions. Not that I wasn't yesterday, but I felt invisible fingers were influencing my will, coaxing me to stay here.

Today, I'm the me I've always been.

I kiss Bragdin's cheek. Ae smells divine. I run the tip of my finger down aer temple, along the outside of aer ear, to the pulse pounding at its base. "There's always tomorrow."

Bragdin's face splits in a grin, and aer pulse jumps slightly.

"Or tomorrow," I finish.

Bragdin's grin fades. Ae nods and takes my forearms. Our foreheads touch, and ae caresses mine, an imitation of a kiss.

"Manot su manot, Qatzsi."

Strangely, hearing my birth name on Bragdin's lips doesn't annoy me like when Qrow says it.

Ae walks away. I expect I won't see aem again before we leave.

I'm greeted with, *'Oiy, Qat,'* several times as I walk through camp this morning. I find the carriage I'd seen yesterday that sells what Bell needs.

The crafter, Olaron, is at work already, shaping a pot with aer hands while the turntable spins with every press of aer foot on a pedal. Aer tail flicks when I veer toward aem. Ae wasn't the only one with a tail here, but aers is so fluffy, I was tempted to stroke it when we spoke yesterday.

"*Oiy*, Olaron." I'm surprised I remember aer name. Our conversation had been short.

When ae looks up, aer hazel eyes catch the morning sun. "*Oiy*, Qat. Good morning."

"Good to see you again."

"And you as well. Are you looking for something in particular, or just browsing?" Aer foot action slows, but ae continues smoothing the sides of the pot.

"I'm looking for small pots with lids that stay on tight. I thought I saw some yesterday."

"Oh, yes." Aer foot stops. "Are you going to be using any of them for food?" Ae stands as soon as the table stops turning.

"Yes. Does that make a difference?"

"Sure." The potter wipes the clay from aer hands with a towel hanging at aer waist. Ae climbs the steps inside aer wagon, and aer tail brushes my hand on the way. The fur is as soft as I thought it'd be. "Come on up, Qat. You're one of us."

Feeling like an imposter, I step up into the vehicle. The inside is painted orange like the clay ae uses to form aer pots. As I step in, a barrel labeled *CLAY* is to the left of the door. Two bales of hay are to the right. On the far end is a table with pots of paint, brushes, and weird metal tools most likely used for shaping or sculpting clay. Along the sides are tables with trunks and crates nestled underneath. Like my pocket home, the top of the wagon is open and shimmering with the outline of a *reasamagila*. Olaron could paint even in the rain while taking advantage of the daylight.

"What will you be using them for?"

"I'm not sure what it's called, but the one Bell had was small. She wore it around her neck. It had something in it for starting bread?"

"Oh, sure. Starter pots. You know they can't stay in the reasacobila when it's pocket-sized, right? The starter fails."

"We found that out this morning. She's crushed. She said she's had the same one since she was young."

"Oh, no." Ae turns to me with one hand on aer heart and a sad tilt to aer mouth. "Tell her I'm so sorry. My ama was a baker. That will be devastating, for sure. But we'll get her back in business. Is it a sourdough starter or a wild-grow starter?"

I shrug. "What's the difference?"

"Well, one is a flour and water mixture. The other is water fed with fruit or bark and sugar."

"I'm pretty sure it's the second one. I saw her feeding it some berries earlier. Is it normal that she keeps the pot around her neck while we're on the road?" It's rather strange to me.

"Sure. It keeps it warm during cold weather. Otherwise, it could go to sleep." Ae smiles at the face I make and then hands me a box from a stack. "Here. Ama was forever collecting anything ae thought might make a good starter. I made these boxes to carry six starter pots. They fit inside a backpack. Now that your friend has a reasacobila, ae can store most of aer belongings there. That will leave plenty of room in aer backpack for these."

"Will she need more than one?"

"With wild-grow starters, you never know what will work or how it will taste. Bread made with fruit starters tastes different than bark starters. Willow bark starters will taste different from pine, and so on. If ae needs to start a new one, ae'll want to gather various ingredients to try. Six may not be enough. My guess? You'll get a lot of bread over the next few months until ae perfects aer recipe. Ae may even decide to keep more than one starter. Just, you know"—ae raises one shoulder and scrunches aer lips—"in case it happens again."

Considering how Bell takes food samples wherever she goes, she'll likely need more than six. She did say she'd need a lot. "Maybe I should get two boxes. Or three. What do you think?"

"I think you know your friend better than I do. Does ae have a good bread pot and proofing basket?"

"She's only been making flatbread so far. What do you have?"

Ae shows me a selection of pots and an assortment of baskets in different sizes and shapes.

I'm going to need more money.

Chapter 30 Qrodin

They leave camp around midday. Their departure takes much longer than Qrodin anticipated. Nearly everyone comes out to say goodbye to the reunited twins. All but Bragdin, it seems. Qrodin wonders briefly what happened between them.

Several hours later, when they stop to make camp, Llani mentions wanting to gather witch hazel, and Kasaandra protests.

"It is an excellent herb for healing, divination, and protection. It is unassociated with genuine witches."

The reminder of their previous encounter with the witches is...unpleasant. Despite the distraction of Sorbslles Magnificent Menagerie, Qrodin hasn't been able to keep the witches' words out of his head.

When he turns, Kasaandra is watching him. "You should write it down," she says.

"Pardon?"

"You're a songwriter."

"Yes." He had mentioned it only briefly while they were riding. He didn't think she would remember such a detail.

"What happened the other night with the Twisted Sisters."

The Twisted Sisters. That's what Bell had called them. How had he let his control slip so much that Kasaandra noticed?

"I draw," she says.

He has no idea how that's supposed to help, but he doesn't want to discourage her. Kasaandra makes odd connections that others don't see. It reminds him of Talim.

"I think about a design. Over and over. Can't get it out of my head until I draw it. Once I do, I can move on."

Ah. And she thinks that if he writes down what happened, he can move on.

"Thank you, Kasaandra. I appreciate your help." They sit for a moment as Qrodin thinks of what to say. Eventually, he remembers the orange rock he had picked up recently. He pulls it from his bag. "This caught my eye during one of our stops, and I thought of you when I saw it. The color matches your hair."

She examines it closely. "I think you're in tune with these more than you let on." She doesn't go into further detail. Instead, she hands it back to him. "Give this back to me when you've finished writing. You need it more than I do right now."

"I don't think it will—"

"There's a reason you picked it up."

He can't think of a good argument for that. "Well. Thank you again."

Before he can finish, she's already turned to go. Watching her leave, he decides that now *is* an excellent time to compose a new song. If it doesn't help, at least he tried.

He retrieves a box of loose-leaf pages from his bag, finds a sunny spot against a tree trunk, and makes himself comfortable some distance away from the others. If Kasaandra can tell that he's off today, they likely can, too. He'd prefer them not to witness his process while he composes.

He uses the box as a writing surface. The task is hard going at first. He doesn't want to remember the battle, let alone enough to write about it. Words are weapons. His song could do more harm than good if he does this wrong.

He sketches an outline of the events while he works on a melody, then starts writing.

Unlike stories and books, songs are short, so every word must count.

He needs to convey everything in a few dozen lines. That's the challenge, and Qrodin crosses out more than he keeps. Pages of discarded verses and scrapped lines build up beside him.

He starts over again. Finally satisfied with the first verse, he moves on to the chorus. He writes two more verses, a bridge, and the final verse.

When he's finished, he thinks of Bell and titles it *The Battle of the Twisted Sisters*.

Finally, he unclenches his left hand and finds the orange stone in his palm. Had it helped?

He tucks the pages away in the box and looks up. The sun is gone, and in its place, a lantern sits next to him. How had someone left it without him noticing?

Qrodin must have sat there for hours. Why didn't they come get him?

His stomach rumbles, but he stretches his legs, arms, and back before entering camp. Only Llani is sitting outside. The others must be occupying themselves inside the reasacobila.

Llani looks up from her book. "Bell said to inform you that your meal is in that covered pot by the fire. Kasaandra forbade us from disturbing you."

"Forbade?" he asks, amused.

"Vehemently."

"Was she holding her axe when she did it?"

"She was unarmed at the ti—" She stops when she notices his smile. "Oh. You were making a jest."

"I was." His smile comes more easily than it might have this morning.

Chapter 31 Qat

19TH DAY OF ZAMDI, 14,887
ROAD TO CRANWOOD, ZEDANA

We stop for camp sometime before sunset. As Qrow scouts for the best place to set up the pocket homes, Llani asks to test their magical resistance.

"I suggest that we test the efficacy of various spells against them. For instance, can magic penetrate the walls from outside? From within? If the former, they are little help as a shield, except from a physical attack. If the latter, but not the former, we should feel quite safe enough to forego keeping a watch. If neither, then a new watch schedule should be prepared forthwith."

I get lost in the *formers* and *latters*. "What kind of spells?"

"Yeah," Bell says. "I don't want you to blow up the Home Dome."

At Kasaandra's urging, we decide to test them after dinner.

Once the pocket homes are set up, Bell asks Llani to try the same flaming green lights she had used against the witches. I stay inside with Bell and watch the flames roll over the top, lighting the rocks around us. Bell dances in the green glow. The light doesn't penetrate the inside.

Qrow says something to the others, and I pop my head out in time to catch the end of his comment. "—meant to blanket everything in its path. We need to try getting through it."

Akin whistles and signs something to Qrow. Llani translates. "Try to get the occupants to exit. Can you attempt to command Qat to leave it as you commanded the witch?"

"Command Qat to do something?" Qrow pinches the bridge of his nose. "Perhaps it will work on Bell. She responds to *Soothe*."

I smirk at Qrow's comment and duck back inside.

"What were they saying?" Bell asks me.

"Boring stuff. They're going to—"

Bell turns away and walks toward her section, away from the group outside. Bollocks! I'd been hoping it wouldn't work.

"They're going to what?" Bell asks. She stops at the table and peeks inside one of the starter jars. "There's bubbles! It's working. We're going to have bread in a few days." She lifts the other lid and frowns, then digs in her bag.

Hmm. Maybe Qrow's command didn't work after all.

Kasaandra pokes her head inside and looks around. When she finds Bell in her kitchen, she pulls back out. She shakes her head and says something to the rest of the group.

I walk over to the table and peer down into the pot. "What are you doing?"

Bell had abandoned her bag and was opening and closing cupboard doors. "I'm trying to feed them."

"Feed what?" I look inside the jars. "The leaves and"—I look in another jar—"and bark?"

Bell is now in Llani's section. She picks up Llani's bag, puts her hand inside, and pulls out a heavy sack. "No, silly. You know the white stuff on the outside of them? Llani said that's what makes my bread puff up."

Back at the table, Bell opens the sack and spoons sugar into each jar.

"They like sugar?"

"Don't we all?"

I do. I lick my finger and stick it in the bag.

"Hey!" She smacks my hand with the spoon without turning. As fast as I am, she's faster.

My knuckles sting from the rap. "Hey! Why aren't you that fast when Kasaandra sneaks meat?"

"She's sneakier than you."

I'm offended. "No one is sneakier than me." To prove my point, I reach over the top of her head, bury my wet finger in the sugar, and then draw a circle on her forehead.

Bell tenses, and I pull back quickly. The spoon whacks Bell on the forehead. "Qat!"

I vault over the low table and run.

"I'm going—"

Her voice cuts off when I exit the structure. I race to the nearest tall tree and climb from the opposite side. Kuu is almost a perfect half circle tonight and throwing enough light that even Bell would have seen me if I'd stayed in view.

"—when I catch you!"

Too bad I didn't hear the beginning of her threat. Maybe I should have waited a little longer before ducking out of the pocket home.

Kasaandra's voice reaches me. "Nope. Just Qat being Qat."

They're still testing the magic?

I'm high enough in the tree to see Llani's frown and Qrow's smile.

Qrow calls out, "We're going to test the inside now. Are you coming or staying up there?"

Well, I do want to see that.

Bell's gaze sweeps the area, but she gives up and goes back inside. Descending the tree is quick work after that. When I finally join them, flames appear and coat the inside of the Home Dome. But instead of green, they're purple.

Bell squeals. "Llani, your arm! You have a shiny star. How pretty!"

The purple lights go out.

No one says a word.

Llani marches directly to her space. She jumps up to a bar she'd made as we rode. I'd watched her assemble it, but didn't ask what it was for. She hangs upside down, facing away from us. Ah.

Qrow clears his throat. "At least we know magic won't penetrate from the inside or out."

Everyone disperses and starts their evening chores.

It rains as Kasaandra and I go outside to care for the horses. Water sheets down, soaking us in seconds. The horses leave the field and gather under the trees. I should be happy, I won't have to chase them down. Instead, I can't stop thinking about Llani's supposed mark.

"Did you see the star Bell was talking about? I missed it."

Kasaandra shakes her head.

"You ever heard of anything like that before?" She grew up inside a mountain with thousands of people. There's a good chance that she has.

She doesn't respond.

I guess it was a stupid question. It *would* be unusual for anyone to see something like that. At least she didn't roll her eyes at me.

When we finish our chores, we enter the structure. Mmm, it's nice and dry. But we'd built the fire outside, and now it's extinguished by the downpour. I hope we don't freeze tonight.

Chapter 32 Qrodin

They'd been traveling all day with the sun in their eyes. They hadn't bathed since they left the Shipdurn River behind a few days ago and had only been able to sluice water over themselves from the streams they'd come across. Washing his hair has been a chore, as the thick mass takes forever to rinse a bowlful at a time. At least his beard has grown enough that it's stopped itching.

Yesterday, the road reunited with Turtle River on the final stretch to Cranwood. While the Shipdurn River had veered south through the swamps to feed Halivern Lake, Turtle River flows north from the lake and eastward, passing Cranwood and Craguesport on its way to the Reef Sea.

Qrodin checks his book for a message from Talim. Still none. He takes a chance and copies his song onto her page. Because they'll be in Cranwood soon, he morphs into his Quentin Browning disguise—the one he uses for international business and shipping. Afterward, he evaluates his business holdings until they mount up and ride the last leg into Cranwood.

On the boat ride to Riversmeet over a fortnight ago, he'd glimpsed what he thought were olive trees growing near the river, but later could find no record of sales from Cranwood. The underutilization of nearby resources is one of the reasons he's glad they're going overland, since none of his transports scheduled to leave Riversmeet stop there.

The price of olive oil has risen steeply over the last year, ever since spittlebugs—or rather, the disease they brought with them—wiped out entire olive orchards north of Craguesport. If Cranwood has viable olive groves, he's confident he will do well to invest in them.

Cranwood is a village now, but it had once been a much larger city constantly under siege, and was eventually abandoned by the merkama who ruled there. Most of the outer city has fallen into ruins and left to be overtaken by plants and wildlife, but it used to be one of the wealthiest cities in Zedana, back before Zedana was Zedana.

Its history is Qrodin's main reason for taking this overland route, for more reasons than one. Its tie to the merkama, for starters. He's curious to discover if there are any artifacts he can acquire. What better place to find them than the only historical land home for that species?

As Cranwood slowly becomes visible on the horizon, Qrodin marvels at the giant statue of a male merkama holding a trident victoriously in the air. There were games and competitions during the time of kings and queens, when Cranwood was one of the most influential cities. When the sea level was higher, Turtle River took half a day to cross, and the very center of the coliseum floor was open to the water.

The city wall is tall and imposing, towering eight bandis high and one bandi thick, wide enough for a sentry to walk the top. Massive stone bricks of varying dimensions are pieced together so closely that mortar is barely visible. It's been impeccably maintained, and the brown, gold, and white bricks can withstand another thousand years. Even Kasaandra looks impressed at the masonry work.

The high entrance has a pointed arch framed with two rows of narrow rocks that protrude slightly from the wall. The open double gate is freshly stained a deep, brick red, and the two round, iron handholds are rust free.

The orchards and fields on the way here may have been disorganized and neglected, but the inside of the city is not. Most of the northern part of the city is ruins, the low walls all that remain of a once-wealthy capital, but every surface is trimmed and brushed clear of weeds and debris.

They bring their horses to the stables. They still haven't seen anyone, although several cats are running about, and a dozen or more horses are in the stalls.

"I don't advise using the pocket homes while we're here," Qrodin says. "If you need something from yours, I suggest you leave town first or find a space large enough to contain it. I will go to the inn to see if anyone's inside."

"Hello!"

Qrodin turns at the greeting. A tall, thin man is walking briskly toward them. The long strands of a comb-over flap and flutter with every step.

"It sure is good to see visitors. I'm Norik Bob. I run the stables. Are these your mounts? Mighty fine if I do say so myself. Especially that one, there." Norik Bob pauses only long enough to point at Starshine, then starts up again. "You probably saw the Jobo as you came in. That'll sleep three. The Uncu sleeps two. Hmmm. That leaves one of you without a bed, but you're small"—he points to Bell—"so I'm sure you can work it out. Settle your things." His eyes rove over the mounts and us and finally settle on Bell's pack. "It seems you travel light. Very good, then. I'll take you on a tour of Cranwood, starting right here." He waves his arm to indicate the gate leading into what he calls the 'inner keep.' On the walk, he explains that there used to be a massive castle in Cranwood, but after it fell during one of the hundreds of invasions, the stones were gathered up and used to build other structures.

Norik Bob points to a monument near the south wall of the inner keep. There are no windows or doors—the top flares from the sides before steepling toward the sky. Unlike the town wall and buildings, the monument is bluish-grey and heavily worn. The ground around it is black and bare. "You won't want to go anywhere near there," he says. "Most people say it's cursed. I think it's creepy."

"Oh, yeah?" Qat immediately walks toward it.

Of course, Qrodin thinks. 'Creepy,' 'Cursed,' and 'Stay Away' are all invitations to Qat.

But after a few steps on the blackened dirt, Qat stops. Ae rubs aer arms as if ae's cold.

"What is it?" Bell calls out.

Qat tilts aer head slightly. "I'm picking up a vibe."

"A *creepy* vibe?" Bell asks, taking a step closer.

"Sure, that fits. Feels like it's dropped twenty degrees." Qat glances at them, then back to the monument.

"What's a creepy vibe feel like?" Kasaandra strides forward.

Bell follows. When she gets to the darkened area, she stops and then starts backing away. "Oh, no. No. No way. That is definitely a creepy vibe." Her face is nearly green, and she's holding her stomach.

Kasaandra stands three feet inside the perimeter, proving to everyone she's not afraid.

Qat's demeanor changes slightly. Qrodin doubts anyone else notices. His twin bends forward almost imperceptibly, then takes a few steps closer and tenses.

"What do you see?" Qrodin asks.

"Huh?" Qat looks back at Qrodin. "Oh. Just checking it out." Qat comes back to the group, followed closely by Kasaandra. The dwarf hadn't gotten further than those first three steps.

Norik Bob shakes his head. "That's the closest I've ever seen anyone get to that thing. The kids dare each other every year, but none get further than your friend there." He indicates Kasaandra with a nod. "Most stop without ever touching foot on that cursed ground. Now, let me show you the other inn." He grimaces. "We don't get many visitors."

When they finally leave the inner keep, Llani stays behind to look at a monument covered in glyphs and sigils. Shortly after, Bell lingers at the communal oven, and Kasaandra and Akin abandon them at the Uncu hotel. Qrodin doesn't notice when Qat slips away.

He and Norik Bob spend the rest of the tour visiting the various businesses and discussing their operational status, occupancy, and availability for purchase. He takes copious notes along the way.

There are so many opportunities in Cranwood.

Chapter 33 Qat

29TH DAY OF ZAMDI, 14,887
CRANWOOD, ZEDANA

I'm so bored.

We've been here for three days.

Three days!

All Qrow wants to do is buy up the town. He made a deal to purchase several groves of olives, nuts, and fruits. He bought grain fields and grapevines, the oil press, the old mill, and many buildings he plans to convert into warehouses.

Bell joined him, and they're re-walking all the fields outside the walls and exploring the ones across the river. When she's not with Qrow, Bell's at the communal oven located almost smack dab in the center of town. A crowd of cooks meets there early mornings and late afternoons, with more straggling by throughout the day. Does no one have an oven in their home?

Kasaandra spends most of her time with the only blacksmith in town, but this morning before dawn, I saw her at the oven, talking to one of the oldest dwarfs I've ever seen. Small and thin with silver hair and red eyes. We called them Dusk Diggers on the ship—but I'd never call her that to her face. She's a nocturnal species called Toicheal. That's probably why she's at the ovens so early. And there was Kasaandra, kneading dough right next to her. I couldn't understand what they were saying, but Kasaandra was doing most of the talking. I could hardly believe my eyes.

All Llani wants to do is explore the oldest buildings. She said they have stuff carved into them from thousands of years ago in a language that no one can read. Not even Horik, the current mayor. Horik spends most of his time deciphering the bubble-looking glyphs carved all over the place, so Llani spends most of her time with him.

Akin has been mostly absent. The few times I've seen him outside of mealtimes, he's meditating or doing his *Idajmbe* workout. In Riversmeet, I thought he was sick or had an ulcer. He seems to be over that, and it looks like he's gained weight.

Which leaves me.

All by myself.

The way I've always been.

But now I'm miserable. If I were visiting Cranwood by myself, I would have left already. There's no one to entertain me, as nearly all the villagers are out fishing.

Earlier today, I found a spot for my hammock beneath a few trees that were sparse enough to let sunlight trickle through the leaves as I slept, but were still shady enough to remain cool through the hottest parts of the day.

Now that the sun has set, I'm awake. Which means I can explore all I want without anyone bothering me. Kuu is nearly full, casting enough light for me to sneak around in. Tonight, I'm checking out the cursed monument Norik Bob showed us.

A search of the ground around it doesn't yield anything promising. Unlike the other buildings in Cranwood with neatly tended flower beds and shrubs at the base, nothing grows anywhere close to this thing. The rumors say nothing will. Everything planted here dies.

The closer I get to the building, the more hesitant I am about searching it. I don't believe it's haunted. I've never believed in ghosts. Whatever it is that's making my stomach squeeze uncomfortably, it's not that.

The hair on the back of my neck isn't even stirring.

I disregard the conflicting signals and approach the building. People say to trust your gut, but I'd prefer the warning system that's never failed me. My danger sense doesn't lie. I would have gone straight up to it the first day had Kasaandra not stopped. I hadn't wanted to alert everyone that there isn't any real danger. None that I could detect, anyway.

That doesn't mean it's easy. Everything in me wants to turn back. My stomach turns inside out, my hands shake, and I'm trembling with cold.

All these factors make me more determined to investigate.

I inspect the entire structure. It's so odd, large enough to be a building but with no entrance. The cracks and crevices in the stone are black, and the entire monument is glistening as if it's recently been hauled out of the sea. When I touch it, it's slimy, and my hand comes away wet.

I scale the wall behind the monument to get a better look at the roof. There are no other structures between it and the wall, so I get a clear view of the roof and spire. The south side has a gaping hole.

Too far to jump from the wall. I'll have to climb the monument. The task won't be easy—the grey stones are slick with moss and algae—but I came prepared with my climbing kit.

At first, I have no difficulty, but at the overhang, my hand slips.

I flail for the wall. My fingers brush slime, and I fly forehead-first into the side of the monument. I taste ocean and mold and rot. Something I'm well familiar with, but don't expect out here.

Bollocks!

I roll onto my back.

When the stars finally morph into constellations I recognize, I sit up. There's a lump the size of a walnut on my forehead and blood dribbling down my face. I pull out a scarf and staunch the flow.

Finally, I stand.

My second ascent is both easier and more complicated. Confident I won't slip again, I grasp the overhang with both hands and swing. One. Two. Three. The momentum takes me up and over the top until my feet enter the gap in the roof. I let go of the overhang and barely catch the edge of the hole.

Phew! That was close!

I hang here long enough to see a giant statue in the center of the room and a table below the hole covered in refuse. I drop. This time, I land perfectly.

The place is a mess. Roof blocks lay where they fell, and leaves and mud coat the floor.

Only the giant statue in the center remains of whatever was used to decorate this space.

Like a few other figures in town, this statue is a merkama. Across its chest is a round chest plate with straps that hold it in place. I spare it no more than a cursory glance until I notice a medallion in the center of the plate. One that depicts a sea monster.

Just like the logo on the paper I'd found in Truffle's room.

Near the west wall is a round room with an opening that faces the statue. The space within it is small, probably only five or six feet wide. The floor in this room is covered with loose stone pavers. I push one of them aside with my foot and find the corner of a steel plate.

My blood rushes at the sight, warming my ice-cold hands. I feel like I've spotted a merchant ship stuffed full to the gills and riding low in the water. Anytime I've had this feeling, it's paid off big.

I push another tile aside and find a ring handle. Yes! A hatch to a hidden compartment built into the floor. Someone had attempted to hide it, but did a terrible job of it.

My pulse accelerates, blood zinging in my veins.

Even my hands are shaking as I reach for the ring.

The hairs on my neck stand at attention.

A few seconds of searching reveals a trap. If I'd raised the handle, a small, probably poisoned dart would have sprung loose from underneath. Not only have I seen these before, but I've set them hundreds of times, so it's easy to disable.

I open the hatch slowly, cautious about crawlies that might swarm out. They don't.

The plate covers a natural round hole in the floor. I sweep my arm into the opening in case there are webs. There aren't.

So far, so good.

Steps descend into a dark room. As I step down, I feel a slight resistance around my ankles, like water. Except that there isn't any water. Cold creeps up my legs with each step, then my torso, and finally my neck. I take a deep breath before dipping beneath the invisible surface. I'm not underwater, but I feel pressure against my body like I'm swimming deep in the ocean.

As I reach the bottom, I release my held breath. There are no bubbles. The pressure is gone. The air isn't warm, but compared to the icy cold from before, it's comfortable. I'm in a natural underground cavern. The stairs were carved into the wall up to the opening above.

A torch sits in a sconce at the bottom of the staircase, and another is leaning against the wall. Convenient. I light them both and take the spare with me. I don't need them to see in the dark, but you never know what you'll encounter. The lit torch at the opening will show me where the exit is if I get lost in a maze of rooms or hallways.

I debate closing the hatch, but decide against it. I may need a quick exit.

The room leads into a hall with small chambers along each side. The sections have no doors but rather walls with shelves and niches of various shapes and sizes. I wave the torch back and forth. The empty rooms shimmer like the outline of the pocket homes, illuminating a treasure beyond belief. It fades as quickly as it appears.

I hate it when that happens.

Captain Rogen always said I have an over-active imagination.

"Qat's late," I hear Bell say, even though she isn't with me.

That's weird.

I open my eyes and nearly flip the hammock in my panic. The sun is high in the sky, and it's already hot. I'm late for mealtime.

I'd fallen asleep under a few trees inside the inner keep. I dreamt the whole thing. The monument of my dream is ahead of me. Is there treasure inside? What does it mean that it faded?

I recognize a particular quality of this dream. Similar ones in the past have been prophetic. I have to get in there now.

But not until after we eat. Maybe not then, either. I doubt the townsfolk would want us crawling all over the creepy place.

Maybe tonight, when no one can witness our trespass. It was nighttime in my dream, after all.

Chapter 34 Qrodin

Qrodin's business dealings with the mayor are nearly done. He and Bell have almost finished cataloging all the adjacent fields, orchards, and farmland that are still available for sale. He'll tell anyone willing to work the land that a fair price will be found here, especially if they mention Quentin Browning's name. He will have workers sent over to tend the remainder.

His notebook is open before him. On one page is a list of the properties he purchased, some of which he'll sell or lease. On the other is a list of necessary supplies. Anything that can't be bought here can be brought by the workers. He's looking forward to Cranwood's future as a neighboring fresh food supplier for Riversmeet and Craguesport. He's also making arrangements to have Cranwood added to the shipping routes.

He closes his notebook and rests his arms on the table.

Qat still hasn't joined them. Bell is very quiet as she carries the hot pie to the table. Her smile is big, but her eyes are sad.

A few minutes later, Qrodin is relieved when Qat finally appears.

"You are not going to believe the dream I had!" Qat says as ae sits down. A frown forms between aer brows when ae sees the evenly sliced bread arranged in a basket. Bell usually breaks pieces off for each person. As their last day in Cranwood, she'd taken great care to make today special. "I'm sorry I'm late, Bell. I screwed up big time, but I think you're gonna love what I'm about to tell you!"

Qrodin listens with growing trepidation as Qat tells them of aer dream. They're supposed to leave tomorrow. They don't have time for treasure hunting. But if that treasure is...Qrodin's pulse speeds up. "Can you describe the items you saw?"

"It wasn't the normal stuff, exactly. I mean, there were jewels, of course, but I also saw statues of crushing clams, sharks, and merkama."

Qrodin masks his reaction. He doesn't want anyone to know how interested he is, especially Qat. If Qrodin doesn't overplay his hand, Qat will want to investigate to see if the hoard exists. "Mmm." Qrodin smiles at Kasaandra. "Did I see you braiding bread this morning?"

When the meal is finally over, Qat suggests they do just that. Of course, ae does. Had Qrodin not predicted this?

Akin gets Qat's attention with a whistle and signs.

Llani speaks for him. "Akin asks why you think your dream is real."

Qat shrugs. "It's happened before."

As children, Qat had always claimed to have dreams about places. Sometimes, they discovered those places within a few hours or days. Sometimes, it was months or even years. Akin whistles again. When he's finished signing, Qrodin frowns. Akin probably wants to go. He hasn't been this animated since they met. That's good.

Bell says, "Me too. I really wanna go." She turns to Qrodin. "What do you think?"

"What about the creepy vibe?" he reminds her.

"If Qat says it's safe, I'm good."

Qat flinches as though ae's been slapped. By a gesture of trust. Has no one ever put their trust in Qat? Qrodin reviews his actions since their reunion. He's ashamed that he hasn't shown aer any trust, either. Quite the opposite. What must've Qat's life been like?

Qrodin's fake resolve not to join the treasure hunt topples in the face of that revelation. "Why not?" he relents with a heavy sigh. "We're not leaving until morning, after all."

Once the table has been cleared and the food put away, they grab some supplies and gather near the edge of the darkened patch surrounding the abandoned building. The inner keep is always empty this time of day, so they don't worry about being interrupted.

They go around to the back of the monument and wait while Qat—the only one willing to brave the sickness of the blackened area—readies a ladder Akin found and starts climbing. There's no use suffering whatever curse or anomaly triggers the uneasiness and nausea unless they receive confirmation that a hole in the top validates Qat's dream.

Qrodin is confident the hole will be there.

Qat climbs up two rungs and looks back. "Hey. You only get that feeling when you're touching the ground." Ae then climbs quickly. At the top, aer face breaks into a large smile. "It's here. I'm gonna go check it out." Qat disappears onto the roof before the last word is said.

"Perhaps we should run across," Llani says. "We will be unaffected when both feet are suspended above ground." She gracefully lopes across the clearing in less than ten strides and is up the ladder before the rest can move.

Bell is the first to follow. She scrunches her face in concentration and rocks forward and back a few times as though to gain momentum, then rushes forward. When she reaches the ladder, her face is green, and she's shaking.

Akin and Kasaandra go next, but only Akin makes it to the ladder. Kasaandra doesn't get any further than she did on the first day they were here.

"Kasaandra, are you okay?" Qat won't wait for them, and Qrodin's anxious to get inside quickly.

"Give me a minute," Kasaandra says. She has the rope they'll be using to drop down inside. In hindsight, they should have given it to Llani.

"Where'd Qat go?" Bell says from above.

"I do believe ae went ahead."

Qrodin groans at Llani's answer. Akin has already joined Llani and Bell at the top.

Bell cups her hands to her mouth and calls out, "Kasaandra. Just run! It's easier! Trust me!"

"I can carry you if you wish," Qrodin says as he draws near. A sickening dread fills his body as he waits for her answer. He nearly turns back, but the despair on Kasaandra's face stops him. He reaches toward her, intending only to comfort her, but she flinches back.

"Over my dead body."

"Then let me take the rope. It doesn't look very roomy up there. Take all the time you need."

Kasaandra hands over the rope. He takes it and runs to the ladder, trusting Llani was right. She was. Running helps. Qrodin hands the rope to Akin when he reaches the top. Kasaandra still hasn't moved.

Qrodin closes his eyes. As he'd done with the manticore, he shrinks the space between him and Kasaandra. He imagines that he *is* Kasaandra. He feels the terror that has her rooted to the ground. *Soothe* vibrates through his entire body. Then, he switches to *Inspire*, imagining himself running, legs pumping high with each step.

He hears her grunt when she reaches the ladder, and he opens his eyes. Only then does he realize that it shouldn't have worked. When they were testing the reasacobilas for magic, she had confided in him that her arm bands are supposed to prevent psychic manipulation. Her father taught her how to keep them charged. If it weren't for her protection, he wouldn't say anything. "Kasaandra, you need to charge your armbands."

Her eyes narrow in displeasure, but she nods a quick acknowledgment.

The rope is tied to the center spire, and Llani is inside the monument.

Bell frowns. "There's no way I can climb down that rope. My arms aren't strong enough."

Akin pulls her away from the edge and puts up a finger for her to wait. He pulls up the rope and ties it around her like a harness. They help lower her down, and at the bottom, she unties herself. Kasaandra goes next. With a quick jump, she arrows straight down. The rope goes taut as she slides to the bottom, and when she's down, Akin motions for Qrodin to go.

Qrodin doesn't argue, but he does pause when he looks down. His hands start to sweat. He hates heights. How had Qat jumped down without the rope? How is he going to get over the edge without falling?

He glances over at the ladder, wishing he could use it, but the floor inside is lower than ground level. The ladder's not tall enough.

Akin motions for Qrodin to sit opposite the rope on the hole's edge. When he does, Akin sits next to him and shows him how to thread the rope between his feet, then demonstrates using it like a brake. He gestures clearly with a few self-explanatory signs and accompanying motions: *Lean back. Release. Brake. Release. Brake.* Then he points to Qrodin, his eyes, himself, and finally, down into the hole.

Qrodin nods, thankful Akin is willing to go first, but worried about how long they're taking. There's no way that Qat waited this long for them. Even the others have disappeared from the room below. Qrodin's hands are now shaking, and sweat dots his upper lip.

Akin takes hold of the rope, clamps his feet around it, and pulls himself over the edge. He stands up on the clamped rope, and his head and shoulders are still clear of the hole. He leans back, slides his feet a short distance, then stops. When he leans back again, his hands slide down. Then his feet. Then his hands. He repeats this a few more times until he's at the bottom.

"Qrow!"

He looks down. Bell is back in the room below.

"We can't find Qat. It's just like ae told us, but at the end of the room, there's a door and a long tunnel. Qat went ahead."

Qrodin closes his eyes. He doesn't feel anything from Qat. He takes a deep breath and *Soothes* himself. Then he grabs the rope tightly, winds his feet around it like Akin had shown him, and pulls hard, testing the brake. It holds. He does it three more times before he's convinced it will hold him.

He pulls himself off the ledge and stands up as Akin had done. He doesn't look down, staring instead at the steeple where the rope is tied.

It's fine until he leans back. His legs shoot forward, and he clamps the rope tightly to his chest until he stops swinging. He loosens the brake, but the rope slips free of his feet. Qrodin's hands slip about a foot before he catches himself.

With his heart in his throat, he kicks wildly for the rope.

"You got this, Qrow!" Bell shouts, clearly nervous.

His hands burn, and his arms cramp from holding so tight. When he finally gets the rope braked between his feet, he takes another deep breath. Fuck. Fuck. Fuck. He does not miss this part of chasing after Qat. After a moment, he lowers first one hand, then the other.

"Akin says it's easier to loosen your hands and let them slide."

Yeah, well. Akin's done this before. Qrodin may be strong, but he wields a pen all day, not a sword. His hands aren't as strong as this task requires.

He loosens his feet again slightly, tracking the slide of the rope between them. But he brakes after only a foot or so. He clutches the rope close to his chest. He's supposed to lean back. Yeah, right. His hand sweat has soaked the rope, so he may not have a choice about sliding down.

His stomach muscles are trembling. He can't hold himself at this awkward angle for much longer.

"Slide your feet more."

He does, and his body straightens toward the floor, easing the tension in his stomach as he brakes. He stands up tall to give his arms a bit of a rest.

"You're doing great!"

He repeats Akin's instructions in his head. *Lean back, release, brake.* He does his best. First his hands, then his feet. He probably looks like an inchworm, but he can't help it. He only goes about a foot at a time.

By the time he reaches the bottom, there isn't a part of him that isn't cramped and shaking with the effort of not falling.

"You did it!" Bell puts her hand up for a high-five. The childish gesture should have felt condescending, but seeing her evident pride, it doesn't. He slaps her hand.

"Now, where's that tunnel?" he says, trying to hide how much he's still trembling from that climb.

He takes a moment to quickly scan the room and get his bearings. Tall statue, detritus littering the floor, and Bell motioning him to follow her.

"Here!" she says. "I know you said that the creepy vibe was only a warding spell to keep everyone out, but I really hated crossing it. It smelled bad."

It takes a moment for Qrodin to realize she's talking about the blackened soil surrounding the monument. Bell's frown says it took everything she had to cross it. Is she trying to distract him? Like when you tell someone about your fears when you see they're afraid?

"Do you feel unwell?" he asks her, remembering the dread he'd felt while he waited for Kasaandra to hand him the rope.

"Don't worry. I'm okay now."

There's an open steel door in the floor.

"Of course there's a secret room like in Qat's dream place," Bell says as she starts down the steps.

Qrodin follows Bell, ducking at the last second to keep from hitting his head. He doesn't feel the cold resistance Qat described. At the bottom, they walk through a hall to a doorway where Llani is motioning them to go through.

The first chest he sees is empty. Llani notices him staring. "They are all empty," she says.

Qat won't have liked that, but Qrodin's not surprised. When they were children, he sometimes wondered if Qat's visions were from the past or present. "Where's Qat?" Qrodin asks.

Llani points to a door at the end of the room, standing open. "I assume ae has gone to scout ahead. Kasaandra went after aem. She told me to wait here for you."

Qrodin doesn't waste more time checking out the chambers and follows where Llani had gestured.

"You think Qat dreamt all that, too?" Bell points down the long hall.

"Ae didn't mention that part, so probably not," Qrodin says. "I hope we can find aem."

Bell pats his hand. "I'm sure ae's fine."

The small reassurance is surprisingly effective. His heart rate slows perceptibly. There's no telling how far Qat's already gone. Descending the rope had taken him a long time, so Qat had plenty of time to get in trouble.

Qrodin leads the way into the dark corridor with Akin at his elbow and Llani and Bell right behind.

The tunnel is almost perfectly round, with rough dirt and stone walls. The floor is dotted with loose rocks, making for an uneven floor. There is only one set of footprints, small and close together. Kasaandra's. Where are Qat's footprints? The walls are nearly two arm-spans wide, and the ceiling is almost as tall. Where did Qat get torches? There's a lit one near the corridor entrance and another one far ahead.

"Llani. I need my bow," Bell says before they get far. "And torches."

Good idea. Bell will be nearly blind otherwise, although the rest of them should be fine. Most non-danaash species see well in the dark. Considering that hablises traditionally lived underground, he's surprised they never adapted. The torches ahead are spaced too far apart for them to help her see in the dark spaces in between. They're more like beacons than illumination.

Llani hands them each a torch from her bag of everything. Qrodin doesn't wait before lighting his. Akin joins him, and they set off at a quick pace. The ukulu's a fast walker and is used to hiking long distances. Plus, he's an experienced fighter. Qrodin couldn't ask for a better partner for this task. Because following Qat into one of aer dreams *is* a task. Although Qrodin won't admit it to anyone, it's one he's missed since Qat's been gone. Qat was fearless, and their adventures were always memorable.

"Why are you going so fast?" Bell calls from behind.

Qrodin feels a twinge of anxiety. "Qat has a habit of either finding or causing mischief."

"Don't feel like you need to wait for me."

He hadn't felt comfortable leaving her behind, but with her permission, Qrodin picks up the pace. Akin keeps up with him.

They catch up to Kasaandra in a couple of minutes. She stops and turns as they join her.

"Kasaandra, any sign of Qat?" Qrow asks.

She shakes her head. "The torches are getting further apart." She points to one up ahead. "I think ae's running out."

Llani is slightly out of breath as she comes up behind them. Her ears twitch forward. "Be silent. I hear something."

Kasaandra nods to something behind them. "That's Bell."

"No. It is musical."

"Like an instrument?" he asks.

"Unlikely."

Without warning, dread churns in Qrodin's stomach, and a tug of awareness pulls at his consciousness. "Qat's in trouble! We need to hurry!"

"Wait!" Llani grabs his arm. "I was going to wait until we left town before trying this. Move aside, please, and don't be alarmed."

At her words, Qrodin moves closer to the wall, but keeps his attention on the first tangible link to Qat since ae landed in that skiff. Qrodin doesn't have time for one of her oopsie spells. Unease swells within him, and Qrodin knows he's feeling Qat's emotions. "Hurry. Qat may need all the help we can give." He looks past Kasaandra, trying to find any sign of Qat.

Whatever Llani's doing, he doesn't feel like waiting. He takes a few steps forward, but ahead of him, Kasaandra's face drops open in shock, and her eyes track upward. When Qrodin hears the unmistakable sound of padded feet and nails on stone, he turns back and stops cold. The hairs rise on the back of his head.

A black wolf towers over them, withers as high as Akin's shoulders, while its head nearly reaches the tunnel's ceiling. Llani's turquoise eyes are the only reassuring thing about it. The wolf takes a second to sniff them. Her fur nearly blends into the dark tunnel as she passes them.

A shiver passes through him. Llani can turn into a dire wolf? Damn. He wishes he'd watched her transformation, but there's no time to bemoan that now. They set out again, but Llani is in the lead this time.

"If you see or hear anything…" Qrodin leaves the rest unsaid.

Llani moves swiftly away, her tail and nose down and ears forward.

"That was so awesome!" Bell says.

Qrodin wonders how Qat will react to a dire wolf. He hopes ae doesn't hurt Llani when she catches up to aem.

Several or more minutes pass before they hear Llani's howl.

Chapter 35 Qat

I am venturing beyond my dream and have no idea what to expect.

There are no turns along the way, only a long, straight path from what I can see. Whenever a torch is but a flicker behind me, I place a new one and light another. I wouldn't bother, but I want them to know which direction I take in case there are other tunnels. As it has several times before, the sloped floor turns into flights of descending stairs, but so far, no other rooms or tunnels have branched off.

There are plenty of sconces. From the spacing, a torch could be placed every five bandis if I had enough. But I don't.

The lower I descend, the wetter and colder it gets. And the more it smells like mildew. Moss grows on the sides of the walls, and the stones at my feet are slightly damp.

I'm curious about who built this tunnel and why they felt it necessary to have a back entrance to a treasure room. Scrape marks indicated that someone had used it at some point to get something heavy out through the tunnel, but they've long since been worn away. I wonder if there will be any treasure at the end of this. I hope so, or I'm wasting a lot of time underground.

As far as I've walked, I must now be at or below the river. Why would there be a tunnel going under the river?

I wish I'd paid attention when Bell and Qrow talked about what's on the other side.

When the time comes to place another torch, I stop. I'll only have one left when I do. Should I keep going or not?

I place the torch and light my last one, thankful that almost all the old torches could still be lit, then move forward into the dark. With my keen eyesight, I can see far enough ahead that I'll have plenty of warning if anything's amiss.

A strange, somewhat musical sound echoes up ahead. My instincts are telling me there's nothing to worry about, so I continue.

There's a small pile of stones and dirt up ahead where part of the wall came down. A round hole where the rocks had been pushed out starts about five or six hands above the floor and is no more than a bandi in diameter. The sound is coming from there. It's not tall enough to stand up straight, and I don't feel like crawling to investigate it, but the sound intrigues me. What could be making it?

I stick my head into the opening to hear it better. Frogs? Or birds? It has a croaky sound, but it's more of a trill than a true croak.

Either way, I don't need to check out frogs. I've seen more than my share living near the water for my entire life. I pass three more tunnels, all of which have the same croaking trill coming from them.

I haven't gone down any stairs for some time now. I'm positive that I'm below the river. Occasionally, when the croaking trill quiets, I feel, more than hear, the melody of water over rock.

Eventually, I look back, and the last torch is a blinking flicker. I wonder if any of them followed me. I'm guessing Kasaandra and Akin did. Llani isn't the type to rush into danger. Qrow probably stayed back with her and Bell to inspect the treasure room. He wasn't too keen to come tonight.

Should I keep going or stop and wait?

I squint into the tunnel ahead. No sign of stairs going up as far as I can see. I suppose there wouldn't be if I'm only halfway across the river. I'll need more torches if the tunnel branches off.

As damp as it is down here, my throat is dry, and I'm thirsty.

Stay? Go back?

I pull out my pouch of gaming dice and grab one at random. Odds, I stay; evens, I go back.

The ten-sided die stops on eight. Go back. Perhaps the others will have more torches.

It's unlikely I can convince everyone to stick around for another day, so tonight will be the only time I can come back. Hopefully, I can get to the end of this mystery tunnel.

I place my torch in the nearest sconce, then start toward the blinking light behind me.

If The Qrow were here, he'd be lecturing me about my thoughtlessness and about going ahead without them. Or he'd give me that look. The one he gives me when I screw something up. Like that one time I tried to make coffee and ruined most of the bag of coffee beans. He's all polite or businesslike with everyone else, but with me, he glowers like I'm some out-of-control kid. It's annoying.

My stomach growls loudly. It's the loudest sound I've made since entering the tunnel. Even placing the torches inside the sconces has been done quietly. I can't believe how loud it was; I ate an hour or so ago.

Thinking about the noise makes me nervous. I can hear Rogen now, '*You never know what might be lurking in the shadows.*' Well, it's all shadow down here.

I distract myself with thoughts of food, something I always did on the *Raven Scream* after weeks and months of eating ship gruel. Now that we're in a town with a proper oven, Bell's been making lots of bread, trying out her different starters. I could eat it plain. Or with butter.

I feel a prick in my neck, more like a tickle than anything.

I pick up my pace, just in case those aren't frogs down those tunnels. Could it be some giant rodent? Don't they burrow? And don't they have large teeth and claws?

I trip over something. A rock, probably. My breath leaves me in a rush, but I catch myself against the wall with the hand holding my dice bag. It falls, but I catch it before it hits the ground.

Bollocks, that would have been loud.

I'm in front of one of the round tunnels. The croaking sounds closer than it was when I passed by earlier.

Something small falls. Then more. They tumble, making a loud clattering noise as they skip along the tunnel.

My dice! I must've caught the pouch upside down.

The croaking stops.

Bollocks! I'm an idiot.

The single little tickle changes. Now there are a dozen sensations.

I pick my way carefully along, trying to find my dice. They're my lucky dice. And the tingling is still more of a tickle. I'm not in any *real* danger.

I may be able to see a lot better in the dark than most, but in complete darkness, my dice look like all the other rocks on the floor.

Before I can take the three steps to reach the eight-sided one ahead of me, the tingling in my neck becomes a prickly stab.

Something's coming.

I forget the dice and pull out my dagger.

When I look back, I can't see anyone or anything, but I can feel it. One stab almost directly behind me. I turn, place my back close to the wall, and crab my way as quickly as I dare toward the light. It's no larger to me than a star and looks nearly as far. I glance back every few seconds, but I don't see anything. Whatever it is, it's staying beyond my field of vision.

I hear a brush of sound, like feathers stroking air, coming from my left, back toward the small opening in the wall of the tunnel.

I stop and close my eyes to focus on my hearing, hoping I imagined it.

The sensation pricks me again. Finally, I hear it—about head-high to my left, twenty or so bandis back. I'm not alone. I already knew I wasn't, but that doesn't mean I'm going to be reckless.

More reckless.

I open my eyes and search for a moving shadow. Anything that will tell me what or how big it is. Whatever it is, it had to have come out of one of the intersecting passages, so it should be smaller than me, right? How many of those openings have I passed on the way back?

I don't remember.

My danger sense has narrowed to one hot, piercing point to my left.

Kraken's teeth! What's in here with me?

It feels like an hour has passed since I heard the noise, but it can only be seconds. Whatever it is, it hasn't made a move to attack, but I feel it following me, just out of sight. How is that possible? I should see something. A shape, at the very least. However, it must stop when I stop, because I would see movement. Wouldn't I?

Unless it's invisible. Like the witches were before Llani lit them up with green flames.

Okay, Qat. Stop. What is wrong with you tonight? What has got you so jumpy? You've been in these types of situations before. Lots of times.

The light is getting nearer. I can make out the color of individual stones about fifty bandis ahead, and I estimate the torch is about another twenty to thirty bandis farther. I sigh in relief.

I wonder what made those passages. The wall had been pushed from the other side rather than from the main tunnel. At least a few of them were. I've heard of giant burrowing mammals that make tunnels. Someone told me once that the creatures look like blind beavers. Some frogs do, too, and those *were* frogs singing away back there. Weren't they?

But frogs don't get big enough to tunnel that large. I've lived on the water my whole life. I'd know if they did.

What lives with—or eats—frogs and burrows in the ground in tunnels? Snakes do, but snakes aren't that big, either. Are they? I've heard of giant water snakes that live deep in the ocean, but we're not underwater.

Well. We probably *are* underwater, but we're not *in* it.

My heart almost stops when I remember what Kasaandra said happened to her brother. That giant spiders came in through tunnels like the ones I've been passing and took him in the middle of the night. Why she doesn't stomp every spider inside the Home Dome is a mystery to me. I would if they killed *my* brother.

It takes me a second to realize that I have one.

A brother. Qrow.

Would I stomp them if they killed Qrow? No time to think about the answer. Not if I have a giant spider following me. They would be stealthy enough to blend into the rocks. And they would have to be big enough to keep up with me. My danger sense doesn't tingle for tiny spiders. Sometimes, I wish it would.

I also wish I'd kept a torch. Most creepy crawlies are afraid of fire.

The anticipation is killing me. My whole body is tense, and I force it to relax. Now my neck feels like it's crawling with biting spiders, and I want to swat at it.

There must be more than one thing down here with me to get my danger sense going like this, but I hear absolutely nothing.

I glance back the way I've come, but whatever it is, it's staying hidden.

Now that I can see where I'm going more clearly, I pick up the pace.

A stab in my neck makes me stop and turn.

There's nothing there.

That makes no sense!

I feel something pass over the top of me. Somehow, it doesn't exactly move *into* the light, but around it.

Then it drops right in front of me.

A shadowy figure with about a dozen legs. Kraken's teeth! It *is* a spider. But no. The body is wrong. Why is it standing there? The body looks like a frog with a giant frog mouth, sitting back on its frog butt. Two legs fold back. But the others are splayed out to its side. Like a spider. What the fuck is it? A frog or a spider? It's only about Kasaandra's height, but if it stood up on its froggy legs, it would be taller than me. With a head and mouth wider than my shoulders, it could swallow half of me if it tried.

Its throat swells, and it starts...humming?

Crooning. The creature is crooning.

This is the creature that's been making those sounds. I'd bet my blades on it. But this time, it's different. More hypnotic. Like it's trying to lure me in.

Ha! I don't think so, buddy. The back of my neck is jangling a warning refrain in response. More like screaming, *Get out!*

The crooning continues.

There's no way you're going to fool me!

In one practiced move, I toss my dagger to my right hand and uncoil the length of leather at my waist. My whip comes to life with a *snap* on the leg nearest me. I manage to move around the beast when it backs away, but it's quicker than I thought it'd be. It leaps, and I dive out of the way, but its mouth opens wide and catches my right leg. Teeth puncture down to the bone just above the knee.

Kraken's claws, that hurts! Frogs have *teeth*?

No, but spiders have fangs!

I wrench my knee up, pulling its fangs free in the process.

My dagger is usually all I need, but I don't have the reach to stay safe. And my whip isn't compelling enough to keep it away. I'm going to need something more.

Its giant mouth gapes open. I dive to the side as its tongue splats against the wall behind me. Oh gross!

I back up until the torch is right behind me. I'm breathing heavily now, and the thick, moist air is heavy with the smell of acrid slime.

With my back to the light, I'm nothing but a black shadow to it. Hopefully, it won't be able to anticipate my movements.

But I can see it now.

It's a frog with four spider legs protruding from each side. One large and several small spider eyes are in the middle of its forehead, while bulging, rotating frog eyes are spaced wide to each side.

What the fuck?

It evades my jab to its large center eye and shoots its tongue back at me.

I'm not as fast this time, and it splats into my hair, yanking some out as it retreats. I'm pulled off balance and use the momentum to thrust my dagger forward. The point goes through its right frog eye and pokes out the back of its head. I use both hands to twist it and slice through bone and tissue.

It drops to the ground.

"That's right! That's what you get for"—I wipe the slimy eye goop on one of its hairy spider legs—"messing with me. What are you, anyway?"

I pick up my whip, coil and stash it, and grab the torch off the wall. When I turn to go back toward the exit, reflective red eyes blink at me.

Beyond the torchlight, the most enormous wolf I've ever seen is running straight at me. But my danger sense is still.

It pads to a silent stop in front of me and howls.

Chapter 36 Qrodin

Qrodin picks up the pace. Almost another minute passes before a torch comes toward them in the distance. His relief is profound.

And familiar.

Qrodin recognizes the feeling even though it's been two decades since it was an almost daily occurrence.

When he can make out Qat with Llani-as-wolf loping behind, Qrodin finally stops so he can regain his composure. Akin slows but continues toward them.

Of course, they're both safe. Qat always is.

Immediately following his relief, Qrodin's anger returns. Until he realizes that Qat is limping.

"You're hurt," he can't help the angry tone.

"Sorry I'm not dead?"

"Don't be ridiculous. Were you in danger or just clumsy?" Qat is never clumsy.

"I was attacked. We may still be in danger, so stop your yammering, and let's go."

They turn back and continue moving at Qat's limping pace, with Llani bringing up the rear. As they go, her giant head and turquoise eyes loom over Qat's shoulder.

"What happened?" Qrodin finally asks.

"I was attacked."

"You already said that. By whom?"

"You mean by *what*. A freaky giant frog with spider legs. And fangs. I wish it was in my dream, so I knew what to expect. They can crawl on the ceiling. Oh, and their singing? If you hear it, I suggest you run."

"Qat! You're safe!"

In the distance, Kasaandra stops and bends to catch her breath, but Bell drops her torch and runs toward them.

"Oh shit! Bell's with you?" Qat whispers. "I was hoping she hadn't come down here."

"Not even the curse around this place could keep her away," Qrodin replies, also in a whisper.

"We've got to get her out of here. Those frog things are big enough to swallow her whole."

Qrodin's never heard of such a thing. He wouldn't believe it now but for the excitement in Qat's voice. Excitement. Not fear. Never fear.

"How do you know there are more?" he asks to be thorough.

"I heard them. I passed four of their tunnels. There are dozens, maybe even hundreds, of those croaking things. I killed one of them back there, but the others could have heard us. Llani's howl was loud."

The wolf's head lowers, and Llani nuzzles Qat's shoulder.

"Sorry, beautiful, but it was."

Qat grunts in pain when Bell runs up and hugs aem around the legs.

"Oh! Sorry, Qat. You're hurt!"

"I'll be okay, but I want you to stay near the front on the way back, you hear me? You're going to need to go fast."

Kasaandra *harrumphs* as she joins them, still breathing hard.

"I want to stay back here with you. Oh!" Bell backs away when Llani slips into the light.

"Don't be afraid. It's Llani," Qat says.

"Oh. I know. I saw her change. But how did you know?"

"I'd recognize those eyes anywhere."

"Oh." The nervousness on Bell's face recedes as quickly as it appeared. Qrodin wonders if she's afraid of dogs and wolves. "Llani, you make a pretty wolfie. I'm going to call you Blackberry! Hey! Maybe I can ride on your back!"

"Maybe later." Qat gives Bell a light nudge to get her on her way. "Right now, we need to get out of here. Now, get up there with Kasaandra. And Bell, if you hear me whistle, I want you to turn around and spray the tunnel behind me with those exploding arrow things you did with the sisters. Think you can do that?"

"Sure thing, but they don't explode. They just splinter into a million pieces. Just remember to duck when I yell, *'Don't look now!'*" She scurries up to Kasaandra, pulls an arrow out of her quiver, and notches her bow, ready to draw the string at a second's notice.

"Good. Oh, and Bell? Keep an eye on the ceiling, too."

"Sure thing. What am I looking for?"

"Think of giant green frogs with a bunch of spider legs."

"Oh, I love frogs! They're so cute!"

"These aren't," Qat says quietly, too low for Bell's ears.

Qrodin does a quick inventory of his things. He'd left the staff back at the inn. Hadn't even thought of carrying it on him. All he has is a torch and his ability to influence the mind. Controlling heated boardroom discussions has not prepared him for fighting multiple frog-spider things.

After tonight, he's going to start carrying the flute everywhere he goes.

They take off again. This time, Kasaandra and Bell are in the lead.

Less than a minute later, Qrodin's stomach clenches, and he fears that Qat's prediction has come true.

"They're here," Qat mutters, and Llani's deep growl confirms it.

It's going to be a tight fit in this corridor.

"Heads up!" Qat warns as two shadows pass silently over the top of them. The third leaps at Qat.

Qrodin wouldn't have known they were there if Qat hadn't said something.

Bell shoots her arrow at the same time Kasaandra drops the torches to reach for her axe. The creatures split up, and the arrow ricochets off the ceiling between them before falling uselessly to the ground.

Qrodin tries to read one of the creature's feelings to understand what it's responding to. They don't like the torches, but he can't get a handle on whether it's the light or the fire they're frightened of.

He hears Llani's wolf attack and wishes he knew what was going on behind him, but he doesn't want to take his eyes off the two creatures in front of him. He tries to *Coax* them with fear and doubt. Anything that will keep them from getting to Bell.

Akin sends a bolt of light toward each of them, just like he had at the manticore. Qrodin cringes, reacting to the light. His scar pulls and burns at the reminder of the battle with the sisters. He recovers swiftly. He can't lose his head now.

One of Akin's strikes hits, and the creature falls between Akin and the girls. Akin swings his torch at it, but it avoids the flame by rearing up on its hind legs and backing into Kasaandra. The dwarf stumbles back, nearly falling, and almost drops her axe.

Bell's arrow pierces its chest. The creature drops down with its mouth open, and a long, white tongue launches Bell's way, then goes limp. The sticky appendage misses her as the creature lands hard and doesn't move. Bell's arrow had finished it off.

The other spider goes after Kasaandra. Its tongue wraps around the hand holding her axe, disarming her and pulling her off her feet. With a stumble, Kasaandra is dragged headfirst into the giant frog's mouth. Only her legs and feet are visible when its large lips close around her.

Akin attacks it first with a fist, then holds a torch to its side. The creature shrieks and vomits her out. She's drenched in bile and cursing in Dwarven. The stench nearly makes Qrodin wretch. The hair on its spider legs combusts, spreading the flames to the rest of its body until the long legs curl toward its distended belly and become fuel for the fire. Coarse hair along its back curls, and its skin smokes, shrivels, and shrinks, curling into a blazing ball of scorched toad.

No wonder they're afraid of the torches.

Those two threats gone, Qrodin turns back to Qat and Llani. The wolf is chomping on spider legs but looks up and growls fiercely. The ruff on her back stands straight up.

"More are coming!" Qrodin warns the others. "Use fire if you have it."

Qat holsters aer dagger and grabs a discarded torch from the ground. Ae stands at the ready with aer whip in one hand and a torch in the other, watching the tunnel. "Let 'em rip, Bell!"

"Don't look now!" Bell yells. Qrodin and Akin duck as splintered arrows fly over their heads.

"I see at least four of them!" Qrodin yells. "Two on the ceiling, two below!"

Qat runs forward. Aer whip sings out at the one in front, the leather wrapping itself around several of the creature's legs. Qat pulls hard but is yanked into the air by aer whip. Ae flips and swings the torch, but the momentum pulls aem close to a wide-open mouth. The creature bites down on Qat's right shoulder, forcing aem to drop the torch. Aer right arm is pinned to aer side while half of aer head and a quarter of aer upper body are inside the creature's mouth.

"Qat!" Two crawlies go overhead as Qrodin runs to his twin. He's barely aware of Llani's growling fight with a fourth one. He ignores the flash of light and searing heat behind him in his attempt to get at his twin. "Hang on, Qat!" He brings his torch down on the back of the frog's neck with both hands. The moist skin fizzes and steams but doesn't ignite. He slides the torch toward a patch of hair low on its back, but it's not enough.

Qrodin hears Kasaandra's battle laugh as Akin thrusts a torch into the hairy spider legs. The creature tries to retreat but falls to the ground as its legs curl under it, and its belly finally burns.

Qat pushes the now-slack mouth open and falls out, rolling and standing up in one smooth move, as if ae hadn't nearly been devoured. And burned.

Llani's growl comes seconds before she lunges forward. More are coming. The wolf launches herself at the closest one as it tries to go overhead. She latches onto its throat and shakes it until it slumps forward.

Kasaandra runs toward Llani and swings for one of the critters as it scurries around the wolf. The spider-frog jumps from the wall, over Kasaandra's head, and lands between her and Qrodin. The dwarf's axe buries itself into the stone wall where the spider had been a second before.

Qat grabs aer torch off the ground and waits for another to attack as it speeds toward aem. As soon as it opens its mouth, Qat tosses the torch inside. The creature stops mid-hop and gulps. Then, its mouth opens, and smoke emerges. I touch the torch to its legs, moving quickly to the other side to light those. Finally, its hairy legs curl, and it collapses into a charred pile. The smell is sharp and acrid, and Qrodin can't wait to leave.

An arrow zings by, but Qrodin can't find its target until it scurries over him, heading toward Bell. The creature is too fast for him to catch. Qrodin uses *Terror*, burrowing his thoughts into the tiny spider mind. It croaks in response, and Qrodin can feel the frog's melody drowning out his thoughts.

It's so soft, like a warm current wrapping around him. His body relaxes in response.

The crooning spider frog leaps from the ceiling, arcing gracefully through space and time and—

"Awe. You're cute—" Bell's comment is cut short as the frog's tongue springs forward and then back, pulling Bell with it. The hablis disappears into the creature's mouth, and it lands right where she'd been standing. Her bow clatters to the ground.

No!

Bell's muffled, agonized scream nearly brings Qrodin to his knees. The creature had managed to charm him until it stopped crooning to swallow Bell. A white bolt explodes into the frog behind its front foreleg. The frog's belly is shuddering with Bell's struggles to free herself, even as the creature hops past them back toward the direction it came. Qrodin starts running. There's no telling how acidic its stomach acid is or how long Bell can last before she's digested. Or before she suffocates.

Qrodin runs faster.

"No!" Qat screams as the frog comes abreast of aem. Qrodin's twin thrusts a torch into the frog's green face. It backs away from the flame, climbs the wall to the ceiling, and over Qat, then drops and hops down the hall.

Qat runs after it—after Bell.

Qrodin can hear Llani and Kasaandra fighting again and hopes this ends soon.

Akin passes Qrodin. Two lights flash from his hands toward the ceiling—fiery orange this time. The heat from the flames scorches Qrodin's lungs. Roasted toad and singed hair assault him from all sides as two creatures drop before him, already blistering from fire. He jumps back, then around them. He hadn't seen them up there.

He can't believe he's running toward more of them.

"Bell!" Qrodin yells as he chases the leaping frog. But unlike the creature, he can neither jump over nor climb up the walls around the charred monstrous bodies littering the hall.

He stops running. He'll never catch it. He can barely see it past their torches. Instead, Qrodin plants himself in the creature's mind. He sends harsh and clashing chords. But this time, Qrodin does what he never thought he would. He twists the beast's crooning melody into the horrifying cadence and hatred of the Twisted Sisters' words. He layers in the terrified croaks of its burning companions. He doesn't stop until it stumbles on its next leap and falls, skidding and tumbling into the wall.

The cacophony in his head stops, and Qrodin nearly collapses in relief. He uses the wall to steady himself, then hurries toward the fallen frog. Its belly is no longer moving.

Bell is no longer fighting.

Qat reaches it and wrenches its mouth open, using a foot for leverage and bearing down on the lower jaw. Akin joins Qat and uses his considerable strength to stretch the mouth wide.

Qat reaches in. "Bell!" Ae pulls the hablis out by one foot, then the other. Qrodin finally reaches them as Bell's head clears the frog's mouth.

She's not moving.

She's not breathing.

Qat wipes Bell's face and eyes, then clears her mouth of frog acid and slime before starting chest compressions.

The Llani-wolf bounds toward them, swiftly transforming back into her natural self. She kneels beside them and inspects Bell.

"Bell! Are you okay? Oh!" She says when Bell doesn't stir.

"Do something, Llani! Heal her!" Qat urges.

"I don't know if I can. She may already be gone." Llani wrings her hands together.

"She's not! I can feel it. Hurry!" Qat encourages through the compressions.

"But what if I—"

"You can do it! Right now, before more come. Right *now*, Llani." Qat says, only a little more in control than before as ae presses on Bell's chest.

"You can do this, Llani. Bell needs you," Qrodin says, infusing his voice with *Coax*. "Just picture it in your mind and let it flow."

Llani's face clears. She turns to Bell, and her hands hover over Bell's face and chest as Qat sits back to make room for her. Thankfully, green light emerges from Llani's hands instead of the necrotic purple.

When Bell takes a gasping breath, Qrodin lets out his. When she opens her eyes, his legs nearly give out in relief.

"Are they all dead now?" Bell asks when Llani is done. Both she and the elf are trembling. "I really hate spiders." Giant tears tremble in her eyes as if they're too frightened to fall.

Qat releases aer breath in a long, shuddering sigh and sits back on aer heels.

"Qat! What's wrong?" Bell brushes Qat's face with her tiny hand. "It's okay. I'm alright. Look! I'm—Hey! Your face is bleeding. Llani, heal Qat, too."

"I'm fine, Bell. It's *you* we're all worried about," Qat replies with a smile and a slight tremor in aer voice.

Kasaandra finally joins them, Bell's bow in one hand. Her eyes are gleaming brightly, and she smiles. Qrodin can almost feel her excess energy thrumming throughout the tunnel. She frowns at Bell. "Now *you're* laying down on the job? You're almost as useless as the princess, there."

Qrodin can see the concern in Kasaandra's gaze as it roams over Bell. He's unsure if fear is making her gruff or if it's a calculated move to distract Bell, but the hablis narrows her eyes and stands up.

"Are you certain there are no more?" Qrodin asks Kasaandra.

Llani answers. "We dispatched the last of them. Kasaandra is a slow runner."

Qrodin laughs internally at her unintentional parry. It fades at her next words.

"I think we have a reprieve—if only a short one. Let us make haste now that everyone is healed. There may be more beyond the range of my hearing."

"Kasaandra, how are your injuries?" Qrodin asks, remembering that she, too, was nearly swallowed whole.

Kasaandra glares at him.

Llani looks distressed to have forgotten. "Oh, Kasaandra. I—"

"They can wait. Let's get out of here." Kasaandra hands Bell her bow. The hablis's green scarf outfit, which she had had made in Riversmeet, looks even worse than the tunic she wore when Qrodin met her.

Qat wipes more of the frog's stomach slime from Bell's hair and face. "Yeah. Maybe we should drag one back. I think I might be in the mood for frogs' legs later. Maybe some spider kabob? With hot sauce?"

"Tough. All you get is leftover pheasant pie. And I'm not gonna heat it up, so no complaining."

"Okay. I can come back tomorrow for the frog legs."

"Qat," Qrodin growls. "If you come back down by yourself, I'll skewer *you* for dinner."

Chapter 37 Qat

Despite my teasing, I can't stop thinking I almost got Bell killed today. She's taking it well, but her darting glances say she can't wait to get topside. I don't blame her. I feel the same way.

We probably all do.

But I will try to convince them to come with me again tonight. Maybe Kasaandra can help me seal those tunnels. And Akin can be our fireguard. He was amazing and could probably have fought them all single-handedly.

And I thought I was good.

Those things were poisonous, too. Or is it venomous? I can never remember. Every time one bit me, I got weaker. I'm still weak. How much longer can I go without collapsing?

But I'm determined to get to the other end of the tunnel before we leave Cranwood.

I don't relax until we enter the chambered hall and close the hidden door. There's no way I could have outrun them alone. I would have died today had the crew not come after me. That's the second time they saved my life. Third, if you count the witches.

Why did they come after me, anyway? I told them to wait while I scouted ahead, didn't I?

"You're lucky we came when we did, Qat," Qrow says.

"Why did you?" I regret the words as soon as I say them.

Kasaandra motions to Qrow. "That one said you were in danger."

How did *he* know?

We're silent as we navigate the final stairway, leaving the room where I saw the dream treasure. Is the treasure real? Something tells me it is. The emblem on the statue's chest says it is, too. I don't think anyone else noticed it. Even if they had, they have no idea about Truffle, the ring, or the list of artifacts. Could the treasure be the artifacts for sale?

"Please tell me there's another way out of here!" Bell slumps to the ground and stares up at the hole in the ceiling.

I know how she feels. I feel like we've been gone a week.

Llani extends her hand. "Climb on my back. I will take you up."

"What? You're not strong enough to carry me up the rope!"

"I assure you, I am. Akin, you go first and grab Bell when I reach the top."

As Akin climbs, Bell rushes to me and pulls me down. "I'm worried about Qrow. I don't think he'll be able to climb up."

I feel one eyebrow go up in response. "Sure, he can. He's a strong guy."

She presses her lips against my ear. "He's afraid of heights."

I frown at Bell's whispered words. "I wouldn't call that 'heights.' It's barely ten bandis up."

"You should have seen him trying to come down the rope."

Llani nods. "Perhaps there is another way out. After all, this hole is not meant to be the entrance to the monument. Perhaps you can locate another while you are down here. You seem to have a unique talent for it."

Was that a compliment? Coming from Llani, it's hard to tell.

Llani squats down, and Bell puts her arms around Llani's neck. "You better not drop me!"

"Hold on and wrap your legs around my waist. Yes. Like that. Wait. You're choking me. Okay. There." Llani grabs the rope and, without using her legs, climbs hand-over-hand until she reaches the top.

Not even I can do that, and I've been climbing ropes my whole life.

When they reach the top, Akin grabs Bell and hoists her onto the roof.

Kasaandra must have had the same thought Llani had. She's standing atop a column behind the statue, running her hands along the wall. Several other columns of different heights act as stairs to the one she's on. I thought they were there to hold more statues.

"You looking for an exit?"

Kasaandra grunts.

Qrow is standing in front of the statue. He's running his finger along the sea monster on the statue's chest.

Does it mean something to him? Why would it? For a second, I wonder if Qrow knows about Truffle's ring. About the list of rare objects. Qrow's wealthy enough to purchase them, but I've never heard Quentin Browning's name in conjunction with anything illegal.

He looks over at me and narrows his eyes. He pushes on the emblem.

The column Kasaandra's standing on drops fast, revealing an opening to the back of the monument. Kasaandra stumbles backward and rolls out onto the black soil.

Either it's timed, or there's a sensor, because the wall slides back into place as soon as she clears the opening.

"You found it!" Bell calls down.

"I think it has a sensor," I say. "Only one person at a time. I'll wait before going through. See how long it stays open."

Qrow nods at my suggestion before pushing the button. Nearly a minute passes before the door finally slams closed.

Time enough for one person to push the button and walk to the exit.

I nod when it's my turn, and Qrow pushes the button again. Outside, I stand on the ladder's bottom rung and search for a door release while waiting for Qrow. It takes me almost until Qrow exits to find it. That will make it easier to come back tonight.

As exhausted as we are, we all run across the *creepy vibe*. Even Kasaandra. Her battle euphoria is probably to thank for that.

We take a few minutes to wash up before reconvening in the inn's dining room.

Worry, leftover fear, and adrenalin start to fade from everyone's faces. Except for Kasaandra's. I wish I had her energy. I'm still feeling the effects of spider venom.

Even so, I want to go back down, but I can't blurt out the announcement. I have to lead up to it. Perhaps get someone else to suggest it. "How long have you been able to become a wolf, Llani?" I ask instead.

"It was prior to our meeting on the roof."

"What meeting on the roof?" Qrow asks.

"The one where ae pulled a knife on me, and Bell shot aem with her slingshot."

"That was you?" Bell asks.

"What? When did that happen?" Qrow asks abruptly.

Llani answers, "The night we met."

I can't help my response. "So, you *did* know it was me."

"Of course. If you were attempting to disguise yourself, you failed. You sat a few tables away from us at the Lightning Strike, flipping your knife. It was quite obvious you were the same individual, despite your altered appearance."

Ouch! That was harsh.

"Ouch, Llani. That was harsh," Bell says as though I had injected my thoughts straight into her brain. It's happened to me before—mostly with the crew on the *Raven Scream*—but never as often as it does with this group.

As to Llani's reference to that night, I realize I haven't thought about taking her necklace in the last few days. I don't steal from people who are close to me. Before meeting this group, that number included Captain Rogen and Goffin—until Goffin broke that trust and became fair game. Even then, the only thing I tried to steal from Goffin was his life. Did I even take that?

Llani waves a hand to dismiss Bell's comment. "My apologies, Qat. I was merely attempting to answer your question relative to our time as acquaintances."

Does she view us only as acquaintances? Double ouch.

Llani frowns. Perhaps she regrets—

"Retrospectively, it may have been clearer had I said I learned the steps to perform a transformation nineteen years ago next trit'quarter. I have memorized numerous spells and incantations but have yet to perform them."

Yeah. Great.

"I just love Blackberry." Bell looks at Llani. "That's what I named the wolfie. Blackberry. What else have you changed into? Oh! When can I ride Blackberry? Maybe we should get her a saddle. Do you think she'd like one? We can probably get her a pink one. Or a green one. Oh! We should get one the same color as your eyes! How come you never changed into her before?"

No one can resist an excited Bell. Even though her shadowed eyes and still shaking hands say she's anything but fine, her enthusiasm is addictive.

"I was hesitant due to my..." Llani pauses, brushing at some slime on her sleeve.

"Oopsies?"

Llani frowns. "Yes, Kasaandra. If I were incapable of changing back, I was afraid I would be mistaken for an animal and..." She glances at Bell's bow propped in a corner and draws her arms close to her body.

"Shot for supper?" I ask.

"Qat!" Qrow says.

"Precisely," Llani responds.

"Oh, Llani. You're my bestest best buddy and bestest best friend in the whole wide world. I would *never* shoot you."

"You might if you mistook me for..." She looks around.

"For not you?" I finish for her again. It's not like her to be so lost for words.

"Yes. Precisely."

"What was it like? Could you, like, smell *everything*? You were *so* tall! And could you—"

"Bell, would you like me to answer your questions in the order you ask them or in the order of my experience? Either way, I do believe three questions at a time should be the limit."

"Oh. Ha. Any way you want. You don't have to answer any of them if you don't want to."

"Of course I'll answer your questions. I believe I will answer in the order asked. Although I can choose anything I have seen before, this was my first transformation."

She's seen a wolf that big before?

Bell gasps loudly, "You've seen a wolf that big before?"

Did I do it again? Did I inject my thoughts into Bell? No. I'd bet my favorite dagger we were all thinking it.

"Yes. Oh. That was out of order. It's unusual for someone to ride a wolf, even one as large as I—"

"You're not that big," I say.

"I was referring to myself in wolf form."

"Call her Blackberry, so we know when you're talking about wolfie stuff," Bell insists.

"Thank you, Bell. I appreciate the clarity of your suggestion. As to riding Blackberry: I believe it is unusual to ride dire wolves. It would be difficult to find a comfortable saddle, but if I were to have one, I would object to pink. Green would be acceptable, but I prefer one that coordinates with my eyes."

I would have to agree with her. Kasaandra, however, rolls her eyes.

"As for my experience. Well. My somatosensory receptors were—"

"Llani. Remember what I said about big words and stuff?"

Thank you, Bell.

"Of course. Senses. *I* have superior eyesight, but Blackberry is dichromatic." At Bell's glower, Llani reiterates. "That means Blackberry can see in only two colors: in her case, blue and yellow, and any combination of the two. The color spectrum was greatly diminished from my usual—"

"What else?" I ask.

"Blackberry's olfactory senses..." At Kasaandra's huff, she says, "Her smell was...better. As such, I was unfamiliar with the myriad scents Blackberry encountered. As a side note, I would like to expand my repertoire posthaste." She hurried through those last few statements because Bell was scowling at her again.

"Llani," I say. "Could you tell how far those things traveled? I mean, how close did they come to the...?" I nod my head toward the inner keep.

"Initially, I scented them only upon your approach. I must wonder, though, if there are more. And if so, will they follow our scent back to the monument?"

"Is the town in danger?" Bell's eyes dart back and forth from the inner keep to us.

Thank you, Bell. That threat should be enough for me to convince them we need to go back down. "I passed four of the tunnels they were using to access the main one. Something had burrowed through and knocked out the stones along the tunnel. If it was them, and if there's more, and if they follow our scent, the folks here *could* be in danger."

"Frogs can't go through stone," Kasaandra says.

"But what about spiders? Didn't you say spiders got into your mountain?" I hate to remind Kasaandra of her brother's death, but if it gets me back into the tunnel, it'll be worth it.

Kasaandra shakes her head. "They used tunnels that had been made long ago by burrowing worms."

"Worms? Like, soft and squishy worms?" Bell asks.

The dwarf's eyes narrow. "No. Like giant worms with teeth that eat through rock. With scales like metal."

"Has anyone heard the locals talking about them?" Qrow asks.

Silence. "Even so," I say. "I think we should go back down and block off their access." That way, I can find out where the main tunnel leads.

"Do you have a death wish?" Qrow's frown is as fierce as I've ever seen it.

"I want fire arrows!" Bell says. "Is there any way I can light my arrows on fire?"

"What?!" Qrow growls. "Bell, you, of all people, should understand the danger of going back down there."

"That's why I think we should do it. I can't leave here knowing a pack of those things could come up here and swallow someone like they swallowed me." Her eyes shimmer with tears, but her chin is high and firm with conviction.

"I agree with Bell," I say. I'm betting on Qrow's protective streak because if it weren't for a possible treasure, I wouldn't give those hopping monsters a second thought. The townspeople can deal with the danger themselves.

"If they can't get through stone, then the town will be fine." Qrow's tone is even harsher than before. "There are several stone barriers between those things and us, including a steel door. Forget it. You're not going back down. I won't allow it." He says the last part to me.

"I wasn't asking your permission, *brother*. What if someone else goes down there? I doubt they will, but if some townsfolk know we've been there and nothing bad happened to us, some braver kids might try it. I would. I already did. Do you want to take that chance? Do you want to be responsible for their deaths? We should at least make it safe. *We* know how to defeat those crooning spider frogs. *We* know fire is their weakness. Someone else who finds themselves down there won't. Akin, how many times can you do that fire thing?"

"I call it Whoosh!" Bells says.

She does like to name things.

"Akin says, 'no limit,'" Kasaandra says in answer to my question.

I continue as though the decision is already a foregone conclusion. "Bell, we can get you set up with a bunch of arrows dipped in oil. You can light them with a torch before you shoot them. And if you run out, pick up a torch. They don't like fire. Kasaandra can seal off the tunnels while we use torches or whatever else y'all have."

"It went after *you* when you were carrying a torch," Qrow reminds us.

"I was in front." And running straight for it. But I don't point that out. There's no need to antagonize him further.

"Hmm," Llani murmurs. "I can collapse some of the tunnels near the main passage. How many are there?"

"I don't know. I didn't go further because I ran out of torches. There could be a dozen more."

"Then perhaps it will be a secondary plan."

"This is ridiculous. We're not going back down there." Qrow stands up and leans forward on his hands. He looks each of us in the eye as if he could implant the command by doing so. Maybe he can, but it doesn't affect me.

What's the matter, big guy? Not used to your demands being ignored?

I decide to try my hunch about injecting thoughts. I look at each of them. I imagine I'm shooting a harpoon straight into their foreheads and sending, *I think we should do it,* shimmering along the ropes running from me to the imaginary harpoons and into their thoughts.

After only two heartbeats, Akin signs, *I'll go.*

Yes! I'm partially stunned.

Bell smells her saliva-drenched top. "Me too! Just. Not tonight. Okay?"

I can live with that. I need to regain some of my strength, too. "We can collect some supplies and head down tomorrow morning. That will give us enough time to rest and recover. We can leave town when we're done," I say to convince the rest.

"Agreed," says Llani.

Kasaandra nods, and with her support, we all start discussing the items we'll need. Except for Qrow. He looks like he's been ambushed. I think he's shocked we're not all jumping at his commands.

Even so, he won't let Bell go down there without him.

I hold back my smile, though. No need to rub it in.

31st day of Zamdi, 14,887

As soon as we start down the long tunnel, Llani changes into Blackberry to warn us if she smells anything unusual. I don't tell her my danger sense will give us enough warning. She doesn't indicate she smells anything until we get close to the burnt ones from yesterday. That's a good sign, at least.

We continue until we reach the first burrow, which is what Llani calls the intersecting tunnels.

As the smallest of us, Bell had insisted—long before we got there—on lighting a fire about five bandis into the creatures' burrows. Not even Qrow was able to dissuade her. She said the smell of the fire would probably keep them from coming toward us. I'm not so sure, but I don't argue. Perhaps it's her way of overcoming her fear of being swallowed again, like getting back in a boat after nearly drowning or on a horse after falling off.

It doesn't take long for her to get the fire going. Afterward, Kasaandra patches the wall with Qrow's help while Llani, Akin, and I keep watch. I feel them coming, and we dispatch three of the creatures before the wall is finished. Akin sends flames that nearly fill the passageway. Only one of them keeps coming, and we take it out quickly while the other two curl up and cook from their burning legs.

The other three tunnels are patched up without any further combat.

"Now what?" Bell says, frowning at her full quiver. I think she's disappointed she didn't get a chance to shoot flaming arrows.

"We're done here. We're returning," Qrow says.

"I think we should keep going. Who knows how many more tunnels there are? I didn't make it much farther than here before I turned around yesterday."

"We're already here, and we still have plenty of supplies. I vote to keep going," Kasaandra says. "I don't want to haul this stuff out of here if we don't have to."

"There is no vote. We're going back now," Qrow insists.

Considering all the noise our conversation is making, we may not have a choice about another confrontation.

If Bell's expression is anything to go by, I'd say at least half of us want to go on, so I push a bit more. "I say we do vote. If you're afraid to keep going, you're free to go back on your own." This time, I don't try to convince them using magic, if that's what my harpoon thoughts were yesterday.

If Qrow's glare could kill, I'd be dead.

"I vote to go!" Bell says.

Kasaandra and Akin both nod a 'yes' vote. Qrow's lips nearly disappear into his frown.

"I'm curious where this will lead. Who knows what may be at the end."

Thank you, Llani! I wonder when she switched back from the wolf. "What's on the other side of the river, directly west of town?" I ask.

"The cemetery," Llani answers.

Really? Maybe they stashed the treasure in one of the vaults. If it weren't for those scrape marks on the ground, I probably wouldn't have bothered to search for a hidden door, but I can't stop looking now.

"That seems safe enough. And it's five to one. You coming with us?" Without waiting for Qrow's answer, I proceed down the tunnel.

Llani moves in front of me and starts tossing fire down the tunnel. They're not like Akin's *Whoosh*. They're more like throwing darts, only with fire. The darts don't travel very far at first, but I show her how to flick her wrist for more distance. Before long, she's slinging fire far enough that we see them coming. Four more of the creatures. They don't even have a chance to start crooning. Llani catches two of them on the way, and Bell uses her flaming arrows.

"Go for the legs," Kasaandra tells Bell. "The hairy spider ones."

"You got it!"

Bell's next shot hits, and hairy legs light up like one of the hablis's little campfires.

"Way to go!" I say, giving her a high-five.

The three that get within five bandis of us are assaulted with Akin's *Whoosh*, filling the entire tunnel. Two of them make it through, but barely. Their legs are already alight. Kasaandra's axe and Bell's arrow take care of them before they stop moving.

And now the tunnel smells of frogs and burnt hair again.

As a sailor, I was taught to fear fire. But I don't think I ever appreciated its destructive force before now. I was too busy trying to stay alive yesterday to watch Akin in action. But today, I have plenty of opportunities. Each time, he grabs at the air—as though he's gathering it with his hands—then lets the fire loose. The air sucks into the flames, pulling me toward it. Making it hard to breathe. And the heat is almost overwhelming.

We find the next burrow and get it patched with only one creepy crawly coming at us. I tell them it's coming. The frog starts crooning long before we see it, and Llani's fire darts illuminate its reinforcements.

Akin launches balls of light that show us their progress as they explode upon creatures and walls. Bell and Llani time their fire darts and flaming arrows to coincide with Akin's lights.

Bell has difficulty lighting her arrows on the wall torch, so Qrow lifts her onto his shoulders and holds the torch for her. Maybe it's Qrow's attempt to make her look taller so the frog creatures won't be inclined to go for her again. Whatever the reason, she has a better vantage point, and while she almost lights Qrow's hair on fire, she eventually learns how to avoid it.

When she yells, "Don't look now!" a spray of fire splinters whiz over our heads. Meanwhile, Kasaandra and I hang back, waiting to see if any get through Akin's *Whoosh*.

Three of them do, but one falls from the ceiling dead and rolls to a flaming stop before me. The other two go for Kasaandra. She takes them both out with one swing of her blade, nearly decapitating one and removing several legs from the other on the backswing.

For good measure, I stab the last one on the top of the head.

Kraken, we're good.

We get the next burrow filled and walled up without incident. A few minutes later, we encounter our first set of steps going up.

I suggest we leave the last of the supplies at the base of the steps. If Llani's bag has a space limit, I want there to be plenty of room for treasure.

After a few minutes of climbing, we finally reach the top of the last set of stairs. In less than a minute, I find the latch that opens the door from this side. I don't see any traps, but I ask the others to stand back while I flip the catch. The door swings open.

And I feel as if I've been stabbed in the gut.

Before me is a mirror of the other treasure room, but longer.

And this one's not empty.

I blink, and it's still there when I open my eyes. It's not overflowing onto the floor or anything, though, not like in my dream. Has someone been emptying it? Or perhaps filling it up?

It might not be as much treasure as I was hoping, but there's enough to go around.

I'm barely aware of the others' gasps and exclamations as they enter.

Like my dream, most of the objects have a water theme. There are countless shells and fish and water plants. There are many statues of merkama with their fully finned arms and legs, webbed feet, and scaly skin.

I wave the torch back and forth, illuminating gold, platinum, copper, and brass. And the jewels! Some of the metal is tarnished green, while others gleam.

The armor pieces must have been custom-made, considering the number, length, and placement of fins that merkama have on their backs and bellies.

Something Llani is saying gets my attention.

"…in a museum! Horik will be thrilled!"

"What? Horik? No! This is ours!" I say.

"These are cultural artifacts! We can't keep them. They belong to the merkama." Llani looks as scandalized as she sounds.

The merkama? Ha! It's ours, or mine if they don't want any.

"Horik is not merkama. He is merely related by marriage. There are no descendants of the merkama here in Cranwood."

Yes! At least Qrow's on my side.

"However, they appear at every Kish conference. I can get word to Queen Sarafeen when we get back to the inn."

Seriously? Leave it to Qrow to ruin even that for me. "You're kidding, right? I say we vote on it. Who wants to keep it? Raise your hand." I look frantically from one to the other, but I'm the only one with my hand up. "Kasaandra. You're with me, aren't you? You, of all people, should understand how much this is worth."

"If this were dwarfish-made, and you said you were keeping it, you'd be feeling my axe."

I stare at her in disbelief. What in Kraken's name is wrong with them?

They'd never have to work again. They'd never want for anything.

There's nothing like these items anywhere in the world!

"There are very few merkama artifacts outside their realm," Qrow states firmly. "You would never be able to sell them without being found out and hunted by the merkama."

I could always melt them down.

Qrow continues, "I imagine they will reward us for finding them."

Wait. What? Reward?

"Reward? What could they give us that's worth more than this? Besides, wouldn't that be like selling them back to them?" Not that I object to the thought.

"Not at all. Of course, requesting payment would be unadvised."

Well, that changes things. But how would we get the treasure to the queen?

Qrow answers my unspoken question. "I imagine she would come here to see the treasure in person. I recommend we not disturb it any further, so she can see it exactly as we found it. This will reassure her of our honorable intentions and may reveal clues to the perpetrator."

Who cares about being honorable? Or the perpetrator? I want the reward! Don't they?

"I will take none of the rewards," Llani says. "It will be enough to know it is returned to its rightful place."

"I would caution you not to turn it down if it's offered. They are proud people. Refusing their gift might be misconstrued as contempt."

Bell says what I'm thinking. "What do you mean *if* it's offered? Didn't you say she would?"

"That's my best guess. In my opinion, Queen Sarafeen is quite adept at reading one's intentions. If she feels that we are trying to force her hand, there is no knowing how she will respond."

So, what do we do now?

"What do we do now? Go back?" Kasaandra asks.

Maybe she's used to being around this much wealth, but I can't imagine walking away from any of this stuff. I want to roll around in it. I want to sleep in it. It can be taken away at any time by anyone. The thought makes me sick to my stomach.

"How long do you think it's been here?" Bell says. Her hands are behind her back, like a small child whose mother has told her not to touch anything at the market.

"The merkama ruled this city more than two thousand years ago," Llani reminds us.

Kasaandra shakes her head. "These haven't been here that long. Maybe a couple hundred years. And these at the front? Less than a year."

"Why do you say that?" Qrow asks.

"The tarnish. See this one?" She points to something that resembles a glove with a shield. "And that one?" She indicates a pauldron. The shield is a very dark green, while the pauldron is much lighter and gleaming in the torchlight. "They're the same metal, but the pauldron looks like it was polished no more than two trit'quarters ago."

Bell gasps. "This could be someone's stash room! I bet someone's stealing from the queen and keeping it here! Just like in *Stolen Heart*!"

Kasaandra harrumphs.

"No, Kasaandra," Qrow says logically. "Bell may be right. I think it would be wise to identify the exit on this side of the river. And we should proceed with caution. Whoever brought this here could be nearby."

I find the hidden door near the other end of the room before Qrow finishes talking. After a few moments, I see the mechanism that opens it. The door is thick stone; it should have been nearly impossible for me to open, but it swings wide with ease.

I step into a room about ten bandis long and six wide with a high ceiling. The stone floor is laid in an intricate coral reef pattern, complete with all kinds of sea life, matching the similarly decorated ceiling and walls. The room has pedestals, tables, chests, and niches carved into the walls. All of which are empty.

There is a set of stairs at the opposite end.

"Whoa!" Bell says as she steps to avoid the sea creatures within the design. Kasaandra's the last one to enter from the treasure room. She joins the others in inspecting the floor designs.

"Wait! Don't let the door close!" I yell.

Kasaandra and Akin turn and try to stop it, but it's too late. The door settles seamlessly into the stone wall. All on its own. I run over to inspect it. There's no indication there's a door here at all. I would never have found it from this end. I search the walls and floor but can find no latch, button, or wall seam.

"No wonder the other room remained undiscovered until now," I say, still searching. "Kasaandra, do you see a seam? It's as if it's been—"

"No. This was sealed by magic. You won't find a seam." She looks around the floor and ceiling. "My guess? There is a clue in all that."

She's got to be kidding! A clue? In the designs? I use my foot to press on different areas of the floor. Maybe there's a button, like the sea monster emblem on the statue. Nothing depresses.

Kasaandra scoffs. "It won't be as simple as a button."

"Oh! Look at these glyphs! This is writing. I've been studying them. Look! This one here…in the shape of an octopus. We think it may represent change or perhaps freedom. Or it could be the number eight. There are so many possibilities."

How do we get back now?

"How do we get back now?" Bell asks.

My guess is the stairs.

"My guess is that way," Qrow points to the stairs.

Yeah. No shit.

Chapter 38 Qrodin

2ND DAY OF PILAMEE, 14,887
CRANWOOD, ZEDANA

Qrodin has spent more time than he'd like to admit thinking about the sea monster button on the monument's statue. Did Qat recognize it as a match to Truffle's ring? If Qat was the one who assassinated Truffle, his twin is perceptive enough to make the connection.

Does Qat know what it represents? If so, what will ae think if ae finds out that Qrodin has the same ring? Does Qat know Qrodin was in town to meet Truffle? If Qat *was* hired to take out Truffle, was ae also hired to take out anyone else with the same ring? Is Qat actively investigating the ring's purpose?

Qrodin knows next to nothing about Qat. Not the new Qat.

All this time they'd been together, he'd been too distracted by their reunion to think about the act that brought them together in the same city. Now, he can't stop thinking about it.

Is it possible Qat was working with the detectives, and that's the reason ae wasn't detained? Qat's never been one for following the rules, and as children, ae didn't see anything wrong with stealing—and perhaps now, even murder—so Qrodin rejects the possibility.

He's still tossing scenarios around when, a few minutes before the scheduled time, the water ripples. The queen has arrived.

When they'd finally found their way out a few days ago, Qrodin wasn't surprised to find himself in the cemetery. The temple stands near the center of the graveyard and is the largest structure, full of giant merkama statues that Qrodin believes are ancient royalty.

When they had returned to their respective rooms, Qrodin took a tiny shell from his bag. It had been a gift from the queen herself. She told him to keep it with him always, for he would likely need it most when he was away from home. She was right. This was the first time he used it. He spoke the activation word followed by her name and a short message. A few minutes later, the shell hummed. As previously instructed, he blew gently on its surface as if it were a feather. He was startled and pleased to hear her voice come out of the center, clear but quiet.

A meeting was scheduled an hour before dawn four days from then, and she cautioned him to be discreet about the meeting location.

That last part is why he's waiting in this cove, one of the only private spots before the river snakes its way around the graveyard and the southernmost point of Cranwood. The cove is protected from view by large trees growing on both sides.

Unfortunately, they still haven't discovered the means to open the two secret doors from this side of the tunnel, so Llani and Bell are holding open a door they found at the top of the stairs behind a crumbling statue, while Kasaandra and Akin are waiting within the second doorway, the one that leads to the hidden treasure room.

Seven merkama emerge from the water about twenty feet out. Well-armed guards surround the queen. They're shorter than Qrodin, but not by much. They have giant mouths, flat noses, and protruding eyes that never blink. Isa's blue light only enhances the magnificence of their polished armor and glassy scales. All merkama have fins along the back of their arms and calves, though their shapes vary. The rearguard has a dorsal fin that immediately narrows into a long, thin, flexible spine that sticks out between aer shoulder blades and nearly touches the ground behind. One of them has a fin protruding from aer sternum.

Their gills are located down the side of each ribcage, so their armor usually covers only their back and chest.

The front guard moves aside, and Queen Sarafeen steps forward. She is a vibrant sea green. Her gill fins are royal purple and flutter around her as she walks. Her armor is copper-colored and sparkles with aquamarine gems.

Glad he'd transformed his armor into a suit, Qrodin moves his head counterclockwise as if he could turn back time one hour on a clock face using only his nose. The gesture is awkward for anyone who isn't merkama, but it's the royal greeting, and Qrodin does it out of respect for their customs. He'd brushed his hair until it shined and pulled the sides back, fastening them with a beautiful shell clip Llani had made. She'd spent two days looking for the prettiest shell for this meeting. Perhaps it's not his best impression, but it's the best he can do on such short notice in Cranwood.

The queen returns the gesture. "Mr. Browning. It is a pleasure to see you again. The beard suits you."

"The pleasure is all mine."

"You said you found some artifact of our heritage." She pauses, and I nod. Her lips twitch in a small smile before it disappears. "I am intrigued you discovered something too large to transport and so important that it required my immediate presence."

"My apologies for the insistence on expediency, Your Majesty. Although I do not presume to know your mind, I believe that—once you see why I've requested your presence—you will agree such haste was necessary. This way, if you please."

She steps forward when he indicates the path to the cemetery.

"Have you been to Cranwood before?" he asks as they walk.

"I have not. I have wanted to visit the ruins, but the current situation"—she glances back at the guards—"has kept me away."

Qrodin's pulse picks up speed. He wonders if the situation she's referring to is the missing treasure. Considering how vast the ocean is, he'd be surprised if there weren't many things that take precedence, and the treasure has been vanishing for decades.

The queen continues, "I have been told there is little of interest remaining here for me."

"Until now, I believe." Qrodin clears his throat. "Forgive my presumption. There is a temple within the cemetery. That is where we are going now."

"A temple to whom?"

"To merkama royalty, I believe. I did not discover it alone. There are six of us, and the others are awaiting our arrival. My twin will meet us outside the temple."

"Your twin?" Queen Sarafeen smiles. "Did I not tell you that you would find what you were looking for? I'm glad you didn't have to wait long."

"Ah! I was never certain to what you were referring." A few years back, Qrodin had learned the queen was clairvoyant, though unlike Qat's dreams, she cannot see events close to her. "We recently found each other in Riversmeet and traveled here overland with the other four." At her inquiring look, he continues. "You will meet them all, but they are keeping the way open for now. You will see."

They pass through the arch at the cemetery's western entrance. The wall surrounding the cemetery is only a few feet high, making it easy to see the tombs and memorials inside. The ground is covered in sturdy wildflowers. Tall grass pushes through stone walkways, and flowering vines cling to minuscule cracks in the stone memorials. There are very few critters at this time of the morning.

"You can see the large temple there." Qrodin indicates the stone structure surrounded by cypress trees. "That is Qat standing outside." Qat is walking back and forth, searching for something.

They proceed in silence until they reach the temple. Qat gives up searching and joins them.

"I think I would have known you had I met you elsewhere," the queen says before Qrodin has a chance to introduce them. But that's her way. "Who are you looking for?"

"My horse. Starshine."

"Starshine?" the queen asks. "You said he was your horse?"

A few of the queen's guards speak in a series of popping and clicking sounds. She responds quickly, and one breaks from the group and heads in the direction Qat had been searching.

"He is. I expect he'll be along shortly. I told him that if I end up walking back to town, he's not getting outside the city walls again until we leave Cranwood. I'm Qat, by the way. Your stuff's in here." Qrodin had instructed them on the proper greeting, but Qat turns and walks into the temple without bothering with formalities.

"I apologize for—"

"No need," the queen replies.

They follow Qat into the temple. Qrodin walks through the door into a hall of giants. The mausoleum is about thirty by fifty feet, with a twenty-foot ceiling. Stone statues are carved from giant stones that couldn't have come from this region, as they are blue, green, and red, rather than the local grey and pale-yellow rocks that make up the city. Some statues hold tridents, while others are surrounded by sea life. Some wear armor, others are clothed in kelp, and a few are unclothed. The surface of several statues is pitted and gouged. Kasaandra had said they used to be covered in gemstones that have since been pried off.

Qrodin had brought lanterns to light the room. As is the space below, the walls, ceiling, and floor are inlaid with colored rocks arranged to resemble an underwater palace. A long table is broken in the center of the room.

Most statues are still standing, but one has crumbled, obscuring the opening to the treasure room below. Llani and Bell are standing in the doorway to prevent it from closing. Llani has been in this vault for several days trying to decode the myriad symbols. She is convinced they contain the secret to opening the door from this side.

Two of the queen's guards stay with her while the remainder spread throughout the room. They inspect every corner and around every statue before returning to her side.

Sarafeen inspects a symbolic rune at the base of a statue. She runs her hand down the leg before turning to Qrodin. Her lips are pressed tight in obvious disappointment. "While these are impressive, I had hoped that when I heard from you next, you'd be calling for something more...significant. These statues have been plundered. In this state, they are practically worthless. Too bad. They would have been a veritable treasure"—glancing at Qrodin—"in their time."

Not wanting to give anything away, Qrodin gives the queen an almost imperceptible nod but doesn't interrupt as she continues, her shoulders relaxing slightly. "We don't create such statues of our dead. At least, those of us who live within the sea don't. Nor do we build the type of structures I hear can be found in Cranwood. Perhaps the Misirin thought they'd be accepted if they imitated *mia luuvay*."

The merkama had initially called this city Misir, so he assumes that Misirin are the inhabitants. "Mia Luuvay?" he asks, having never heard the term.

"The people of the land," the queen answers almost absently as she inspects some of the markings at the base of the nearest statue.

Llani rushes over. "I have been attempting to decipher the script. A reliquary in town full of tablets, stones, and obelisks is covered in the merkama script. I was hoping you or one of your historians would...Oh! Forgive my breach of conduct." Llani takes a few steps back and presents herself as Qrodin had done, but far more gracefully.

Queen Sarafeen returns the gesture and then nods to Qrodin.

"Queen Sarafeen, let me introduce Llani Deairheann of the Tumi."

The queen displays the insides of her wrists in the elven greeting. Delighted, Llani does the same. As the queen examines Llani's gesture, Sarafeen's eyes widen slightly, and she scrutinizes Llani's face closely.

Llani drops her arms to her sides quickly.

"It is a pleasure to meet Llani Deairheann ane..."

Llani shakes her head quickly. "Just Deairheann. I-I...the pleasure is mine, Queen Sarafeen."

Qrodin's curiosity is piqued, but the queen said the visit must be brief. "The reason for your visit is below. This is merely the entrance. One of two. The other entrance comes from the city and is how we found the...I'd rather show you. We will be going through here"—he gestures to the open door and Bell—"and down a series of stairs. We will allow the door to close behind us if you are comfortable with it. There is a latch from the other side, but not this one. Or we can have someone stay in the doorway to keep it open."

The guard with the spear-like fin comes forward. "Show me."

Qat leads the way, and Bell finally rushes from the doorway. She's practically vibrating with excitement.

Qrodin introduces Bell to the queen while they wait. Bell rotates her head three times before finally stopping. "You are soooo pretty! I love your armor. It's so sparkly!"

The queen smiles, but the door opens before she can respond, and the guard nods. She turns back. "Thank you, Bell. Let us speak more after we see why I'm here."

"Oh, yes, please!"

They descend a series of stairs before entering the large, empty room they found a few days ago. On the far end of the room, the door is closed.

"We believe this room was full of treasure. This is how we found it. The reason for your visit is on the other side of that wall." Qrodin crosses the room and raps on the wall with the hilt of a dagger. The door swings open, and Kasaandra and Akin appear in the open doorway. Behind them, the treasure glows in the soft torchlight.

The shocked silence is finally broken when the queen takes a step forward. Then, it's filled with the clicking and popping sounds of the guards' conversation.

"This door will also close behind us. If you would like, Qat can demonstrate how to open it before we proceed."

The spear-fin guard follows Qat. Qrodin waves Kasaandra and Akin in and introduces them to the queen, who inspects them almost as closely as she did Llani.

However, when the door opens again, whatever she is looking for in their faces is forgotten. She steps into the room and gasps.

Chapter 39 Qat

I don't get it.

How could they give it all away?

We found it. We should keep it.

But I'm the only one that feels that way.

What is it going to matter to the fish folk, anyway? It's not like they knew it was here. They never would have missed it.

The last few days, I wrestled with staying and waiting for them to come to take it all away or taking what I could carry and leaving. Taking Starshine and riding off to Craguesport. I even asked about boats.

But I couldn't do it. I couldn't leave.

What stopped me?

Maybe it was Kasaandra. She guarded the treasure as if her life depended on it. She and Akin moved their pocket homes to the treasure room, and Bell brings meals down several times daily.

I tried multiple times to sift through the treasure, but Kasaandra stopped me each time.

"I'm not going to take anything. I just want to see it."

"Qrow said not to touch it."

"Since when do you do what Qrow wants?"

"Since he's right not to touch it. There might be clues as to who took it."

"Clues? What are you talking about?"

"How it's arranged might say something about who put it here and why."

I'd rolled my eyes at Kasaandra's explanation.

Recognizing several pieces from the list I found in Truffle's room, I could tell her why the treasure's here. The pieces are going to be sold. Most likely auctioned. I wonder if the sea monster symbol on the statue inspired the ring's design and the logo at the top of the page. Most likely. I'd never seen it before I saw Truffle's ring. Now, I've seen it three times. Is it on any of the pieces?

The theft wasn't Truffle's doing. He wasn't smart enough, nor could he have gotten access. He was probably one of the buyers—he was wealthy enough to be. I kick myself for not having broken into his place in Riversmeet. He'd have had some nice stuff. I might have done it if his disappearance hadn't been discovered so soon.

I finally moved my pocket home down here, too, so I didn't have to worry about anyone messing with my witches' stone. We didn't want the merkama to question why there were large boulders in the treasure room, so we moved them out this morning. Mine is now near the cemetery. I don't care where the others are.

Qrow told us very little about the merkama queen. Now, she's here. Picking up my treasure. Holding it. Caressing it.

The clicking and popping sounds of their conversations at first annoy me but then quickly become no more than background noise as I watch Sarafeen. Unlike her guards, she speaks only in Oramische, when she speaks at all.

She names all the monster statues, even the ones I've never heard of. That says something because pirates love songs and tales about sea monsters. Sarafeen tells us stories of the ones we've never heard of. Who and what they were, what they're legends for having done, who killed them, battled them, or were defeated by them.

She also tells us about the artifacts. I mentally compare the names of the artifacts to those on the list. Many of them are there. I'd also finally looked at the notebook the list had come in. The pages were full of random notes and scribbles. I was tempted to throw it out, but there may be something useful in all that mess.

I wonder if one of the six that came with the queen is responsible for the thefts. It has to be someone close to the queen. Wouldn't that be a twist?

When one of the guards—the one with a stiff, spiny fin that runs from the crown of aer head to the base of aer spine—approaches the queen, I can't help but follow aer progress. I've dubbed aem the Finder Fish, as nearly everything ae's brought to the queen's attention is an item on Truffle's list. Ae's carrying a jeweled trident that's more than two bandis long. The engraved stone tablet that the queen and Qrow are studying slips in her hand, and she barely catches it before handing it off to her shadow, a tall, blue merkama who resembles the queen. Ae hasn't said a word and follows Queen Sarafeen wherever she goes, accepting items and fetching others. Ae towers over the queen and glares at everything as if even a slight breeze is threatening. Qrow mentioned the queen has a son. Perhaps this is him.

The queen's hands tremble as she accepts the weapon.

"The Thunderlight Trident," Queen Sarafeen whispers as she inspects the lightning-shaped forks. "This was used to defeat the kraken Akxoss. It disappeared from our vaults nearly four hundred years ago."

Another artifact on Truffle's list.

I've heard of Akxoss. And the trident. Even before I'd seen the list.

My hands itch to grab it from her and run. But that would be suicide. And I like my life, despite my lack of caution the other day.

But to touch the Thunderlight Trident? To hold it?

I look around at the rest of the treasure, regretting that I hadn't rooted through it when Kasaandra was sleeping and found the trident for myself. There's no consolation that Bell was right about this being a stolen hoard. The queen admitted these items have been disappearing for centuries, and the culprit has never been caught.

When the Finder Fish is done digging up the good stuff, ae joins Llani in inspecting the runes and symbols until Bell returns. I never saw the hablis leave, but she arrives with a cart of food. I wonder what she brought for the fish folk?

I walk over to investigate.

Seafood. Of course. I look closer. Fish eggs, live crabs, sea urchins, and something that resembles the green slime that coats the bottom of the *Raven Scream*. I shudder.

I feel as though I'm going to wake up from another dream. This can't be real. But even I couldn't imagine the merkama language, nor the weapons or armor. Or the slimy stuff they're putting in their mouths right now. One of them is slurping something out of a shell. Live crabs try to escape as their legs are ripped from their bodies and eaten, shell and all.

I grab a few pieces of fruit, but I can't eat while they are. The sounds they make—all that slurping and chomping—are worse than the ones Goffin the Black made in the privy after a milk-drinking contest.

I go outside to look for Starshine instead. Since the fish folk arrived, at least one merkama guard has been at each door between the treasure and the cemetery. I don't bother telling them I'll return later. I haven't gotten a reward, so it should be obvious I'll be back.

Qrow had said the queen would be staying longer than they initially thought due to the volume of treasure that needs to be guarded until it's transferred elsewhere. She wants to meet with us again tonight in the temple room.

On my way out, I notice that the table has been repaired but still stands empty.

They should load up the table with the food.

How will they avoid going into town to get back into the vault without at least one person in each room to open the doors? Unless one of them figured out how to open them from this side.

Oh well. Not my problem.

I don't see my four-legged, silvery companion anywhere amongst the graves, monuments, and shade trees. I can't imagine why he would leave. Neglected though it is, the cemetery has plenty of wild grass and shrubs. I whistle a few times on my way toward the water—just in case he got thirsty and went to drink. When I don't see him, I follow the river toward the bridge, thinking he'd likely go that way to return to town. As it turns out, I don't have to go far. Around the south wall, I find him grazing under a tall tree next to my pocket home. He does love his shade. "Hey, buddy."

His whole body reacts violently until he realizes it's me.

"Didn't you hear me whistle for you?"

He shakes his head before lowering it slightly away from me.

"Sorry. I didn't mean to be gone so long. Honestly, I think I'm a bit bored from it all."

The horse chuffs and swishes his tail.

I can't help but laugh. "Yeah. You're right. Like I could ever be bored in a room like that. But the more I'm in there, the more bummed I get. Qrow says she'll reward us, but..." But I can't imagine what she could offer me that I would want more than that trident. "It's not like I can take much with me, anyway."

Starshine turns to stare at me.

"You're right. It would nearly all fit in my pocket home."

Starshine shakes his head, and his mane blows in the soft breeze.

"Hey. Did I tell you it's a stolen treasure? Bell was right. Someone's been stealing it for more than four hundred years. I bet it's that spiny-finned one. Ae keeps digging out items on the list. I told you about the list, didn't I?"

Starshine blows out through his nose so hard that horse snot sprays the ground. He stomps his hoof twice, rears up on his hind legs, and comes down so hard that the ground trembles slightly.

"Whoa! Careful now. What's got you so riled up? At least you didn't have to listen to them eat. Slurping that slime?" I imitate the sound and shiver in disgust.

Instead of calming down, Starshine whirls away from me. He stomps forward and then kicks back with his hind legs. He spins, kicks, and huffs, agitatedly repeating his frustrated actions. This must be like watching me with my knives, trying to decide what to do.

I've never seen him like this. He's not wearing a saddle. There are no stinging wasps or biting flies. What has gotten him so riled up? I shrug and give him some space. He obviously needs to work through something. By the time he's done, he's heaving. Foam drips from his mouth, and his coat gleams with rage sweat.

"Sorry, Bud. Had I known you'd work yourself into such a state, I'd have brought a brush. Look what a mess you've made of your mane. Bell's going to be so mad. It's going to take her hours to brush it out. She'll probably braid it, too, as punishment for throwing a tantrum. Maybe I'll pick a few flowers while we wait so she can weave them in."

Starshine snort-blows his nose again, but it's more of a reproach than an outburst of rage this time.

"Serves you right. Now, if you're sure you can control your temper, I'll get some rest before the next round of whatever they have planned for us."

I sit down under the tree. I don't know what kind it is, but it's got a smooth trunk comfortable enough to lean back against and a sparse enough canopy that I don't feel as though I'm still underground. I nibble at the apricots and berries I'd stashed in a scarf on the way outside. Sun patches shift and wink on the grass as the light penetrates the spaces between delicate leaves and pink flowers in full bloom. Hummingbirds are flitting from one flower to another or chasing each other off until they realize the tree has too many flowers to defend adequately.

That's how I'd feel with a load of treasure. Like I had to spread it everywhere and try to keep everyone else away. How does Qrow do it? The weight of all that wealth and responsibility would probably break me. I can barely manage one green egg.

It's much better this way.

After we finish with the merkama, I'll gladly stay topside for a while. Being underground for so many days has done a number on my good humor. And my sleep.

I close my eyes briefly to refocus on what I want to do once I reach Craguesport.

Pounding hooves wake me from a dreamless sleep. Starshine is galloping away, his tail high.

What the…?

I rub the crust from my eyes and get up. It's nearly sundown. I've been napping for several hours.

It takes a few seconds before I realize Bell's chatting to someone nearby. They sound like they're coming my way. Starshine usually adores Bell. But today, I don't blame him for running. If I were him, I'd run too. I wouldn't want her to catch sight of that straggly mane.

I slowly walk back toward the river. Bell is with one of the fish folk, the spear-finned one that I showed how to operate the door latches. I must be careful not to call them fish folk in anyone else's presence anymore. Qrow and Llani lecture me, Bell looks at me with a sad and disappointed face, and Kasaandra laughs. Akin scowls. He probably disapproves of it, too. They'd never survive a pirate ship.

"Qat! I was looking for you! Queen Sarafeen wants to meet with us now." She puts her hands up to her mouth and continues in a loud whisper. "I think it's time for"—she glances briefly at her companion— "that thing Qrow was telling us about. You know."

I know. Our rewards.

If we get one.

I wish that part had been in my dream. Should I be angry or anxious? Mad that I'm still here, or nervous about what the queen will give us? Or, more specifically, what she'll offer *me*?

Will she reward the group as a whole or individually?

I nod at Bell and turn toward the cemetery entrance. Inside, the table is now loaded with fruits, nuts, and everything Bell had gathered from the nearby fields.

Qrow is pacing. He stops when I walk in. His gold stare pierces me. Then he returns to pacing. Kasaandra's cracking nuts on the table with her smithing hammer and brushing the shells on the floor. Qrow looks annoyed with her, but at least she's not using her axe. I wouldn't have as much restraint.

Akin is sitting cross-legged on the floor with his eyes closed, meditating.

Llani walks in through the door beyond the broken statue. She looks worried—an expression I usually see on Qrow. She nods her head at Kasaandra.

It's already begun. I don't see any indication that Llani's received anything.

Kasaandra is next. Everyone is quiet while she's gone. When she returns, she looks a strange combination of stunned and annoyed. She points at Bell.

Bell comes back with tears in her eyes and a bottle of wine. What could be so bad that she'd want to start drinking before mealtime? And where did the wine come from? I didn't see any in the treasure room. I'm tempted to leave, but she looks at me. My turn.

This isn't the reaction I had expected from a group of people being rewarded. No one is talking. No one is sharing their great news.

Kraken's maw, what's going on here?

How did we screw this up so badly?

At Bell's watery smile, I throw back my shoulders. May as well get this over with.

I descend the winding staircase. I had initially thought we'd be in the treasure room and there would be small piles of stuff to choose from. We'd put jewelry on. We'd weigh a sword for balance or admire a precious item.

I didn't expect to enter the larger of the two treasure rooms and find two benches facing each other in the center. Where did they find the benches? The queen is already seated on the one facing me, her shadow standing guard behind her. I don't bother with the head circle greeting thing. Doing it now would imply I only do it when I'm being paid.

Am I being paid?

"You want to know why none of the others returned with part of the treasure."

Do I?

Maybe. But really, I want to know if *I'll* be leaving here with part of the treasure.

She smiles as if she can read my mind.

That's maybe not such a good idea, considering I feel like strangling her scaly neck after putting us all through this.

I'm staring at her throat, so it wouldn't be a stretch for her to perceive my thoughts. Her armor winks in the lantern light when she adjusts herself. I hadn't noticed before, but it comes over her shoulders and clasps in front with a metal disc inlaid with jewels that look curiously like the eye on a peacock feather. I'm only familiar with it because the captain used one for writing. It's a strange symbol for a water person to wear.

But she's a strange being.

I thought I'd be more impressed, as she is a queen. Llani's been nervously preparing for the visit, and Bell's been so excited that she's had to leave town every day for fear she'd mistakenly tell someone.

Now, here I am, sitting before her, and she's just another person to me.

I hold more respect for Captain Rogen than I do for her.

"I willn't tell you what I gave your companions. That is their choice to say or not to say. But I will give you the same choice I gave them. I can tell you something about your future or give you a gift."

"I don't much care about the future."

"I thought you might say that." She withdraws a spyglass from within her armor. "Some would say what I offer you may be as much a curse as a treasure. That will be for you to decide." She lays it flat in both hands and presents it to me.

I take it from her. The scope is small enough to fit in a fold of my belt or slide into the top of my boot. Or, as the queen had, I can tuck it into my armor. Unlike most spyglasses I've used, this one is not made from metal or wood but from gemstones and coral. The outer sleeve is a piece of opaque greenstone in varying shades of green and black, carved into a long sea serpent coiled around a branch of genuine coral. The scales are etched exquisitely. Each one is a different color. The serpent's eyes are dark green and translucently flowing, like looking into a deep well of algae-green water.

At first, I wonder if this is another version of the sea monster logo, but no matter what angle I hold the spyglass, it doesn't match the version on the ring. The sea monster on the ring has four legs, whereas this is a legless snake with gill fins like the queen's.

I pull, but the scope won't slide open. Nor can I twist it free.

I look at it more closely.

Finally, I pry the mouth open. Hidden fangs slide out like daggers from their sheaths, releasing the other sections. I twist the scope slightly to draw the second section to its fullest. The barrel is made from the same greenstone as before, but this section is also marbled with purple. The third sleeve is made entirely of a vibrant blue stone with iridescent blue and green highlights. The fourth and last sleeve is an unnatural shade of translucent greenish-yellow.

Before I can bring it to my eye, the queen stops me. "You should understand what you'll be looking into before you attempt to discern its visions."

I lower the spyglass and wait.

"Looking through it while fully collapsed will enlarge what is before you. The next section will show you events of now, but not here. The third will show you what was. And the last will show you what will be."

I collapse the spyglass and latch the serpent's mouth.

My breath stops, and my heart races. I feel as though I might suffocate.

I could see the past.

I could see *my* past.

My hands start to sweat. I tuck the artifact into my waistband to avoid dropping and shattering it. What should I say? I can barely remember what *she* said. Something about here and now and what could be? If I weren't sitting, I'd fear falling.

What had she said before showing me the scope? Something about a curse?

"Why a curse? Wouldn't seeing be a good thing?"

"It is said you cannot direct what it will show you. If you look to the future, it may not reveal yours. If you look to the past, it may divulge an event long before you were born. And if you look to the now, you cannot change it. You might spend your life staring through the glass and never discovering what you are looking for."

"Then why are you offering it to me?"

"Because I believe you have the strength to wield it wisely."

Strength and wisdom? Me? She obviously doesn't know me well.

"I can see you doubt me."

"Yeah. I don't think anyone who knows me would agree with you there." I pull it out and inspect it again. I notice something etched into the stone surrounding the large lens. The writing is in the same bubbly-looking language Llani has been trying to decipher. "What does it say here?" I hold it out for her to inspect.

She runs her finger along one edge. "Knowing is UnSeeing. And here," she says, tapping along the opposite edge. "Seeing is UnKnowing."

And yet she says it's a gift of sight. Is it worth more than the treasure? Why would I want a scope that shows me things? I don't need the past. I don't want to see the future, and the only present I care about is mine. As far as I'm concerned, it's useless to me.

"You're disappointed."

"Not really." I bet I can sell it in Craguesport.

"Don't underestimate the importance of sight."

Yeah. Whatever. "Does it have a name?" All the cool stuff does.

"The glass? Not that I know of. Perhaps you should give it one."

Naw. I'll leave that to Bell. She likes naming things.

Chapter 40 Qrodin

9TH DAY OF PILAMEE, 14,887
ROAD TO CRAGUESPORT, ZEDANA

Only Bell's nightmares mar the beginning of their trip to Craguesport. Qrodin tries talking to her about them, but she denies their existence each time. Qat and Llani—and probably Akin—are aware of them. Only Kasaandra sleeps through Bell's outbursts. Sometimes, she struggles in her sleep as though she's still inside the frog's belly. At those times, Qrow *Soothes* her until she settles back down.

Queen Sarafeen shared that they had discovered the secret to opening the vault from the temple side. Two of her most trusted guards will be stationed there until they finish transferring the treasure. With the queen's urging, Kasaandra had repaired the hole in the monument's roof within the inner keep. The queen wanted to ensure that no one else had access to the merkama treasure from the city side.

Once the repair was completed, the queen assured him there was nothing on her end to keep Qrodin and his friends in Cranwood if they needed to leave. So, they did.

The first few days, the horses are fresh from their fortnight stay in Cranwood and make good time. The weather holds beautifully, and the road is straighter and more accessible. They pass meadows and work their way over small hills and around larger ones. There are trees to rest under, sufficient food to forage, and animals to hunt.

The next several days go without incident. Heavy rain and the resulting mud slow them down in the morning, but it no longer poses a problem by midday.

Today, the sun is so hot that, by mid-morning, they all agree to stay in the shade until it cools. Even the horses venture out only to get water from the river, then return quickly.

Bell waves a hand in front of her face. "These flies are so annoying. We should set up the Home Dome until it cools down. I won't use a fire, but we can still set it up in a doughnut."

They combine their reasacobilas in a large circle, leaving a hole in the center. It was an accident the first time they set it up like that, but the shape is quite useful. Come nighttime, a tiny campfire in the center hole gives off enough passive light that they can see easily enough to move around without bumping into anything, and having it outside the reasacobilas prevents smoke from coming in.

Thankfully, they don't need the heat and benefit from the reasacobilas' climate control. No matter what the weather is outside, the inside is always comfortable.

Instead of joining the others around Qat's table, Kasaandra sits in her section and whittles. Qrodin was surprised the first time he saw one of her completed pieces, a squirrel. The small figure was quite detailed, standing up with one ear cocked slightly. Qrodin could almost see its nose twitching, looking for the scent of an intruder.

Qrodin recalls Bell's comment that Kasaandra could carve the manticore spikes he'd kept as trophies. Perhaps Qrodin can commission her for the project, and she can work on them once they reach Craguesport. That would keep her progress a secret from Qat. The spikes will make a wonderful Proximus gift. Throughout Kish, Proximus is celebrated in the spring with festivals, games, and gifts. Some people call it the most loving day of the year. The problem is that Proximus is still half a year away. There's no guarantee Qat will still be around by then.

Proximan, on the other hand, which is in two days, is the time of the fall harvest. A time for festivals and feasts and family. And a time to give thanks for a successful harvest. This will be the first Proximan Qrodin spends with family since he was abandoned in Riversmeet. Even so, Qrodin doubts it will feel much different than any other day. Every day is a feast with Bell cooking for them, and he has been incredibly thankful every day since finding his twin.

Speaking of gifts, those who opted for the queen's prophecies haven't shared them. He's not too surprised. Most of the time, they make little sense until they've come to pass.

Much like the UnSeeing Eye. That's what Bell named Qat's spyglass when Qat told them what the inscription said. They'd all agreed not to look into the future when using it. If the future it shows them isn't theirs, it won't make any sense until after it's happened, anyway.

Qrodin was given a giant clamshell that Bell calls the Music Mouth. When opened, it emits melodies, increasing in volume the wider it's opened. Closing and opening it again changes the type of music. She said it was for his home. It was the perfect gift. The entire apartment was soundproofed so he could play his music without bothering his neighbors, but the silence is too loud for him to be entirely comfortable there. Maybe that's why he travels so frequently.

After a quick and cold meal of leftover meat and bread, along with a few fruits, Bell asks, "Qat, have you used the UnSeeing Eye? What did you see?"

"Not much. You can't ask what you want to see. You get what you get."

Qrodin shifts in his seat, thinking about what he'd request to see if he could. Who killed Ama. Would Qat want to see what happened that night? "What would you wish to see if you could direct the UnSeeing Eye?" he asks the group at large.

"Oh! I want to go first! I want to see my husband."

"Of course, you do, Bell," Qat says. "But what would you do if it were someone you didn't know?"

"At least I'd know who he was when I met him. But I don't have to worry about that. I'm going to marry Robyn. Robyn Tripleaf."

"Isn't he engaged to marry Meriski?" Qat asks.

If looks were a cleaver, Qat would be dead.

Qrodin is surprised that Qat knew Meriski's name. He hadn't. Does Qat have some interrogation skills Qrodin is unaware of?

"He'll change his mind because I'm not there, and he's going to realize how much he misses me and loves me and...and...wants to marry *me*. Me. Not her. Now, don't any of you want to see who *you'll* be marrying?"

Qrodin doesn't plan on marrying. Not ever. He'd contemplated it once and got his heart broken. It took him longer than he wants to admit to get over her. Never again. He's decided to follow the Karatolii customs he was born into in that regard.

"I don't," Kasaandra says.

"Why not?" Bell asks. She looks shocked.

"I might not like him."

"You're going to *marry* him! There's *no way* you're not going to like him!" Bell touches her bosom as if looking for her future wedding beads.

"Maybe for you, but not for us," Kasaandra replies.

"*Riiiight*," Bell says. "Who marries someone they don't like?"

"Lots of people do," Qrodin says, thinking of all the marriages he's witnessed over the years. Businesspeople who cheat on their spouses. Wives who throw themselves at him even when their husbands are watching. Sometimes, the husbands do when their wives aren't there. Someone is complaining about their spouse in every bathhouse he's been in. It's a miracle he ever contemplated it, but when he met Doscia, he couldn't imagine life without her. She hadn't felt the same.

"How does one correlate affection with a successful marriage?" Llani asks Bell.

"What?! Because you should only marry someone if you love them! That's how." Bell rolls her eyes.

"Elves seldom marry for love. It's not practical."

"What do you marry for, then?" Qrodin asks, curious. He doesn't get a chance to talk to enough elves on such a personal level.

"Usually, we look for the qualities we want in our children. Marriage partners seldom live together, and once a child is weaned, it stays with the parent agreed upon within the contract." At Bell's shocked expression, Llani continues, "Why are you so surprised? Not everyone wants to raise a child."

Qrodin is impressed with the practicality of the arrangements. She's right that not all people want to raise children. The Karatolii have amas instead.

"And then what? You divorce?" Bell asks.

Llani shakes her head. "No need."

Bell looks scandalized. "But what if you want to stay together forever?"

"Our marriage contracts can be renewed after expiration with the approval of both parties."

"Marriage contracts? Negotiation? Expiration? To me, that sounds more like a business deal than a marriage. Where's the romance? The flowers and sweets and clandestine kisses?" Bell clasps her hands around herself and kisses the air.

She falls back laughing when Kasaandra grunts, "Clandestine kisses?"

"Yeah. Like the book, *Clandestine Kisses*! It's about this woman who falls in love with a...wait...how do *you* do it?" she asks the dwarf.

"Do what?"

"Hello! Find a husband."

Bell's sigh is almost as loud as Kasaandra's harrumph.

"Anyone else want to volunteer what they'd like the UnSeeing Eye to show them?" Qrodin asks to change the subject. He's still hoping Qat will show some curiosity about their past.

"What about you?" Bell asks Qat. She doesn't wait for a response. "Wouldn't it be cool if it showed the World Burn War? You could see what dragons looked like! *Real* dragons! If I had dragons, I'd name them Bosco and Brutus!"

"Dragons would never be named Bosco *or* Brutus," Llani states emphatically.

"How do *you* know? Maybe they would. Do you understand *their* language?" Bell asks.

"Well. No. I...No one knows the language of the dragons."

"The witches did."

Kasaandra's statement shuts everyone up. But not for long.

"Incorrect. They were speaking an ancient form of Elvish," Llani says.

Qat leans forward, staring intently at Kasaandra. "You told Qrow that you knew what they were saying. Does that mean that you understand Ancient Elfish?" Qat asks her.

Llani's lips press tightly together. "Elvish, Qat. Not Elfish."

"It was Drakk, the language of the Drakkaen," Kasaandra says, sounding as though she's clearing her throat with her mouth open while speaking.

A chill runs through my body at the sound.

"What's a Drakkaen?" Bell asks, trying to imitate Kasaandra's inflection.

Kasaandra grunts again. "Drakkaen are dragons."

"It was Ancient Elvish," Llani can be as stubborn as Kasaandra.

"Drakk," Kasaandra says again, low and throaty.

"Kasaandra understood the witches and was talking to them. Maybe it *was* dragon," Bell says, sticking her tongue out at her friend.

"Unless you are familiar with the language, your assumption is pure speculation," Llani surprises everyone into shocked silence when she sticks her tongue out at Bell.

"I understood their conversation. They were speaking to each other in the same language," Qrodin says, though he'd rather he hadn't understood them. He still hears their words stream through his consciousness when he least expects it. He heard worse insults on the streets as an orphan, but while he was writing the song, he realized it was the venom with which the words were spoken that he was reacting to. Pure hatred and contempt.

"Drakk." Kasaandra rarely stands firm against Llani, but she's not backing down, and there's something in the dwarf's expression that says she's not happy doing it.

"You are mistaken. I distinctly recognized several words from my studies."

"And I recognized *every* word. I know what I'm saying."

"How could you possibly know Ancient Elvish?" Llani's ears are almost straight out to the sides of her head.

Kasaandra's voice lowers to a deep baritone. "Drakk!"

"*How did you understand them?*" Llani shouts, clenching her fists tightly in front of herself.

Bell's eyes fly open, and she shrinks away.

Akin signs faster than Qrodin can translate.

Llani nods and closes her eyes.

Qat retreats to the wall of the structure.

Qrodin has never heard the elf raise her voice. He doesn't think the others have, either, based on their reactions. It's disconcerting. And telling. Someone else has knowledge of a topic in which Llani considers herself competent, if not an expert. Was it worse because it was Kasaandra?

Qrodin wants to help Llani, but he fears that asking her if she needs help will worsen the situation. Her last outburst shows that she feels inadequate in some way only she understands.

"Llani," Qat says, pushing away from Qrodin's armoire. "I need a salt block for the horses."

"It is in my bag," Llani says quietly, finally coming out of her stupor. "If you bring it to me, I will get it out for you."

"No worries. I've got it." Qat reaches into the bag and fishes around inside. "I think. No, I don't. Are you sure it's in here? The bag's empty."

Llani is up quickly. She puts her hand out to take the bag when Qat flips it upside down, muttering under aer breath.

Suddenly, the bag's contents explode outward. Clothes, books, bags, and trunks fill Llani's space to the ceiling faster than Qrodin can blink. Qat and Llani are completely buried. Clothes are flattened, conforming to the invisible barrier of Llani's space—because nothing can leave it unless it's carried out.

"Qat! Llani!" Qrodin sprints to the pile and starts pulling things into his space. The items are packed so tightly that several clothing items tear as he yanks them free. "Quickly!" He commands the others. "The border is keeping everything inside. They could be crushed or suffocating."

"What the...?" Kasaandra says, joining him.

"What is all this stuff?" Qrodin says aloud as he frantically yanks at clothes, bags, and small boxes. So much stuff, he thinks. At this rate, it'll take them an hour to reach them. They could be dead by then.

"The contents of Llani's bag." Bell is flinging each piece between her legs like a dog digging for a bone. "Llani! We're coming!" she hollers as she runs into her space to tackle the pile from that side.

"Can we just collapse the Home Dome?" Bell calls out. "They'll be left outside. You know, like the bread bugs!"

"Do you know her symbol?" Kasaandra asks, methodically taking large handfuls of items and putting them in the space in the center of the six pocket homes where they usually build a fire.

"No. Hurry faster! You're going too slow!" Bell screams.

Kasaandra sighs. "Sometimes, slower is faster." She appears coming out of Bell's space with a large trunk and walks it over to her area, out of the way. "You're throwing things on your bread starters, Bell."

"What?" Bell yells, sounding frantic. "I'll fix it later. Llani could be dying!"

Akin climbs onto the pile as he clears a space. He lifts the upper layers of stuff above his head, pushing it through the shimmering border. When he lowers his arms, the items stay outside the structure. But inside, the pile grows until it reaches the dome's edge again.

"Qat! Llani!" Bell hollers. "Can you hear me? We're digging you out. Just hang on!"

Qrodin *Soothes* and tries to mix in some *Haste*, aware of the contradiction. "Akin! Llani was ahead of you. Be careful! You don't want to crush her."

Akin pushes armload after armload up and out of the reasacobila. Finally, the mound stops growing, and Qrodin can see space between the top of the pile and the dome's edge.

Qrodin has been trying to dig through midway up the pile, but stops when one of Akin's armloads reveals curly black hair. "I see Llani. Akin, uncover her face." Kasaandra moves to help clear the area in front of the elf.

"Llani! I'm here!" Bell starts climbing the pile, kicking items toward her space with her feet. They hit the unseen border and pile at the edge.

"Hey, Princess," Kasaandra says. "Stop lazing about and get yourself out of there. You have to clean up this mess."

Akin continues clearing around Llani's head and face. When it's clear, he checks her breathing. Fear spikes through Qrodin when Akin shakes his head. He puts his cheek to Llani's mouth, then places his lips over hers and blows his breath into her. Kasaandra and Bell work to clear the pile from her chest. Akin blows again.

Qrodin can see her chest expand with the breath. When Llani takes a breath of her own accord, Qrodin works faster to find Qat. If Llani was prevented from breathing, Qat may have been, too. He climbs up the pile and uses Akin's strategy of pushing items to the top of the dome. Ae shouldn't be far. Llani was only steps away from aem when it happened.

"Llani! You're alive!" Bell cries.

Qrodin spares only a glance as Llani opens her eyes. He can't stop. He pushes armful after armful until the entire sky is blotted out. Even in his rush, he notices the outside is littered with clothes, bottles, and books. Bags are open, the contents spilling. Crows are clawing and pecking at the refuse. He presses another armful toward the center where Akin and Kasaandra had piled theirs.

"Llani. Is Qat near you? Can you feel aem?" Qrodin can hear the near panic in his voice and tries to calm himself. He lifts another armful and tosses it, mindful not to dump it on Llani, Kasaandra, or Bell as he aims toward the center.

"Ae was pushed away from me when the bag emptied. I think ae's over there." She points to Qrow's left. He starts lifting where she had indicated. Akin joins him, confident now that Llani is uninjured. After nearly another minute, Qrodin wonders if they're in the right spot. They've removed nearly a cubic bandi's worth of stuff from the spot Llani had indicated, but there's no sign of Qat. There's so much resting on top of the structure now that he can't push another armful through the barrier. He tosses it down the side of the mound instead, toward the center, where it is filling up fast.

Llani, finally free of the pile, climbs around the structure to the top and starts pushing the pileup to the center, giving Akin and Qrodin more room. Kasaandra and Bell work to pull items from below.

"Qat! Can you hear me? Say something so we can find you." Qrodin's voice is hoarse, and he can't perform *Soothe*, which he needs right now.

"Qat!" Bell adds. "Please be alive! I'll make you all the pheasant pie you want if you just come out of there!"

"Qrow! I see Qat!" Llani says from above. She drops down, pushing Qrodin to the side. She lifts a small chest and tosses it down the pile. "Quickly! Clear this away. Ae's still alive, but aer chest is crushed." She uncovers and tugs at the end of her hanging bar. It had fallen across Qat's chest and was pinning aem down into the pile.

Qrodin lifts, but it doesn't budge. He squats until his shoulder is underneath the bar and tries to stand, but it's wedged underneath something solid inside the pile. "Kasaandra, can you clear that area?" His legs start to tremble from squatting. "On second thought, hold this up. I'll clear it." He and Kasaandra trade places. She rests the bar on her shoulder while he clears the obstacles. How did a table fit inside that bag? Kasaandra raises the bar. There's not enough room to get Qat out. He pushes the table up more, finally freeing it enough that he can twist it off the bar so Kasaandra can pull the bar off Qat.

Llani slides between the bar and the pile and places her hand on Qat's face. "Green, like Kasaandra's eyes," she whispers and closes her own.

Chapter 41 Qat

"Wake up, Qat. It's time to wake up."

Something soft strokes my cheek. I can smell the unique blend of spices Ama uses when ae cooks my favorite meal. It clings to aer clothes and in aer hair. It's aer particular scent. "Five more minutes," I say.

"You said that five minutes ago."

"Please, Ama. Just five more minutes." I open my eyes.

Ama's long, dark hair gleams in the candlelight. Ae holds one lock to my forehead. My eyes close as ae strokes it down my cheek.

"It's still dark outside."

"Okay, my love. Five more minutes."

Ama kisses my forehead. My heart smiles.

"Wake up, Qat. It's time to get up."

"Five more minutes."

"You said that five minutes ago."

No, I didn't. Besides, Ama said I could have five more minutes. "Go away, Qrow. I don't want to get up."

"Okay, but I'm telling."

That's okay. Ama loves me best.

"Wake up, Qat. You've been sleeping all morning."

"Five more minutes."

"You said that five minutes ago."

I know. But I can't. My head hurts. Leave me alone.

"I need you up in the crow's nest. Uci's sick."

I am, too.

"Wake up, Qat. I need you to wake up now."

Something soft strokes my cheek. I feel sad but don't know why. "Five more minutes."

"You said that five minutes ago."

"No, I didn't." I can't see any light through my closed lids. It's still dark outside.

"Yes, you did. And if you get up now, you can have some of the pheasant pie I made you."

Pheasant pie sounds good. "Bell?"

"Yes, Qat."

I open my eyes.

Bell's nose is a finger's width from mine. Her chocolatey brown eyes crinkle in a smile. She presses her forehead to mine. "Can I tell you a secret?"

"Sure."

She scrunches her nose. "You really need to brush your teeth."

I laugh. It hurts.

"Why do I hurt so bad?"

"You don't remember?"

I try to. "All I can recall is..." I close my eyes. My chest hurts. I feel as though an elephant sat on me. Elephants. Karatolii. That was days ago. No. Longer than that. Cranwood. The queen. The UnSeeing Eye.

Llani yelling at Kasaandra.

The bag.

"I was looking for something."

"Salt for the horses."

"Did I find it?"

"Sort of."

An overwhelming sadness comes over me. I close my eyes. "Five more minutes. Please, Bell. Then I'll have some pie."

"Okay, Qat. Five more minutes."

My heart aches, and I feel tears slide down my cheeks.

I wish I knew why.

Chapter 42 Qrodin

It takes all evening and half the night to clear up the mess. They split the task by item type. Qrodin starts with the clothing. They're extraordinary and elf-made. He recognizes the complex stitches along the hem. Only elves put that much effort into their hemlines. Qat learned how to make garments, but Qrow had been far more interested in their history. He gained his extensive knowledge of textiles from Ama'ani.

These clothes are ancient but in impeccable condition. The fabrics are high quality, as are the brass and copper buttons—still gleaming even though they must have been stored for quite some time.

Bell digs out food, cooking utensils, and kitchen items while Llani collects books. She places most of them on a bookcase she'd purchased from the Karatolii, though Qrodin doesn't think it will be big enough. Kasaandra and Akin select the heavy stuff. There are trunks, tools, climbing gear, ropes, pulleys, and heavy canvases. They repack most of the trunks.

Llani gifts Kasaandra with a leather knapsack of Smith's tools and a case of metal scraps. They could have used many of the supplies on their journey. He doesn't say so, but Kasaandra does.

"It was my pata's bag. Mata gave it to me the day I left. I was unaware of the contents until tonight."

Kasaandra grunts. "I thought she didn't know her pata," she says quietly to Akin.

"What makes you say that?" Qrodin asks her.

She shrugs. "She's never mentioned him."

But she had mentioned him to Qrodin. Sort of. He wonders if Llani's parents had a marriage contract. Can elves prevent unplanned pregnancies? He got the impression she didn't know who her father was. And most of this stuff is his?

What surprises Qrodin most is the size of some of the items. How did they even get in the bag? The opening is so much smaller. He discovers the secret when they attempt to put a table back inside the bag. They place the mouth of the bag over one leg, and the opening stretches to accommodate the other. They all stare in disbelief as the entire length of the table slides inside before the bag shrinks back to its standard size.

"Why did the bag explode, anyway?" Bell asks.

"I saw Qat tip the bag upside down. Could that have done it?" Qrodin asks.

"No. I did the same when Mata gave it to me. I believe Qat somehow instructed the bag to empty."

"And you didn't know any of this stuff was in here?" Bell asks.

Llani's lips compress. "As I said, the bag's contents were undisclosed. I doubt Mata knew its specifics."

"And you didn't inspect it when you got it?"

"Had I known how to empty it, I would have done so before now. One must request an item to retrieve it. I know only those items I placed inside."

"You say the bag belonged to your father?" Qrodin asks.

"That is my understanding."

"These clothes look nearly new, but I don't recognize this style as from this century. Where was your father from?" Qrodin didn't want to say it, but the clothing didn't look from this millennium, let alone this century. Even though elves have been known to live nearly one thousand years, their average lifespan is less than eight hundred. There's no way these clothes could have belonged to Llani's father.

"I need to check on Qat. Ae is still sleeping. Please excuse me," Llani says instead.

"Of course."

It wasn't the first time Llani had avoided questions about her father.

They continue cleaning and sorting, leaving the center portion for last, until Qrodin remembers the crows eating from a bag earlier. "We need to get the items outside."

"I'll go," Kasaandra says. Most of the bulky items have already been moved or stored, and she doesn't seem keen on sorting through the small stuff, especially the clothes, of which there appears to be an inordinate quantity. She doesn't wait for a response before leaving.

"Hey! Look at this! It's a crown!" Bell puts it on her head and smiles, her face softening and losing the worry grooves that have been etched there since Llani healed Qat. "How do I look?"

"A crown?" Qrodin and Akin join Bell.

Akin signs something. *Don't*, and *Kasaandra* was all Qrodin could make out.

Bell laughs. "Oh, yeah! The princess jokes would never stop!"

"It matches her necklace," Qrodin tells them, staring at the twisted branch-like design and large gemstone.

"Really?" Bell takes it off and squints. She holds it as far away as she can. When she notices Qrodin watching her, she holds it closer to a light. "Oh. Yeah. I see that now."

Qrodin doubts it. He'd realized almost immediately that Bell was far-sighted. She can spot a rabbit nearly a coot away, but not the stains on her bosom. He can't imagine how she's been able to read all those books she's constantly referring to. He's never seen her wearing glasses.

"What kind of wood is that?" Bell asks, handing the headpiece to Akin.

Instead of inspecting the piece, Akin closes his eyes. The lines that are usually etched deeply around his mouth smooth out, and for the first time Qrodin can recall, Akin looks relaxed and at peace.

"What is that?"

Qrodin hadn't seen Llani approach. "How is Qat?" he asks her.

"I was able to complete aer healing, finally, but ae is still sleeping. We will not know if Qat sustained irreparable brain damage until ae wakes up." Earlier, Llani had said that, when she was trapped inside the pile, she couldn't move to clear her face, and there was so much pressure on her chest she couldn't breathe. When the contents were released, they compacted so tightly that Qat's ribs were broken and aer chest compressed, preventing aem from taking sufficient breaths.

She pauses a moment. "Some injuries cannot be healed with magic."

Yes, he's well aware of that. He'll probably never regain full strength in his side.

Qrodin has been trying to occupy his mind with clearing and sorting to keep him from worrying about the fate of his twin. Llani's words don't alleviate any of it.

Akin hands Llani the headpiece. As soon as she touches it, her body spasms. Bell gasps. Qrodin flinches as though he's been shocked. Llani's breathing becomes harsh, and her eyes grow large. Her face seems to elongate. Akin growls and grabs the crown back. Llani immediately relaxes, and her face returns to normal.

"Llani!" Bell asks, "Are you okay? What happened?"

"I...I am," Llani responds. "Thank you for asking. I do believe I am feeling the effects of my ordeal. Bell, would you help me make some tea?"

The two dip into Bell's space, leaving Qrodin to wonder if he had been seeing things. What had happened to her face? It's like looking in a mirror when he changes his appearance using *Deziré*. Has Llani been in disguise this whole time? Is it possible that she could be a strong enough magic user that she can hold a disguise indefinitely, and the crown interrupted it? What is its connection to her necklace? Is it the necklace that allows her to hold the disguise? Or is it an elf trait?

The witches held their disguises until they died. And they were also elves. Do elves have some advantage in that area?

Bell breaks the silence, poking her head into Llani's space and looking over. "Here comes Kasaandra."

Akin folds the jeweled crown in a soft cloth and carefully fits it into the box from which Bell had removed it. He places it back in the bag.

Qrodin has no idea what just happened. It's not Kasaandra that speaks next, though.

"Hey. What happened in here?"

Qrodin flinches and turns to see Qat sitting up, rubbing aer chest as though it hurts.

A sense of relief shudders through him. "How are you feeling?" he asks.

Qat squints at him. Aer hands rub in circles over aer heart. "Like I've been drowned, died, and reborn." Ae looks at the remaining mess. "Did I do that?"

"Yeah." Kasaandra points to the center, where items are still piled up and are suspended against the nearly invisible barrier. "Now, you can help us clean it up."

Qat gets to aer feet and walks around it, obviously impressed that the items are defying gravity. "That's pretty cool."

Part 3 Craguesport

Chapter 43 Qat

15TH DAY OF PILAMEE, 14,887
ROAD TO CRAGUESPORT, ZEDANA

We're going to arrive in Craguesport today.

Thankfully, the road stayed close to the river, where we replenished our water and bathed daily. For the most part, the weather is cool enough that Kasaandra only complains about the heat a few times a day. How can she spend all day in a forge heated by magma but can't ride on the back of a horse in autumn?

There have been enough trees along the way to keep Llani stocked with new cuttings. I've tried to tune her out whenever she shares a specie's properties and uses. How someone can keep that much knowledge is beyond me. I wouldn't want to learn that much if I lived a hundred years like her. I like the mystery of not knowing something. Mystery fuels the imagination.

She's been doing the same thing with birds. She and Akin have worked up different bird calls for warning alerts we might need. They've even incorporated them into our drills. There's an alarm for an attack from above and another for snakes. One for animal predators, one for umanid threats. Plenty more, but when will we ever use them? We'll be in Craguesport soon.

Akin spends much of his non-travel time meditating. I've learned a few more signs, mostly the signs we use when sparring, but they're inadequate for conversation between us.

Thankfully, we've had plenty of time in the evenings to spar after camp is set up, especially as it takes less time with the Home Dome. Considering how often we've encountered the unexpected, we've switched things up during our practice sessions. We sometimes practice in teams or all-against-one, in addition to one-on-one matches. Akin uses whistles and simple hand gestures to communicate. He's the most skilled of us all and usually directs our practice, but sometimes, he puts one of us in charge of it.

Starshine has gotten involved in our sessions as I practice dismounts and mounted combat. He learns so fast, it's as though he understands what I'm saying. Or maybe I'm learning to understand him. I get it, now, why some people claim they can communicate with their pets.

I'd never been this close with an animal before, but they're not so different from people, now that I'm paying attention. The horses sigh when they're frustrated or bored. They quiver and pick up the pace when they realize they will get fed. But Starshine is extraordinary. I'm not able to teach the other horses anything, but he is so responsive. And he and Llani seem to have made up. One time, she even practiced launching her fire darts from his back while he was circling us. The feat was quite impressive.

When we're not training, we've been taking turns looking through the UnSeeing Eye and sharing what we see. We started with the past. It was disorienting at first. The visions were from a person's perspective, complete with eye blinks, as if we were viewing a memory.

Qrow has been writing everything down.

Sometimes, the visions are horrifying, and for Bell's sake, I'm thankful there is no sound. I've seen battles and fires. I think one of them was from the World Burn War. An entire town was on fire. The smoke was so thick and dark that my eyes started watering. Out of the corner of my eye, I swore I saw a giant wing arc over the burning building my bucket brigade was trying to put out. The wing was red, or I probably wouldn't have noticed it. I—or rather the person whose visions I was viewing—put an arm up and ducked, then ran when flames *Whoosh*ed from around the side of the building.

I was so surprised, I pulled the scope away. When I looked back, the vision was a new one.

I lied when they asked me what I saw. Dragons were real. And terrifying.

We looked at the present a few times, but none of it was recognizable. There were lands we'd never been in, although Akin may have recognized a few based on his expression (or lack thereof). I hear he's traveled to every country with his aunt.

We'd all agreed not to investigate the future yet. I told everyone about the queen's warning that we wouldn't be able to change the future, even if we saw it. Or was that the present? I can't remember her exact words.

"You think if I ask, it will show me who took the treasure we found? That would be so cool! I would tell the queen, and she would make me her new best friend!" Bell looks over at Llani. "Don't worry, Llani. *You'll* still be *my* best friend."

"I think the queen can find who took the treasure. She has an entire merkama force at her disposal." Qrow looks annoyed, as if the thought of that many riches bores him. Well, maybe it does, but that's because he's rich. The rest of us have never seen that kind of treasure. Well, maybe Kasaandra has. She looks as bored with the subject as Qrow whenever it gets brought up.

Llani hands the UnSeeing Eye to me now because we'll be arriving in Craguesport soon. She seems unwilling to part with it. The closer we've gotten, the quieter we've all become—except for Bell. She is so excited she's practically bouncing in the saddle, kind of like Kasaandra with battle euphoria. Even though none of us respond, Bell keeps a running commentary of equal parts nonsensical babble and squealing.

I've tried to prepare her for the sheer size and magnitude of the city, but there's nothing I can say that will effectively do so. She thought Riversmeet was gigantic, and Craguesport is at least three times the size.

That's one of the reasons I'm usually comfortable staying here. The city is large enough to remain anonymous, I'm never bored, and it has the best sourdough bread on Oram. I know the fishing district like I know the damascus pattern on my daggers. I'm up in the forestry and crafting districts when I'm not there. The shops there can't be beaten, and the forestry district has the only brothel in town and, ironically, the best seafood restaurants. If I ever settle down, I've contemplated getting a place in one of those districts.

"Hey, do they celebrate Proximan more than one day here?" Bell asks. "There is this amazing dessert we make especially for it with honey, cinnamon, and super thin layers of crispy pastry. I want some so bad right now."

"The farming and crafting districts do," Qrow says. "You can probably find your dessert in the farming district." Qrow's voice changes slightly when he continues. "You know that we met Kasaandra during the Proximan festival twenty years ago?"

We did? I look at Kasaandra for confirmation.

She nods. "On the fifteenth."

"On Mordkanee?" Bell asks.

Mordkanee. Rogen used to call it the Shadowstich Solstice. Other cultures have different names for it, like Gathering of the Unbound Souls and Twilight of Echoes, but they all celebrate it today, on the fifteenth of Pilamee. The day when the veil between the living and the dead is thinnest—if you believe in that stuff.

"You mean, today?" I say, wondering why Kasaandra never told me. She and Qrow talked about it. Did he tell her not to say anything? If so, why did he bring it up now?

"That's today?" Bell asks and groans when I nod.

I'm always surprised at how few people keep track of the days unless they follow a rigid schedule. Llani journals, so I'd bet she knew what today was. And Qrow is constantly checking his business ledgers, but Bell seldom seems to know what day it is. Four days ago, she prepared a special Proximan meal for us at the last minute because she hadn't discovered until the afternoon that it *was* Proximan.

Twenty years ago today, I was with Qrow when we met Kasaandra outside Dwarf Mountain. Qrow said I was abducted in Riversmeet a short time later. All I remember is that—after waking up onboard the *Raven Scream*—Rogen's first stop was Craguesport, and it was wintertime.

Today, Qrow, Kasaandra, and I are riding into Craguesport on the twentieth anniversary of the day we met. Life is a strange set of coincidences.

"We'll be in Craguesport soon," Qrow says.

"In that case, we need to put on masks!" Bell stops her horse and digs in her bag. "Kasaandra, at least you can wear your bear rug cape thing. Llani, do you have something in your bag I can use?"

Pirates love Mordkanee, one of the best times to visit large cities since so many cultures, including hablis, wear masks or costumes. We don't have to worry about trying to blend in since most city-goers are in disguise. Some cultures say it hides their true form from ghosts or demons. I guess I understand why you might want to hide from the ghosts of your ancestors, but what would it matter to a demon? They don't care who you are, do they?

I look over at Bell riding next to me. "If you were at home, what would you wear?"

"We combine as many animal parts as we can," she says. "At least three. I wish I'd thought of bringing mine. I have the cutest looking rabbit ears."

Hearing that, Kasaandra gives her a cloak of rabbit furs she's been making. Llani hands her an antler helm she'd retrieved from her bag. I'm surprised it hadn't broken when the bag discharged. Lastly, Akin places a mask of feathers to cover her face.

Once she's disguised, I entertain her with stories about the seedy parts of the city as the others change. She can't get enough of them.

The final approach is through rolling hills. The roads are better here. They're paved and maintained because they're constantly used to travel north, south, and west into the Manntar mountain cities we'd just passed between.

I tuck the UnSeeing Eye into my belt. We look like a well-traveled bunch of misfits. Qrow transformed his clothes into a tight-fitting, lion fur outfit. With his hair down and a bit of magic, it made a convincing enough mane. With that costume, there is no need to put in his colored eye lenses. I tied my hair back, and I'm wearing my black leather breeches. I tie the red scarf around my head and put on an eye patch. Why not embrace the stereotype?

Kasaandra draped her white fur around herself with the head of the bear resting on top of her wild red hair.

Akin and Llani have chosen to look like royalty. Somewhere in Llani's bag, they had retrieved long robes belted at the waist and worn over matching leggings. Llani is resplendent in silver. Her hair is piled high with tight ringlets, and her necklace gleams at her throat.

Llani had given Akin something to help polish his ropy dreads, and now sunshine reflects off their bouncing locks. Even his tusks look brighter and whiter than before. His blue robe is belted lightly at the waist and split down both sides to allow ease of movement. Running from shoulder to hem on the front is a multi-colored band about the width of my splayed fingers. His pants are cut loose and long, nearly hiding his sandaled feet. And on his head rests the matching circlet. He's almost as dazzling as his fire and lightning.

I don't know if I'll stay with them when we get to town. I'm more worried about Starshine than anything else. I turn him back and motion the others to go forward, leaving Kasaandra in the lead. Today, Qrow's in the rear of the group.

"Qat," Qrow says in greeting when I join him.

"What are your intentions with"—I nod to the back of Starshine's head. Though it seems like it sometimes, the horse can't *actually* understand Oramische. But he does at least recognize his name.

"Why do you ask?" At my silence, Qrow continues, "You may keep him if you'd like. If not, I'll give him a permanent home in my stable. He's far too grand to be traded in as a cheap rental."

I swallow the sudden lump in my throat. "I'm worried about how much I travel."

"You may keep him in my stables as long as you want. I will inform the stablemaster."

Starshine nods his head forward and back as though he agrees. I feel my stomach relax. "I appreciate that."

"There is another matter I'd like to speak with you about. Regarding Balaerdo's," Qrow says, keeping his voice low.

Balaerdo's? He can't be talking about me snaking the flask. I wait until he continues. It takes longer than I thought it would.

"It's yours," he finally says.

"Mine? What do you mean, mine?" That was the last thing I thought he'd say. "I don't need your charity."

"It's not charity. I listed you as a co-owner when I opened the first one. I arranged for a portion of the profits to be transferred into an account for you ever since then."

What?

My brain feels like it's frozen again.

Balaerdo's is mine? Part mine?

What does that mean?

"At your convenience, I'd like to show you how to access the account."

I have an account?

With money in it?

My belly does a flip-flop, then settles into a non-stop flutter. Or maybe it's a trot. No, more like a steady gallop.

I've never even been inside a bank. There was no need. They're nearly impossible to steal from.

My hands start shaking, and I clench them tightly to prevent the tremor from showing. I swallow hard. My mouth is so dry that it hurts to do so.

What am I going to do with money?

What am I gonna do with a store? With many stores?

"You can be as involved as you want to be with the business. I have managers and buyers in place who have been overseeing the business for years. Let me know if you'd like to meet any of them or make any changes."

Buyers and managers and bank accounts?

If we were in town, I'd be dipping down an alley and running right now, but there's no place to hide here on this empty road.

I can't wrap my head around it all. Instead, I nod and nudge Starshine forward. I wish the UnSeeing Eye could show me what I'm going to do because right now, I'm clueless.

To take my mind off my conversation with Qrow, I halt next to Bell, who is riding by herself but still babbling nonstop to her horse. Llani has moved up, and Akin is teaching her more sign language. I had asked her once how she picked it up so quickly, and she said she had learned it when she was a child but hadn't used it since. She'd clammed up afterward and wouldn't answer any more questions about it.

"Hi, Qat! Are we almost there?" Bell asks.

"I think so, but I'm not used to arriving by land. If we were closer to the river, I'd be able to recognize a few landmarks, but that hill is in the way. You'll know we're getting close if we see an old shipwreck on one of these hills."

"What's a ship doing way up on a hill?

"Sometimes at night, through the cracks in the beams?" I pause.

"Yeah?" she asks.

"I see colored lights moving around inside."

"I want to see that!"

"Maybe I'll take you there one night. Of course, you have to be sneaky if we go. Can you be sneaky?" I wouldn't let her get close, but we could look from a distance.

"Oh. I can be sneaky, all right!"

I hold my hand out for a high-five, and she obliges.

I can't tell her it's the entrance to the Winged Death Guild for faeries. That would be an unforgivable breach and could cost me my life. Besides, she probably wouldn't believe me, anyway. Faeries aren't supposed to be real. I only know about the lights because I followed one of their members back to the ship, and she disappeared between the slats. How did she fit through the small gap? I could only guess. She was a faerie, after all. And no one truly knows what faeries can do.

Thinking of her, I get nervous. She had said I wouldn't remember her or our escapade that night, or the bet she won, or her admission that if she could have anything she wanted, it would be her freedom. I'll never forget the look in her eyes when she said it, or her surprise when she realized I could see her. But I did see her, and I do remember her.

What's worse, she wasn't the only faerie I met. She was just the first. A few nights after I met her, a male faerie accosted me. He came up behind me and whispered in my ear while I was playing cards. And in a crowded tavern, no less. He told me his name was Frostbite Flickerfall, and if I wanted to live, I'd never reveal the guild's location, and I'd forget I ever saw his daughter.

No one else acted like they saw him, so I pretended I didn't know he was there. I don't know how I did it. Frostbite Flickerfall is a stupid name, but he's a legend—one of the most successful assassins in Kish. I can't imagine anyone knows he's a faerie. I doubt anyone believes he's real. Legends of him have been passed from generation to generation in the assassin guilds. Jobs no one else could complete were eventually attributed to him.

Like I said. A legend.

And I couldn't even brag to anyone that I'd met him. Or that he had a daughter. What would happen to her if anyone knew he was real? And still alive?

And had a daughter?

The best assassins have no familial ties. That kind of weakness can be used as leverage.

It's one of the reasons I've always valued not having a family.

But now, I have Qrow.

"Look, Qat! There it is!"

And Bell. If anything happens to her... I rub the sudden ache in my chest and follow her pointing finger. The ship. It's daytime, so there aren't any lights. I look away quickly.

Starshine sneezes.

"Oh, Starshine. You're so cute when you sneeze."

I laugh, thankful for how easily she gets distracted. I feel a release in my shoulders and back and take a deep breath. I hadn't known how tense I was.

I suddenly realize I'm more vulnerable now than ever. And after today, the faeries will know it. My spine tightens, but I refuse to look around for whoever's watching us.

The faeries already know it.

Knowing about Qrow and our relationship makes me vulnerable. And that might make him a target.

I hadn't thought about that when we announced we were siblings to Sorbslles or Queen Sarafeen. I don't want to think about it now.

I haven't seen either of the faeries since. Or any faerie since. But I have seen the lights nearly every time I sail by the shipwreck at night. I never saw them before that night, and I've never heard anyone else say they saw lights there. I wonder if the lights are the faeries' way of telling me they know I'm sailing by. As if they know where I am, always.

My spine tingles again. I ignore it. If it is them—especially Flickerfall—I don't want them to know *I* know they're there.

Up ahead, another road is meeting up with the one we're on, widening this one enough that we can all ride side-by-side if we wish.

I look over at Bell with her antlers and rabbit cloak. She looks like a little kid. "Let's join Kasaandra in the front so I can show you the city when we get there."

"You bet!"

Chapter 44 Qrodin

Craguesport is the only city in which Qrow has a personal residence, and if there's any place Qrodin considers home, it's this city. Riversmeet has too many bad memories to ever feel as welcome or as safe.

Craguesport started as a mining outpost at the mouth of Turtle River, north of where it dumps into the Reef Sea. The mining outpost changed hands too often to record over the centuries, but eventually, six families settled in Craguesport, and the city's current districts are named after them. The tiny mining outpost was transformed into a metropolis of giant warehouses and the largest and most important seaport on Kish's east coast. Many guilds are set up here, from smithing to tailoring to shipbuilding. In addition, Craguesport hosts Zedana's naval headquarters and supports a substantial military. An old coliseum was eventually refitted to house and train them all.

As they ride toward his home in the Jalu district—a roomy *domi* that takes up the entire top floor of the complex—he realizes he's strangely reluctant to give up his natural face again. Not needing a disguise for weeks at a time gave him more energy to focus on everything else around him. He hasn't done that since he was a child, since shortly after he woke up on that dock in Riversmeet.

Not focusing on keeping a disguise in public would be a relief. There were times he'd look at himself in his bedroom mirror and not recognize himself until he realized he was still holding his disguise hours after he got home. It takes him a moment to realize that he can remain disguised in Craguesport by *not* using a disguise. Everyone knows him as Quentin Browning. When he doesn't want to be Quentin, he can be himself.

The streets are so crowded that Qrodin tells the others to stay mounted as they work their way down Kaibur Street, the main street that runs from the city's entrance to the cliffs overlooking the sea. Since passing under the arched entrance to the city, Bell hasn't stopped oohing and aahing, but at least she's no longer screeching. With most of the townsfolk in costume, their small group gets no more attention than anyone else.

Qrodin's been here so long he's ceased paying attention to how amazing the city is. He's forgotten what it looks like to an outsider. Seeing it again through Bell's eyes—her very wide eyes—gives him a new appreciation for the city he lives in.

Her interest wanes when they reach the fishing and financial districts. There are fewer vendors here. Merchants hawking their wares and townsfolk bartering are left behind, replaced by guild halls and government buildings.

When they approach the stables near his home, they dismount.

"We can leave our mounts here. The stablemaster will see that they get taken to a rental agency."

"What? Who will give Ginger carrots? And who will braid her hair? I want to keep her! You want to stay with me, don't you, girl?" Bell hugs Ginger. The horse ruffles Bell's hair when the hablis finally releases her.

"Of course you may keep her, Bell. As can anyone else who prefers to. They will have a home here for as long as you like."

"I think Ginger wants all her friends to stay, too."

"You speak horse now?" Kasaandra asks.

Bell responds by sticking her tongue out.

After changing into their costumes outside the city, they'd removed everything from their saddlebags, so there is nothing to unload when they leave their mounts with the stablemaster. Before starting on the final stretch to Craguesport, they left everything except the small bag Qat had given Bell for her bread starters, Qat's small pack with the green stone, and Llani's bag, inside their reasacobilas.

"Where is the hotel?" Bell asks.

Without thinking, Qrodin replies, "You're welcome to stay with me. I have plenty of room."

They look as surprised as he is at making the offer. He had entertained the notion briefly on the walk through town but had dismissed it. Now that he's made the offer, though, it feels right. After all, they had been living together in their combined reasacobilas. This will be a roomier and more comfortable extension of that.

The only one he worries about is Qat. On the one hand, it will be nice having aem near again. On the other hand, Qat's the most curious person Qrodin's ever met, and Qrodin can't afford to have Qat impede his business dealings. There's too much at stake, including his reputation. Of course, in some circles, having a professional assassin as a sibling might give him *more* credibility, not less. But those are the circles he's sworn to keep secret. Qat can't find out about them. None of them can.

Qrodin leads them to his home. Across the street is the round training facility of the Tiolapin Monastery, where Akin told them earlier he would be staying. Qrodin had purchased the abandoned facility long ago, shortly after arriving here. He hadn't had a plan for it at the time, but when he met Akin's Aunt Imolena, he knew it would be the perfect location for their monastery in Craguesport. It was their first collaboration.

Qrodin points out his domi. "I live on the top floor. You are welcome anytime. Would you like to accompany us upstairs?"

Akin declines with a shake of his head.

"How about dinner after you settle in, then. At the fish market around the corner?"

Akin nods and crosses the street.

The building that houses Qrodin's domi is six floors of red brick with large windows framed in white. The front doors are glass and open to a vast hall that ends in a staircase. As they ascend, each level looks the same as the first, only with fewer and fewer apartment doors. Only Qrodin's apartment takes up an entire floor.

Qrodin unlocks the door, and they pause a moment in the spacious lounge room in the center of his home. Strategically placed columns and decorative archways anchor an open floor plan and separate the main areas while providing necessary architectural support. The walnut hardwood flooring gleams in the filtered light from tinted skylights set into high ceilings. Gentle shadows caress steel-blue walls decorated with original artwork. Large windows in the room opposite the front door provide picturesque views of the setting sun and the garden below. A variety of instruments hang on the walls and nestle in floor stands, and a harpsichord sits comfortably in the far-left corner.

Purchasing such a large home was impulsive, and his reasons elude him still. Perhaps it was a holdover from his childhood and their enormous gatherings. He always imagined it would be perfect for hosting large family parties, despite not having one anymore. Regardless, the only other person invited inside is Garmand, who comes by twice a fortnight to clean it and water all the plants resting in corners and on fixtures, in sconces on the walls, peppered amid the many bookcases and priceless antiques, and hanging from the ceiling in front of the windows.

Qrodin gives them a quick tour of his home. Llani, Bell, and Kasaandra select their rooms. Qrodin offers Qat the blue and grey suite adjacent to his rooms.

Qat grimaces. "I'll be more comfortable nearer the water."

Qat slips out while Qrodin's showing the others how to fill the bathtubs with warm water and where to find the towels and other toiletry items.

Finally alone, Qrodin's careful not to mar the all-white décor of his bedchamber as he strips off his travel clothing. After a long, cool bath, he admires his beard in the mirror and decides not to remove it all. Instead, he trims it, then shaves the sides, leaving a mustache and goatee.

Though he's exhausted from the trip, he enters his office. It has the best views at sunset, painting the room in brilliant yellow, orange, and red, reminding him when it's time to eat—something he forgets to do otherwise. Right now, though, the midday sun brightens the room without revealing the hidden walk-in vault.

He sits at his desk and makes a list of things to catch up on. A list of questions for his business managers. A list of vendors and potential buyers for Cranwood. A list of supplies he needs for his house guests. A list of ideas to entertain his guests. A list of...

Chapter 45 Qat

In a city with so many people, the silence in Qrow's apartment is eerie and unnatural. I thrive in places where I can pass without a sound. At the very least, I should've heard neighborhood kids playing or people moving around in other units. But there was no clanking of pots and pans. No chitchat. Nothing. It gave me chills.

As I get closer to my side of town, I shake off the feeling. The sooner I find out if Rogen is here, the better I'll feel.

My last intel was that he'd be heading to Craguesport sooner or later. The influx of visitors means he'll likely be here for either Mordkanee or the Longest Night celebrations. More visitors mean more ships, which means more targets to choose from. This wouldn't be the captain's first time visiting Craguesport around Proximan and Mordkanee. He could already have come and gone, but I don't think so. Tonight is his favorite holiday.

My first stop is the fish market around the corner. Even though it's where we'll be eating tonight, I could eat every meal there. With my deep-fried, battered fish in hand, I take the back alleys to the bathhouse to avoid the crush of tourists in the streets.

Unfortunately, there's no word of the captain or the *Raven Scream* along the way.

The bathhouse is so busy, I don't have time to relax and soak in the tub like I usually do. I don't even get a proper bathtub. They pour a few buckets of lukewarm water into a metal tub traditionally reserved for washing clothes, hand me another bucket for rinsing, and leave me to my business.

I step in and sit down, folding myself into a pretzel, and close my eyes.

I'm alone.

Finally.

"I knew it was you!"

My eyes fly open.

Sitting on the side of the tub opposite me is a faerie. She, too, is purple, but unlike Llani, the faerie is an aubergine shade, and her hair is midnight purple—so dark, it's nearly black. Her legs are crossed, and her feet dangle just above the water. She can't be more than a foot tall—even though her horns have doubled since the last time I saw her and are now protruding well above the top of her spiky hair. Gold shimmers on dragonfly-shaped wings and within inquisitive eyes.

"Nightshade?" How did I not feel her presence before she spoke? Maybe because she's not intending to harm me. At least I don't have to worry about covering myself. I'm already twisted up enough that my knees come up to my chin. "What are you doing here?"

"I had to see if it was really you. Who was it that you were riding with? A new mark?"

"How did you know I was with…?" I recall the twinge I'd felt when riding by the shipwreck earlier. "Oh. That was you spying on me when I rode in?"

"You knew I was watching you?"

"I knew someone was." I shift uncomfortably. Why had I felt her then and not now? Maybe I'm getting soft. If so, I'll need to change that. "What are you doing here?" I ask again.

"Are you a bodyguard now? Or were you hired to take out that fancy couple? They look important. Who are they?"

"What fancy couple?"

Nightshade rolls her eyes. "I thought you were smarter than that."

I smile. "Does your daddy know you're here?"

Her eyes widen, and she nearly falls backward. Her wings flutter as she rights herself, although I remember she doesn't need them to fly. Something about their design catches my attention. When I try to focus on them to figure out what it is, she pulls them behind her. "How do you know about my dad?"

"He came by to warn me to stay away from you and forget I ever met you."

Her eyes narrow. "You must have been born under a lucky star. How are you still alive?"

"It's my charm."

"I doubt it."

"Can I help you?"

"I don't know yet."

"Okay." Suddenly, I realize how *she* might be able to help *me*. I can't forget about the treasure we found in Cranwood. "Since you're here, do you know anything about a secret auction happening anytime soon?"

She shrugs. "Sure. At least a dozen. What kind of stuff?"

I debate telling her anything specific. "The expensive kind?"

Instead of answering, she wiggles her fingers, and a conical hat made from glittering dust particles forms between her hands. She places it on my head.

"What's that?" I ask.

She waves her hands, and the hat dissipates. "My humor is wasted on you."

"My sincerest apologies," I say, mimicking Qrow. What were we talking about? Oh, yeah, the auction. "I'm looking for one that requires you to wear a special ring to get in. You ever heard of anything like that?"

"Maybe. What's in it for me?"

"What do you want?" All the faerietales say you need to be careful giving promises to faeries.

She narrows her eyes. "I want to go with you when you leave here."

"And have your daddy come after me? No thanks."

"I'm an adult now. He can't kill you if you're paying me to do a job. It's against guild rules."

"Ah. So, now you want payment."

"Isn't that the going rate for information?"

Only when I can't get it for free. "Why do you want to leave?"

She crosses her arms.

I raise one brow. Last time, she said she wanted to be free. I'd been confused at the time, but now I wonder if maybe she wants to be out of her father's shadow.

She sticks her chin out stubbornly.

I put my arms behind my head and lean back.

She purses her lips.

I smile.

She huffs loudly. "I want to see the world. All I've ever known is Craguesport."

I believe that. I decide to leave it alone for now. I'm already late. "Do you know what time it is?"

"Time for you to get a watch."

Ha ha. Only the wealthiest people have watches. "And it's time for you to leave."

Her eyes narrow again, but then she focuses on my side. She flies close, looming over me. "Those tattoos aren't very good. Why would you want cat tattoos, anyway? I swear those nasty creatures are demons in disguise."

I look down. I'd uncovered my birthmarks. "What's wrong with cats?"

She scowls. "It's a faerie thing."

"I guess if I looked like a bug, cats would go after me, too."

She hisses and bares her teeth, revealing two rows of razor-sharp teeth that look as lethal as a piranha's.

I swat at her, but she somersaults backward and lands softly, sitting on the tub's rim again. She smiles and crosses her legs. "How long are you going to be in Craguesport, anyway? I want to know when we're leaving." She looks over her shoulder as if the answer is unimportant.

She can leave anytime, as far as I'm concerned. "Does that mean you'll tell me what you know?"

"Of course! I told you I want to go with you. When are we leaving?"

I shrug.

"When you figure it out, let me know." She floats up and seems to disappear, but something swoops toward the gap beneath the door.

She's gone before I can ask her how I'm supposed to find her. Not that I would, anyway.

The last thing I want is a rogue faerie assassin with a daddy complex following me around. Especially when that daddy is Frostbite Flickerfall.

I soap up quickly, then stand and dump the pail of tepid water over my head. After I dry off, I use my damp towel to clean off my leather breaches before putting them back on.

When I get to the fish market, Qrow sees me first. "You're late," he says. "We're almost done eating."

"Then I'm right on time." When Bell frowns, I say, "For dessert."

18TH DAY OF PILAMEE, 14,887

The last few days have been spent crisscrossing the fishing and crafting districts, the docks, the guild halls, and the back alleys. Not one word of the captain. Almost like he's disappeared. Or never existed.

Instead of visiting the brothel as I originally planned, I decide to find the old woman Rogen used to visit. She lives—or at least she used to—in one of the few homes in the fishing district, a small place directly behind the fish market. Not the marketplace we ate in last night, but the open-air market a few blocks away that sells fish newly unloaded from the fishing boats.

In the mornings, large carts filled with fresh fish are crowded behind tables full of butcher blocks, weighing scales, and stacks of newsprint. Shrimp and crab are sold by the bucket. The stench is so foul by afternoon that everything is scrubbed with salt water and vinegar after the carts are wheeled away. A few hours later, the place swarms with vendors hawking everything from nuts to self-published zines until they're kicked out in the early morning.

This evening, cast iron grills on wheels are loaded with kabobs, grilled vegetables, and one of my favorites. I buy two scorpions on a stick and amble around the side of the market. The old lady's apartment is the closest of six that line the back of the marketplace. There are two windows on the side wall. The first is shuttered closed, but the second is open. I move to the far side of the window and lean against the wall, which gives me a good view of the inside. This is where I used to spy on the captain when he'd visit.

A lamp burns brightly through the window, revealing a couple of chairs and a side table. The old woman is sitting in the same chair she used to when I was younger. Her hair is entirely grey now. Her hands are gnarled, her knuckles are swollen, and the needle in her hand looks a bit unsteady. Even so, the piece she's embroidering doesn't have a wrinkle in it. From what I can see, the stitches are even and flat, but that's not what holds my attention. The design she's embroidering is the same design that was on my red scarf so long ago. The same pattern that's on the scarf I stole from Balaerdo's in Riversmeet. Stars and the three moons in their different phases. This time, she's embroidering them in various colors along the bottom hem of a garment.

Two men walk by, arguing loudly. At first, I don't pay any attention to them. I barely register their presence because I can't take my eyes off the woman. But she hears them. Our eyes meet, and hers fill with surprise, then joy.

"Aleena!" She stands up and drops her sewing. She waves me toward the front door, calling, "Come in! What are you doing standing out there?"

Who's Aleena?

Do I stay, or do I go?

I don't have time to roll the dice. Or draw my dagger. My instincts kick in, and I duck into the shadows.

I refuse to contemplate whether fear spurred me. After all, she's an old lady. There's nothing she could do to me.

Except tell me about my past?

No. If I wanted to know, I could ask Qrow.

She might tell me who Aleena is?

Who cares about some random woman?

She might tell me how Aleena is connected to me?

Why would she think I was connected to Aleena?

Maybe because she called you Aleena?

Whatever!

I don't need to talk to her tonight. Knowing she's still in town—and alive—is enough for now.

Chapter 46 Qrodin

28TH DAY OF PILAMEE, 14,887
CRAGUESPORT, ZEDANA

Qrodin holds the pen over the page, but his fingers can't form the words he wants to write. Ever since their argument, he's wanted to tell Talim everything about the ring, the auction, and the list—even if he can't. She'll be furious when she finds out he kept it from her. Will she understand that his oath prevents him from telling her? That's the thing about magical oaths. You can't break them, even if you want to.

The worst part is that Talim wouldn't think less of him for making the deal. Only keeping it from her. After all, their childhood was spent on the questionable side of the law. Some would even say they'd never have made it out of the streets if they hadn't bent—or broken—some of the rules.

But this particular task will be much easier with her help, which will only be possible if he phrases the request properly.

What have you discovered regarding the person who hired Stolgut? Qrodin finally writes. *Are they after Qat or something else?* There. 'Something else' is vague enough that it doesn't break his oath. He wouldn't have been able to write it if it had.

Her response is almost immediate. She must be scribing with Xan. Some pirate. Didn't give his name, just signed it as 'First Mate.' Stolgut said that when the guy left, he got on a ship called the 'Raven Scream.' Here's the thing, though. Stolgut wouldn't tell this guy anything about his contracts unless he paid for it. So, the guy said he'd pay for whichever job Qat accepts. Stolgut said he was okay with that, especially when this job came to him anonymously. Can you believe it? Who does that?

Someone who's looking for Qat.

Did he give you a description of this pirate?

She doesn't respond right away. Qrodin's lips compress. Perhaps he should ask his guy to install a system to notify him when a message comes in. But then he'd be getting notifications nonstop.

It takes her nearly five minutes to reply. *I didn't ask.*

Do it. And get back to me.

He doesn't expect an immediate reply.

Chapter 47 Qat

I've checked on the old woman every other day since I saw her, being careful she doesn't see me again. I change the time of day and direction of my approach and alter my appearance in case someone is watching her place. I wouldn't put it past Rogen. Even if he needed her existence to be kept secret from the rest of the crew, he may want her watched. He's always been quite protective of his things.

Sometimes, I pretend I'm one of the homeless and camp out in a doorway. Sometimes, I'm on one of the rooftops, like I am now, spying through the window with a 'borrowed' scope. Other times, I've wandered past or browsed the market in one disguise or another.

The only thing that changes is the garment the woman is working on or wearing. She doesn't leave, and she doesn't have visitors, at least not that I've seen. So, how does she get food? Wash her laundry? She just sits in that chair and sews.

After nearly a trit'quarter of waiting and watching, I finally get my answer. A woman carrying a basket of food arrives and lets herself in. A brown scarf covers her hair and hides her face. She moves like someone past the prime of their life but not yet bent with age. She slides a chair over and sits with her back to me, across from the old lady. She removes the scarf. Her hair has streaks of grey and falls in soft waves halfway down her back.

After they finish their meal, she leaves the room for a short time—probably to clean up—but eventually returns and repacks her basket. When she leaves, it's full of embroidered garments.

She's my only clue now as to the old woman's identity.

I follow her until she enters the market, and I lose sight of her. I traverse the rooftops to a spot that gives me a better vantage point. I finally spot her. She's one of the vendors. Her basket is sitting on the ground, and she's stringing a line between two lighted posts. Once it's secure, she pins the garments onto it for display.

After a few hours, I leave my perch and enter the market. It's late enough that it's still crowded, and I want to get a closer look at the woman.

Up close, her headscarf is quite extraordinary. Lamplight reflects off metallic strands in the cloth. A delicate gold chain is attached at four points, making three loops around her face. The center one has a cat pendant that rests in the center of her forehead. Another chain is draped from a piercing in her left nostril to the forward curve of her left ear.

I forget the chains when her bright yellow eyes meet mine.

I'm about to duck out when she says, "Qatzsi, wait!"

I stop and turn. How does she know my name?

"It is Qatzsi, isn't it?"

I hesitate at first. But then I remember something else Rogen taught me: When the seas get rough, you ride out the storm by turning into the waves. If you turn away from them, they can sweep you away, and if they catch you broadside, you risk being flipped or capsized.

I face her squarely and nod.

"I thought so," she says. "I'd know those eyes anywhere."

I hadn't bothered with my lenses today. I was on the rooftops, so I didn't think I'd need them.

"I'm Qat," the woman continues. "My mother calls me Qataleena, but everyone else calls me Qat."

Like me. A chill runs down my spine like raindrops that somehow sneak beneath your collar when you're trying to escape a downpour.

There's something about Qataleena that is so familiar. She's tall for a female. Considering her height and the fact that the captain used to come here, I wonder if they're family. I'm hesitant to bring up his name, though. It's not wise to admit to being related to a pirate, after all.

"How do you know me?" I ask instead.

"We met once when you were young—barely this tall." She holds her hand waist high. "Your mother came to visit us. She said you followed her. She was so mad at you, but she forgave you when she saw the effect you had on Ama."

Ama. My gut twists at the confirmation that this woman is Karatolii. I point my thumb over my shoulder toward the old woman's home and raise my brow.

"Yes," she says, her voice high in surprise. "That's her."

"How does…" Can I say it? Out loud? "How *did* my…mother… know yours?"

"From my understanding, *her* mother—your grandmother, Qataleeha—and mine were related. Cousins, I think? They didn't call each other that, but that's what my dad used to call them. I suppose that would make her and me second cousins, so you and I would be second cousins, once removed. Your mom used to visit when she was in town, even after her mother died. She and Ama were close."

Cousins? If Qataleena and Rogen *are* related, that will make me a distant cousin of his, too.

"Your father?"

"He died a long time ago, when I was in my teens. He's where I get my height."

Captain Rogen is also tall.

If the old woman is his mother, it makes sense that he would come to visit. And it made even more sense that he wouldn't want his crew to know about her.

Or a sister.

After a few minutes of silence, she says, "You and I were named after your grandmother. You probably call her your Ama'ani Qataleeha."

I don't say anything. How can I? The Sorbslles elder hadn't mentioned Ama'ani's name.

I shake my head.

"You don't remember her?" She looks almost hurt by that thought. "I'm sorry. I…" She looks around nervously, then starts removing a garment from the line. "I shouldn't have said anything."

I want to run, but something stops me. Why am I still here? Why didn't I go when Qataleena called my name?

Oh, right. The storm.

She stops folding. "If you don't remember, why are you here? Why did you follow me?"

I must not have kept my eye on the waves. I've flipped over. Or maybe I'm being swept away. How did she know I followed her? I was right to compare this to a storm. She's as unrelenting a force as I've ever met.

"Why do you say we're named after…my grandmother…when my name is so much different?"

"Ama says it's because we shouldn't say the name of the dead. Names are altered so we don't say them out loud after someone's passed." At my raised brow, she says, "Something about calling their spirit to you and preventing them from moving on. I've never been very good at that. My dad wasn't either.

It's my mother's way, not his. I'm a mix of both worlds. I mostly resemble my mom, but I have my dad's eyes." By this time, she's finished packing her basket and stands up. She inspects me closely. "You have his eyes, too, I bet."

What is she talking about? The color? The shape? It isn't the pupils.

Wait. How would I get my eyes from her dad? Aren't we related on our moms' sides?

Qataleena must have read my mind. "I'm sorry. I shouldn't have said that. I have a very active imagination. I've always thought your mom and my..." Her eyes open wide. "Um. Never mind what I just said. I've got to get home and help put my brood to bed, but I'd like to see you again. That is, if I haven't messed everything up with my big mouth."

I don't respond immediately, still rolling in the waves of everything I've heard tonight. I search for the bubbles, those little pockets of air that rise to the surface so you know which way to swim.

Pockets of air.

I take a deep breath. Then another. I feel my head peak above the waves.

"Unless you'd like to join us?" she continues. "It's just my husband and me. And our kids. And their kids. Like I said. A brood. Are you staying nearby? You're welcome to..." She trails off at my continued silence. "You know what? No pressure. I know this is all pretty crazy."

Crazy is putting it mildly.

"Please say you'll at least think about it. I can't tell you how much I've wanted to see you again. Oh, there I go again. You know what? Let me give you my address. Then, I'll shut up." She names a street over in the crafting district. "Come by whenever you like. If I'm not there, I'm here." She pauses, takes a deep breath, and asks, "Would you like to meet Ama? I know she would like that. I'll warn you, though, half the time, she doesn't know what day it is. She might even call you your mom's name or something."

My mom's name. I wouldn't even recognize it if she did. Qrow calls her Ama. *The old lady called me Aleena.* Is that my mom? I almost ask her, but don't. I'm barely staying afloat as it is.

Qataleena tilts her head again. "You look a lot like her."

An undertow drags me down again.

I struggle to breathe.

"There I go again. I said I would shut up, and here I am, babbling on. I'm going to go now. I hope to see you again, Qatzsi." She pauses, studying my face, then turns on her heel and hustles away.

It takes me a few seconds longer for the waves to recede and to get my feet moving.

The market is much emptier than when I entered it. Did we talk about our family in the middle of the market? Where anyone could have overheard us?

What is wrong with me?

I don't dare to peek in on the old lady. I never asked her name. All that talk, and I have no idea what to call her other than 'the old lady.'

The captain would be so ashamed of me. He always saw storms coming.

His eyes. He has icy blue eyes. Not like Qataleena—her eyes were a stunning yellow.

But he does have sunbursts in the center.

She had said I have her father's eyes, too, even though mine are a dark golden amber rather than sunflower yellow, like hers. How could I have his eyes unless we're related?

What was she saying before she interrupted herself? That she always imagined my mom and her...

Her who? Her father? That they used to hook up?

Was she implying that he was *my* father, also?

No. She said he died when she was young.

Could he be my *mother's* father?

And what about Rogen? Where does he fit in with all of this? Qataleena's brother? He's the right age.

If the captain *isn't* her brother, why is he visiting the old lady?

And if he *is* her brother, is that why he took me?

Has he known this whole time that I might be his...his *what*?

His half-sister's child?

Does he know about Qrow?

Does Qataleena know about Qrow? She said *I* followed my mother. She never even mentioned Qrow.

Does Qrow know that the man he thinks killed our mother might be Ama's half-brother?

Doesn't the possibility that Rogen might be our uncle make it *less* likely that he killed our mother?

Or maybe it makes it *more* likely. Perhaps he was angry that his father cheated on his mother and blamed it on Ama.

I stop before I go out of my mind and remind myself that Qataleena didn't finish her statement. She said it was her imagination. I filled in the rest. I might be torturing myself for nothing.

But now, I have even more questions for Rogen when I find him.

"This is all very touching, but I have to talk to you."

I look around. No one is anywhere near me. I flinch and slap at a gnat flying around my ear.

"Hey! Stop that!"

Something drums against my eardrum. "Fucking bug!" I put my finger in my ear, and something sharp jabs my fingertip. When I remove it, a tiny bead of blood forms.

"What is it with you and bugs?" a tiny voice booms inside my right ear.

This time, I recognize it. "Nightshade?" I duck down a side street and climb up to a roof. I've had enough public conversations for one night.

"Who else? Now, shut up and listen. Who's the first mate of the *Raven Scream*?"

She appears out of nowhere in front of my face. My heart lurches, and my foot slips on a slimy tile. Nightshade grabs my ear to steady me. I'm surprised she's strong enough to do it. Once I'm righted, I sit down hard. Nightshade lands on the toe of my boot.

"Thanks," I say, rubbing my ear where she'd pinched it to keep me from falling. "Why do you wanna know?"

"I asked first."

"With any luck, the only one I know of is a ghost by now."

Purple and gold lights shimmer on her wings. She shakes her head.

What does she know that I don't?

"He's been paying to put his name on any contract you accept, from here to everywhere."

"Why would he do that?" I never see the contracts between my contact and the person who hires them. I don't care who's paying for the job. I only care about who pays me. But if Goffin's offering to pay for any contract I take, it's because he's interested in me, not the job. And he would be told which contract I took. He'd know where to find me.

More importantly, it also means he's still alive.

"You tell me. After you screwed up the one in Riversmeet, why would he want you? You're the worst assassin I've ever met."

"I didn't screw up in Riversmeet."

"That's not what I heard."

"Find out anything about the auction?"

"What does the ring look like?"

"Gold. Blue stone. Sea monster design."

"I'll let you know." She's gone before I can blink.

I hate it when she does that.

Chapter 48 Qrodin

18TH DAY OF ITRANY, 14,887
CRAGUESPORT, ZEDANA

It's been thirty-six days since they arrived, and Qrodin still hasn't returned to his old routine. Having house guests changes things.

The additional noise in the home is a delightful change to the tomblike silence it held before. The Music Mouth, as Bell named it, is nearly always in use. This morning, it was wide open, and Bell sang along while she danced to the music. At other times, it's nearly closed for background noise only. The sounds of talking and laughing, of Bell cooking and Kasaandra grumbling, are welcome intrusions into his life.

"Qrow?" Llani says outside his office's open door. "We are leaving. I'll be at the library if you need me." Llani has spent her time either cataloging the contents of her bag or visiting the city's museums and guild halls—or, as she calls them, educational centers.

"And I'm going to the school. My sourdough turned out flat again." Bell doesn't sound happy. Her new sourdough starter lives on the kitchen countertop and seems to have a life of its own, but her loaves seldom achieve the high, domed shape they do at the baking school where Bell is an intern. It's probably the only thing she's baked that isn't perfection. And her Pure Gold starter is still tarnished. Her words, not his.

Akin had initially stayed at the monastery but moved into the yellow room a fortnight ago to make room for visiting acolytes when the city started filling up for the winter solstice festivities, but he leaves at dawn most mornings.

Kasaandra has been in the Searbaltoir district almost daily, mainly visiting the various blacksmiths. Unlike her home, there are many female smiths here. Although she hasn't joined a guild, she's been hired by one of them to help make multiple items for tonight's Longest Night celebration.

Even Qat is keeping aer bag in the grey room now. Ae comes in at dawn and joins them for breakfast, often bringing rare or different foods and trinkets for each of them.

"Enjoy your day," Qrodin says.

Most days, Qrodin catches up on work in his office or visits his local businesses.

Shortly after arriving, Qrodin and Qat visited the bank to have him removed from aer account. Qat was nearly speechless when the balance was disclosed. Even so, ae withdrew a minute amount and declared that it would keep aem for a full trit'quarter, at least. Qrodin was saddened at the thought, but Qat seemed quite satisfied.

Qrodin opens his ledger to Talim's page.

You're supposed to be getting a TFDG in Craguesport. Some new hotshot Toolium is sending out. I heard they're going to visit Quentin Browning. Anything I need to know?

Toolium is Zedana's capital, located up in the Manntar mountain range.

TFDG stands for Two-Fist Detective General. Long ago, Zedana's Senate created the Two-Fisted governing system. The Right Fist is the military arm, while the Left controls trade. Most detectives work locally or for the Right Fist. TFDGs work for both, investigating international underground trafficking of trade goods. The position's upside is that they can access intelligence from both sides. The downside is that each fist believes they are the dominant fist and should have direct authority.

TFDGs need to be tough, loyal, determined, and, above all else, impervious to distraction and corruption. They seldom have close family and never get married.

That's just what Qrodin needs.

How did they find out that Quentin was involved with Truffle? Was he stupid enough to write Quentin's name in his day planner? Qrodin rereads Talim's message and scribbles a response. *When should I expect this visit?* Out loud, he mutters, "If Truffle weren't dead already, I'd have him killed again for his stupidity."

Qrodin closes the ledger and then opens it again. And have you discovered what this 'First Mate' looks like? While you're at it, has Stolgut delivered the ring yet? If so, find out how and to whom. If not, I want that ring. I don't care what it costs me. And get me that TFDG's name.

He closes the ledger and looks around the office. Sealed shut. The rest of the home is empty. Everyone will be gone for at least another two hours. He sighs, trying not to think about the impending TFDG visit. Instead, he takes a package out of a drawer in his desk. Kasaandra had given it to him this morning, and he wants to inspect the contents before storing them in his vault. She's been working on them for more than a trit'quarter—since they arrived in Craguesport. After seeing her whittling skills on the journey, Qrodin couldn't imagine anyone else crafting them.

He unrolls each piece as he removes it. Six of the original dozen manticore tail spikes are ornately carved. They are beautifully done. Each one is uniquely crafted to represent a different member of the group.

The first one he picks up is Llani's. The butterfly birthmark on her inner wrist is there, as is the three-pointed symbol that flashed when she had been testing the reasacobila. Qrodin had forgotten seeing it until now.

He picks up another one and chuckles when he sees the word *Obey* engraved as though it's escaping a carved mouth. Kasaandra must have seen his birthmarks—probably after the Battle of the Twisted Sisters—for they are each represented in different locations on his spike.

He recognizes Akin's tusks amongst the designs on a third spike. And what might be a fist and a tree? Qrodin turns it around. A gnat lands in the center of an eye that is staring at him from the center of the spike.

Why an eye? he wonders, swatting at the gnat. It buzzes loudly in protest.

The clock on his desk dings the hour. He rewraps the spikes and places them in the vault next to the glass case housing his sea serpent ring. He opens the case and picks up the ring.

"You are quickly becoming more trouble than I bargained for," he says to the sea serpent.

The only way to get one is through the death of someone who has one. Qrodin waited years to discover the woman who had owned this one. He wonders who ended up with Truffle's. Probably Qat.

"I hope Talim never finds out what I did to get you. Even though she'd probably be proud of me."

"Oh, yeah?"

Qrodin whips around at the whispered words. Had he imagined them?

"Eeek! Another one?"

"Who's there?" He searches the vault, but it's empty. So is his office.

Qrodin rubs his eyes. He hadn't slept well last night. He had gotten in the habit of thinking out loud when he was at home alone, just to hear noise. Now, he's either answering himself or hearing voices that aren't there.

Through the nearby window, Qrodin watches several people strolling along the walkway. Perhaps the soundproofing spells need to be refreshed.

"Either that, or I'm going out of my mind."

He'll ask his head of security to inspect the domi for any breach, just to be certain.

Qrodin puts the ring back in its case, and his eyes settle on the case next to it. He'd been trying not to look at the necklace, but it won't be ignored. The rarest of gems, primatite sparkles with more fire than diamonds and can be found in clear, white, violet, purple, and all shades of blue. But its rarest color is pink.

He'd wanted to get Doscia a blue necklace to match the midnight blue of her eyes. But she didn't like blue. Her favorite color was pink. He purchased the pink. But she broke off the relationship before he could give it to her.

Six years ago, their romance had been so new that Qrodin hadn't told anyone about it. Doscia was a professional athlete. They'd met in Alonard. She'd won the local competition, and as the largest sponsor of the event, Qrodin was the one who handed her the medal. They'd been inseparable for over four trit'quarters until her coach told her she needed to choose one—him, or her career.

"I hope your career was worth it, Doscia."

Chapter 49 Qat

I wake up with a start. Something is sitting on me. It leans forward, and two rows of sharp teeth appear.

"Boo!"

I flip the hammock and land face down in a bed of dead leaves and dirt.

A giant bug lands a few inches from my face. "Ask me nicely."

"What the kraken, Nightshade!" I yell. I want to wring that faerie's neck and pluck off her wings. Slowly. I sit up on the cold ground and get tangled in the hammock above me. I wrestle with the ropes until I pull myself out from underneath.

"Well?" she asks.

"It wasn't a question," I grumble. I pull a pine needle out of my hair and hold it threateningly in her direction like a mini rapier.

"If you don't want my news, I'll tell someone else." She disappears. Just like that. Pop! She's gone.

"Wait!" I toss the pine needle and turn in circles, looking for her. "What news?" I shout into the air.

"I said *nicely*." Nightshade lowers down in front of me. Upside down. Her gravity-defying hair looks the same as when she's right side up.

I glare at her. Why do I tolerate this nonsense again?

She smiles, and lights chase each other in circles around her wings like daga on a racetrack.

"What news do you have for me?" I ask her, as nicely as I can manage.

"That Quentin guy you're staying with isn't who you think he is."

I doubt that.

Nightshade must be following me. For nearly a trit'quarter, I'd only gone to the domi a few times, but recently, I've been sleeping in the blue-and-gray room every few days when everyone is gone. I've also been joining them for at least one meal a day. "I didn't ask you to spy on me. Have you found out anything about the ring?"

Nightshade rolls her eyes. "If it were a snake..."

"It is a snake. A sea snake. And?"

"And you should ask your roommate about the one he has in his safe."

Chapter 50 Qrodin

Qrodin has no idea what Qat gets up to at night. Ae often leaves shortly after their evening meal and doesn't return until early morning. Qrodin only knows this because he is notified on a page in his ledger anytime someone enters or leaves the domi.

Qrodin is in his office when Qat slips through the door. They're alone in the domi. Qat swats at a gnat and looks back at Qrodin cautiously. There's a strange look on aer face, and ae's noticeably distracted.

"What's up with you tonight?" he asks.

Qat looks away, but Qrodin can sense that something is off. Qat shrugs, but worry cuts three deep grooves into the space between aer eyes.

"Qat. Talk to me. What happened?"

"There's a detective here in Craguesport from Toolium. Ae wants to talk to you. Seems like someone you were supposed to meet in Riversmeet was murdered?" Qat waves away something near aer ear.

Qrodin frowns at the judgment in Qat's tone. He wasn't the one who killed Truffle. Qat was. He's certain of it. And the act has turned out to be more than an inconvenience for Qrodin. "Where did you hear that?"

Qat raises one brow.

Qrodin sighs. "I hadn't heard," he lies. He can tell immediately that Qat doesn't believe him.

"Why didn't you tell me?" Qat asks, proving his hunch.

He sighs again. "Because it's not important. Bernhard Truffle and I were merely going to discuss legal matters resulting from a new property tax law scheduled to go into effect at the beginning of the year." Another lie, but Qat seems to believe him this time. Boring business details usually suffice. And it isn't exactly a lie. That's the reason he gave Truffle for the meeting. Truffle had no idea Qrodin was trying to befriend him. As a wealthy businessperson, he'd hoped Truffle would give him information about the auction. Truffle's known to share secrets when he's inebriated.

Talim has since reported that none of the Valore she sent to Cranwood to purchase farmland have reported back about anyone showing up looking for Quentin, or anything to do with Qat or Truffle's murder. Since the TFDG is already here, ae either bypassed Cranwood altogether or got there before Talim's people did.

Qrodin didn't ask Talim if there was any talk of treasure. She would have told him.

One thing is for certain. Finding the loot and turning it over to Queen Sarafeen has made his task much more difficult. Thanks to Qat's insistence that they search the tunnel to the end, the contraband is back where it belongs instead of waiting to be acquired by Qrodin. He needs to discover the person responsible for hoarding them in the first place. Only then will he be able to achieve his goal. He hopes there are other stashes. It was just his bad luck that the hoard was in Cranwood.

Talim assures him that nothing unusual was with Truffle's belongings when the Valore searched his house in Riversmeet. The special paper would have dissolved in the river if the list were on Bernhard when he was tossed overboard.

That's another thing that he has Qat to blame for. The missing list.

If Qat weren't his twin...

But Qat is his twin. They may have been separated for twenty years, but Qat has always been the most curious person Qrodin has ever met. If Truffle had the list on the ship, Qat would have found it.

He searches his twin's eyes and face for a clue.

Qat blinks slowly.

Ae's trying to protect Qrodin from something.

In a flash, Qrodin knows without a doubt that Qat took the list.

Qat had been too calm while the merkama were digging through the treasure. Ae hadn't even tried to steal anything. Ae hadn't been cracking jokes or insulting the merkama. Normally, the only time Qat's quiet is when no one's aware ae's there. But Qat hadn't tried to hide. Ae hadn't slunk around in the shadows. Ae'd sat there watching. Then, ae went out to take a nap.

A nap.

As a child, Qat would have been in the middle of it. Ae would have tried to distract everyone. Had them looking in one direction while ae was up to no good in another. Qrodin hasn't seen anything to convince him Qat's changed.

So why the change in behavior with the treasure?

And why is ae warning Qrodin of the detective's arrival?

Qrodin had been waiting for days to hear from the detective. What are they waiting for? He can't prepare properly for the visit, since he has no idea what they want from him. He's gathered what little correspondence he's had with Truffle and the paperwork regarding the tax law changes. It's all he can do for now.

Chapter 51 Qat

24TH DAY OF ITRANY, 14,887
CRAGUESPORT, ZEDANA

"I told you he's hiding something."

I've been staying at the domi every day since I told Qrow about the appearance of a detective. I wanted to get a look inside his safe the moment Qrow left. Besides, the city's filling up. Nearly every room is full for the upcoming Longest Night celebration. It's impossible to find a place to stay. At the domi, I push the bed out of the way and erect my pocket home so I can hide the witches' stone there. I never showed anyone else the symbol to access the space, so it should be safe there for now.

Nightshade and I are back in Qrow's office. The last few days, Qrow hasn't left the domi, so today is the first time I've had a chance to look inside the vault.

"It's in here." Nightshade disappears under a door cleverly disguised as a bookcase. Why is it always a bookcase? Or a mirror? At least he didn't hide it behind a giant painting of himself.

I tense, half expecting some alarm to go off, but I hear nothing.

I'm a little nervous about what I'm going to find. I lied to Qrow. I have no idea if the detective is already in Craguesport. I wanted to see Qrow's face when I told him. The lines in his brow furrowed slightly. The reaction was just a twitch, there and gone so fast I would have missed it had I not been looking for it.

What does it mean, though, except that Nightshade's right? He's hiding something.

The vault door opens.

The room it reveals looks bigger on the inside than the dimensions I'd estimated based on the surrounding rooms. I wonder if it's spelled like Llani's bag.

Nightshade—at her full size—lifts a box and presents it to me. Inside is the serpent ring. I open the box and remove the ring. It's heavy, like the one I took off Truffle, but this one shines like it's never worn, whereas Truffle's ring had scratches, and the gold serpent's tail had worn away where Truffle used to rub it when twisting it around his finger.

For fun, I try it on.

It fits me perfectly.

I don't tell Nightshade this isn't the ring I took from Bernhard Truffle. That one was a few sizes too large. No matter how much she's done to help me, I don't trust the faerie. I wonder why she's showing me this. So I'll take her with me? Is she secretly trying to leave the Winged Death? She said she wants to leave Craguesport and everyone she's grown up with, since they all still treat her like a child.

I don't blame her for that.

Even if Goffin hadn't done what he did, I'd have only stayed with the *Raven Scream* for another season or so. They all treated me as the child I was when I woke up on board. It didn't matter that I could out-fight, outmaneuver, and outsmart all but Captain Rogen.

I understand Nightshade's frustration.

But I still don't trust her.

I don't see anything that resembles the merkama treasure. Does that mean he's not interested in the artifacts, or that he hasn't purchased any yet?

I don't want Qrow to discover we were here, so I put the ring away, take a quick visual inventory of the items in here. Beside the ring is a woman's jeweled necklace. It's beautiful, but why would he have that? I've seen enough antiques to recognize that this isn't one. Therefore, it isn't an investment unless he anticipates it increasing in value. I shrug and scan the shelves, stopping only when I see the manticore's tail spikes. They're now carved. I recognize Kasaandra's handiwork. They're gorgeous.

Picking one up, I roll it between my hands and inspect the design. Its smooth surface is cool to the touch. I run my fingers along the grooves Kasaandra had carved. Recognizing a shape, my breath catches. Why is there a pyramid carved into this one? Rotating it in my hands, I feel the blood drain from my face when a two-headed snake appears. Those are the same symbols carved into the stone's wooden box. Why would Kasaandra carve them on one of the spikes? How did she know what they looked like?

Has she been spying on me? My brain almost crashes at the thought, and I laugh.

"What's so funny?"

"Nothing."

I'm tempted to stash the spike in my boot, but Qrow would know it was gone and immediately suspect me. He did say I was prone to taking what I want.

I briefly glance at the rest of them and realize each one represents one of the six of us. The symbols I'd recognized were on Bell's. Now that I'm not distracted by them, I notice the splintered arrows and carved pie. The other spikes have markings I've never seen, like the tree on Akin's. When I turn that one over, an eye stares back at me. There's something familiar about it, but I can't think what.

"I'm bored. Ready to go?"

"Huh?" I say, looking up. Nightshade is perched on the edge of a shelf with her chin in both hands. She flops back into a half-prone, half-dangling from the edge position. "Oh, sure."

Reluctantly, I set the spike with the rest and leave.

Chapter 52 Qrodin

It's been fifty-one days since Qrodin and his companions arrived in Craguesport. Today is the first day of Samdi, the first trit'quarter of winter. And the winter solstice—otherwise known as *Longest Night*. The celebrations are always exceptional in Craguesport. Nearly every home will be lit up, inside and out.

Qrodin has an extensive collection of candles that would be suitable for tonight, but Kasaandra had proposed a candle-making party a few days ago. During her spare time, she had made custom molds with sigils and designs she said were customary for dwarven Longest Night observances.

Now, as evening draws close, they decide to wait to light the candles until they return from the celebrations.

Qrodin is using his Quelen Brown disguise for the evening, the one he uses most often around town unless he's conducting business. His brow and chin are less pronounced, and his nose is more rounded at the tip. His coal-black hair is pulled into a high bun. He's used this disguise often since they returned to the city.

The first time Bell saw it, she cocked her head to the side and looked him up and down. "You know, that disguise kinda makes you look more like Qat. I think it's just as handsome as the other ones, but I like your real face the best."

They go out to eat in the Piladata district first. Each course is served glowing with different colored flames to celebrate the holiday. They finish their meal before sunset, and Qrodin suggests watching the bonfire lighting next.

Kaibur Street is closed to all but foot traffic. From now until morning, a throng of people loops from the city's entrance to the cliff and back again, detouring to each district's primary celebration site. Meanwhile, fireworks burst overhead, displaying the daga races' winning team color after each competition.

Cheers and boos can be heard throughout the city as people cheer for their favorite team, or boo at their rivals. Bell, of course, is rooting for the green team. Every time pink lights the sky, Qrodin wonders if Doscia competed in that race. It's a grueling day for the competitors, since the races start earlier than the rest of the celebrations.

Qrodin leads the way through the crowd of people to the city arch and beyond. There's a non-stop parade of people carrying candles or torches or bowls of burning incense, dancing and singing as they go. The lighting of the bonfire is the official start of the evening's celebrations. Qrodin's seen it a dozen times, but the others haven't, and everyone should experience it at least once.

Large round drums line each side of the main street. The drummers stand motionless, arms forward, holding unlit torches.

Bell pats his hand. "I can't see. Will you put me on your shoulders?"

Qrodin lifts Bell. They approach the unlit bonfire as the sun winks out on the horizon.

The drummers' torches light as if by magic. Up and down. Low and slow. They beat in sync with perfect precision. Qrodin's heartbeat slows to match the rhythm. The drumming increases in volume, power, and speed before the drummers break from each other, each pounding out a different sequence that complements its neighbor.

Hidden bells ring from everywhere at once. People throughout the audience start to dance. Bell claps when the person to their left rushes forward with the other dancers. Their regalia's long strands stream behind them as they fly through the crowd. As if powered by flight, the faster they go, the brighter their clothes glow until their movements light the entire road.

The performers converge on the pyre, an assemblage of tree trunks more than two stories high. The dancers circle it, moving closer with each rotation until nearly ten rings of glowing bodies surround it. The drumbeats change tempo. The dancers' clothes burst into flames. Some of them rush inside the pyre. Others start climbing the trunks that make up its frame. Sparks fly up through the center, straight to the top. The blaze consumes the dancers. Those that had scaled the trunks are no longer there, replaced by a roaring fire that is drowning out the beats of the drum as the drummers' movements get smaller, quieter, until—all at once—they stop.

A hush falls over the crowd. The dancers stream out from within the blazing inferno. The crowd cheers. Akin whistles. Kasaandra hoots, pulling Qrodin's attention. Her green eyes are sparkling, and her mouth is stretched wide in a smile that shows straight, broad teeth as perfectly formed and placed as the city wall in Cranwood.

When it's over, Qrodin lowers Bell. "What did you think?"

"It was spectacular!" Bell yells to be heard over the crowd. "Where to now?"

They start in Wusdweit, the district founded by a hablis family, and the one closest to the arching entrance of the city. The all-night party is held in a garden park that changes year round. The landscaping is choreographed as intricately as any theater production. Fire pits of all shapes and sizes are lit and placed within courtyards and parks along the way. Braziers and light posts illuminate walkways and alleys.

Bell ignores the disapproving glances at her lack of traditional attire and tall hat and instead focuses on teaching them the very energetic, wiggly-jiggly dances of her people.

"You try to scare away the night and entice the dawn to return," Bell explains, alternately growling at and beckoning the night.

Llani and Akin make the dance look more erotic than intimidating as they gracefully move in time to the music. "Oh! This is quite fun!" Llani says, glancing at Akin shyly during the beckoning portion of the dance.

"You should dance with her," Qat tells an old dwarf ogling Kasaandra and smiles when he moves toward her, jerking his hips lewdly in mock imitation of the dance.

"Troublemaker," Qrow says.

"I just want to see her whomp his ass."

Qrodin laughs. "Me too."

Kasaandra—having seen the aging dwarf's approach—says something to Akin as she turns toward him and away from the dwarf, wriggling to the side and making room for the stranger to pass. He dances right on as if that were his intention all along. He finally stops and turns. He looks confused and sad when he notices that Kasaandra has turned again and now has her back to him.

"Wow! That was smooth," Qat says.

"I'm impressed."

"I'm disappointed."

"Then maybe you should go dance with the old dwarf," Qrodin suggests. This is the first time he's been alone with Qat since they were in his office, but it's not the right setting for a confrontation.

Bell eventually pulls them away. "On to the next celebration!" She's out of breath, but her face and eyes spark joyfully.

The grimm festival in Jalu is opposite of Wusdweit.

Grimm are very tall and somewhat bulky around the middle. They are hairless, have no ears, and blink only a few times per minute. Despite their awkwardness and lumbering gait, they are controlled and graceful dancers.

Because the grimm have a shared consciousness, they seldom speak out loud. Their ceremony consists of sitting silently in concentric circles around a large fire pit while holding hands and swaying their arms and upper bodies to a beat only they can hear. Their movements are punctuated by abrupt changes in tempo, followed by bowing forward until their forehead touches the ground—which the Grimm can do, but many others can't. The dances are synchronized by subspecies despite them being intermixed amongst the assembly. Their dances do not share the same rhythm. Nor do the repetitive moves match each other in length. Even so, they skillfully avoid knocking into their neighbor. And despite the dissimilarities, the overall choreography is spectacular.

Bell sits down, pulling Llani with her on one side and Qrodin on the other. Llani reaches for Akin. Qrodin sighs deeply, hoping to avoid the dance, and looks to Kasaandra for rescue, but she grabs Akin's other hand and sits. Qrodin looks around for Qat, but as usual, ae's disappeared. Qrodin joins Bell.

Not wanting to disturb the atmosphere with whispered conversation, Qrodin doesn't ask anyone if they saw Qat leave. Instead, he sways, lifts his arms, and bends forward with the rest of them. After a few minutes, the movements become almost hypnotic, and he's calm and relaxed when Bell eventually jumps up.

"What's next?" she asks.

On their way to the Hondjikal district, Qrodin slows down to let the others get ahead as he searches the crowd for Qat. Llani appears between two people shuffling ahead of them.

"Qrodin? Qat? Is something amiss?"

"Shh!" Qat says.

Qrodin turns around. Qat is directly behind him.

"Don't be rude, Qat," Qrodin says, frowning. Qat's much better now at sneaking up on him than ae was as a child.

"I said, 'amiss.' Who are you shushing, Qat?" Llani looks closely at Qat's hair. "Yes, I can hear you whispering. I can see you, too. Qat, your faerie companion is quite rude."

"Who *are* you people?"

Qrodin's head jerks toward Qat. That was the same voice he'd heard in his office. His head of security hadn't found any problem with the office's spells, and no one else had appeared in his security journal, but at least now, Qrodin knows he hadn't imagined the voice.

Qat blinks slowly. "Faeries aren't real," ae says. "Ouch!" Qat flinches and bats at a fly buzzing nearby.

The slow blink. What is Qat trying to protect Llani from?

"Your faerie doesn't agree with you," Llani says.

Could faeries be *real*? Remembering the gnat in his office, Qrodin tries to get a closer look at the fly Qat has been batting away, but Llani grabs Qrodin's arm. "If we tarry, Bell will send reinforcements." Her ears flick back toward Qat. "I say 'tarry.' It is a perfectly acceptable word. And short. What is that faerie's problem with vocabulary? She is even less tolerable than Kasaandra."

Qrodin looks back at Qat. Ae's talking to aerself but following behind them. Qrodin will talk to aem about it later.

"How is there a faerie in Qat's hair?" he asks Llani.

"She shapeshifted. Obviously."

Obviously.

Faeries are real. And one of them was in his office.

What had she seen? And what has she told Qat?

Chapter 53 Qat

Hondjikal is a delight and one of my favorite districts. Populated chiefly by arghor and markali families since its founding, the district climbs up into the forested hills until it ends at the cliffs overlooking the sea. Most of the year, the homes and businesses are hidden in the depths of the forest, but tonight, the hillside is ablaze with thousands of candles and torches.

The roads are easily accessible, but the homes aren't unless you are one of the two mountain-climbing species. Both have hooved feet, short, flat tails, and wide-spaced eyes with pupils that run horizontally. But that's where the similarities end. The arghor are peaceful, preferring to live in large family units in long houses. The markali, on the other hand, have spiral-shaped horns they use when sparring. They love nothing more than rousing fights. They excel at one-on-one competitions and usually live alone. Once you know the difference, it's easy to determine which houses belong to which species.

Flames snuff out as quickly as they ignite in the reflections of tiny mirrors hanging in the trees and spinning in the breeze. Polished shields are placed along wooden fences, multiplying the light of thousands of candles. Woven mats are placed at the bases of trees.

I drop onto a mat and roll underneath a low branch. Each tree is a galaxy of fireflies and mirrors placed to reflect the night sky. Even the part of the sky that's currently on the other side of the world. "Lie down on that mat and look up," I say to Bell. "You should be able to see constellations. I bet I can name more than you can."

"Not fair! You know them all!" Bell crawls under and places her face right next to mine. "What's that one?" She points up.

"That's Akxoss."

"Like the trident?"

"Like the kraken that the trident killed."

"Cool! Oh! There's Veri." Bell points to a large mirror that's hovering above a triangle of mirrors.

"The Goddess of Creation."

"And the North Star. I always know because of the three below her."

"Can she hear me, too?" Nightshade whispers, interrupting. I wonder why she's following me again. I thought I'd gotten rid of her earlier.

"Only when you pray to her," Bell says, looking at me strangely.

"Oh, cram it!" Nightshade buzzes loudly as she flies away.

"Qat!"

Bell thought that was me? Do I sound like Nightshade? Apparently, Llani hasn't told her about Nightshade. "Sorry," I say.

"Do you pray to Veri? Do you believe she created all of us?"

I shrug. "I haven't thought about it much. Is that what most hablises believe? The skunks don't."

Bell doesn't respond.

When I look at her, she's frowning. "What's wrong?"

She turns on her side and props her head on her hand. Her eyes search mine. "Why do you do that?"

"Do what?"

"Call people names." She doesn't look away. She's serious.

"I don't call *you* names," I point out.

She lies back down and stares up at the twirling mirrors and fireflies in the branches.

"Everyone else does."

"What do they call you? Queen Cook? Princess of Pies? How about Sweet Stuff? Or Creampuff?"

"Ugly, crybaby, skinny."

"Skinny?"

"Yeah. That's one of the worst ones for us hablises. Boys don't like us skinny. They want us to be very curvy and plump. They call me Bony Bell and say no one will ever want to marry me."

"What?" I sit up fast, barely missing a branch above me. "They're dumb. Obviously. Anyone who's ever tasted your cooking would want to marry you."

She turns her face away. "But no one wants to get to know me."

"What about Robyn? He's your best friend. I bet he doesn't call you names."

Her face scrunches up, and for a moment, I think she will cry. "Why do people have to be mean to people just because they don't know them?"

Because in my experience, most people aren't friendly. Of course, I mainly associate with pirates and assassins. But I can't tell Bell that. I doubt she'd like me much if she knew what I was. That thought hurts. My stomach twists, thinking of Bell looking at me in horror or distaste.

"You should be nice to everyone and only be mean if they're mean first." Bell pauses a moment and looks at me. "Skunks isn't a very nice name."

"I'm sorry, Bell. I won't call them that around you anymore."

Her eyes narrow. "How about you try not to call them that, whether I'm there or not." She rolls away from me. "I don't want to play this game anymore."

"Wow," Nightshade says, popping out of nowhere and hovering inside the branches. "That makes *me* feel bad, and I don't even know her."

"Tell me about it." If I'm around her much longer, I'll forget how to be me.

"What are you going to do about Qrow? He has the ring you gave Stolgut. Are you going to show him the list?"

I glare at her.

"Yeah, yeah. I know about the list. Where'd you get it?"

I don't answer her. I can't tell her about Qrow's involvement. What I *think* I know of it, at least.

"I did some digging. You know the only way to get one of those rings is to inherit it or assassinate the owner?"

That's how I got the one from Truffle. I can't decide if I'm proud of Qrow or disappointed. I didn't think he had it in him to have someone assassinated. In Cranwood, he acted like keeping the treasure was a despicable thing, and the entire time, he was planning on bidding for the items at auction. Why did he hand them over to the queen? He could have gotten them for a steal.

The pun almost makes me laugh.

So why *did* he contact the queen? Could it be because the others were with us? How magnanimous would he have been had it just been me and him?

I wonder if I should show him Truffle's notebook. I've hidden it inside my pocket home, but it's always possible Nightshade was near me when I set it up. If so, she can go in and out of the dome whenever she wants. Which means she might have access to the green stone, too. Every time I enter the dome, I check to ensure it's still there. I only look at it when I'm inside the dome, too, in case opening the box continues to affect everyone like it did before. Sometimes, I feel that weird vibration in the air when I enter the dome. The same sensation that led me to it in the first place, and it only goes away when I open the box and take out the stone.

It's been happening more often lately.

Chapter 54 Qrodin

Qrodin asks Llani to accompany him to a stall for coffee. The hot drink always calms his nerves, and right now, they need calming. "Llani. What were you talking about back there? Did you really see a faerie?"

"Of course."

"What did it look like?"

"She. She was flying about Qat's face. Did you not see her?" Llani flicks two curly locks over her shoulder.

"I thought that was a fly."

"Yes. I believe their natural size is about three hands."

Qrodin tries to picture someone that size. Would she look like a person or an insect?

"Have you never seen one before?" Llani asks.

"Most people don't even believe in them. I never have, to be honest."

"Yes. Faeries take advantage of that fact. I have always been able to see them."

"And this one? Do you believe Qat saw it? Her?"

"Oh, yes. Qat has been talking to her since we sat down with the grimm."

Qrodin feels a sense of foreboding. "Talking to her? What about?" No wonder Qat left them.

"There were so many people about, it was difficult to isolate their voices, but I believe Qat was inquiring about an auction. The faerie mentioned a ring."

Qrodin feels the blood drain from his face. He's thankful when they arrive at a coffee cart, and Llani focuses on the people around them. Qrodin is quiet until after he orders his coffee.

Llani declines his offer of one. When they start back, Llani apologizes. "You asked what the faerie looked like. She is my coloring, with violet hair that spikes up—rather like Bell's—and bright gold eyes." She touches his arm to get him to stop and looks deeply into his eyes.

"Like yours but lighter and brighter. And they lack both your brown and red variegations." She turns away.

Qrodin releases his breath, frustrated and worried about what the faerie saw and was telling Qat. Had she gone into the vault with him that day?

"Her wings…" She suddenly looks uncomfortable.

"What about her wings?" Qrodin asks.

"They are shaped like dragonfly wings. They have magical flight. Flapping their wings is unnecessary. Had they been flapping, I would not have seen their design."

"What design?"

"I could be wrong, but I believe it was the same as Akin's…what do you call them…marks from birth?"

"Birthmarks?"

"His scarring nearly obliterates it."

"On his forehead?" Qrodin asks. He'd wondered at the number of puckered scars that had been intentionally made. Could they have been put there to cover his birthmarks?

"Oh, no. Those are archaic ceremonial attestations of his rank among the Tiolapin. They are unusual these days. I am referring to the scarring here." She waves a hand toward her throat. "The mark looks like an eye, though I can only make out a fraction of the outline. It was much clearer on the faerie's wing."

"I've never noticed a mark there. On Akin," he elaborates at her confused look. He's curious that neither Imolena nor Anada had such ceremonial scarring, but even more intrigued that Akin has a birthmark covered by his injury. "How did you see it? The faerie's mark. She was so small." Qrodin remembers the gnat in his office. She had been sitting on the eye carved into one of the manticore spikes.

"Practice. And exceptional vision. Faeries usually panic when they discover I can see them. I have learned to observe them without looking at them. They are much like souls in that regard."

Qrodin's thoughts halt. Souls? "You see souls?" he asks her in his most conversational voice.

Her face flushes. "You do not believe me."

"No. I do." Akin's aunt Imolena sees souls, too. She used to talk about ancestor souls and how their custom is to craft a vessel to capture the soul when they die. She told him a story about Soul Soarers—people who can separate their soul from their body and travel great distances when still alive. She said both she and her nephew were Soul Soarers. Qrow had forgotten the story until now.

Qrodin glances toward Akin. Imolena must have been talking about him. When she'd told Qrodin the story, he hadn't known Akin personally. But now that he does, the story is too unbelievable.

Llani catches his glance. "Have you seen it, too? When Akin leaves his body?"

"I haven't." The thought is disconcerting.

"That was how I met him. His soul was wandering the forest, looking for a way out. I followed it back to their camp. I joined them the next morning."

"How did you convince Kasaandra to let you do that?"

"I told them they'd never find their way out without my help."

"I bet she loved that."

Llani frowns at the memory. "She was displeased." She continues to watch their companions for a moment. "I have shared several confidences with you tonight because I believe you will keep them." She looks at him directly. "Am I wrong?"

"You are never wrong, Llani."

She sighs. "Would that it were so."

When Llani leaves him, Qrodin pulls out his notebook and navigates to the page showing his personal vault notifications. Qrodin hadn't felt comfortable leaving the domi while there was a chance his security had been breached. His head of security had checked the domi and vault on the twenty-fourth. Qrodin was annoyed that it took a few days, but he'd given the man a vacation, so it took several days to reach him. Qrodin had been assured that all was in order. He hadn't looked at the notices since then.

He should have.

Qrodin had left the domi after the inspection. Less than an hour later, the vault was accessed.

Whoever it was, they were only inside for three minutes and sixteen seconds. The intruder had to be Qat.

Singing and drinking are the themes of Searbaltoir, the district founded by a dwarf, Turaisi Searbaltoir, who made selling anything more potent than ale within the district's boundaries illegal.

The main event is held at the end of Kaibur Street, overlooking the cliff where a row of bonfires lines the edge to keep partiers from toppling over the side. When Qrodin first visited Craguesport as an adult, he was surprised that dwarfs lived so close to the sea. He had remembered visiting Kasaandra's home, and the dwarfs there couldn't swim. Then he'd learned that Asairtsall dwarfs love the water and are some of the best shipbuilders on Oram. Despite that, their Longest Night celebrations are all on land. And they involve copious amounts of alcohol.

Spontaneous musical duels and feats of strength are aplenty, and eruptions of cheering and laughter quickly follow as bets are won and lost. Up and down the district's main streets, vendors serve lager and mead in custom drinkware for this year's event. Visitors come every year to add to their growing collections, and traders accumulate as many vessels as they can to sell elsewhere across the country.

Qrodin finally locates Qat as ae dips into an alley.

He watches to see if the faerie shows up again. He wants to get a close look at her. A minute later, Qat emerges wearing a full, ruby-red skirt and round-necked blouse. Qrodin's breath catches. Qat looks like Ama—almost enough to erase the anger he's feeling. Almost. The scarf previously around aer waist is now a headband holding aer hair back and loose, while long bangs frame aer face on each side. Qat stops a woman on the street and kisses her full on the lips. A few men whistle and cheer. When Qat lets go, aer lips are coated in the cherry red lipstick the woman had been wearing.

Qat joins Kasaandra and Akin, who'd already entered the dueling competitions. They don't acknowledge aer presence. They probably have no idea it's Qat. The three are paired separately.

As soon as Qat starts fighting, Qrodin realizes he'd have recognized Qat's style if not the fighter. This is the Qat from his childhood. Here, ae's entertaining a crowd, but Qat's much more skilled now. If Qrodin were a betting man, he'd bet Qat's more adept at other things, too, such as acquiring items.

Qrodin's thoughts swerve back to the vault. Had Qat gone in there? If so, how? Qrodin has searched the safe twice since the twenty-fourth. He hasn't noticed anything missing or out of place.

"Hey, Qat's missing all the fun!" Bell searches the crowd.

"Qat's fighting now," Qrodin mumbles tightly.

"Ae is?" Llani looks surprised. She inspects the fighters closely. "Oh! How clever."

"I don't see aem. Where is ae?"

"The one in the red skirt," Qrodin whispers, afraid his annoyance will spill over. He doesn't want to ruin their fun.

Bell's mouth drops open, and then she laughs loudly. "Go, Qat!" she yells.

At that moment, Llani sounds one of their alarm bird calls. Akin instinctively turns, avoiding a kadal's lizard-like tail that would have swept his feet from under him. Unfortunately, Qat also turns, and the person ae was sparring scores a hit. The point is the first scored against Qat this evening.

"Llani! You're cheating!" Bell says, still laughing.

Llani looks embarrassed. "It was purely reflex. I will rein in my instincts."

After the duels, Qrodin hopes to pull Qat to the side, but a bell clangs loudly, and a squat dwarf announces, "All participants are welcome to our Until-the-last-one-standing, No-holds-barred brawl. The only weapons allowed are wits and fists. The prize is a full keg of Yowl at the Moon lager from our sponsor-of-the-hour: Feral Eclipse Brewing Company."

Kasaandra cracks her knuckles. "I'll be getting an early birthday present when I win!"

"When's your birthday?" Bell asks.

Kasaandra shrugs. "The thirteenth."

"The thirteenth is my mata's nascency day," Llani says.

"We have to have a party!" Bell cries. "I'll cook!"

"I'll drink to that!" Qat says, coming up behind the group and removing the skirt ae'd thrown on over aer favorite leathers. Ae wraps the skirt around aer waist as a makeshift belt.

Kasaandra does a double-take, then laughs. "Only if I win."

"Or I." Qat sprints as the bell rings for all contenders to meet in the courtyard's center.

Kasaandra and Akin race after Qat.

"Qrow! You should go in and help them win," Bell says in a loud whisper.

"Wouldn't that be cheating?" Llani asks.

"No way! There are way too many people in there for it to be cheating. And I bet they're all going to be helping each other. Go!" Bell pushes Qrodin toward the courtyard.

Qrodin lets her. Maybe a good brawl will help get rid of this extra tension.

The courtyard's center is decorated with concentric rings, reminding him of the grimm sitting around in their circles. Somewhere, music starts playing a fast and rowdy tune. The dwarfs cheer and grunt at each other. They pound their chests and knees, stomp three times, and turn with the music until all participants enter the outer ring.

Qrodin watched the competition in previous years but never participated. Not that it matters. The rules are simple. You're out of the competition if you get pushed out of the fiery ring. Every minute, the next smaller ring is lit. If you're stuck outside the new ring, you're eliminated.

The outer ring bursts into flames nearly as tall as Qrodin. The dancing stops, and the brawl begins.

Qrodin heads straight toward Qat, angry that ae had broken into Qrodin's vault, even if ae hadn't taken anything.

As if alerted, Qat turns.

Qrodin charges.

Qat twists away at the last second and taps him on the back of the head as he passes. Angrier now, Qrodin turns around. Qat's fist skims his jaw. He retaliates, but Qat deflects the blow and jabs at his throat.

Qrodin coughs to clear the spasm of pain. He grabs the skirt around Qat's waist and pulls, wrapping his arms around his twin and lifting aem into the air.

Qat reacts quickly, snaking an arm around one of Qrodin's. A quick second later, Qat breaks his hold. Before Qrodin knows what's happening, Qat has his arm twisted behind him, and he's bent double.

Then Qat releases him. He stands up and rushes forward. He hadn't been keeping track of time, and he barely clears the next ring when indigo flames shoot out of the ground. Qat also made it inside the ring. Good. He's still angry.

Qrodin's taller than nearly everyone in the ring, but it's a disadvantage. Now that they're more densely compacted in the smaller ring, nearly a dozen participants turn toward Qrodin. He races toward them, trying to imitate Akin's natural intimidation. Only a few back away, the others swarm him. One of them crawls behind him, tripping him. A few follow him down while others pull on his arms and legs. He can't return to his feet, so he rolls clear of the crowd instead. When he gets his bearings, he's outside the ring. He stands up and joins Llani and Bell.

"I wasn't much help, was I?" Qrodin says, lifting Bell onto the tall base of a statue nearby as cobalt flames eliminate a dozen or more participants.

He's glad he joined in. The brawling has wrestled some anger away, if not all.

"To the contrary," Llani states. "When they converged on you, Kasaandra and Akin gained the center ring."

"Look! They're going after Qat!" Bell laughs.

His twin sprints, jumps over several contestants, and slides under and through the legs of a danaash. Qat unwraps the red skirt from around aer waist, flicks it at one person, and then trips another with it. Half of the combatants are trying to catch aem. When the next ring lights up—emerald green this time—nearly a third of them are left outside, including Qat.

When ae gets close enough, Bell whoops. "Way to go, Qat!"

Qat bows. "That ought to thin the herd."

"Oh, it did!" Bell says, then whistles a warning when someone tries to sweep Akin's feet from under him. "Sorry." She wrinkles her nose. "I couldn't help it."

Although they are somewhat back-to-back, Kasaandra and Akin don't acknowledge each other. Qrodin recognizes several tactics from their training sessions. They sense where the other is. Somehow, they manage to keep the center ring without exposing their alliance.

The subsequent elimination catches more than half of the participants outside the bright yellow flames. There are only two rings left. Two more participants are pushed out. Only nine remain when the orange ring lights, including Akin and Kasaandra. Of the other seven, six are dwarfs.

Qrodin blinks in surprise when he focuses on the last of the nine. He'd know her anywhere. Her short stature kept her hidden from him until now, but there's no mistaking it's her.

She calls herself a mutt: part daga, part danaash, part markali. He always joked she was one hundred percent gritty determination.

She and Kasaandra square off.

"Time to go," Qrodin states tightly.

"What's wrong?"

"There's someone I'd rather avoid if at all possible."

"Who?" Bell scans his face and then the crowd. "Who is it? The one in the ring? Oh. She's beautiful! Did you love her?"

"It's not like that, Bell." Qrodin's annoyed she's so close to the truth.

"Did she break your heart?"

Qrodin frowns. Did she? Doscia hadn't stuck around long enough. All this time, he instinctively knew they'd see each other again. Doscia was an athlete, and he often attended the games. He'd even wondered if she would compete tonight in the Piladatan races. "I'd rather not discuss it," he says to Bell.

Qrodin tries to *Coax* Akin out of the ring, but he should have known better. He doesn't have any better luck with Kasaandra. She must have charged her armbands.

The dwarfs gang up on Akin. Meanwhile, Kasaandra picks up Doscia and drops her outside as the red flaming ring appears. On the way down, Doscia grabs Kasaandra's shirt and bends low, pulling Kasaandra with her. They somersault together, and Doscia lands on top before swiftly jumping to her feet.

Kasaandra grabs the hand Doscia holds out to her. Doscia may be slight at under five feet (including her horns), but she's strong from years of training. She has a daga's small and erect ears, markali horns, a danaash upper body, and daga long legs. She doesn't have daga fur, but she does have pointed teeth unlike any he's seen. The only time she's not self-conscious about them is when she's competing. Then, her smile is as joyful as it is fierce.

Qrodin pulls his eyes away from her as Akin falls to the ground at the inside edge of the ring, pulling several dwarfs with him. He kicks his legs up, knocks two out of the ring, and then backflips. Three dwarfs catch him before his feet hit the ground. They toss Akin out of the ring headfirst as though they'd rehearsed it. He rolls to a stand and shakes his head.

Akin joins Doscia and Kasaandra, and the three of them approach Qrodin's group.

"Smooth move," Doscia says to Akin.

She had said the same thing to Qrodin once. Her voice is just as Qrodin remembers. Low and husky. His face burns hot at the memory. Seeing her again is twisting up his insides. He'd hoped he was over her, but all he wants to do is take her in his arms and whisk her back to the domi. At least he's using a different disguise than the one she knows.

"Kasaandra! Introduce us to your friend!" Bell smiles when Qrodin growls. "You sound just like Akin," she teases, jumping down. To Doscia, she adds, "You were great out there! Where'd you learn how to flip someone like that?"

"At the Academy."

"The one here? Are you a Stormwall cadet?" Bell asks.

How does she know about the cadets? And what does Doscia mean, the Academy? What about her career as an athlete? Did she get injured? It hadn't seemed so when he'd watched her in the circles.

Doscia gives Bell one of her closed-mouth smiles. "No. The Academy of the Adamantine Fist. I graduated last year."

Qrodin's foreboding increases. The Academy of the Adamantine Fist is part of the Zedanian military.

"That's so cool! I'm Bell, and if you teach me how to flip Kasaandra, you'll be my new best friend!" She sneaks a glance at Llani. "I mean, my new second-best friend."

"I'd like that, Bell. And I'm Doscia, or TFDG Theo, at your service. It's very nice to meet you."

A round of cheering and stomping erupts as the brawl winner accepts aer prize, hopefully covering up the sound of his pounding heart. TFDG Theo. She can't be in town to see him, can she? To see Quentin Browning? He can't be that unlucky. Can he?

"Whoa! You're a detective?" Bell high-fives Doscia.

Faerie laughter erupts behind Qrodin's left ear. "Oh, you're fucked."

Llani's ears twitch and swivel toward him.

So do Doscia's.

Yeah, Qrodin thinks. Don't I know it.

Doscia's appearance tonight has soured Qrodin's mood. He's thankful she's never seen his Quelen Brown disguise. And that, although she has the hearing and speed of a daga, she doesn't have their keen smell, or she'd already know who he is. Although he can disguise his voice, he's unsure how effective it will be, so he hopes she doesn't stay long.

"It was nice meeting you all, but I need to go say hello to my former teammates. Cheer them up a little. They're not doing well tonight."

"Oh! What color are they?"

"Pink, of course." Doscia's eyes twinkle. "It's my favorite color."

It was why she'd joined that team despite being recruited by several other teams.

"Oh. Too bad they're not green."

Doscia smiles at Bell. "I'm sure we'll see each other again soon." Her eyes flick toward Qrodin as she says it.

"I like her," Bell says to Qrodin when they start toward the next district. "And I think she likes you, too!"

Qrodin decides to ignore her comment. "You're going to enjoy Androi's show. Did I tell you it's my favorite?" He pushes all thoughts of Doscia out of his mind. There's nothing he can do right now, even if she is the one who's investigating Truffle.

When they reach the Androi district, ships are lined stem to stern away from the docks with lanterns hung along their lengths. Performers line the sides of the boats and the dock, and more swim below. An acrobatic show featuring water, fire, and air dazzles the crowd with lights and torches flying from ship to shore. Water cannons are shot, and mist is swirled into elaborate creatures that chase or consume the missiles. Along the docks, jugglers show off their fire-handling abilities in a display as spectacular as the one over the water. The performances won't end until the bells ring at dawn. Meanwhile, street vendors are peddling seaweed wraps and flaming food on a stick.

It's been several hours since they ate, so when Bell decides it's time to move on, they grab food before heading to the Stormwall Coliseum in Piladata. Fireworks announce the race winner.

"Woohoo! Green won again!" Bell yells when fireworks burst overhead.

"Selecting a team by color is not practical, Bell. Statistically, the yellow team has outscored the green team by nearly half," Llani says between bites of her fruit kabob. "Besides, we have yet to witness a single race. You may change your mind once we do."

"Nope! Green is my team, no matter the game. Hey, Kasaandra, how do you pick 'em?"

"Best-looking legs," she answers.

Qat laughs. "I go for the—"

"Heart. Every time," says a voice from their right. "Hello, Qat. I've missed you."

The deep voice is humorous but threaded with steel as a tall man emerges from the crowd. His face is brown from years in the sun, and his long, platinum hair turns jade green from the fireworks.

Qrodin's heart stops, and his stomach takes a steep dive as recognition hits him in the solar plexus.

The stranger's eyes meet Qrodin's.

Qrodin is eleven again, and this man is wrenching Qat away from Ama.

Chapter 55 Qat

Qrow hisses like a cornered cat.

I react instinctively, jumping between him and Captain Rogen. My hands go to my blades, but I don't draw them. Akin and Kasaandra also react to Qrow's hiss, surrounding the captain.

Too bad Nightshade already left. A faerie assassin would be lovely to have on my side right now.

"Call your friends off before I invite my crew in," Rogen says.

It takes me a second to respond to the captain's bluff. "Your crew isn't here," I tell him. I would have recognized them if they were.

"You've been gone a long time, Qat." Rogen nods, and several strangers appear behind Akin and Kasaandra. When he nods a second time, they back into the crowd.

Bollocks!

The captain must have kept them back far enough that they didn't set off my danger sense.

Either that, or he's not here to kill me.

Akin relaxes his stance outwardly, but I know him well enough by now to know he's ready to react instantly. Kasaandra tucks a handaxe back into her boot and stands with legs splayed wide. Her green eyes narrow on Rogen. They flick to me and back again, but I see nothing in them to alarm me. She's as controlled as Akin.

I hadn't heard that Rogen was in town. His prolonged absence had assured me he had skipped Craguesport this year for Alonard. I figured if the captain were here, he wouldn't be downtown on this of all nights. He should be staking out businesses that don't have candles burning in their windows—a guaranteed sign they aren't occupied.

"How did you know I was here?" *Please don't say Qataleena.*

"You've been careless to stay in one place so long."

"Qatzsi. How do you know this man?" The Qrow must be rattled to use my full name.

Rogen's eyes narrow at my name, but otherwise, he doesn't react.

"This is Captain Rogen...my former mentor." And possibly our uncle. Half uncle?

Bell squeals. She turns to him and bobs, bouncing back up so fast her feet leave the ground. "*Griss frem*, Mr. Captain Rogen. I'm Miss Bell Liddlyri of clan Tubaks from Bierenan. Wow! You are so gorgeous!" Then, in an aside to me, "Is he married?"

I shake my head at her. I almost don't recognize Rogen. He's clean-shaven, for one thing. He also looks smaller than I remember. I thought he was taller, but he and Qrow are the same height. I guess everything looks bigger when you're young.

"What? He's not married? Or you want me to be quiet?" Bell asks in a loud whisper. "I know that look. Llani gives it to me all the time."

I smile at her, worried that Qrow still hasn't responded to my introduction but thankful for the distraction. Even though he hasn't said anything, he seems to have regained his composure. "Captain, this is—"

"Quelen Brown. Real Estate," Qrow says, coming around my side to introduce himself. "It's very nice to meet someone who's had such an influence on Qat," Qrow says, full of charm as if he hadn't nearly attacked the captain a moment before. Qrow's hands are relaxed at his sides, and his mouth is only slightly tighter than usual. Other than that, there are no signs he's anything but curious.

And that worries me.

How does he do that?

When he smiles, I hear alarm bells in my head. However, my danger sense isn't tingling, so I don't believe a fight is imminent.

"Tell me, Captain, how did you and Qat meet?"

Oh, cannonballs.

"It was so long ago, I scarce remember. Qat just appeared one day."

I release my breath slowly.

Until Rogen continues, "And then disappeared without a word. Naughty, Qat."

Although he says it jokingly, I can tell he's angry. Which surprises me. I usually haven't a clue what he's feeling.

"Worried I'd fallen overboard and drowned?" I ask in my most nonchalant tone as if requesting what he ate for breakfast.

"Not at all. You're an excellent swimmer. And we were at port."

That, we were.

"I was a bit concerned when I found this." The captain removes my red scarf from an inside coat pocket.

My heart skips a beat, then races out of control. If Rogen hands it to me now, my hands will be shaking. Thankfully, he doesn't.

"Ah. I never knew you cared, Captain. You must have missed me a lot to come all this way to give it back."

"Don't be flip. You owe me an explanation," Rogen says tersely. "And. A. First. Mate."

That last part was short and clipped.

"Oh yeah? What happened? Goffin take off on you?" I hold my breath for his answer.

"In a manner of speaking."

So, does that mean he left, or that I killed him? I hope it's the latter. Knowing he's not here with Rogen is enough to get my trembling hands under control. I hold out my hand. "I'll take that off your hands now. I'd hate for your trip to be for nothing." I smile with my mouth but not my eyes. They're too busy looking for a clue to his real motives for being here.

"How about we make a trade?" he says instead.

If my stomach could clench tighter, it would. I raise my brows.

"Come with me, and we can discuss it." He turns and takes a few steps.

Back when I sailed with him, I'd have followed him without question, but I don't work for him anymore. "My mates and I were about to check out the races. Want to come with? We can bet on the outcomes to see who gets what." It's not much of a gamble, to be sure. I seldom win any of our bets, but the longer we put off the inevitable, the more time I'll have to...

What? Breathe?

My neck is fine, so I doubt I'll be harmed.

"Haven't you been paying attention? It's the yellow team this year," Rogen says.

"That is what I was telling them," Llani says. "It is all about statistics. At this point, there is a seventy-two percent chance they will win the night."

Seriously, Llani?

"I don't care. I'm still rooting for green."

Llani and Bell's comments must have reminded Rogen that we weren't alone. "My apologies," Rogen says with a nod that includes Kasaandra. And then to Akin and Qrow, "For detaining you. We'll let you get to the races. Qat will be along shortly. You have my word."

As they reluctantly walk away, I hear Bell telling them Captain Rogen reminds her of the romance novel *Stolen Heart*. I'm not surprised. His blonde hair and icy blue eyes have always attracted the ladies.

The captain turns again and starts walking.

But like I said, I don't work for him anymore.

He pauses a moment and turns.

I cave under his stare and follow him. I always have.

It's a wonder I've been able to keep ahead of him for so long.

"Imagine my surprise when I turned around and saw you standing only an arm's length ahead of me," the captain says as we finally outdistance the crowd and settle on two boulders overlooking the ocean. "Have I taught you nothing, Qat?"

"I was just thinking the same thing. What are you doing here, Captain?"

"I deserve an explanation."

"And you came all this way to get one, did you?" Despite my taunts, he wouldn't come into town tonight just to talk to me.

"I'm here on business."

Of course, he is. That's what he always says.

"Who's Qataleena?" I barely get the words out before he has me on the ground with a dagger to my throat. With the knife I gave him, no less. The one with a piece of amber embedded in the handle.

"How do you know Qataleena?" he growls low. But there's caution in his words—like he doesn't want his men to hear him. That's probably why I can push him off with a move he taught me and roll away. I'm on my feet quickly, but so is he.

"Another surprise lesson?" I ask loudly, for his men's sake. Of course, I'm protecting Qataleena, not him. He doesn't need anyone's protection. "You must be getting old to let me get away so easily."

"Only in your dreams," he says before lowering his voice. "Now tell me how you know her."

"Funny thing, Cap. She knew me. Came right up and said my name." He doesn't respond, and I can't read his expression. "How do you know her?"

"What says I do?"

"Your reaction just now. You can't take that back."

He sighs loudly, and three lines appear between his brows. Seeing them makes me pause. How could I not have remembered them or seen the resemblance to Qrow?

Maybe because the captain never lets his feelings show. If I've seen them before, it was too rare to have remembered their existence.

Their presence means he's vulnerable right now.

Qataleena *does* make him vulnerable.

"Did she say how she knew you?" he asks.

"I propose a trade. You have something of mine. Give it back, and I'll tell you everything." Maybe I will. Or perhaps I'll take my chances with the side of the cliff. We're not that far up the mountain. How hard could it be to climb down a dozen or so razor-sharp rocks?

When Rogen's hand dives into his pocket, I can't believe my luck. I've never seen him so pliable. So obviously off balance. Even so, I still can't tell what he's thinking when he tosses me the length of red satin I'd left looped around Goffin's neck.

I sit back down. As I fold the satin over and rub the rough sides together between my fingers, I feel as though I'm back in the hold of the ship, hiding after a beating. The tension between my shoulders eases a fraction.

The captain follows me back to the boulders. He stands with his hands on his hips in his power position.

"She said my grandmother was her mother's cousin—if that makes any sense."

He sits so fast it's as though he lost his legs, and his face searches mine closely for several seconds before he speaks. "What's your mother's name?"

I shake my head.

"Qataleena didn't tell you?"

"Nope, only that she and I were named after my grandmother, Qataleeha."

The captain closes his eyes, and something flashes briefly across his face before it vanishes. When he opens them again, Rogen studies me like I'm some gem he's deciding if he should purchase.

"Aleena," he says, caressing the name. At my silence, he continues, "Your mother's name was Aleena." His voice is rough, and his eyes are haunted.

He loved her. Aleena. My mother. That changes things.

"And you didn't know she was my mother? That wasn't why you took me when she was murdered?"

"What? No. I had no idea you knew her." He closes his eyes. "Or that she had a child. I thought you were part of the crew that killed her. I took you to find out why they did it."

I *knew* Qrow was wrong. I knew Rogen couldn't have done it. "Why *who* killed her?"

Maybe if I find that out, I can keep Qrow from going after Rogen.

His frown deepens. "The sword that killed her was Karatolii in design. I saw only a boat leaving the shore and you screaming, *'Don't leave me.'* When

I dumped you into our skiff, you fought my crew. One of them cuffed you. Knocked you out cold. I thought he'd killed you. When you woke up two days later, I hoped you could tell me, but…"

"But I couldn't remember."

The captain nods. He's staring out to sea, and I can only see his profile, but a vein is pulsing on his forehead. Another Qrow trait.

"Is Qataleena your sister?"

He's silent for so long that I figure he won't answer, but then he nods. One very slow nod.

I hesitate before asking the next question. "Was Aleena your half-sister?"

He looks startled at first, then laughs and shakes his head, then shrugs. "No."

He'd said *a* child. Not children.

That means he doesn't know about Qrow. And his Quelen Brown disguise didn't give him away tonight.

Something else suddenly occurs to me. Qrow had mentioned they got their slit pupils from a many-times-great-grandmother. The trait skipped generations. Could that be the same for eye color, too?

I look at Rogen. He and Qrow have so many similarities. I see that now with the captain right in front of me. Maybe I didn't realize it before because it had been so long since I'd seen Rogen. Or perhaps I've learned more from Llani than I thought. I spent a lot of time with Qrow on our journey here. I studied every one of his expressions and compared every trait to mine. I should have been comparing him to a man I hadn't seen in over a decade.

And tonight, Rogen's mask has slipped more than once. The only other time I saw that was when the captain's ruby went missing, and he found the man who'd stolen it.

His ruby.

Aleena's ruby. A memory bombards me.

I'm sitting cross-legged on the floor of the captain's quarters, polishing the pendants spread out on the floor and handing them to the captain to pin to his new jacket.

He places a rough-cut ruby into the breast pocket.

"Why don't you wear the ruby on the outside like the other ones?"

"You don't wear your heart for everyone to see."

He always called his ruby his heart. I thought it meant he loved treasure more than anything else in the world. But now I know better. He was talking about Aleena.

Which means… "Are you my *father*?" I don't see how he can't be.

His eyes rest briefly on my face. Then, he shrugs again and turns back to the sea.

"It's possible."

It's possible.

That's it?

That's all he's going to say?

Qrow did say I looked like Ama. Maybe Rogen doesn't see himself in me.

I guess I understand that. I never saw a resemblance between Rogen and Qrow until now. Rogen is blonde with blue eyes. We may have the same eyebrows, but they're not that rare. I have his angular jaw, but my chin is round rather than square. I'd never noticed before, but now, with the captain's bare face, our matching, barely-there chin dimples are identical. As are his and Qrow's. To be honest, he looks like an older version of The Qrow's real face, the one I haven't seen since we arrived in Craguesport.

Picturing Qrow with light hair and a tan, he looks so much like the Rogen I met as a child, I'm ashamed I didn't see it. I excel at noticing details.

Rogen taught me to.

Does this mean I only bother when there's something in it for me? When I'm getting paid?

Maybe I'm not the only one who failed. Rogen never saw Aleena in me. Qrow says I look like her. Shouldn't Rogen have noticed?

Maybe the captain didn't want to see her.

Maybe the idea was so foreign it never crossed his mind.

Maybe I only started resembling her after I left the *Raven Scream*.

Either way, it doesn't seem like the news carries much weight for him. I'm surprised it isn't such a big deal to me. He's the only authority figure I've ever had. That means he's always been the closest thing I had to a father. It just never bothered me that I didn't have one.

Sure, I wanted a family to claim me and take me away from the bullies, but I never really thought about what having one would have been like. How can you, with nothing to draw upon? It's not like most pirates sit around talking about their families. They talk about how many limbs they've severed or how many women they've plundered.

I decide not to tell Rogen about Qrow. The less everyone knows, the better.

So. Now, what do we do?

"Now what?" he asks.

Did I just...? No. Rogen would be immune to any mind tricks I might have. "That depends on if Goffin is still alive," I say to change the subject.

"When I got back, you were both gone, and that"—Rogen nods at the red satin I'm twisting around my fingers— "was on the deck. I haven't seen or heard news of him since."

"What about me? Have you heard about me since I left?"

For the first time tonight, Rogen smiles. "You're not as invisible as you think."

Well, that settles it, then. Goffin must be dead, or Rogen would have heard about him. Does that mean Goffin wasn't the one buying up my contracts? I stand up and stretch my back.

"You never said what happened that day. Why did you leave?"

I can't detect anything from his tone. Did he worry about me? Did it bother him that I left without a word? I sneak a peek at him. His brows are still furrowed. "I thought I killed him." As I said, the less everyone knows...

"You must have felt you had a reason. You don't kill for fun, Qat. Just for money. Or survival."

That affirmation melts something inside me. He would have believed me. "I wasn't paid to assassinate him." I raise my chin, daring him to call me a liar.

His face hardens. His eyes probe mine, but he doesn't ask me to elaborate, just nods his acceptance of my explanation. "One more thing," he says before I can turn around.

"What's that?"

"How did you know your mother was murdered?"

My heart lurches sideways. I feel as though I've been hit broadside. I messed that one up. "What?" I prevaricate.

He stands up but turns to face the sea. "You asked if I took you because your mother was murdered. How did you know she was if you can't remember anything?"

If I tell him about Qrow, it could place him in danger. Their father/son connection could put them both in danger.

I'd be less nervous if Rogen were looking at me.

I almost mention Qataleena's name, but something stops me. I still don't know what *she* knows, and I'd hate to cause her problems.

"How do you know!"

At the sound of Rogen's raised voice, the back of my neck goes on high alert. Rogen and I both turn as footsteps approach quickly.

"Because I saw you kill aem!"

"Wait!" I say, too late to stop Qrow as he launches himself at the captain. I'm afraid they might go over the cliff's edge, but the captain's too stout to let that happen.

And too skilled in close combat.

And too fast.

He uses Qrow's forward momentum against him, tripping him sideways into one of the boulders, but The Qrow keeps his feet. When his throat starts flexing in that odd way it does when he's soothing Bell, Rogen punches him in the throat, interrupting the spell Qrow was probably casting—just like he taught me. Qrow tries to push off the bigger man but is at a disadvantage.

Anyone fighting the captain is at a disadvantage.

I reach for my whip to immobilize the captain before realizing I left it at the domi.

I check behind me at the jabbing in my neck. At the same time, I hear a bird call and instinctively look up.

A falkira lands in front of me, his taloned feet spread wide. Uci was forever trying to compete with me for the captain's attention. It pissed him off that I didn't have to try. Looks like he's finally got what he always wanted. I brace myself at the telltale clicking he makes before casting a spell. His wings flap forward, pushing a gust of wind my way. Before it hits, I step out of its path.

Only then do I realize the bird call I'd heard was one Llani and Akin had taught us. I guess it was a good idea to practice, after all.

"You know better than to interfere in the captain's business, Qat." Uci clicks his beak shut on my name.

I go for one of my daggers. "Uci Coochie. Fancy meeting you here." He hates the rhyming nickname. At least I know *his* weaknesses.

"It's First Mate to you. And I wouldn't do that. I've learned a lot since you left. I won't be as easy to beat."

First Mate? *Uci? He's* the one who bought out my contracts?

Just then, an arrow pierces one of Uci's wingtip feathers, and it folds backward from a nearly severed spine.

Way to go, Bell! Thank the gods below that Llani doesn't leave the domi without her bag.

Uci searches behind me. I take a quick second to check on Qrow. His face is slightly battered, but he's still standing. And what little disguise he'd engineered is still there. He's using his two-toned stave to keep Rogen at a distance. I bet Rogen didn't anticipate a magical staff. Our practices have paid off, too. Qrow's showing some skill, but I can see the weakness on his left side from the Twisted Sisters' injury. And if I can see it, Rogen can, too.

"Is that the best he can do?" Uci sneers, still searching behind me for the person who shot the arrow. Good. He still hasn't found Bell's hiding spot.

"*She* doesn't miss. That was a warning shot. I bet the flaming arrows come next. She loves her flaming arrows." Or perhaps Llani's flaming darts or Akin's *Whoosh*? I hope it doesn't come to that, but I wouldn't mind the smell of scorched feathers right now.

At Uci's worried look, I almost pity him. Fire and fowl don't go well together, and flying outside an arrow's range would take him too far away from the captain to protect him adequately. Not that the captain needs Uci's protection. At least the idiot bird hasn't made another move. Even now, he's pulling his wings tight behind him.

I sheathe my dagger. I'm not going to interfere again soon.

I turn my focus back to the fight. Rogen ducks under the stave and comes up with a wicked uppercut that knocks Qrow back a few steps. Rogen disarms Qrow and uses the weapon to flip Qrow's feet out from under him. I hear his head hit the ground and wince. I'm relieved when he struggles to sit up. Rogen tosses the stave and tackles Qrow to push him back down, then straddles him. The captain lands one stunning blow after another. Qrow is no longer fending him off.

I hold my breath.

"Qrow!"

Bell's cry snaps Rogen out of his rage haze, and his fist halts midair.

Qrow's disguise is gone. Rogen and his crew stare in stunned disbelief at what could have been Rogen's face twenty years ago.

I take a step, raising my weaponless hands when Uci moves to restrain me. When he finally steps aside, I run to Qrow's side and kneel in front of Rogen. "Captain," I say softly so my voice doesn't carry. "He's my twin." I lower my voice to a bare whisper, "Aleena's son."

Rogen searches Qrow's visage. His eyes flicker in pain, then go completely blank.

He stands and gives the sign for his men to retreat. He nods to someone behind me, and Llani rushes forward. The others finally approach and gather around Qrow. They must have been held back, too, same as I was. I'm surprised Qrow got through in the first place.

Llani kneels at Qrow's side and checks his pulse. "He is still alive. I need to heal him now, or he will perish." Her eyes shoot sparks at Rogen. "Impede my progress, and I will siphon the moisture from your body until you are a shriveled corpse."

I shiver at her tone.

"I won't interfere." Rogen's voice sounds strangled. It can't be from fear. Rogen fears no one. I can't imagine what's going through his head right now.

When Llani's healing green light appears, I sigh in relief. Qrow will be okay now.

"Can she do that?"

"Do what?" I raise my brow at Uci, who had come up beside me in defiance of the captain's orders.

"Turn someone into a shriveled corpse?"

"Of course she can," I respond. And she probably can, too. If she can remove water from wood, she can probably remove the water from a living body. And even if she can't, there's always that purple thing she does. "Aren't you supposed to retreat a hundred feet?"

"I'm not leaving the captain with you. I don't want *him* to disappear."

"Like Goffin the Black?" I ask.

His answering laugh is ugly.

"Uci!"

"Captain. You don't know these people or what they can do."

He's even more reckless than I remember to question the captain that way. And in front of others, too.

"I know I'll have a new first mate tomorrow if you're still standing there by the time I..." He trails off as Uci leaps into the air. The falkira circles the group five times, ascending with each loop before he finally swoops away and lands the requisite distance behind me. I can't believe the party is still going strong, and no one is bothering to interrupt us. They probably think we're drunk and rowdy.

After all, at least a dozen duels are commencing as we speak.

"Uci? First mate? Really, Captain?" He must be hurting if Uci is the most qualified person for the position.

"The crew respects him. Unlike you, they don't question every decision he makes."

"Then they're as stupid as I remember." It's comforting to know that some things don't change. "But you've changed. I've never seen you so out of control."

"Why did the little one call him Qrow?"

Think fast, Qat. "She was yelling at the birds. I think I saw one trying to push a mouse over the cliff. Did you know that crows are scavengers?" I can do this all day if necessary to throw Rogen off Qrow's scent. "They don't kill their food, but they'll chase a rodent into the street to get hit by a cart. They're also—"

"Does the name Kqrogen mean anything to you?"

"...thieves," I continue. His lightning-fast change of topics is meant to disconcert his opponents, but I grew up with them. He's going to have to work harder than that to rattle me.

"Kqrogen was Qataleena's father."

That rattles me.

Because that would make Kqrogen *his* father, and he's never mentioned his family before.

My conversation with Qataleena splashes over me like the waves on the rocks below. Or a bucket of water in the face. *'Names are altered so we don't say them out loud after someone's passed,'* she had said.

Kqrogen and Rogen.

His eyes haven't left Qrow once during our conversation. Not even when he was dressing down Uci.

"His real name isn't Quelen, is it?" he asks.

I shrug. Sometimes, it's better not to say anything at all.

"Do you know why I named you Qat?"

I shake my head.

"Because you reminded me of Qataleena when she was your age." He takes a deep breath and lets it out slowly. "And I used to call her Qat."

Something else occurs to me. "What is Qataleena's mother's name?"

"Aleeha."

And her cousin was Qataleeha. Whose daughter was Aleena. Who bore me and named me Qatzsi.

It would make sense that Qrow would be shortened from a variation of Kqrogen, whose son is Rogen.

"What's his real name?" Rogen asks, still staring at Qrow.

"He told me his name is Qrow."

The captain indicates I should follow him. "Give us a moment alone with him," Rogen says as he kneels next to Qrow.

Everyone moves away, but only a few feet.

I kneel on Qrow's other side.

Rogen whispers. *"What is your real name?"* But this time, he's speaking in Karatol.

Qrow turns his head, and his swollen eyes glow with gold fire. "Qrodin Balaerdo. Now, who the fuck are you?"

My chest hurts. Why had he never told me his real name?

Chapter 56 Qrodin

Qrodin sits up slowly. He only heard the end of their conversation, but it was enough to know that Captain Rogen is not who Qrodin thought he was.

After a few seconds of silence, Llani comes forward and, for once, must realize the gravity of the information she imparts because she whispers to Qrow, "He's your father."

"How does she—"

"Don't ask," Qat interrupts the captain. "Unless you want the long answer."

Kasaandra *harrumphs* as she kneels next to Llani. "Yeah. She'll say stuff like 'recessive' and 'dominant,' and they won't mean what you think they will."

Not wanting to get in the middle of that conversation, Qrodin looks at the man Llani claims is their father. Karatolii don't keep track of fathers, so he's never really wondered about his. He'd never even heard the word until he was on the streets of Riversmeet. He was always amazed to learn some orphans were devastated that they never knew who sired them. At that age, he hadn't even learned how babies were made. Conception wasn't something anyone ever talked about. He had no concept of the typical family unit until much later.

Having listened to many of Llani's lectures about trait inheritance, Qrodin inspects the captain for similarities. Rogen's light, while Ama was dark. Ama had the Karatolii characteristic black hair and reddish-brown eyes. Rogen's ash-blonde hair could have given Qrodin and Qat their bronze highlights. Imagining Rogen with dark hair and brows, gold eyes—and twenty or so years younger—Qrodin can see the resemblance for what it is.

But none of that answers the question of Ama's death.

Or Qat's abduction.

He doesn't want to discuss his personal life publicly. "We should continue this conversation elsewhere and perhaps at another time? Tomorrow at my place should be sufficient." If they must have this conversation, at least his domi is spelled to keep it private.

Rogen agrees, and he and his men disappear into the crowd.

The walk home is subdued. Llani didn't heal him completely, and the bruising and scratches on his back and face are quite painful. He can't concentrate enough to keep his disguise for the walk home, so he leads them through the back roads to avoid as many people as possible.

"How were the races, Bell?" Qat asks.

"Oh, we didn't make it that far. Qrow didn't want to leave you. We circled back until Llani could hear you guys talking."

What Bell didn't know was that, when Rogen had asked how Qat knew Ama was murdered, Qrodin had felt his twin's anxiety spike, and he could wait no longer.

He wishes they'd gotten there earlier because it's evident Rogen is very familiar with the Karatolii and the language, and Qrodin wants to know how he met Ama. At least he'll be able to grill Qat before Rogen arrives tomorrow.

At least, that's the plan until they arrive at the domi and Qat is no longer with them.

He should have known Qat would run.

They collect their Longest Night candles and bring them into the music hall. Llani lights them while Bell rustles up some snacks. Qrodin, Kasaandra, and Akin move the sectionals to one of the picture windows. They make one large bed and climb on top of it to wait for the sun to rise while the candles release their perfumes.

Outside, the celebration will continue all night until the first rays of the sun touch the top of the arch over the city's entrance. Once it does, bells will ring, and everyone will extinguish their lights, but Qrodin doesn't care about that right now.

2ND DAY OF SAMDI, 14,887

Qrodin wakes to the smell of coffee and sunlight in his eyes. He's still in the music hall. Kasaandra and Qat are sleeping at the opposite end of the makeshift bed. He wonders what time Qat came in last night.

A quick scan of the room shows Qat's candle. The flame is slightly higher than the others, so ae must have come in shortly after everyone settled down. Nevertheless, Qrodin can still smell the lingering scent of roses and...pine? He wrinkles his nose. Not his favorite combination.

He shakes the slumber from his limbs and climbs out of bed, wincing at the pain between his shoulder blades. He can't believe he slept so late. But then again, healing is exhausting.

The Music Mouth is playing forest sounds. Llani must have selected it this morning. Qat usually picks the under-ocean theme.

Usually, his morning routine is to bathe and dress immediately, then review his financials over coffee. But this morning is a holiday for all businesses. There won't be anything to review. His head is a bit muggy, and his cheekbone is still sore from the beating he took last night.

A quick look in a nearby mirror reveals a black right eye.

"I would have siphoned energy from Rogen last night if I'd needed to, but I am relieved it was unnecessary. Once you sat up, I knew you could make it home. Would you like me to continue the treatment this morning?"

Qrodin declines Llani's offer. Perhaps the pain will remind him to keep his head when Rogen arrives. Rushing the man last night was stupid of him. No good ever comes from that kind of mindless action.

She looks ready to argue, so he excuses himself and retreats to his quarters. He quickly washes and puts on comfortable slacks. He doesn't bother buttoning his shirt, though. Llani will probably insist on inspecting his injuries when he rejoins them.

He looks at the time. Rogen said he'd come by midmorning. That could be any time in the next two hours or so, if he comes by at all.

When Qrodin returns to the kitchen, everyone is up, and the sectionals are back in their usual places. All but Qat are at the table. Even Kasaandra is dressed, and her hair has been freshly braided. That had to have taken some time. Qrodin sighs. Today's going to be one of those days when he moves much slower than the clock.

There's a knock at the door before he has time to sit down.

When Qat opens the door, Rogen ushers an elderly person into the domi. Aer shoulders are bent from decades of sewing—like his Ama'ani Qataleeha's had been. "My mother insisted on coming. I hope you don't mind," he says.

At Rogen's statement, Qat rushes into the room and stops short at the sight of the elder.

"Ama. These are Aleena's twins. Do you remember them?"

When she lifts her eyes to Qat's face, they fill with tears, and she presses one hand to Qat's cheek. Qat clasps her other wrist and bends forward, resting aer forehead on the elder's wrinkled one. "*Oiy, varsome shay valore, Ama'ani.*"

"*Oiy, valore,* my sweet *pisitas.*" She kisses Qat's cheek before turning to Qrodin.

Aleeha shuffles over and hugs Qrodin tight before greeting him in the Karatolii fashion. When she pulls back, she looks confused. Then she sees Qat again, and her expression brightens. "Aleena! I'm so glad you came to visit. What are you wearing? Come sit with me and tell me all about those precious babies of yours!" Aleeha looks around, confusion creasing her brow. "I...Aleena? Where are we, dear?"

Rogen takes her hand. "Ama, we are visiting Aleena's children. They have invited us for a meal. Come sit down, and I will serve you." He glances at Qat. "She gets confused easily these days. Qataleena says it's easier on her if we don't try to correct her."

"Kqrogen. My love. Where are the children? Where is Rogen and Qataleena?"

"They are at home. Come. Let's eat."

Aleeha inhales sharply when Qrodin moves to sit next to her, and his shirt gapes open. "I've seen those marks before." She looks at Rogen. "You have the same birthmark. Here." She touches his left side. "And Aleena had that other one there." She looks at Qrodin intently. "So did aer ama."

"That sounds very much like a *jurva-tetu*," Llani says, frowning. She focuses again on Qrodin's bruising. "Would you like me to heal you? It must be difficult to see with that eye swollen shut."

"We can do it later. I want to talk to Ama'ani Aleeha."

During the meal, Aleeha drifts between present and past, unknowingly answering questions that haven't yet been asked, slipping back and forth from Karatol when she thinks she is with Aleena, to Oramische when she finds herself in the present.

Aleeha effectively—if not chronologically—presents a list of events that tell the story of Qrodin and Qat's familial relationship with the captain. She said she fell in love with a man named Kqrogen Browning when the Balaerdo caravan came to Craguesport. Aleeha stayed with him when the caravan left. Because the Karatolii don't believe in marriage, they'd never married. Because of that, Aleeha didn't inherit any of Kqrogen's wealth when he went missing. Left destitute when Kqrogen vanished, Aleeha raised their children in the only way she knew how—her craft.

The nickname 'The Qrow' only became widespread after Kqrogen's disappearance when—many years later—it was given to the 'Specter of Death' who killed everyone believed to have murdered him.

Watching Rogen's face during the retelling, Qrodin wonders if Rogen was the cause of the disappearing business partners. He had been old enough by then to exact revenge on his father's murderers.

Qrodin doesn't tell them how *he* came to use the nickname, nor that he and Talim were the ones who unraveled the mystery of Kqrogen's death. That's a story for another time.

"Your Ama always visited me whenever Balaerdo's was in Craguesport. And always brought you, my sweet Aleena." Aleeha looks at Qat when she says it, again mistaking Qat for Ama. "You never stopped visiting me. Even after..." She pauses, and her eyes fill with tears. "Oh. I miss your Ama. And I always look forward to your visits. Where are your babies? They must be nearly grown now."

"You never mentioned Aleena had children," Rogen says roughly.

Qrodin cringes at hearing his mother's name. He doesn't blame Aleeha. After all, her dementia is excuse enough, but Rogen should know better than to speak the name of the dead. Qrodin can't imagine Aleeha didn't teach him. It's another example of the pirate's lack of respect for the rules of civilization. It reminds him of someone else. Qrodin can't help but glance at his twin, who is more like Rogen in spirit than looks.

"You have never been interested in babies," Aleeha says, bringing Qrodin back to the conversation.

Sometime later, Rogen admits he was Aleena's supplier of crafting items—and the reason Aleena was on the dock that night in Riversmeet. Rogen was too late to save her.

Even though Qrodin knows several of the people they are discussing, with all the similar names, he finds himself constantly trying to catch up. He isn't the only one. Llani starts jotting down names and relationships. They're still hard to follow. Even Bell looks confused. Finally, Kasaandra turns the page of Llani's notebook and quickly sketches a family tree, placing each name in its corresponding place.

"How did you keep track of all that?" Bell asks.

"This is nothing compared to our family trees."

Bell's nose twitches slightly. "How are Aleena and Rogen related again?"

"They are second or half-second cousins, depending on who fathered Aleeha and Qataleeha. If you remember, I hypothesized their relationship based on the recessive inheritance of—"

"Right. Well, I think Ama needs to get home." Rogen says, already used to Llani's complicated explanations. Aleeha had fallen asleep sitting up. He gently wakes her and tells her it's time to leave.

Qrodin presses his forehead to Aleeha's. "I'd like to visit you when I'm in town. Would that be okay?"

"Of course," she replies.

A moment after they leave, there is a knock on the front door. Rogen must have come back for something. "Did you forget...?" Qrodin says as he opens the door but stops when he sees it's not Rogen.

Doscia is standing on the landing, peering down the stairs, looking small and too delicate to be a detective. How deceptive that is. She's all hard muscles under her winter clothes.

"What are you doing here?" Qrodin's voice is harsher than he intends.

"I was wondering when you started hanging out with pirates." She quickly looks back at Qrodin and visibly starts. Her eyes narrow. "Quentin? What's wrong with your eyes?" The voice isn't the sweetly mellow tones of his previous lover. No. The tone belongs to the detective she's become. "And what's up with the disguise?"

Qrodin hadn't thought about his appearance when he opened the door. After all, Rogen knew his natural face. Last night, Qrow had kept silent around his ex-lover, afraid she'd recognize his voice. He was right. She'd known it was him when he answered the door from those few words alone.

"Who are you calling a pirate?" he asks instead, hoping to distract her.

She eyes him for a minute before answering. "The man who just left. That's Captain Rogen, isn't it? He captains the *Raven Scream*?"

Qrodin narrows his eyes slightly. How does she know him? "His name is Rogen, but I don't know the name of his ship. I wasn't aware you two were acquainted."

"We're not. And I'm surprised you are. We've been trying to catch him in the act, but he's a slippery motherfucker."

"Catch him in the act of what?" Qrodin asks.

She looks at him squarely. "Piracy. Now, you answer my question. Why are you in disguise in your own home?" When he doesn't answer, she takes a deep breath. "I see. Are you going to invite me in? I'd like to ask you about your association with Bernhard Truffle."

"Uh, oh! You're screwed now, buddy!" Qrodin can barely hear the whisper over the Music Mouth sitting on the table near the door.

Qrodin glances down. A fly is perched on his shoulder. Qat's faerie? Was she here the whole time Rogen was, or had she come in when he opened the door just now? He'll have to inquire later.

Doscia notices his glance. Her eyes narrow on the fly, then flick back to him. "Oh. You can see...?" Several emotions flicker across her face. Finally, she straightens to her full height. "I should tell you I lied to you about something." She removes her knit cap and reveals the horns she usually keeps hidden.

Qrodin hears the swift intake of breath from the faerie on his shoulder.

"I've already seen those," Qrodin says, remembering his surprise when she'd first shown him the small corkscrew horns hidden by her hair.

"You always assumed they were markali. They're not," she says, looking away. "They're—"

"Faerie!" The fly on his shoulder flies forward and pops into a faerie nearly a foot tall before backing toward him again. Her wings flutter his hair, and lights emanate outward from the center of them. She sits back hard on his shoulder.

"Bell, you shouldn't interrupt them!" Llani says as Bell runs in from the dining room.

Doscia's eyes grow wide. "I thought the three of us were alone," she hisses.

He's not surprised. She's still in the outer hall, and the others have been quiet.

"Qrow! You have a faerie on your shoulder!" Bell says, running over to them. "Hi, faerie! I'm Bell."

"What is *with* you people? Can everyone here see me?"

Llani comes to the door. "Oh. You again," she says to the faerie. To Doscia, she says, "Did I hear you say you are part faerie?"

"Llani! Why didn't you tell me you met a faerie?" Bell squeezes her way to the door. "Oh! Hi, Doscia! How did you know we live here? You must be a really good detective. Is she right? Are you part faerie? That must be soooo cool!"

Doscia pushes inside. She stops when she spies Akin, Kasaandra, and Qat coming toward them. "The gang's all here, I see."

The faerie flies straight at Kasaandra. "Can you see me?"

Kasaandra winces at the alarmingly high tone. "I can hear you, too." She rubs her ears. "Wish I couldn't."

The faerie detours to Akin. She stops short when he snarls. Lights flicker on and off on her wings. Akin's staring at them as though he wants to rip them off.

"What in Leha's name is going on here?" The faerie flies at Qrodin. She stops a foot from him and places her hands on her hips. "Is it this room? Is there some spell here that lets you all see me?"

Qrodin shakes his head.

Kasaandra rubs her ear and scowls at the flying purple faerie, then at Qrow. "I wish you had a silence spell."

"Except for Qat, no one has ever been able to see me before. Now, a whole room of you can see me. Something's happening here, and I want to know what it is."

Qrodin thinks she mutters '*before my father finds out,*' but can't be certain.

"Qat!" Bell cries, nearly in tears. "You didn't tell me you knew a faerie, either."

"Sorry, Bell. It wasn't something I was allowed to talk about."

Kasaandra steps forward. "I think I know why, but I'm not saying it in front of her." She points at Doscia.

"Why not?" Doscia says, "I'm part faerie, too."

"'Cause you're not marked."

"Marked? What are you talking about?" Doscia's eyes dart to Qrodin's sides. She knows about Qrow's birthmarks. Used to scowl at them, for some reason. "You mean like a tattoo?"

Llani said the faerie and Akin have similar markings. So much has happened since then, Qrodin hadn't thought of it since. He inspects the wing closest to him. An eye glows back at him. Just like the eye Kasaandra had carved into the manticore spike. He recalls the gnat that had landed on that spike when he was inspecting them.

"Kasaandra," Qrodin says slowly. "Are you saying we all have a mark that allows us to see things others can't?"

Earlier, Ama'ani said the marks are inherited. So did Llani. If that's the case, and Akin and the faerie share the same mark, does that mean they're related somehow?

Chapter 57 Qat

Un. Fucking. Believable.

The detective from last night somehow knows Qrow. And Qrow knew Truffle, too? I glare at Nightshade. She hadn't mentioned that part when she told me Qrow was lying. Should I run from the detective or stick around to hear Kasaandra's explanation?

"Like Llani's butterfly and Qrow's cats?" Bell asks.

Kasaandra nods.

Yeah. I think I'll stay.

Doscia glances at Qrodin, and he nods. "In that case, I should stay," Doscia says, turning and lifting her shirt in the back to show two marks between her shoulder blades. One is a tree. The other resembles an ocean wave. "Whoa!" Bell says, turning to Kasaandra. "Where are yours?"

Kasaandra takes off first one and then the other armband. Upon each arm is a brown symbol that nearly blends into her freckles. One looks like a crescent moon. The other, like fire.

Llani sighs. "Those are merely formed by an overabundance of melanin."

No one pays her comment any attention.

"My brother has the same marks. Dadair," she says, pointing first to the left mark, then the right. "Mamair." She scowls at Doscia before continuing. "I believe we're all descended from the Drakkaen Nakkla," Kasaandra says.

"What is that?" Qrodin asks.

Llani huffs. "It means Hunter of Dragons, and it is preposterous."

Dragons? I'm staying. I doubt anyone will be thinking about Truffle now.

"Why do you say that?" Doscia asks.

"The stories have been passed down through my father's line since the World Burn War. I grew up on them. The same birthmark has been passed down to every generation."

"Oh. I see." Llani says quietly. "They *are* jurva-tetus."

"Like yours?" Bell asks.

"Yes," Llani replies. "They are the marks of birth received from your parents. It's scarce. Even rarer to have two. Elves have them on the inside of our wrists." Llani shows them the butterfly mark on her left wrist. "The right side is from your mother, a *jurva-mat-tetu*; the left from your father, a *jurva-pit-tetu*." She frowns. "I was unaware that non-elven species could have them."

I remember the iridescent star that Bell said showed only briefly when Llani was assessing the Home Dome's defenses. Why does that one only appear sometimes?

When Qrow had his shirt off earlier tonight, Ama'ani had said Rogen's mark was on his left side, and Aleena's was on her right.

I didn't tell them I have identical birthmarks. I wonder if Qrow knows about them. I've had them as long as I can remember. Did we talk about them when we were children? I remember being surprised the first time I saw Qrow's and wondered if it's common for twins to share birthmarks.

Does Kasaandra know about mine? She seemed to think we all have them.

And what about Akin and Bell?

And what do the marks have to do with seeing faeries?

"What about me?" Bell asks. "The only birthmarks I have are on my...Oh." She blushes furiously.

On your where? I think.

"On my..." Bell looks embarrassed and closes her lips tightly.

"They're on her butt cheeks."

"Kasaandra!" Llani admonishes.

Kasaandra shrugs.

I can't believe Nightshade's been silent for so long. I inspect her wings for markings. Before Qrow's revelation, Kasaandra had said only Doscia wasn't marked. That would mean she saw Nightshade's. I only see an eye directly in the center of her left wing. On the right wing, something that looks like a danaash heart. I've seen my share of those often enough to know the shape.

Interesting.

And what about Akin?

And what does Bell's look like? I can't be the only one wondering unless I'm the only one who hasn't seen her naked while bathing.

"Everyone's marks are different," I finally say. "Why would you think they're all from Dragon Hunters?"

"I was told that many heroes fought the dragons during the World Burn War. The Drakkaen Nakkla were marked by the gods and given extra strength, wisdom, and knowledge to defeat the Drakkaen. The marks are passed down to their children so that one day, when the dragons return, we can fight them."

"And you think that's going to be us?"

"I do."

"Why? No one has seen dragons in nearly fifteen thousand years. Don't you think they're all gone by now?" My green stone flashes briefly in my mind.

"It is said that the Drakkaen attacked during Darknight and will do so again."

Darknight is a night when all three moons are absent from the sky. It happens no more often than once in nineteen years. Sometimes, there are hundreds of years between Darknights.

Kasaandra's explanation doesn't answer my question, but I leave it alone. Hadn't Rogen and I wondered what might happen the next Darknight? When it coincides with Mordkanee? Could this be it?

Bell pipes up next. "We've had a lot of Darknights since then. We don't even know when the next one is." She looks at me and cringes. "Do we?"

I almost don't want to answer her, but I do. "The next one will be in fifteen years."

"But we've had some in the last hundred years, haven't we?"

Llani shakes her head. "The last complete Darknight was in the year 11,263. The ones since were incomplete, as at least one of the moons was visible. I will calculate the exact date of the next one, but it is preposterous to assume dragons will attack in our lifetime, let alone in fifteen years. It would take them hundreds of years to fully grow enough to attack. Why should the next Darknight be significant?"

I wasn't aware Llani knew anything about the stars. She's never expressed any interest in them before, but everything she said was correct. "The next one is on the fifteenth of Pilamee," I say.

"Hey! The fifteenth of Pilamee was the day we came to Craguesport!" Bell says.

"It's also the day we met Kasaandra twenty years ago," Qrodin adds.

"How do you know the date?" Llani asks me.

"It's Mordkanee," I respond. I've known the date of the next Darknight since Rogen told me the World Burn War began on Darknight nearly fifteen thousand years ago. Ever since the war, people have tried to predict when dragons will return. Every Darknight since, there have been vigils, rituals, and preparations to ward off an attack if one happens. Rogen and I used to guess what crazy things might happen this next Darknight since it falls on Mordkanee. Will dragons come back from the dead? Will their ghosts?

I don't share those dark thoughts.

"Why do you think we're the ones that are supposed to defeat them?" Qrodin asks Kasaandra. "We don't even know if there are any dragons."

Akin signs.

"Yes, we do," Kasaandra translates, looking back and forth between Akin and me.

We do? I stare at her blankly. Why is she looking at *me*?

Akin cups his hands together in the sign for 'egg.'

The witches' stone flashes again in my mind. He then points to Bell and tugs at his robes.

Green. A green egg. Akin sighs and signs again, looking at Kasaandra and Llani as he does. They're the only two who can translate such a long message.

"He says it is the green stone you carry." Llani's lips are tight as she looks me up and down. "Why have you not told us of this stone?"

How does Akin know about that? I've never taken it out in their presence. Not since the night I was in the tree and saw how it affected them.

"Akin thinks it's a dragon egg," Kasaandra says, frowning at Akin. She looks hurt that Akin kept it from her.

Akin signs again, and Llani translates, "He was uncertain before, but now he believes it is so."

"What stone is this?" Doscia finally joins the conversation again.

"I don't have it anymore," I lie.

"Well, that sucks," Nightshade snorts. "What did you do with it?"

Her comment indicates she doesn't have access to my pocket home. Otherwise, she'd know about it. I look back at Kasaandra. "I asked you about stones. Remember? I didn't get the impression it was valuable. I tossed it in the ocean." I point in the direction of the Reef Sea. "Why didn't you tell me dragon eggs look like green rocks?" I say to put the blame and attention back on her.

"No one knows what they look like," Kasaandra grumbles.

"The witches said you took something." Qrodin is angry. Angrier than I've ever seen him. "Your carelessness almost got us all killed, and even then, you didn't tell us what you took."

"It was a rock," I say now to defend myself. "I found it in the caves under Riversmeet."

Qrodin's face flickers with surprise. Because he wasn't aware of the caves? Or surprised that I am?

Akin's hands fly. I don't pick up even one word.

"He says it was in a box carved with runes and symbols. Where is this box?" Llani asks.

"I—"

Kasaandra interrupts my next lie. "The witches spoke Drakk."

"It was—"

"Drakk," Kasaandra says forcefully, cutting off Llani. "What more proof do you need? Qat stole a dragon egg."

"And now it's in the ocean," Nightshade adds.

"Green dragons lived in the swamps," Kasaandra informs us.

Doscia's face twists in disbelief. "How do you—"

"That's where the Twisted Sisters attacked us!" Bell cries.

Doscia frowns. "Who are the Twisted Sisters?"

"Green elves," Kasaandra says.

"They also live underwater, although more are living on land lately," Llani adds.

"Elves can breathe underwater?" Bell asks.

Llani's eyes widen. "Some of them do. Is that not common knowledge?"

"Uh. No!" Bell says.

"If what you say is true," Doscia says, sweeping us all with a decisive look, "I'll need to get divers out there immediately. We can't have a dragon egg hatch this close to land. What does it look like?"

"A green rock," Kasaandra says. Her eyes slide in my direction before returning to Doscia. What was that look for?

"What size?" Doscia persists, asking question after question about detailed markings and the specific shade of green. She finally leaves, rushing out the door with athletic swiftness.

I'm just glad she seems to have forgotten about Truffle and Rogen.

But I haven't.

"Akin, come with me, if you will," Llani says, and they walk to the dining room. It's sundown, and she lights a few candles with a flick of her wrist when they enter. Thankfully, her *oopsies* are less common nowadays. She retrieves her notebook and hands it to Akin. "Can you draw the symbols you saw on the box?"

She doesn't trust me to draw them, even though I could do it blindfolded. I can still feel the wood beneath my fingers as I trace the outlines of an odd pyramid and a two-headed snake.

Llani gasps when Akin shows her the drawing, and her eyes go directly to Bell.

"What?" Bell asks. She pulls the drawing down so she can see it. "What?"

Kasaandra sighs loudly. "Those are your marks. How do you not recognize them?"

Bell's eyes narrow at Kasaandra. "Duh! They're on my butt! Can you see your butt?" Then she looks at Llani. "Are they?" she asks, pointing at the drawings.

Llani nods. "Both of them."

Bell's birthmarks are the same as the symbols on the dragon egg?

What the fuck does that mean?

Chapter 58 Qrodin

In the two fortnights since Longest Night, Qrodin has spent as many evenings as possible visiting Aleeha or Qataleena and their family. Being in their home reminds him of how it was before that fateful night in Riversmeet. Qataleena's four children (Qat and Qrow's cousins) all have children of their own, a total of sixteen grandchildren between the ages of two and fourteen. Qataleena's youngest daughter, Dylan, lives with her, and Dylan's two-year-old son, Dai-Gi. But the other grandchildren visit every Fullkuu for a family get-together.

Thankfully, most of them have more unique names, although not entirely. Qrodin had to ask Kasaandra to draw the family tree again on the inside back cover of his notebook so he could keep track of them all.

Qataleena and her husband refused to allow Qrodin to buy them a home, but they did take him up on his offer to sell her goods at Balaerdo's. They also agreed to come to his house for Hearthsglow, the mid-winter celebration tonight, which is usually spent with family or close friends.

He's happier than he's been in a long time and wishes that he and Qat were closer. He got over his anger at Qat for taking the dragon egg, even though ae lied about tossing it in the ocean. The slow blink gave it away.

It also appears that Doscia has wholly forgotten about Truffle and Rogen. Or perhaps she was reassigned. She hasn't contacted Qrodin since, nor has any other TFDG.

How she had believed that Qat would throw away something of such value, Qrodin has no idea. Of course, she didn't know about Qat's propensity for stealing or aer past with Rogen. She also didn't know the dragon stone looked like a giant gemstone. In Doscia's defense, she had never seen the egg, and no one had mentioned its apparent value.

None of them had seen it, after all, except Akin.

After Doscia left, Llani explained that Akin had seen the egg while he was Soul Soaring. Then, she explained to Qat and Bell what Soul Soaring was.

"You mean every time we thought he was meditating, his soul was inspecting the area nearby?" Bell had glared at Llani for not telling her.

Qat hasn't been around much since that night. Ae still visits the domi—the logs tell Qrodin that, but ae hasn't returned to the vault. The stablemaster also said Starshine often goes missing at night. Sometimes for days at a time. Qrodin told him not to worry about it.

As for Kasaandra's claims about them being Dragon Hunters, Qrodin doesn't know what to believe. It's all a little far-fetched. She says their marks must have drawn them together. That the knowledge imparted to their ancestors still flows through their blood. She claims that being double-marked must have some great significance. Why else would there be so many of them all together at the same time? The final piece for her was the similarities between the dragon egg's box designs and Bell's marks.

Every night, she tells stories about dragons. Each color has unique strengths, weaknesses, and magical abilities. She teaches them how best to fight each subspecies, which she learned from her father. She's also been teaching Llani how to speak Drakk. And Llani has let her.

On a good note, Qrodin is pleased to have finally heard from Queen Sarafeen. All the missing treasure was recovered in Cranwood. She, therefore, no longer requires him to find the missing Merkama treasure. But she hasn't released his oath of silence. She's still searching for the culprit. She said she'll contact him if she needs further assistance and asked him to hold onto the serpent ring in case items turn up missing in the future.

A part of him wishes he could talk to Qat about it. But Qat's not around much.

Chapter 59 Qat

I still can't believe they're gone. Llani, Bell, Kasaandra, and Akin left this morning.

Saying goodbye was more challenging than I thought it would be.

So, I didn't do it.

I couldn't.

After a winter of randomly dropping in whenever I felt like it and consuming the food Bell always left for me in my room, how would I manage a lifetime without them? Without Bell's waffles? Without Kasaandra's muttered complaints about Llani's vocabulary and Akin's quiet steadiness? And without Llani's unexpected oopsies?

It's not like I can count on running into them, considering they're going to the opposite end of the continent. Llani wouldn't explain her sudden need to leave or why she chose to visit the other side of the world. Kasaandra seems to think it has something to do with our status as Dragon Hunters.

Dragon Hunters. Drakkaen Nakkla. The title makes me laugh.

There are no dragons.

The rock isn't an egg.

I've looked at it closely in the last two trit'quarters since Longest Night. Nothing about it has changed. Eggs hatch, don't they? And their shells are fragile. This one isn't fragile. The outside isn't broken, and wouldn't it have cracked when it dropped out of the pocket home at the Sorbslles camp?

But I still get that weird vibration sometimes, and it no longer stops right away when I take it out of its box. But it does stop when I talk to it.

I find myself talking to it when Starshine isn't around to talk to.

That Qrow didn't go with them is curious. He claims it's because he has no business interests west of the Bien'fil. I think that would be the best reason to go, but he repeatedly declined their offer.

I haven't talked to them since Qrodin told me that Doscia told him Rogen was a pirate. I somehow missed that part of their conversation.

"Is it true?" he'd asked me.

"The less you know, the better, little brother."

I'm doing it for their sake. Plausible deniability and all that. The situation's bad enough that Qrow knows I was a pirate. I'd hate for the others to find out. I couldn't stand the look in Bell's eyes. Or Kasaandra's.

I think Llani knows. With those ears, she probably heard Doscia tell Qrow. Llani hasn't treated me differently, though, so I'm not sure.

I agreed to sail with the captain again. He recently returned from Qreelport and will be leaving in a few days for Alonard. I'm just killing time until then. I told him I don't start working for him until we sail, so I won't help clean or stock the ship while they're in port.

Now that I understand Rogen's my father, I feel foolish for running off after the Goffin incident. After Rogen announced that I was returning to the crew, Uci tried to discredit me. He took great pleasure in telling Rogen he'd found Goffin dead in the water with my red scarf around his neck. The bastard must've finally tumbled over the railing after I left. Or maybe he'd had just enough life left in him to stumble overboard and accidentally drown himself. Uci said he'd tugged my scarf loose from the sinking corpse before it could disappear beneath the waves and left it on the deck so everyone would know who to blame.

He got to be first mate and rid of me all in one swoop.

Surprisingly, Rogen took my side.

I could tell it bothered Uci, which is probably why he took credit for finding me. He said he'd been the one searching high and low for information about my whereabouts to give to Rogen. That he'd paid good money to convince the various middlemen I could find work with to rat on my commissions. He'd been *useful*, he kept insisting.

I got to stay.

Uci flew into a temper, then flew off. He'll return before we leave for Alonard, I'm sure.

All those years running around by myself, I could have been doing what I love most. Fighting by the captain's side. But, of course, we hadn't been aware of our relationship, so maybe it was wise of me to leave after all.

Perhaps one day, I'll run a crew of my own.

The captain's getting up there in years. Maybe I'll inherit the *Raven Scream* when he's gone. I seriously doubt he'll ever retire, but the life of a pirate is a dangerous one. He's already considered old for a pirate—not that I'd ever say that to his face.

Leaving with him is my best option. Fleeing will get me—and my not dragon egg—away for a while.

Now that I have a bank account with more than I'll ever need, I feel reluctant to return to petty theft. But what else am I going to do? I'm not cut out to run a business like Balaerdo's, especially one I can only mess up if I manage it. I could always join the assassin's guild now that I'm no longer running from the captain. But if I decide I don't like it? Well, there's only one way to leave an assassin's guild. Nightshade's made that clear.

Making decisions is the worst part of working alone. At least, it is for me.

Half the time, I roll the dice. Let fate decide. That wouldn't go over well with a crew, though. I laugh at the thought of it. I guess that means Captaining the *Raven Scream* is out.

But leaving it to chance is fine when I'm alone. Take now, for instance. I don't even know the name of the tavern I'm in. I got hungry and picked the first place I found that served food. I have all afternoon with nothing to do. I could take a nap, check out the UnSeeing Eye, sharpen my daggers, find Rogen or the crew and hang with them, wander the docks for gossip, or visit my grandmother.

The last possibility would be more for me than for her, considering she doesn't recognize me half the time, but I may not see her again after we sail. At her age, she could go anytime.

I'll let fate decide.

I pull out the set of dice Kasaandra made for me as a going-away present. She felt terrible that I lost mine in the tunnels. We were so busy fighting those frog things that I completely forgot to look for them.

I select the six-sided die and give it a half-hearted roll. It's circling and about to stop on the four. Not wanting to wander around searching for the crew, I bump the table slightly. The die flips and lands on the two.

Okay, so I *mostly* let fate decide.

The UnSeeing Eye it is. Now, do I choose past, present, or future?

I roll the die again.

A six. The future.

Why not? That's all I have ahead of me, isn't it?

I pay for my ale and wander outside to the same rocky ledge where Rogen and Qrow fought. I find a shady spot under a crooked oak tree that leans toward the ocean and remove the scope from my belt. I unlatch the snake fangs and flip the cover open.

With each slide and click, my stomach tightens a little in anticipation. We had all agreed that looking into the future was too risky. We might see something and want to change it. But the queen said it wouldn't be our future, so what's the harm? The dice said future, so risk be damned to the depths of the ocean.

When the scope is fully open, I take a moment to inspect the beauty of the piece. Why did the queen entrust me with it? I'm perhaps the most untrustworthy of the six of us. Why didn't Queen Sarafeen give it to The Qrow? Or Llani? They appreciate the scope's visions more than I ever have. Qrodin could have recorded history and composed songs about it. And Llani would have had half a millennium's worth of research into the past.

To me, the scope is pure entertainment. How can I care about something that doesn't affect me personally?

I make myself as comfortable as I can on the rock and lift the glass to my eye. I lower it again. If only I could direct it to show me what I want to see. If only I could inject my thoughts into the scope, the same way I do with people. If only I...

Tried.

If only I tried.

Okay, then. Why not?

I wet my lips in anticipation.

Now. What do I want to see?

Well. That's an easy one.

What will my traveling companions find when they get to where they're going? Llani was too secretive about their destination.

I look at the scope.

Show me their fate, I direct it.

I lift it back to my eye.

At first, all I see is black. I'm about to check if I remembered to remove the cover when I see a light ahead in the distance.

Something flies through the gap between me and the lens. "What are you looking at?" Nightshade says.

I almost wrench the scope away, but the image will be gone if I do. Possibly forever. I need to see if I was able to direct the scope. I might only have this one chance.

Nightshade sits on the bottom edge of the eyepiece, obscuring a part of the vision. "Whoa! You never told me about this! Are we in a cave?"

I think so. The walls are rough stone, like the tunnel in Cranwood. I can almost hear feet crunching on the gravel floor. I finally emerge from the cave into the moonlight. I'm very high off the ground and moving back and forth as I fly forward. Almost as though I'm riding on the shoulder of a giant as it exits a cave, but the long nose I see in front of me has scales instead of flesh, and sharp teeth.

There is a meadow in front of us. I don't have time to inspect it as the image tilts up.

All three moons are out tonight, and Kuu is shining overhead.

The image tilts back to the horizon, moves left, then right.

When it tilts toward the ground, something moves in the trees. Four horses.

Everything speeds up as we rush toward them. Clawed hands appear below me and tear into the closest horse. Claws nearly rip it in half while the other horses scatter, rearing in fear. Their eyes roll back in their heads.

I urge the horses to run faster.

"Faster!" Nightshade says.

They do.

For a moment, I feel like I'm back in the crow's nest of the *Raven Scream* as we fly across the land, cutting hard right and left as if pursuing an enemy ship. But in this case, it's a horse we're chasing, not an enemy.

And this ship has wings.

Large, leathery wings.

We swoop in fast, and two more mounts are incapacitated in nearly no time.

My belly somersaults when I recognize the fourth one.

It's Bell's pony, Ginger.

There's something else about the visions I can't accept. Is it the moons' influence? Dread shivers on the back of my neck as I wrench myself away from the UnSeeing Eye's lens.

Nightshade pops into full view in front of me. "What is that thing?"

"What are you doing here?" I ask her instead.

"I've been keeping an eye on you. That's our deal, remember? I'm leaving with you."

She was serious about that?

I don't have time to argue with her. I grab my bag and start running.

When I reach Qrow's front door, I pound on it.

"Qat? What are you doing here?" Qrow says when he opens the door. His lips pinch, and he nearly slams the door in my face. Not that it'd do any good. His lock isn't a match for my skills. Besides, Nightshade could get us in, even if I couldn't.

"Do you have a horse that can keep up with Starshine?"

"What? What are you talking about?"

"Look. We don't have time to argue. You need to pack."

"Pack? Why?"

He still hasn't opened the door enough for me to enter, so I push my way in. "I was bored, and I looked through the UnSeeing Eye."

"And you want to tell me your vision now?" The Qrow rubs his face.

He hasn't shaved, and I can tell he didn't sleep well last night. His clothes are wrinkled. Did I wake him up? Was he napping in the middle of the afternoon?

When his gold eyes flash my way again, I wonder how I missed his resemblance to the captain. On the other hand, maybe I didn't want to see it.

Just like I don't want to accept what I saw in the scope earlier.

"Well?"

"I looked into the future."

His anger is swift. "Why would you do that?"

"I rolled the dice."

"You what?"

"Never mind. Just trust me that we need to go." When he just stands there, my patience snaps. "Look. I did it, and now you need to listen to me. We need to go *now*, or they're all going to *die*!"

His eyes narrow. "Who's going to die?"

"Who do you think? The only 'they' we both know!"

"Don't be—"

"There were dragons!" Nightshade says, finally showing herself and sitting on my head to be eye-level with Qrow.

"What?" Qrow says, clearly frustrated now.

"I told it to show me their fate. And it did." I clench my hands tight and pace his landing, but he stands there looking like an angry bear.

"And there were dragons!" Nightshade says again.

We need to leave. Now! I silently direct him.

His face pales. "We need to leave. Now! Stay here. And don't touch anything. I'll grab my things. On second thought, get the horses ready. I'll take the one to the right of Starshine's stall. And then I expect you to tell me everything. And Qat? You'd better not be fucking with me."

I'm not. I don't think.

Nightshade appears before him. "Ae's not. I saw it, too."

Qrow spares her only a glance, then nods.

I rub the back of my neck. It's still sore from the muscle contractions I had during the visions.

I wonder if Rogen will be upset when I don't show up.
Oh, well. Nothing I can do about that now.
Sorry. Not sorry.

Appendix A: Family Tree

Qat and Qrodin's family tree as Kasaandra drew it.

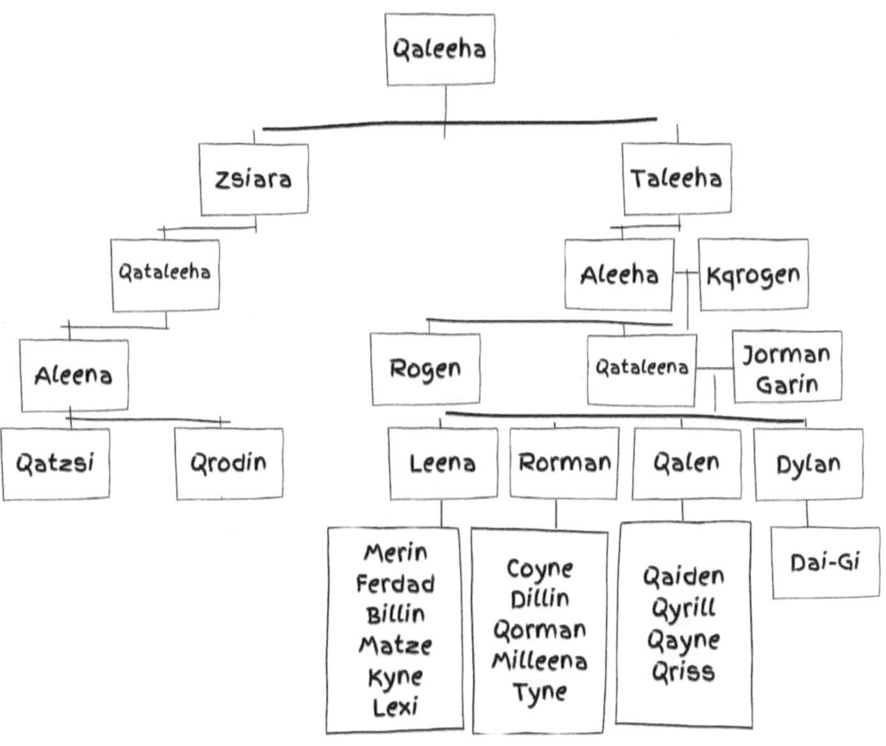

Appendix B: Dates and Times

On Oram, the new year starts on the Spring Equinox, the first day of spring. The summer and winter solstices mark the first days of their respective seasons, and the autumnal equinox is the first day of autumn. Each season is 99 days and is split into three trit'quarters, each of which is 33 days (see table below).

SEASONS AND TRIT'QUARTERS

Season		Trit'quarter	
1	Spring	1	Mamdi
		2	Netamee
		3	Elany
2	Summer	4	Bamdi
		5	Kazamee
		6	Ojany
3	Autumn	7	Zamdi
		8	Pilamee
		9	Itrany
4	Winter	10	Samdi
		11	Tihamee
		12	Anany

Of Oram's three moons, Kuu has a dependable fourteen-day cycle and inspired the term fortnight. Each day of a fortnight was named, starting with the first day Kuu is visible and ending (ironically) on Newkuu, the day Kuu is absent from the sky.

Fortnight Days

1	OnKuu
2	TuKuu
3	TiKuu
4	FoKuu
5	FiKuu
6	SiKuu
7	FullKuu
8	EtKuu
9	NiKuu
10	TeKuu
11	Elkuu
12	TaKuu
13	ToKuu
14	NuKuu

Appendix C: Measurements on Oram

Items and lengths were originally measured by using one's body parts. The hand and foot were the most frequently used but varied greatly due to variances between species. That wasn't a problem until multiple species started comingling.

A dwarf engineer's feet were vastly different in length from those of a danaash engineer. When a blueprint was created by a dwarf and built by a danaash, it was much larger than intended. Supplies ran out. Arguments ensued. It was a nightmare.

Something had to be done. An abandi named Ium Koot—the local mathematician—was volunteered to chair the committee for standardizing measurements on Oram. The rest of the committee was a combination of species, but predominantly danaash. They eventually agreed that using danaash hand and foot measurements should be the standard. Ium argued that, since the hand was three and one-third the size of the foot, they should use one or the other, then create new units of measure in multiples of ten. He was overruled.

They did, however, agree that multiples of ten were a great idea.

Ten hands (the width of a palm; Ium never understood why it wasn't called palms) equaled three feet, which, coincidentally, was the exact height of abandis all over Oram. The committee joked that they should call it a "bandi" because Ium was fond of saying, "I am not danaash. I am abandi." The team echoed, "Ium. A. Bandi. Get it?" No matter what other terms Ium suggested, the team insisted on bandi.

Skootch was unanimously selected for $1/10^{th}$ the length of a hand because the term had been universally used for moving something "just a skootch." Unfortunately, it was also the width of an abandi's middle finger. Before Koot sticks were commonplace, carpenters all over Oram asked nearby abandis to put up their middle finger so they could see, again, how big a skootch was. Terms like 'skootch me', 'skootch you', and 'skootch this' became common epithets heard by all species, although predominantly by abandis.

Oram measurement	Oram reference	Earth equivalent
Skootch	1/10th the length of a hand; also, the width of Ium's middle finger	1 centimeter
Pinch	1/10th the length of a foot;	~1.3 inches; ~3.3 centimeters
Hand	10 skootches; the average width of the adult male danaash hand	10 centimeters; 1 decimeter; ~4 inches
Foot	10 pinches; the average length of the adult male danaash foot	~13 inches; ~33.3 centimeters
Bandi	10 hands; 3 feet; the height of an adult bandi	1 meter; ~40 inches
Dinghi	10 feet;	~11 feet; 3.3 meters
Koot	1000 bandis; 3000 feet; named after Ium Koot	1 kilometer; ~3300 Earth feet
Flock	Area equaling 10,000 square koots (100*100); the amount of land large enough to raise 25 ewes and their lambs (the size of Ium's flock)	1 hectare; ~2.5 acres
Mock	42.6667 koots; the distance between one degree of latitude on Oram.	42.67 km; ~26.5 miles

Appendix D: Glossary

AE PRONOUNS

ae: he/she/they
aem: him/her/them
ae'd: he'd/she'd/they'd
ae's: he's/she's/they're
aer: his/her/their
aers: his/hers/theirs
ae'll: he'll/she'll/they'll
aerself: himself/herself/themselves

HOLIDAYS AND EVENTS

Bucuatoari: annual Karatolii festival
Hearthsglow: midwinter holiday
Longest Night: winter solstice, the longest night of the year
Mordkanee: midpoint between autumnal equinox and winter solstice; similar to Halloween, All Hallows, and Samhain
Proximan: one of two days the planet is closest to the sun; usually celebrated with harvest festivals
Proximus: one of two days the planet is closest to the sun; also known as the Day of Sharing

PLACES

Androi: fishing district in Craguesport, originally founded by a danaash
Biennora-Abfil (Bien'fil): two mountains that bisect the entire continent of Kish from north to south
Hondjikal: forestry district of Craguesport originally founded by an arghor. The surname was adopted by 'spiral horn' arghor
Jalu: financial district of Craguesport, originally founded by a grimm.
Middlequet: the valley where the Biennora and Abfil ranges overlap
Oram: the second of three planets orbiting their sun
Piladata: military district in Craguesport, originally founded by a daga. The word means 'yellow tooth'.

Searbaltoir: crafting district in Craguesport, originally founded by a dwarf. The name means 'bitter digger' and adopted by a family that survived the Bitter Caverns' collapse in the year 143 AWB.

Whaligator: caves under Riversmeet formed by an ancient sea creature

Wusdweit: farming district of Craguesport, originally founded by a hablis. It means 'willow' in Hablis

SPELLS

Aagut/Tugaa: transforms Qrodin's magical flute into a staff/back to a flute.

Coax: a deep hum—so low it cannot be heard by most danaash—layered beneath a spellcaster's words that lulls the target into doing as the spellcaster wishes

Deziré: a form of illusion that alters how light reflects on an object, changing its size and appearance

Don't Look Now: transforms a single arrow into splinters that separate before reaching the target

Haste: a form of psychic magic that encourages the target to increase the speed or pace of activity

Inspire: a form of psychic magic to inspire the target

Keep Up: allows the caster to increase their walking speed

Privacy: placed around an area or room to keep sound from escaping

Soothe: a form of psychic magic that encourages the target to relax

Terror: a form of psychic magic to create fear in the target

Whoosh: flames shoot from the caster's fingers

ABANDI

talim: alone

DWARFISH

Mamair: Mother

Dadair: Father

drakkaen: dragon

Drakkaen Nakkla: Hunter of Dragons

sia'damhalla: cloth made by the dwarfs of Dwarf Mountain, which has similar properties to leather armor with the look and feel of silk

ELVISH

Mata: Mother
jurva-mat-tetu: birthmark inherited through the maternal line
jurva-pit-tetu: birthmark inherited through the paternal line
Pata: Father
Siroha suskirta: response to the greeting, "Tama musari vasidara" which has no direct translation but conveys health and happiness in return
Sueh ba' mira: formal greeting when meeting for the first time. It is accompanied by stacking one's forearms such that the inside of one's wrists is stacked one above the other and facing the person being greeted
Tama musari vasidara: roughly translated to "blessings on your journey [through life]"

HABLI

Griss frem: Nice to meet you

KARATOL

Ama'ani: term of respect for a relative or very close friend within a Karatolii troupe
Ama'nu: elder
bramzi: a pepper stuffed with meat and thick, creamy cheese
cobila: mushroom-shaped carriage homes
itan: magic
Magila(s): mobile shops
Mano su mano: tomorrow or tomorrow; a farewell
motas: kitten; an endearment for children (under teens)
Oiy varsome shae valore: initiated by a host to another Karatolii visitor extending the wish to share the bond of kinship amongst the Karatolii
Oiy: Hello
pisitas: kitten; endearment for babies and toddlers
reasacobila(s): a collapsible home. Also known as a pocket home. When connected, referred to as Home Dome.

reasamagila(s): a collapsible warehouse. Also known as a pocket warehouse.

valore: the members of a caravan outside of one's immediate family

varsome: the bond that forms between members of a caravan who are outside of one's immediate family

Yu nu pot prita o Qat tu o Qrow: phrase often recited by Qat that translates, "You can't catch a Qat with a Qrow"

MERKAMA

mia luuvay: the people of the land

ORAMISCHE

bandi(s): form of measurement equal to one Earth meter (see Appendix D)

domi: luxury, individually owned condominiums

ha-sheesh-shun: an assassin's blade specifically designed for left-handed assassins

Sati lida ane tari takaro: motto of a secret society

umanid: non-animal species given the ability to speak languages and communicate across species

OWANULAFA

didi atete: until next. A salutation said when one departs.

edi: command to rise (from a kneeling position)

ero ami: my friend

gia faa: the high priest in charge of all decisions in a monastery

Idajmbe: a form of martial arts practiced by the Owanulafa

iniki: greeting

keka: a student. An acolyte of the Tiolapin religion

Nigbe: Mr.

oku: an assistant instructor. One who is a specialist in their field working in a junior position while continuing their training/research

Author's Note

As an Anthropology student studying different cultures and genetics, I learned about a condition known as 5-alpha reductase deficiency (5aRD), where male testes may not develop until puberty due to a deficiency in the production of dihydrotestosterone (DHT) hormone before birth. Those children are often initially raised as females.

Studies were done in a small community in the Dominican Republic, where individuals born with this condition are called "Guevedoces." You can watch the second episode, "Against the Odds", of BBC Two's *Countdown to Life: The Extraordinary Making of You*, for interviews with several adults who discuss what it was like growing up with the condition.

I had wondered what a culture might be like if all children were born with 5aRD. Would an isolated community in a fantasy setting have words for each gender, such as boy and girl, mother and father, brother and sister? Would they have a typical family structure? What would happen—to the parent or child—when a child was born with a penis? Would they be shunned? If so, would those children be abandoned as babies?

I wanted this culture to be nomadic as a nod to my maternal great-grandfather's circus family. I also knew they'd have ancestral traits from an extinct species. I rolled the dice. The Nonyx had feline traits.

That was the inspiration for the Karatolii.

Catching Qat is not a story of gender identity or transformation. I don't go into detail about what Qrow felt or experienced during that time. I can't begin to know.

And if you're wondering if Qat is male or female, I have to say...I don't know. Ae won't tell me. I first met Qat as a female. Then a male. Most of the time, it seemed like Qat was playing with me, so I finally asked. After all, as the author, I should know, shouldn't I?

Ae just smiled.

Regarding Qat's feelings at others' confusion, that was my experience in college when I cut my hair, stopped wearing makeup, and dressed in comfortably shabby, indiscriminate clothing. I became familiar with that look of confusion.

Speaking of confusion, have you ever tried to describe a battle scene about a group that included someone using they/their/them pronouns? I couldn't tell who I was referring to: the group or Qat. For clarity's sake, I chose to use ae/aer/aem for Qat's pronouns. To me, they were the most natural by leaving off the 'th' from *they*, *their*, *them*, etc. It became standard in Oramische.

I hope you enjoyed *Catching Qat*. It was a labor of love. And laughter. And frustration. A few tears. And a lot of learning.

The story continues in *Legacies*, where Llani and Akin go in search of theirs...with a little help.

Acknowledgments

It's amazing to me that one Facebook post changed my life. It was the start of a series of events for which I will be eternally grateful. What would have happened had Mom never seen that post and sent me those Archaeology magazines? That gift helped me realize that I could go back to school; that I could change my career. That opportunity led to the *Magic, Witchcraft, and Religion* class, where I converted D&D into a religion and reincarnated my first Dungeons & Dragons character to help me understand the most recent version of the tabletop game.

Of course, one character led to five more, and before I knew it, they were meeting each other. They told me who they liked and who annoyed them and why. They told me where they grew up, all about their families, and why they left their homes to explore the world. When my sibling prompted me to write their story, I laughed. Then couldn't stop thinking about it. I had to create a database to keep track of their world.

Their stories prompted me to add a writing minor when I transferred to university. Even then, I may never have completed the book if it hadn't been for COVID-19. The subsequent quarantine prevented me from continuing my education in graduate school, as all the labs were closed until further notice. To stay busy, I wrote.

I'd like to thank my family and friends for supporting me through that process. I'd also like to thank my professors, classmates, and workshop buddies for their time and invaluable feedback. I'd especially like to thank my beta readers: Margaret, Tracee, and Mom. Your insights, comments, and advice encouraged me to keep refining the story. And to my coworkers who had to listen to all the versions, edits, delays, cover changes, and more...thank you.

Lastly, I'd like to thank my editor for encouraging me to do the hard things. You were right.

Turn the page for a sneak peek at

Legacies

Book 2 of the *Drakkaen Nakkla* saga.

Chapter 1 Ki-Llani

I searched the world over for a very special female.
One that had just what I needed.
I found her.

124 YEARS AGO

14TH DAY OF SAMDI, 14,764
TUMI, BABUM

Ki-Llani watches as everything around her dies. Tiny fern leaves crinkle and curl, then shrivel and turn brown before dropping to the forest floor. Vines break and slither to the ground, catching limbs on the way down, flailing before breaking again. It is as though hundreds of snakes are plummeting toward her on all sides. Birds, lizards, squirrels, and insects flee as their homes are sucked dry of moisture and wither away. Trees drop their leaves.

A sadness she has never experienced before assaults her, even as her body absorbs the released energy of those deaths. She is helpless to stop the devastation as it spreads, and her heart breaks when she feels the life force extracted from those majestic beings and flow into herself.

Trees are life. She should be protecting them. Instead, she is killing them. Again.

She collapses to the ground in defeat. Each death is a personal failure, and she will never forget it. What is worse, she will be energized for days unless she releases it back into the world. Some may consider her magic a great benefit. A powerful skill to wield in battle, but Ki-Llani regards it as a weakness. A curse.

One of these days, Ki-Llani vows, she *will* control her magic. And it will be long before she finally reaches adulthood on her one hundredth nascency day and drops the Ki from her name. To distract her, she does the math in her head. She has another eighty-one years, ten trit'quarters, and eight days to master it.

Well, she thinks, *she will reverse the spell*. It is, after all, the opposite of what she had been attempting. It is supposed to be easy. She shifts the ground with her foot, looking for twigs or leaves she may use, but there are none. She should have collected some before she started this afternoon.

Oh, why had she thought she would succeed this time when she had failed so often before?

No worries. She has plenty of twigs in her bag.

She places several on the wasteland left in the wake of her mistake. If she does this correctly, she will repair the damage, and no one will know.

"Ki-Llani," Mata had said the last time Ki-Llani destroyed something with magic, "if I need to repair the injuries you make to our home again, *you* will need to choose a different career path. Perhaps you would be better suited as a soldier."

"Like Ni-mata Sanka?" Ki-Llani asks, shuddering at the thought of her grandmother, leader of the Tumi army, doing drills and swinging a sword all day. "Never!" Ni-mata Sanka would love to have her curse. Has urged her to cultivate it. Llani would rather die.

"You may like it," Mata had responded. "Besides, you will find your true calling during your Sodafari. Not before."

As far as Ki-Llani is concerned, a destiny quest is only necessary if you are uncertain of your destiny. She already knows what she wants to do with her life. She wants to study biology, anatomy, and genetics. And the magics to understand it all. And languages. You can never know too many languages. Other than her native Elvish, she already has a perfect working knowledge of Oramische. Of course, everyone on Oram is taught Oramische from birth, but Ki-Llani is completely conversant in it, whereas her classmates struggle to remember all but the most basic words. She also knows Dwarfish. And a smattering of Ancient Elvish, although her teachers tried to dissuade her when they discovered her interest.

"Your daughter is cursed," one of the librarians told Mata after she had caught Ki-Llani in a restricted area. "Everything she touches disintegrates to ashes. She is forbidden from accessing the ancient texts until she learns to control herself. Can you imagine the damage she could do with that knowledge?

Hopefully, she will forget what she has learned soon; otherwise, she may well destroy the entire city."

Mata was furious with the librarian. It had been years since Ki-Llani had accidentally destroyed a book.

Ki-Llani is unconcerned with the librarian's claim that she would forget the words she had already taught herself. Her professors are unaware that when Ki-Llani sees a word written down, she remembers it forever. All these years later, she has still not regained access to those books, but she remembers every word.

Unfortunately, remembering—and repeating—words she has *heard* is more difficult for her.

"Ki-Llani, you must say it *exactly* as I do," her professors always say, along with other, more hurtful things. "The proper inflection is important. How are you tone-deaf with ears like that?"

When other students' magic fails, nothing happens. Nothing changes. Nothing grows. Nothing moves. Nothing, nothing. Ki-Llani, on the other hand, always makes something happen. And it is usually destructive. They call it *myrtu*. Death magic.

Ki-Llani looks up. The blue moon Isa is full and glowing green tonight. If her *di-mata*—her great-grandmother, as they say in Oramische—were standing next to her, she would tell Ki-Llani, "Isa is the Trickster Goddess for a reason. She is up to her shenanigans again! That must be why your magic failed you tonight."

Ki-Llani knows better. Her magic fails her nearly every night.

She looks away from the treacherous moon and stares at the forest floor instead, bare now of even the deadened vegetation. Only the twigs she had placed on the ground are still there. The rest had died, decayed, and then disintegrated entirely.

Utter Desiccation. That should be her nickname. Not all those terribly unimaginative ones her classmates call her.

Ki-Llani swivels her ears around, listening for any sign of life nearby. When she hears nothing, she readies herself, touching her tongue to the tip of her new, tiny little fangs. She has recently discovered that the small amount of discomfort diverts her thoughts from all other distractions and enables her to focus.

She will succeed this time.

Ki-Llani studies the fingers of her right hand. Someone once told her she was the color of a pale plum, but she has never seen a plum before. Are plums as destructive as these fingers? Is it the somatic gestures that she is doing wrong? Or, like her professors say, is it her inflection?

Mata says the words and gestures are immaterial. She says Ki-Llani must imagine it first. Once she has success securely in her mind, she should let her magic flow.

Ki-Llani closes her eyes. She chooses to forego the gestures. To forget the words.

Instead, she imagines the twigs growing roots that burrow into the ground. As they do, the roots pull the stems upright, and those stems grow nearly as tall as she before sprouting branches and leaves. She imagines the trees' roots spreading out, carving new life into the soil. From them, new trees sprout and grow tall, reaching toward the sky and eventually creating a canopy so thick it hides Isa's duplicitous face.

Depleted of all the energy she had received and more, Ki-Llani stops, hoping she was successful.

She opens her eyes and sighs in relief. She is surrounded by trees again. Relief surges through her. She did it!

Then she frowns. She had chosen the wrong twigs from her bag. These are not the tall, red trees of her homeland. Nor the spruce, the bay, nor fir. They are fruit trees. Short and flowering and not even close to blotting out the laughing face of Isa.

And she forgot the ferns and various vines.

Ki-Llani is going to be found out.

Again.

Her only consolation is that she had come to this spot because it was well outside the city limits. Tumi's safety remains uncompromised.

Unlike before.

Chapter 2 Akin

He was born one of three.
And only he was mine.

19TH DAY OF ANANY, 14,798
ILETITUN, URUK

A woman enters the room. She is a swirl of color and the most beautiful creature I have ever seen.

"I am Imolena, and you can stay with me if you want to," she says to the boy on the table. She frowns at his jagged canine and at the men and the file on the ground.

Before she had walked in, the men flew across the room, crashed into the walls, and rolled to the ground. I still smell shaved bone, sharp and hot.

I glide around the room, seeing her from all sides at once.

She is circles and spheres, colors and contrasts, curves and contours; not a straight line or angle to mar the perfection of her form. She is a spring breeze, settling and soothing, cooling and calming.

The boy is breathing hard.

The men sprawled below him cringe and back toward the small room's door.

The boy is savage, not like the men trembling in fear. His legs are shorter, arms longer, chest deeper. And he is heaving with rage. His neck is thick, his muscles rigid and flexing convulsively, fingers curled, nails clawed.

Her face is round, her skin polished ebony. The light reflects off her prominent cheekbones, the button chin, and the curves of her nose. Her hair is a perfect halo, curls spiraling out, black at the roots, fading gradually through all the colors of brown to beige to the palest blonde, and silver at the tips. Her eyes are almost black and large but shine brightly, lit from within with a kindness he has never seen or felt.

The boy's hair is ash brown, the same color as his skin, and sticking straight up, spirals pulled tight from his magic. His nose is short and shallow and scrunched up as his lower jaw juts forward in a silent growl, exposing tusks, one blunted and cracked from the file. His forehead is low and slopes sharply back from protruding brows that shadow eyes set deep, small for his face, and black—solid black—with no whites at all.

I tremble.

So much anger in that small body.

I momentarily forget him when she turns. I am reeled in, helpless to resist. I move forward and hover above her. She looks straight up at me.

I tear myself away and fly back to my corner.

"You can come down now, Soul Soarer. They are gone, and I will not hurt you." Her voice is as melodious as her movements.

I am so engrossed by her that I hadn't even noticed the men leave.

How does she see me?

The men hadn't seen me. They hadn't felt it when I'd tried to stop them from filing the boy's tusks.

She strides closer. She is fluid and grace. Her clothing a riot of colorful scarves flowing around her as if pushed along by tiny sprites swimming in the air, their rhythm musical notes, each color a different instrument. She stirs, her hands sweeping, scarves a melody in their wake, her eyes alight, her feet floating, dancing. I can hear the song of her movements, and it tames me.

What had she called me? Soul Soarer?

"Until you're more experienced, it's not safe for you to leave your body unprotected." She glances at the young boy still perched on the platform, quiet now.

My body?

That boy is me?

His—my?—clothes are dirty and torn from struggling with the men.

"You cannot leave without your body." Her voice reminds me that she is still here. I can tell that, unlike the locals, she is not afraid of me. "And your body will not survive without its soul. If you don't return to it soon, another soul will—or perhaps a demon. Do you want a demon to control your body?"

I fly toward the boy, not certain what to do but knowing that I don't want anything else to control something that is mine.

"I thought as much. You are so like your father."

I have a father?
I debate for only a moment.
I want to know more.
I fly toward the boy, crash into myself...and follow her out.

Chapter 3 Llani

31st day of Kazamee, 14,888
Onboard Brave Mortal, off the shores of Innard

A cannonball crashes through the wall of Llani's cabin. The impact catapults her away from the gap. The projectile tears into the base of the far wall, leaving a gaping hole in the floorboards beyond. The storm is raging outside. Boots pound on the deck above her. Frightened, she tries to stand, but the ship dips suddenly, and Llani is suspended in midair for several moments before landing hard on her feet.

Where's her bag? Qrow told her to pack it quickly before disappearing again. She cannot lose it now! It contains her whole life, and more importantly, what is left of her father's. There! At the edge of the hole. She leaps toward it, grabbing it just before it skids into the hole. She peers down at the devastation below, shocked at what she finds. The horses are terrified, their eyes rolling to the back of their head.

Another hit sends her forward. Heart pounding, she drops the backpack and grasps for a broken floorboard to keep from falling into the hold below.

The door opens beside her.

"Llani!" Qrow pulls her up and rescues her bag. Thankfully, it had also caught on a broken piece of flooring. Qrow puts a strong arm around her and rushes her toward the door. "Come on! We need to get Bell!"

"Where's Qat?" Llani doesn't waste time telling Qrow what she saw below. Llani stumbles as the ship shakes from another hit.

Their ship, *Brave Mortal*, returns fire, and the deck shudders under her feet.

"I don't know. Akin and Kasaandra went to free the horses." Qrow opens the door to Bell's cabin. "Bell! Where are you?"

"I'm here! I can't get my pocket home!" Bell is half underneath the bunk. Her plump bottom is too large to fit now that she has finally gained back some of her lost weight.

Their pocket homes contain all their belongings, shrunk to the size of a large chicken egg.

"I'll get it," Llani says, knowing how crushed Bell would be to lose all her new cooking gear. Llani crawls under the bunk as soon as Bell wriggles out.

The green stone had rolled into the far corner.

"We don't have time for this," Qrow says. "We have to go!"

"I almost have it. If the ship would—"

The ship does, and Llani catches the rolling stone as it careens toward her. She shuffles out from under the bunk and hands the pocket home to Bell. "If you lose this, we will—"

"Likely starve. You think I don't know that?" Bell says. She stuffs the item into one of the many pouches dangling from her belt and glares at Llani.

How long can one person hold a grudge?

Bell nicknamed the combined pocket homes *Home Dome*. There is a total of six of them. One for Llani and each of her companions, but only Bell's has food and cooking utensils. Even so, Llani is certain they would find enough to eat. Once they make it to Innard, they'll be able to resupply, anyway.

The ship lurches again. Llani and Bell both stumble for the doorway. Llani takes her bag from Qrow and pulls the straps over her shoulders. It has her entire life inside. She cannot lose it.

"Who is attacking us?" Llani asks, after another round shakes the ship.

"Pirates!" Bell's eyes shine as she says the word.

Llani cannot believe Bell is more excited by pirates than she fears drowning. How are they best friends? They are complete opposites in both looks and personality. At two thumbs taller than three feet, the hablis barely reaches Llani's waist. Her spiky blond hair is sticking out in all directions from her foray under the bed. But that is normal.

"Why would—?"

"I don't know," Qrow says, interrupting Llani, "but the ship is taking on water now. Look!" He points to the porthole.

A wave splashes onto the glass and retreats. But that does not mean they are sinking. There is a storm blowing outside. Waves have been splashing onto the porthole for days, and it is only a foot above the waterline when the sea is still. If they were sinking, it would be under water.

"We have to get up top. Fast!" Qrow grabs Bell as the ship tilts again and guides her out the door. Llani follows. "Careful! Keep to the right," Qrow tells Bell as they pass Llani's cabin door and the hole in the floor. They hurry along the empty deck where crates and barrels are usually stacked.

"I thought pirates kept the ship intact until *after* they plundered its treasures," Llani says when they reach the steps ascending to the upper deck.

"Normally, they do," Qat says on aer way down the steps.

"Qat!" Bell grabs Qat's hand, and they brace themselves when the ship tilts further to portside.

It was bad enough that one of the masts broke yesterday during the storm, damaging the railing and part of the deck as it flung about. When it finally went overboard, it took a deckhand with it. The dwarf was tangled in the ropes and drowned before anyone could respond. Everyone was too busy trying to cut the rigging and set the mast free before it pulled the ship down.

And that was only the most recent of many disasters that have plagued them since leaving Craguesport nearly two trit'quarters ago. They were only a few days from their destination when the storm hit. They've been floundering for days, trying to ride out the storm.

Now, there are pirates. When will it end?

"Qat," Qrow calls to his twin. "Do you recognize them?"

They had recently discovered that Qat used to sail with Captain Rogen, a known pirate.

Qat shakes aer head. "I've been away too long."

Llani can barely hear aem over the storm and shouting above. She had gained her sea legs shortly after leaving Craguesport, but she struggles to stay upright as she climbs up behind Qat.

The ship lurches upward, then drops again.

Wood splinters. Something rolls and bounces overhead.

Qat stumbles, and Llani grabs aem just before ae falls into her.

She can hear the captain shouting above. "Abandon ship!"

"*Brave Mortal*, my ass!" Qat says.

"The horses!" Bell says, stopping suddenly.

"Akin and Kasaandra are with them," Qrow says. "We'll only get in their way."

Llani can hear the clomp of hooves on the stairs below, ascending from the hold.

Bell turns back again, but Qat leaps down between Llani and Qrow.

Qrow reaches for his twin, but Qat avoids him. "Get them topside! I'll be right back."

On deck, sailors are scrambling. Waves crash over the port side railing. The pirate ship had come around to starboard. Grappling hooks wrap around beams, lodge into the decks, and tear through canvas. Rain beats down on them all.

Instead of cutting themselves free, the crew waits armed and ready, yelling at the pirates and each other.

"They're trying to pull the ship back up!"

"Idiots! We're going to take you down with us!"

"Serves you right for attacking an empty ship!"

Qrow had chartered the ship. They were the only passengers, and he'd paid a cargo hold fee to sail the same day.

"Can you swim?" Qrow asks.

"I guess we'll find out!" Bell says.

"I never learned." Llani had always intended to but had never gotten around to it. Her home in the forest was devoid of lakes, and the streams were too shallow to swim.

"When we go over, hold onto me," Qrow says, looking at her solemnly. His cat-like pupils are thin slits in his golden eyes. "I won't let you drown."

Thank You for Reading!

I hope you enjoyed this journey. If you did, please consider leaving a review on your favorite book-buying site—your support truly helps new readers discover my stories!

For more books, exclusive content, and to join my VIP Reader List for sneak peeks and special updates, visit my website:

KTPike.com

Connect with me online:
Facebook @KTPikeAuthor
Instagram @k_t_pike

LinkInBio: linktr.ee/ktpike